SEA OF ROSES

A Pirate Romance Duology
Book One

OPAL REYNE

Cover art by: Irene Zeleskou
www.imaginedcovers.com

<u>Author's note on language</u>

I'm from AUSTRALIA.

My English is not the same as American English.
I love my American English spoken readers to bits.
You're cute, you all make me giggle, and I just wanna give
you a big 'ol hug. However, there are many of you who
don't seem to realise that your English was born from British
English, which is what I use(although a bastardised version
since Australians like to take all language and strangle it
until it's a ruined carcass of slang, missing letters, and
randomly added o's).

We don't seem to like the letter z.

We write colour instead of color. Recognise instead of
recognize. Travelling instead of traveling. Skilful instead of
skillfull. Mum instead of mom. Smelt is a past participle of
smelled. We omit the full-stop in Mr. Name, so it's Mr
Name. Aussies cradle the word cunt like it's a sweet little
puppy, rather than an insult to be launched at your face.

Anyway, happy reading!

Inspired by the TikTok App

This duology is dedicated to all the creative people on TikTok who were inspired by the copious amounts of Sea Shanty music covers in 2021.

All of the cosplays, the costumes, drawings, and animations people did inspired me to write this book. Artists find inspiration from anywhere and everywhere, and everyone's collective joy in spreading pirate and sailor fun helped me visualise this story, especially one video in particular.
Thank you.

CHAPTER ONE

Beautiful clear skies, tranquil rolling waves, and strong steady winds to fill his sails – what a perfect day to get completely fucked over. Not that Captain Alistair Paine, one of the most notorious pirates on the seven seas of Old Gaia, knew treachery was on the horizon.

No, instead, he lowered his nautical telescope from his good eye with a confident, beaming grin. He closed its bronze, tapering layers with a deep chuckle, his gaze narrowing on the horizon to focus in on what was approaching.

Placing his telescope in the fixed wooden box on the navigation table next to the helm of his ship, he felt the familiar rumble of excitement and lust for death rising in his chest.

"Raise the jolly roger, lads!" he yelled with mirth, palming one of the eight handles of the steering wheel in front of him.

His men sprinted at his command, immediately doing as they were told with cruel smirks. They already knew exactly what was coming.

Within moments, a black flag, with a white skull and two long swords crossing underneath it, rose through the worn and patchy cream-coloured sails of his ship.

He knew, the entire crew knew, that it would be seen by the ship they were coming into range of – like an angel of death preparing to clutch at their souls. If they didn't surrender, they would greet Davy Jones' locker at the bottom of the sea.

If they did, they *might* spare their lives.

Watching it flap in the steady wind with a twinkle of glee in his good eye, Alister lowered his gaze to narrow it back on the ship sailing towards them.

One of his brows raised when it didn't change its course to run away, nor raise its own flag in communication.

They aren't running, he thought.

"Pierre!" he shouted to his first mate. His was one of the very few pirate ships that had one.

"Yes Captain?" Pierre answered, his lean frame sprinting up the steps to the quarterdeck two at a time.

Although the crew often called him by his name when merely sailing, they called him 'captain' when he was in charge of a takeover.

The man, only halfway through his twenties, grabbed the corner of the railing to swing himself forward with his own grand smile; yet there was a serious glint to his features. His green eyes were filled with the same brightness as Alister's. His long blond hair swished around his shoulders and would have been in his face if he didn't keep it tied back in a high, messy ponytail.

His skin was heavily tanned; many days at sea did that to most riding these waves, but he still managed to keep some hint of his paler complexion.

"Get Derek to man the wheel." Derek was his quartermaster and third in charge of the ship. Alister moved his eyes from Pierre, his grin widening as he watched the enemy ship sailing closer. "This is not going to be a chase."

"They plan to fight?"

Alister nodded. "Oh aye, lad. They plan to fight."

"Do they not recognise our figurehead?" Pierre's own eyes widened as his face turned from Alister to the oncoming ship.

"Does it matter?" he laughed. "Whether they do or not, it doesn't matter to us."

"If they want to feed the fish..." Pierre trailed off, his look of concern fading to something more malicious.

"Then we feed 'em," Alister finished for him.

With a nod, Pierre swung himself back around the corner of the railing to sprint down the stairs, shouting for Derek to man the wheel.

It didn't matter if the enemy knew his ship or not; they were knowingly heading towards pirates.

They're either mad... or they thought they could best them, which was a hilarious notion to him.

They didn't know Alister had a large crew of sixty-six good men, all of them seasoned sailors. Most of them had been ruthless pirates for a minimum of a decade – himself included.

His quartermaster came bounding up the steps, peg leg thudding against the distressed timber.

Somehow, even though man had one normal leg and another made of wood, it never hindered his speed nor made him any less formidable than the rest of them.

His leg had been cut off just below the knee. It wasn't completely useless, since it wasn't stiff, and he could still bend it at the knee. He often liked to kick people with it, something Alister witnessed regularly with humour.

He was a short, older man with boundless energy. It was hard to tell if he was frowning or grinning with his long, brown, scraggly beard, but his eyelids often crinkled at the sides, making his hazel eyes almost twinkle.

They were meant to be laugh lines, but Alister often thought they made him appear conniving.

"Aye Cap'in?" He wiggled his long-haired eyebrows up and down, not seeming to notice a few hairs trying to poke him in the eye. "They lookin' for a fight, are they?"

Derek was only eighteen years older than Alister's twenty-nine, but with the short life span of pirates, it meant he was the wisest of them all. It didn't make him any less deadly with a weapon, though.

He was one of his best men and he trusted him explicitly.

"Aye, you old seadog." Alister moved out of the way so Derek could take the helm in his wrinkled, dry, calloused hands. It often looked as though they were dried with salt from the ocean. "And if you let any of 'em take my ship, I'll gut you myself."

"Oh ho!" Derek exclaimed. "I'd like to see ye try."

With a laugh, Alister patted him on the shoulder.

Then, he calmly made his way to the front of the quarterdeck, the level he was on, to stand between the railing and the helm.

His type of frigate warship was one of the largest, the sturdiest, and, proudly, the fastest on the seven seas. He'd commandeered it from pirate hunters with an artistry he hoped was a popular tale on land. He wanted to instil fear into all who heard about the roaring grim reaper – the figurehead at the bow.

He and his crew never had to run from another ship.

It was made of cedar wood, giving it a deep reddish colour when compared to ships made of oak. It was bleached by the sun and dirtied to look a dark brown by waves that often slammed the hull.

His beloved ship had seen better, cleaner days, but she was in perfect working condition.

Below him was the main deck, where he could see his crew manning the many sails and rigs. Two tall, thick beams stood before him – the main mast and the foremast. Each had three white sails bowing forwards, leading them steadfast to battle.

There was a third, smaller mast, called the mizzenmast, behind him on the poop deck, the highest deck of this ship. It sat behind the quarterdeck on which he currently stood.

Underneath the poop deck was the navigation room; it was also where Alister slept. It gave way for his first mate and quartermaster to share the large room beneath the quarterdeck. On a ship like this, they tried to share the few cabins available, so the crew could sleep more comfortably.

A crowded crew would lead to disease and sickness.

Although he was captain, and therefore spoilt, he tried to be as little an inconvenience to his crew as possible, who could rise up and mutiny against him. He'd gotten into his position through an overwhelming vote, and he could find himself walking the plank with another one.

He doubted his loyal crew would ever commit such a heinous act against him, but that was because he made concessions like this. They also knew he wouldn't go down without a fight, and they feared that.

"All hands on deck!" He threw his right arm forward and swiped it to the side, like a blade cutting through air. "I don't want to see a single man standing still!"

The wind cut through his loose clothing and long black hair as they approached, exhilarating him with its cold energy.

"Aye captain!" some of them yelled, telling him he'd been heard.

"Gunmen!" He pointed to the right of the ship. "I want those gun ports open on the starboard side, and the cannons filled with powder. The rest of you, prepare to board. They want a fight? Let's give 'em a fight!"

Not moments later, the figureheads of both ships came into near colliding range. If it wasn't for each steering to come side-by-side with each other, they would have collided.

The enemy's ship was much smaller, and from what he could gauge, it only had eight cannon ports. None of them were open like his were in preparation.

The sound of cannon fire boomed. Eighteen balls were released at the same time, since this was a thirty-six-cannon ship. Half smashed into the smaller ship's side, and the rest blew up explosions of rain when they hit the ocean's glittering surface.

Splintering wood flew in every direction as the enemy ship concaved from the weighted cannonballs and tilted away momentarily. The thunder of cannonballs hitting the timber was enough to understand just how damaging they were.

There was no return fire.

No, and instead of Alister and his crew boarding the ship, men swung from ropes to theirs.

His gaze found Pierre's wide-eyed stare as Alister made his way down the steps to assist.

"Captain!" one of his men shouted, pointing at the skies.

A heavy gust of wind seemed to resonate with the heavy emotion swelling in his chest. It blew his long hair back as he unsheathed his long, curved cutlass sword from the scabbard attached to his hip.

A curved weapon was perfect for slashing, going with the swing of an attack from above, rather than the embedding swing of a straight blade. It's why Alister had chosen this kind of sword.

They're trying to take over my ship!

He watched a man knock into one of his crew, landing on top to stab him in the chest. *Brutus!*

Another landed on top of the crew mate next to him, slicing his throat from ear to ear. *Hammond!*

There were grappling hooks attaching to the railing, allowing his enemies to swing across from below and climb the side of the hull.

A shadow blocked the sun. He looked up to see a man with a determined face, his eyes calculated and gleaming. Men were falling from the sky like terrifying rain, their swords pointed to strike – and Alister was next.

Gnashing his teeth with unyielding rage, he prepared

himself for impact and pointed his blade upwards.

At the last second, he stepped forward to narrowly miss a sword and sunk his own into the enemy's stomach. They both went tumbling back.

Alister kicked him away, off his blade, so he could roll back to his feet with a swiftness, despite his large, muscled frame. Turning just in time towards the thud he heard, he slashed sideways to gut the man who landed next to him, stabbing again just to make sure he was truly dead.

A roar of yells sounded from below the deck. His gunmen were charging to greet the enemy on the surface. *Any moment now.*

Any moment and he'd have dozens of men prepared to fight the crazed flying enemy. *Like a swarm of fucking monkeys.*

The *ching* of multiple swords crossing filled his ears. Yells. Shouts. Gasps. His men were violently defending his ship. The pungent smell of burning timber from the other ship and blood on his own invaded his nostrils.

A yell caught his attention and he turned to find a man running straight for him, his own curved cutlass blade raised. Alister blocked it, using the swing of his sword to direct it away from him, and then punched the man in the eye. The man stumbled back, giving Alister an opening to slash him across the throat.

A small boom echoed. A cannonball grenade blew men across the main deck, surprising him; none of his crew had such careless weaponry skills. He had to turn quickly to avoid being hit by sharp splintered wood and metal shrapnel as it flew in every direction.

Shit. The last thing he needed was for his other eye to go blind. Alister wore a black eyepatch on one side of his face. He'd be useless if he needed bloody two!

The turn meant he was able to see Derek, still manning the

helm, cut down the enemy trying to take the wheel. *Good man.*

But they were being overrun. *Where are my gunmen?* What about the rest of his crew who'd been below deck?

He turned his gaze towards the stairs, watching as an enemy ran over the top of his rowboats – upside down and strapped to the deck – to leap onto Pierre. *No!*

The blond-haired man stepped to the side, slicing his sword beside him to cut into the enemy, who instantly crumbled.

Relief washed through him.

Once more, Alister tried to find the stairs below deck, only to find someone had closed the hatch and turned the locking mechanism shut.

It was stopping those below from coming to the surface.

"Get the hatch open!" he yelled, stomping his way over.

Stepping over dead bodies, both his crew and the enemy, he cut the ropes of the grappling hooks. He heard the men who'd been climbing them shout as they fell into the sea.

He couldn't let anymore reach his ship, not until he had more men on the surface. Otherwise, at this rate, they'd circle the small crew manning the sails.

Pushing a tumbling man with a dagger protruding from his jugular out of his way, he finally found the hatch just as one of his crewmen was stabbed in the back for trying to open it.

Richard! He was one of Alister's best men.

Richard must have understood, just as he had, why they were being overrun.

Despite his fondness for the man, Alister booted Richard's dying corpse out of the way before the enemy could take out his sword.

He reached out and grabbed one of his crewmen by the collar of his tunic to protect his back. He crouched down to move the heavy locking pin, sliding it open.

The hatch flew open so fast, he stumbled back. A mass of angry, sword-wielding men emerged from it.

He pointed to the top of his main sail. "Take back my ship!"

The roars grew louder in response, and he turned to watch them circle the outside of the main deck near the railing to surround the enemy.

Within moments, enemy men realised their predicament, and there was a shuffling pause.

The tips of their blades moved from side-to-side, clinking against different sword tips pointed at them, as if they were unsure who to attack first.

"No mercy?" one of his crewmen shouted.

Alister stomped his heavy frame through the crowd, the fighting halted for now. "Nay. I want answers."

He also knew he'd lost many of his men, and this ship required a large crew to function properly.

They fought well. Now, he would make them work like slaves under his employment – by force.

"Search their ship before it sinks!"

Some of his crew backed away to swing onto the enemy vessel at his command.

He could hear fighting in the distance, but it didn't last; most of them had already jumped from the ship. As he'd been cutting the grappling hook ropes, he'd noticed some them had released their rowboats.

They probably expected to be fished out of the water once they'd taken over his ship.

"Who is your captain?" he asked the group of men, who stood frozen, their swords poised.

None of them answered.

"I will start tossing you, one-by-one, into the depths until you tell me."

Silence followed, but he noticed their eyes narrowing into squints. Glares deepened with every second that passed.

Swiftly, he stepped forward and slashed his sword

sideways, cutting the nearest man's throat. Two of his crew grabbed him as he fell back, tossing his dying body over the railing before he even had a chance to touch the ground.

The sound of crashing water filled their ears.

No one spoke, and he gave a gruntled laugh. "I will gladly do this all day, lads."

They began to shuffle their feet, their eyes darting to each other as the white of their eyes became more visible.

With a tsk, his tongue clicking the roof of his mouth, he stepped forward once more.

His target dropped his sword and raised both his hands. "Wait."

"Captain!" someone yelled from behind him.

Alister's head swung to the voice. "What is it?"

Dale, another one of his men, pushed his way through the crowd in a hurry.

He was huffing, his chest rising and falling quickly as he pointed over the railing. "Captain, there is a woman aboard their ship!"

He rolled his eyes, as though the answer was obvious. "Then get her off it!"

He focused his gaze back to the man who may have been about to tell him who their captain was.

Good gods, it isn't hard to get a woman off a sinking ship! She could be trying to flee it. *What are they doing with a woman, anyway?*

They rarely sailed with women; they caused too many issues. There were also myths about how sailing with one could bring on terrible luck.

Alister wasn't so superstitious.

"She's barricaded herself in the captain's room. She sounds terrified."

His head shot to the side once more, his brows creasing into a frown. "A captive?"

"Aye, seems like it."

A captive woman with a crew of, from what he could tell, pirates like themselves. *That could only mean one thing.*

She was a scared, traumatised woman who'd been kidnapped.

Why should I care for her wellbeing? If she didn't want off a sinking ship, why should Alister care? *I would be doing her a favour, letting her drown.* She wouldn't remember whatever misery she'd been faced with for goodness knows how long.

Just as he turned back to the man in front of him with his sword raised, he paused.

Whatever you do with your life, Alister, a feminine voice in his memory softly echoed. *Fight the strong and help those who cannot help themselves.*

His lips thinned as he thought about that gentle voice, the words spoken to him years ago. A growl-like sound of irritation flung from his throat through clenched teeth.

Curse this bleeding heart! the pirate thought, right as he cut down the man in front of him, his hands raised without mercy.

"Move!" he yelled at his crewmen as he entered the crowd, pushing them to the side. "Keep them where they are!"

Sheathing his sword at his hip, he grabbed one of the ropes attached to the main sail, twisting it around his hand before running for the side of his ship. He jumped from the main deck railing and flew into the air.

With a distinct thud against the thick timber, his boots landed on the enemy's ship, already halfway sunk.

He didn't have long.

It didn't take a genius to know where the captain's quarters were. He immediately headed for the closed door.

Turning the handle while at the same time ramming his shoulder into it, it refused to budge. He pushed off it so that he could boot the door right where the lock was with a thick muscled leg.

His first powerful kick made it cave in. The second flung the door wide open with a loud boom as it hit the wall and nearly flew off its hinges.

His head flinched backwards when he felt something thrown at him, copping him on the bridge of his nose.

He looked down. *A candlestick?*

Looking up, he saw a woman cuddling herself into the ground next to a bed. It looked as though she was trying to hide between it and a small, mounted table.

"Not more pirates!" she cried, blindly reaching to grab something from the side table behind her.

"Aye, more pirates." He stepped forward, just as a book was thrown at him. He swiftly dodged it. "Look, lass. This ship is going down."

"Then let me drown!" He watched her clutch at her frilly, pale-yellow dress with one hand, while reaching behind her back again. Unfortunately for her, there was nothing left on the little side table. "I won't go through it again!"

Blue eyes stared at him, obviously terrified. Her dirt-brown hair was tussled around her head, knotted and windblown. She looked frail, trembling and shaking.

Water sloshed around his dark brown leather boots, small waves of water reaching further and further inside the room with each swish.

I don't have time for this shit! He stomped forward, despite her cries and screams, and grabbed her around the wrist to drag her to her feet.

She attempted to pull away, bashing on his arm, and he used it to flip her onto his shoulder.

"Put me down!"

She kicked her knees into his broad chest while slapping him in the back. Her soft attacks barely left a dent, and he continued to cart her over his shoulder.

Wading in almost knee-deep water, he walked up the stairs to the poop deck, the highest point of this sinking ship.

Holding onto her legs tightly, he brought his free hand to his face to place the tip of his thumb and pointer finger to his lips.

A whooping whistle sounded.

Catching the rope tossed to him, he twisted his forearm around it. With the kicking, bashing, screaming woman on his shoulder, his men hoisted him up the side of his own ship.

Only one thought came to mind: *this is annoying.*

CHAPTER TWO

After giving the woman to his crewmen so he could climb over the railing himself, Alister grabbed her wrist and started dragging her to his chambers.

"Unless those men want to fight to their deaths, tie them up," he yelled to his crew as he dragged her up the steps. He could feel her staggering and tripping over her own feet behind him.

Once he opened his door, he tossed her inside so he could make his own way in. He closed it behind him. She stumbled but stayed upright on her feet before quickly turning around.

"Stay away from me!" Her voice was a high-pitched screech, making him wince.

"Calm down, lass," he sighed, swiftly making his way over to her. He placed his hand on top of her head, bending over to be eye level with her. All the while, she uselessly punched her fists into his chest. "I ain't gonna hurt you."

She froze at his gentle touch and words. Her eyes trailed from where her hands lay on his torso to search his face, a stark fear to her features.

"I don't know what you've dealt with, but we won't harm you, and the next time we port, we'll drop you off."

"P-pardon?" Her brows crinkled and he noted the wild freckles splattered across her sun-kissed face.

"We may be pirates, but on this ship, we don't take

unwilling women." It wasn't his way, and he refused to allow his crew to do the same under his watch.

A flash of emotion crossed her face, one of confusion and strangely, thought. Her face screwed into a tight crinkle as she leaned her head against him, only to start pathetically weeping. Alister rolled his eyes.

Great. He now had a sobbing, fragile woman on his fucking ship. *Where the hell is she going to sleep?*

He wouldn't let her have his quarters. He'd have to ask Derek and Pierre to empty theirs so she could rest without the prying eyes of men. He grimaced; the men would hate that.

"You." He shook her. "Stop your weeping."

It did nothing but irritate him. He felt little pity or sympathy for anyone, regardless of what they'd been through.

She clutched his tunic tightly in her little fists. He could only imagine what she'd been through if she was so desperately clutching him, a stranger, like this.

"I-I want to go home," she whispered, a tremor in her voice.

"Where'd they take you from?"

"D-Dunecaster port."

"Ha!" he laughed. They'd taken her from a port frequented by pirates and criminals. "Looks like you're in luck, lass. We're heading that way."

Alister had been sailing his ship to port after running low on supplies and not finding many ships to raid in the process. He rarely ported if he had to.

He noticed her crying had started to settle already.

"So, would you like to point out which men hurt you so you can watch them drown?"

"Excuse me?" She stepped back to frown once more at him, and he noted her cheeks weren't a tear-shed red. *Must be one of those pretty criers.* "Aren't you going to keep the crew?"

"Oh aye." He folded his arms across his chest, turning his head to the side. "But I don't want those who think it's fine to hurt the weak. We may be lawless, but we aren't dubious on my ship. Men like that turn on others easily. Last thing I need is a crew who will mutiny against me."

Now that they were apart and she wasn't screaming and struggling, he was better able to take in her features.

No wonder they took her. She's a pretty little thing.

Her wild freckles dusting her skin made her look feminine and innocent, almost like someone had thrown a handful of brown sugar across her face. Her hair looked like mud, but it was long and wavy around her face.

Her blue eyes were light, like when the sunlight hit the shallow waters of an island.

She looked as though she had a medium bust under her pale-yellow, frilly dress with elegant stitching. It was obviously a high-quality garment; since she was taken from Dunecaster, a generally impoverished area, the crew must have given it to her from their spoils.

She only came up to his chin, and her frame under that frumpy dress looked small.

Alister hated women like her, women who were frail, broken, in need of saving. He was ill-tempered on the best of days, and he knew, looking at this kind of woman, she'd flinch if he so much as raised his voice in her direction.

"If you don't want to watch them die, I can figure it out on my own." *Perhaps her heart is too gentle.*

He turned to step away, realising he'd offered a meek woman the opportunity to see men die.

"No." She grabbed his wrist to stop him. "I-It was only the captain."

Figures, he thought. *She must have been a prostitute he fancied.*

"And I do want to watch him die, more than anything.

Please, please don't leave me by myself. I-I don't want to be alone."

He nodded, walking forward to open the door, leading her outside. *At least she has some resolve.*

Once on the main deck, he noticed she'd grabbed the back of his black canvas doublet coat with thick brown cuffs and seams. It was the most expensive thing he wore, and it came down to the backs of his knees.

He figured she was afraid and didn't want to be separated from him. He sneered at the idea of being a knight in shining armour when he was nothing but a blood-thirsty criminal. He hoped she didn't come to idolise him; he hated clingy women.

When he tried to enter the crowd, she pulled on the back of it. She didn't want him leading her into the middle of it.

Sighing with defeat and a shake of his head, he stood on the edge of it, his crewmen stepping out of the way to reveal their prisoners.

They were bound with their hands before them, standing in two neat rows along the deck.

"I'll ask you all again. Who is your captain?" He eyed them roughly. "I'll start slitting throats if I don't get an answer."

"Who says ye won't once we tell ye?" one of them snapped.

He gestured to the sails of his grand warship.

"If you haven't noticed, this is a frigate and you've killed much of my crew. You will either join it, or find yourselves at the bottom of the ocean. Thank the sea gods I'm offering to spare your lives." Then the skin on bridge of his nose crinkled tightly in aggression. "Since you broke the code."

Pirates didn't attack pirates.

It was an unspoken code – they all had the same goal and respected their commonalities. If they had raised a black flag, Alister wouldn't have attacked, would have diverted his direction completely.

"You attacked my ship under your captain's command. Therefore, only *he* has to die." He placed his hand on the hilt of his sword to seem more menacing. "Unless you want to join him? I don't keep prisoners."

Too many useless mouths to feed. He wouldn't waste his supplies for such a stupid reason.

"So, I'll ask one last time." He opened his mouth to continue, then, as if on cue, they all stepped away from one man.

A thin but strong-looking brown-skinned man was left by himself. He wore a brown doublet coat similar to his own black one. Like many who sailed, he wore a tricone hat to shield his face from the harsh sun that often bared down from above. He could see the drops of sweat beading on his forehead beneath the hat, glistening against his dark skin.

The man greeted his gaze with a glare before spitting on the ground near Alister's black boots. "Traitors."

"Nay. They're just smart enough to save their own necks." With a large grin splitting his face, Alister shouted, "Alright, onto the railing."

He bumped into the woman behind him as they shuffled out of the way. A bigger space was created so to watch the man jump to his own death with glee. It was one of their favourite sources of entertainment and would be spoken about with much humour later.

Did they scream? Did they cry? Did they toss themselves with courage or did they eventually get pushed off because of their cowardliness?

Much about a man could be deciphered in his final moments.

Alister could cut his throat, but he knew this was a much better way to make him suffer. He'd spend days out at sea, alive, starving, dehydrated, burnt by the sun, before either dying or being eaten by a monster in the depths below.

It was cruel, and it would show just how sinister he could be as commander of his vessel. It should ensure the newcomers fell in line.

Alister unsheathed his sword and pointed it at the man, now forced to stand on the railing, his hands unbound so he could hold onto the netted rope of the shrouds.

"Jump," he chuckled loudly, poking his belly with the tip of his cutlass blade.

The man smiled wide with white teeth. "I think not."

Something cold and round pressed against the back of Alister's head. His eyes widened while gasps of surprise echoed around him.

We missed one?

How could his crew not notice one of the men standing with them wasn't one of their own?

Just to make sure they all knew the owner of the gun pressed to his skull was serious, they cocked back the hammer with a clicking sound that resonated in his ears.

"If anyone moves," said the man on the railing, "she'll blow your captain's brains across the deck."

She? He tried to turn his head to look over his shoulder with his good eye, but the barrel of the pistol was shoved against his head, pushing it forward once more.

"Get off the railing, Naeem," the woman behind him said. "Before I have to fish you from the sea."

This Naeem threw his head back with a jolly laugh, grabbing his hat with his free hand so it didn't fall from his head.

"Aye, Captain."

He nodded as he stepped down to the safety of the deck, his feet thudding against the timber.

"*Captain?*" Alister asked in disbelief.

There couldn't be. There was no way this weeping, crying, fragile woman was actually a pirate, less so a *captain*.

"So, boys," she called to his crew with a hint of humour in her voice. "This is what is going to happen. My crew and I are taking over this ship. If you wish to stay on it, you will follow my command – unless, of course, you don't care for your sweet, gullible captain. I'm more than happy to blow a hole in his skull before you get to me."

Naeem stepped forward to take Alister's cutlass from his hands. He surrendered it willingly, more in shock and confusion than in weakness.

"Why should they care if you shoot me if you are going to kill me in the end?"

"Who said I planned to kill you?" She shoved her pistol harder against his head while Naeem began cutting at the ropes binding her men. "I have no intention of killing you, if you do what you're told."

"You don't plan to kill him?" Pierre asked incredulously.

Alister found him in the crowd of his frozen men, unsure of what to do. He may be able to be voted out as captain, but Alister had a history with his crew. They respected him, had pledged their loyalty; they would never betray him.

If there was a chance to spare his life, he knew they would take it, which meant she had them by the balls.

"No. I have a proposition for all of you, but first, tie his hands; I don't trust his twitching."

Shit. She noticed he was going to make a move to overtake her – and hopefully not get shot in the process.

With a disgruntled curl to his upper lip, he let them bind his hands behind his back, forcing him to turn around to face her.

The smirk she gave him was devilish.

She tricked me. She played the part of tortured damsel in order to get behind him with a gun. She'd gained enough of his trust in such a tiny amount of time; he'd *let her* get him into a vulnerable position.

He thought he'd seen a few moments of calculated thought, but he'd mistaken it for confusion at his kindness. Why would he, a pirate, be so considerate of a woman? He'd have sworn she'd been frightened and confused.

It was also now that he remembered he'd never actually seen her face flushed from crying real tears. *She'd falsely wept.*

Even though he had seen had tear or two, he knew they must have been forced.

"That's better!" she exclaimed with delight once he was bound and unable to move.

She kept the gun trained on him, while the rest of her crew picked up their weapons, pointing them at his. Naeem had Alister's sword notched at his throat as an extra precaution.

One of her men came to stand against her back. He saw she could see behind Naeem as he could behind her.

This obviously wasn't the first time they'd done this.

"I will give you all a choice," she started. "Sail with me, follow my command, and you will share in the bounty we find, the treasure we steal, and the kills we take. Or, you can be imprisoned with your captain and dropped off at Dunecaster when we arrive, alive, unharmed, and free."

"You're soft hearted for a captain," Alister bit, wiggling his wrists, which tossed his shoulders side-to-side as he struggled. "My crew will never follow someone like you."

They liked him because he was ruthless. She was offering to spare his life, giving his crew a choice – it showed her weakness as a commander.

"And we won't follow a woman!" one of his men shouted, raising his fist in anger.

Her gun pointed toward the man who spoke. The bang that sounded was loud and deep as she shot the man in the head with deadly accuracy.

No hesitation. No fear.

She reached into a tear in her skirts. She pulled out a new bullet from a hidden pouch and pushed it into the barrel, before refilling the gunpowder.

Her men looked prepared to fight while she was seemingly distracted, but he could see her eyes trailing across them all. She was ready to defend herself within a moment's notice.

Once the gun was loaded, she pointed the pistol at Alister's head again.

"I am aware my sex is an issue for many – which is the only reason I am giving you this choice. Rather than killing you for your idiotic views, I am showing mercy. Be thankful I am giving it at all. Like your captain already mentioned, this ship requires a large crew, and many have died this day." She turned her head to face the crew with a bored expression. "Make your choice. Fight us and watch your captain die before the first swing. Drop your weapons and put your hands forward to be bound, and you will be dropped off in Dunecaster with him. Or, sheath your weapons and follow me, a woman, as your captain."

Her eyes found his once more and he squinted into a hate-filled glare.

"You," she said to him, cocking the hammer of her pistol. "Help them make their decisions."

After a few moments, he nodded upwards silently.

Some of his men dropped their swords; those who would follow him anywhere, even to the grave. Others sheathed their swords, but they eyed him as they did.

None fought. None were willing to risk his life after watching her shoot someone.

"Bind those who have their hands forward and put them in the cells!" she commanded. "Who else is in command?"

"I," Pierre said, stepping forward with his hands already tied.

"I," Derek seconded as he was shoved down the stairs.

"Two? Well, aren't you a lucky man?" she said while raising her nose up at him, as though he was some inferior creature. "Tie them to the main mast with their captain. We can't have them plotting with their men. Everyone else, you will answer to my crew and will not be unsupervised until you have proven your loyalty."

Finally, she stopped precariously aiming her cocked gun at his head and pulled the handle of a sword through the tear in her skirt.

How did I not notice that when I was carrying her?

"Naeem! Get me out of this godforsaken ugly dress!"

She turned her back to make her way up the quarterdeck steps while Alister was gagged, then tied to the thick mast pole. Naeem quickly followed behind her, and Alister realised he was her next in charge.

"If any of you try to mutiny against me, you will quickly find a bullet in your teeth. My men don't care that I am a woman, and they won't tolerate it if you try to turn against me," she spoke as the ties of her dress were loosened. She shoved it off, revealing the clothing hidden beneath.

Whereas Alister wore loose breeches with buttons clasping it to his hips, she wore high-waisted black tights tied with corset laces over her stomach. A simple white tunic with frilly cuffs was tucked into her tights, the top three buttons undone, showing her obvious cleavage like she didn't care she was around a crew of unloved men. Plain brown boots came halfway up her calves.

Alister watched as Naeem shed his brown doublet coat and wrapped it around her. It was baggy, but she rolled the sleeves back to fit better, leaving the front of it hanging open.

He moved the tricone hat from his head, revealing his short, curly hair.

Now that she was dressed, a sword belted to her hip, she actually looked like a pirate.

She braced the bottom of her boot against the railing of the quarterdeck while Naeem took the handle of the helm.

"If any of you come close to me, I will, without a doubt, shoot you in the cock. If you point your swords at me, I will cut you with my own. Until you can be trusted, you are to relinquish your guns; you must earn them back. If you are found with one, or they are in your belongings, I will hang you from the railing of this ship. Know that I sleep light, I test what I eat and drink, and you will all be watched carefully."

Then she rested her forearm across the knee bent above the railing, a grand smile crossing her pale pink lips, revealing white teeth.

"And you may call me Captain Rosetta Silver."

CHAPTER THREE

Rosetta pointed to the small map pinned to the table at the helm.

She was speaking to Mr Smith, a trusted crewmember, about their current path through the ocean pacific. He was the only person besides herself and Naeem who she allowed to touch the helm.

Mr Smith was her protection, a trusted advisor who communicated her orders to the rest of the crew. With so many strangers aboard, she had to be cautious.

His full name was John Smith, but she only called him John when she felt like it. The rest of the time, though, she knew he liked to feel like a gentleman. Mr Smith it was.

He was a tall man, one who had once been fat but lost the weight after being out to sea for many years. He was still a happy chap, enjoying that he could climb the shrouds without his gut getting in the way.

His dark hair was peppered with white while his well-shaped, short beard hid his roundish baby face. His small circular glasses made him appear sophisticated despite all that hair.

Naeem, who was at helm, listened in on their conversation.

"No, this is a shallow hull frigate, Mr Smith." She shook her head, before fingering the path she was intending to take on the map. "We needn't worry if we come into contact with any shallows near the Sthrill Islands."

She may have never commanded one of these ships before, but she knew them well enough to direct them safely.

"I want to stay our course. It's the fastest route, and I want those men off my ship as soon as possible."

"I know you're impatient, but we can't be reckless. We took this boat by a miracle only."

"Ah hem!" Naeem cleared his throat dramatically. "What you mean to say is 'she stole this boat with such a brilliance that even the war gods would applaud her.'"

A heart-felt smile spread across her features as she looked over at Naeem.

Mr Smith promptly ignored him. "Look, I know you want to get back to sea to hunt for the head fleet, but I do not think it's wise for us to throw those men overboard without stopping to restock."

With a sigh, Rosetta pushed off from the table, holding the hilt of her sword as she made her way down the steps.

"Show me how bad the supplies are." She knew the three men currently bound, gagged, and secured to the main mast of the deck were staring at her. She didn't spare them a glance as she walked past. "Did we happen to get all our own supplies aboard?"

They had tied barrels of grog water and food to the row boats of that useless ship she had been steering.

Mr Smith nodded. "Yes. We grabbed everything, even the gold, but this ship barely had enough supplies for themselves."

"They must have been headed to port in desperation." She rubbed at her chin as she bounced down the steps to the lower decks. "They may have tried to trade with us had we raised our own black flag."

She could have used that to her advantage to trick them, rather than the tear-filled act she played with their captain.

I'm still rather surprised by his response. It wasn't what she had been expecting.

"You there." She nodded her head to a man she didn't know, one of the previous captain's crew. "Take us to your supplies."

He squinted his eyes, his nose crinkling on one side in disdain, but he led the way. In every corner, she saw her men watching the rest of the crew with a suspicious eye.

Hostile takeovers. She shook her head. It would be a while before the tension went down.

When she entered the large cargo bay below deck, dim of light and smelling musty like mould, the man described the state of their supplies to Mr Smith as she listened. She didn't join in, preferring not to speak to a stranger if she didn't have to.

There were only a handful of barrels secured to benches, a small number of crates littering the ground, all containing odd bits of food that wouldn't make good meals.

Most of the crates were half-empty, and stacks of empty ones had been carelessly dumped into a pile in the furthest corner.

"It seems me overtaking this vessel was a god-send for them," she said as she and Mr Smith walked back up top together. He went through the math so she could have a count of the supplies they now had.

"In estimating the new size of our crew, plus the prisoners, we will have just enough supplies to make it to Dunecaster. Then, if we divert straight away to Vinil port, we should be able to restock before we run out."

Dunecaster was a large piece of land that took nearly an entire day and night to circle, but most people stayed near the only section of the crescent moon-shaped island that allowed ships to port all the way inland. The rest of it had long sand banks – meaning they had to row in.

"Feed our goat to the crew." *Poor Reginald.* She had been

rather fond of her long-bearded, stubby-horned goat. He used to bleat in joy whenever he saw her. "It'll help gain their favour if we feed them well."

It was the last big chunk of fresh meat they had, and the easiest animal they originally had on their old boat to transfer to another. A cow was too big, and chickens... well, they had one left.

"I want that chicken cooked and a small feast of smoked meat prepared in my new quarters, enough for a few bellies." She eyed Mr Smith from the side before they reached the lower deck stairs to reach the surface. "Then meet me in the navigation room."

She had to go through the information and maps on this ship, then add them to the collection she brought over. What's more, she needed to map their course, then their future plans.

"Yes, Rosetta," he nodded, breaking away to find their chef hands. They were just general men who knew how to cook, nothing special, but it was better than nothing.

She held the hilt of her sword as she, alone, walked across the worn timber. The sun shone bright in her eyes, so she lowered her head to let the front point of her hat shield them from the glare.

Paranoid, she kept her ears open in case someone suddenly decided to attack. Her eyes may have been searching, but she kept a calm and unbothered expression.

"What are you all gawking at?!" she yelled at the crew standing on deck. There were only a few that weren't busy with their duties – those who weren't her usual crew. "I want this deck shipshape by the end of the day and this boat sailing at full wind strength in the next thirty minutes, or I'll flay your skin and use it to patch the holes in these sails!"

There were still plenty of blood puddles from bodies they had already tossed into the water. They were sticky under her boots and left a pungent smell in the air she couldn't stand.

Immediately, men sprang to action, scrubbing the planks with seawater and soap, their wide, two-handed brushes scraping against the reddish timber. Others began climbing the shrouds to check on the sails and secure any loose rope.

"Captain!" A voice sounded from above in the crow's nest, a small lookout for someone to keep watch above the sails. It didn't escape her attention that she wasn't the only one who responded to that particular call, even though the other was currently bound. "Sail, ho!"

Another ship?

"Naeem!" She waved her hand forward. "Keep an eye out. If they direct to us, avoid. We aren't prepared for another battle yet."

She barely even knew the damn ship!

"Aye, Captain!" He gave her a lazy salute with one hand.

I don't even know the cannonball stocks yet. She may need the supplies on that ship, but she wouldn't take a perilous risk.

Not yet at least.

After passing Naeem at the helm, she entered the navigation room for the first time. She placed her hands on her hips as she looked at the large bed in the corner with a hammock swinging above it.

There was a large desk made of cedar wood, covered in maps, a chair behind it. Typical navigation devices were messily scattered across it with vials of ink and other writing apparatuses mixing into the organized chaos.

What surprised her the most, though, were the extensive maps of constellations, stars, and changing day length cycles with their occurring seasons. The octant the paper drew her attention. She fiddled with the tool before setting it back down when she realised she didn't know how to use it.

The only other items of furniture were a chest of clothes and a small table with three chairs, most likely used as seating for food and drink. Cupboards were mounted into the walls as permanent fixtures.

He made room so that more of his men could sleep comfortably. There was no other explanation for this space. It was something she never thought to do, but a good idea nonetheless.

Like the rest of the ship, it had a funny smell to it, like wet timber and mould, but it wasn't as terrible as below deck.

The sunlight was dim, battling through the murky, dirty gridded windows at the back. Deciding to use whatever sunshine she could get, she made her way to the fitted cabinets, sifting through the drawers and opening the doors.

Rosetta wanted to know all about her new sleeping quarters, where she would be staying for God knew how long. Mr Smith eventually joined her and together, they mapped their course for the next two months. They might have to make some alterations depending on the weather, but they should be where they wanted to be by then. *Hopefully.*

Rosetta had big hopes and even bigger goals. It was why she had decided to take this ship when she first saw it on the horizon. A warship like this frigate was just the weapon she needed.

As they made plans, their food arrived, placed onto the spare table. She'd gone out of her way to make it known she would be staying in this room since it was already prepared. She'd change the sheets, if they were available, since she didn't know how long ago a *man* would have changed the bedding.

Then again, she'd probably sleep in the hammock, since it was more comfortable to go with the swings and sways of the ocean waves rather than fight them in a rigid framed bed.

"That looks like a lot of food just for yourself," Mr Smith laughed, giving her a hard pat on the back. "Good to see you eating properly."

"It's not just for me," she answered, reaching into the

pocket pouch that constantly hung from her waist. Usually it held gold coins, but it also held one other item. She stood, making her way to the mirror on the back wall.

He raised an eyebrow at her, straightening his back as he adjusted his round glasses by his index and thumb to hold the frame's edges.

"Are you inviting me to dinner, Rosetta? I'm sure the other men will be rather jealous."

She gave a hearty laugh. "As handsome as you are, no; I intend to play with someone else tonight."

"I can only imagine what you mean." He wagged his finger at her, a special gleam to his eyes. "I know how you can be."

Without truly caring how it looked, she applied a bright red tint to her lips. She hated the colour, but it was all she had.

"Yes, well, I'm expecting you to watch out for me tonight. We have a new crew on board, after all."

With a nod, he followed behind her as she stepped out onto the quarterdeck. The darkness draping down on them from the setting sun was brightened by multiple flame lanterns.

She patted Naeem on the shoulder. "How's that other ship Keat saw?"

"Haven't seen sign of it for quite some time. This girl's pretty fast." He patted the wheel he was holding. "Once we caught the wind, the other ship fell off the horizon."

"Excellent. Once I'm done with my supper, I'll take the wheel while you get some sleep."

"Are you sure?" He lowered his head closer to hers. "I don't like the idea of you being by yourself since old Johnny boy there will need to sleep as well."

"You know he doesn't like that name." Rosetta shook her head with a light chuckle. "I'll be fine. I have these." She patted her side, knocking her pistol and sword against her thigh. "If anyone tries anything, I'll yell out for you two, since I expect you both to be sleeping in the chamber below. There are two beds already."

Although Naeem was her second and Mr Smith just a normal crewmember, she tried to not show favouritism toward Naeem. He already dealt with the crew's misplaced judgment, due to the tint of his skin. He had once been a slave, but Rosetta freed him when she first set sail. They'd been friends ever since.

Just as she had won over her crew, even with her gender, he managed the same as her second in command.

A slave and a woman, commanding a ship together. They were an odd pair, doing an odd thing, and she was sure polite society would shake their heads if they saw them. *But there is no one better at my side.*

"Now, it's time to play a game."

"Try not to poke the bear too much." Naeem nodded his head, pointing with his chin. "He already looks angry."

Her eyes found the man Naeem was looking at. He was facing them, his hands bound by metal shackles behind his back, cloth tied around his head, rope coiled around his torso that tethered him to the thick pole with two others.

His legs were in front of him, slightly bent into a relaxed position, whilst the rest of him slumped forward comfortably.

The way his arms were stretched back opened his doublet coat, revealing the plain white tunic beneath. It also showed just how broad his chest and shoulders were, near bulging out of them.

He's manned the wheel through many storms.

A black patch covered one eye, the other one narrowed on them with a glare she hadn't seen once since he'd been tied there. Her lips pestered with a smile she couldn't contain.

"I would say he looks rather jolly."

Rosetta descended the stairs with an echo of footfalls following behind. Mr Smith gave her some distance; he never followed behind too closely, since they didn't want to give the impression that she was afraid.

Her eyes fell on the older gentleman tied to the mast with him. Since he had been manning the helm when they'd taken over, she instructed Mr Smith to grab him, and she followed behind as he pushed the man towards her chamber. He grunted and shouted through the cloth between his teeth.

After shoving the man into a chair, Mr Smith left them alone. Rosetta wasn't afraid to be alone with one man, whether he was armed or not. She was quick with her pistol, willing to shoot a man dead, and she had a knack for sensing when they planned to launch. She'd trained her eyes to watch their muscles twitch with anticipation of a move.

"If you want to walk out of this room still breathing, you best keep your hands to yourself," she told him while using the key she'd taken from Mr Smith to unlock his shackles.

Then, she walked to the other side of the table and took her own seat. She leaned against on the arm of the chair while crossing one knee over the other, grabbing her chalice full of wine. This ship had only one bottle, and she was determined to savour every drop of it tonight in celebration.

"Ye a silly one, little lassie," the long, scraggly-bearded man said, after ripping the mouth gag from his teeth and narrowing his coal black eyes on her.

"For what?" She gestured to the food between them. "Inviting you to dinner?"

She smiled around the rim of the chalice before she took a sip.

"Do you not know whose ship this is?"

She gave a small shrug with her shoulders, folding her arm on the available rest and leaning her cheek on her fist.

"Was," she rebuffed. "Why should I care who it belonged to when it now belongs to me?"

"He is Cap'in Alister 'One Eye' Paine, the Bloody Storm of the Seas!"

She gave him a grand smile, her eyes twinkling with humour. "Am I supposed to give a fuck about who that is?"

"Are ye not a pirate? Ye should know 'bout our crew. He got his name by sinking ships and killing almost everyone he's met."

She swirled the tip of her index finger in the wine, giving it a stir before bringing it to her mouth. "I don't care to speak to other pirates, or hear their tales. They are often myths, or egotistical stories to pretend a man's achievement cock is large, when, in fact, it's quite small."

"Then ye are a stupid girl." He shook his head, his long beard swaying side-to-side, the beads in it jingling, as though it wanted to tickle the table. "He will take this ship back."

Rosetta stabbed her fork into the chicken in the middle of their table to cut herself a slice.

"He can have it back." She placed her meat on her plate before going for a bit of smoked... she wasn't sure what it was, but she'd eat it regardless. "Once I'm done with it. Let's just say I'm borrowing it for now."

"Well, ye won't have it for long." The way he said it made a small shiver roll down her spine. His eyes were on her, but it felt like he was looking into her future – so much unwavering confidence he'd be right.

Could Alister really be that dangerous? She'd heard of more famous pirates.

"Every word you speak pushes me closer to slicing his neck." She looked up at him through her lashes, leaning over the table, her lips downturned into an irritated frown. "Refrain from continuing unless you want his last moments to be staring at his own blood."

She watched the hairs around his mouth draw in as his lips puckered. She nodded to the food.

"Eat. Tell me your name and position."

He was quick to manhandle the poor chicken with bare

hands, ripping a leg and wing from it, along with the smoked meat and some bread.

"Me name is Derek Von'tuken, and I am the quartermaster of this ship."

"Were," Rosetta corrected, her smile returning. "Currently Naeem is the quartermaster, while you are a prisoner. If you are what you say, who is the other man who came forward?"

"Alister's first mate."

That made Rosetta frown. "Pirates don't usually have first mates."

"Aye, girl, but ye do if ye command a complicated ship like this one."

She stabbed the point of her knife into the wooden table with a booming thud, startling Derek, who dropped the chicken leg he was about to bite into back onto his plate.

"Call me girl one more time, and I'll stab you in the back of the hand with my eating knife."

He gave a snort of laughter. "What are ye? Sixteen, seventeen? Wee lassie like yeself shouldn't be on these seas."

"I'm twenty-one! I have been sailing these seas and managing a crew for three years, you ill-mannered piece of shark bait."

"Still young." He shrugged like he didn't care that he'd angered her. "What do ye want from me?"

"Join my crew," she huffed.

The belly jiggling, bellowing laugh he gave surprised her, enough to make her eyes relax from their squinting glare.

"No miss, I don't think I will."

"Why not? It's better for your crew if you do. They won't like my new authority."

"Because where me cap'in goes, I go." He gave her a grand face, bright with a smile she could barely see with all that hair. "And there ain't not'ing you can offer me that'll change me mind."

"Fine." She drank from her chalice before nibbling on her food in thought. "Where is the key to the safe?"

"I won't tell ya nothing you want to hear, missy. Yer better off putting me shackles back on."

She gave a grumble. She knew he was telling the truth. *Stubborn man.* He reminded her of her father.

"Finish eating, because I *won't* be feeding you tomorrow." She was going to dish out punishment.

While he was eating, and being quite messy with it, Rosetta got up slowly after draining her chalice.

Time to poke the bear. She didn't *need* to, she just really, really, really *wanted* to. Derek willingly allowed her to shackle his hands and then stood for her.

"Aye! Lassie, what are ye doin'?" he asked in outrage when she unbuttoned his faded brown breeches to the point that they were almost falling away from him.

"Mr Smith, I would like for you to take him now," she yelled, knowing he was on the other side of the door, but not before she used two fingers to smear her red lipstick across her own face and then to his lips – mainly his beard. His head reared back, as if he was trying to escape her.

With a pat on the cheek, she pressed the gag back between his lips and shoved him out.

Once Derek was back against the mast pole, Rosetta stood in front of the blond man, just noticing that his hair was so long, he tied back into a long, messy ponytail that did little to restrain it. He was seated in the middle of the two men, and all three watched her like a hawk.

"Well, well, well," she tsked with a smile before crouching down in front of him. She gripped him by his clean-shaven chin, moving his head around to examine him. "Aren't you a pretty boy?"

Leaning closer and placing her other hand against the mast pole, she noticed him raise his brow at her. Then his eyes dipped to her cleavage; she'd placed her chest in his face for a reason.

"I bet all the women have gotten hurt at all the ports you've been to."

Even in the firelight of the lanterns, she could tell he had green eyes women could lose themselves in. They reminded her of a large forest – easy to get turned around and lost in. His cheek bones were high, his brows arched, his jaw sharp but not wide.

He almost looks like a woman, if it wasn't for the thin, white scar running from under one nostril, past his lips, to end on the side of his chin. He even had a beauty mark under his right eye near the corner and long dark eyelashes that fanned above it.

"Promise not to break my heart if I bring you to my chambers this evening?"

She gave a cute pout, which she knew looked promiscuous with lipstick smeared across her mouth.

To her utter surprise, de did something that made her brow twitch to a frown and her eyelids flicker. He leaned forward and nuzzled the tip of his nose against her own.

"Ha ha! I like him." She rolled back to her feet. "Bring him Mr Smith. He'll be good fun."

"Looks like she's hungry tonight, boys!" Naeem shouted from the helm, a few of her crew chuckling wildly.

The best part of the entire interaction was the dumbfounded look on *Captain* Alister Paine's face as he watched the whole encounter.

The man was brought to her quarters and seated in the same spot Derek had been placed in, and she gave him the same warning as she unshackled his hands.

Rosetta refilled her chalice and sat, folding one knee on top of the other. He was much slower to lower his gag; he arched a perfect blond brow at her as he did.

"You're a strange woman, aren't you?" he asked, noticing the empty plate in front of him. She'd gotten a new one before she'd left.

"Strange to some, but most say I'm unhinged."

He nodded like he actually understood.

"So." He gestured to the food. "You give me dinner, then have your wicked way with me like old man Derek?"

"Perhaps," she smiled. "Depends on how much you please me beforehand."

He placed his hand over his heart. "Why, my sweet, beautiful rose, I believe you'll be quite entranced."

Her lips curled into a small smile of humour. "You're a sweet talker. How many women have you made cry?"

"Endless." He waved his hand as if gesturing to a painting. "Can you not hear them weeping as we speak?"

She gave a giggle, almost a mocking snort, as she brought her chalice to her lips. "What's your name?"

"I am the great Pierre Price, first mate of the infamous Howling Death warship."

"Oh my!" she gasped, her eyes growing wide as she placed her hand against her chest. "I've heard of you!"

His smile widened, one that would have made a weaker woman's heart throb with tenderness.

"Really?" The cheer in his voice was delightful.

"No." She let her hand fall against the arm rest.

His smile fell.

"Eat, Pierre." She nodded to the food.

He obediently heaped food onto his plate like a man who hadn't eaten in weeks. *Big stomach for such a skinny man.* She could tell he steered many ships in his time. He wasn't as broad as the captain, but he had defined muscles peeking out from his barely buttoned white shirt, one button at the bottom holding it together.

"I want you to join my crew."

"Depends on how well you please me," he answered. "Or if you promise to invite me back to this chamber."

She squinted her eyes while taking a sip of her wine. "Perhaps."

"Come now, I'm no fool." He spoke with his mouth full, chewing loudly and obnoxiously. He even shamelessly licked at his lips while smacking them. "Derek wouldn't have betrayed Alister, in his deranged mind, by bedding you. Why are you really doing this?"

"You're quick to catch on." There was a pause as she mused on telling him the truth. "It will help me keep control if I have one of you by my side. The old crew will respond better if one of you declares loyalty to me."

"Ah, and Derek, I'm guessing, said no?" It was spoken as a question, but the way he said it was more like he already knew the answer. "That old salt is Alister's dog. He will only bark and bite for his master."

"And what about you?" Rosetta leaned forward and cut herself more chicken before this brute decided to eat everything on the table.

"As enticing as you are, my answer is the same." He gave her a wide grin, showing a full mouth of teeth. "Plus, the idea of being dropped off in Dunecaster is agreeable. Haven't gotten my cock wet in months." He gave a chuckle. "The prostitutes do so love me there."

Her lips pursed into a thin lip. *He's found men who will follow him anywhere.* Just like she had. It was rare for pirates like them to garner that kind of loyalty. Rosetta thought she'd always been a special case.

Figures I was wrong.

"Where is the key to the safe?"

"In my pants. You might have to fish around in it for a while. You know, really rub around in there."

"You're the first mate. That would mean you actually

know its whereabouts or have it on your person."

There was a mischievous twinkle in his green eyes as he brought a bit of smoked meat to smirking lips. "Come and find out."

"I will, in due time." She nodded to his half-finished plate. "Finish eating first."

"If you didn't really take Derek to bed and don't plan to take me to it, although I would be most willing, what is your plan here? Why are you doing this?"

The smirk she gave was broken. "Green is a wonderful colour on men. It makes them unbelievably stupid."

"You're trying to make Alister jealous?" The laugh he gave was almost her undoing. *He's mocking me.* "Good luck with that. He's too pissed to be anything but disgusted."

He brazenly reached across to grab the stem of her chalice so he could drink from it.

"Perfect," she answered, using the tips of her fingers to grab the rim of her cup to stop him. "It means what I do next will be even better."

Once more, he raised his brow, but with worry this time.

CHAPTER FOUR

Rosetta held a lit lantern high as she followed Mr Smith and Pierre down the quarterdeck stairs.

This time, he was no longer gagged, but his pants were unbuttoned as she had done to Derek. Both their faces were smudged in bright red lipstick.

She may have done it more enthusiastically to him since his face was clean shaven. This time, she removed her doublet coat and undone a further button of her tunic. It would mean someone could easily see into her shirt.

I hope my tit doesn't fall out.

Once he was retied, and Mr Smith stood away to watch, she stood in front of this so called 'Bloody Storm of the Seas'.

She raised the lantern above his head to see him completely in the shadows, his face an expression of arrogant swagger. Mean looking, but arrogant.

The jewellery he'd adorned himself with glinted and shone in the light she held up to him. One golden ring hung from his ear, the silver locket around his neck sparkled slightly. From memory, she knew each of his fingers bore a ring.

A certain silence filled the ship – all they could hear was the sloshing waves of the ocean hitting the hull, the creaking of the rigging, the flapping of the sails.

The entire deck was transfixed, watching what she would do. She'd been putting on a good show this afternoon.

It was the first time she'd truly met eyes with him, and the way the light hit his eyepatch, shadowed his face, and made his good eye gleam made something lance through her chest. The scar running from his forehead, under that patch and down his cheek in a deep line, made him seem even more villainous.

Was that fear she felt? No, it couldn't be. Rosetta would never be afraid of a helpless, bound man.

Still, there was something about his look. A promise; one of death and fear.

He looked like a murderer.

Dark, evil, and... sinfully wicked to someone like her, who liked her men a little twisted, bent, and cold enough not to ask too many questions. He was bound, helpless, and unable to do anything but grunt at her with that cloth shoved between his back teeth, yet she felt *interested*.

Like a hunter inspecting her prey while licking her lips.

She fell to her knees into his lap, straddling him intimately, closely. His legs had been spread into an unfinished cross-legged position. It put her knees beside his hips while her ankles came back to rest over his legs in the space between them.

The haunting look in his eyes disappeared as he reared back.

Rosetta didn't react – instead, she reached above his head to hang the lantern on a hook above him. It pushed her nearly exposed breasts right into his face and she could feel his breath fan against her chest.

She lingered for a moment, keeping herself pressed so tightly against him, her breasts slightly moulded around his head. When she sat back, she leaned her elbows on his shoulders, finding his confusion had vanished in exchange for a sneering glare. Being so close to him, she could see the bridge of his strong, pointed nose crinkled with anger.

The lantern above allowed her to see his brown eye had turned nearly bright yellow in the light. The black eyepatch was convex, giving the impression that he still had an eye under it rather than just a basic, skin-hugging patch.

"So, Alister Paine," she murmured, gingerly pushing back the black hair that had fallen from his tie with the tips of her fingers. The top half was tied back into a folded bun while the bottom was loose. It was long, loose hair resting over his shoulders and reaching the top of his chest. "Apparently, I am supposed to be afraid of you."

His eyelid crinkled on the side, making his cheeks lift in an arrogant smirk, or as much as he could beneath the gag.

"Unfortunately, I cannot be afraid of a man I do not give a shit about." His smirk fell, and she grabbed his entire jaw with one hand in a firm, cheek-squishing grip, moving his head around to inspect him. "You *are* rather handsome, aren't you?"

He exuded masculinity. With strong features, his wide jaw and his cheekbones, he looked like intimidating and *manly*. Coupled with his large, defined muscles, she knew he could probably kill a man with a simple punch.

She released his face to stroke his black stubble, caressing his cheek. "Sorry about stealing your ship," she said, oh so sweetly.

His eye narrowed at her insincere apology. He was clearly unsure as to why she'd even tried.

"I thought it was a shred of luck when I saw a warship coming my way. You can only imagine my surprise when the ship flew a jolly roger."

Teasingly, she stroked a single finger over the side of his face, and he shook his head in vain to get her to stop.

"I was expecting to dupe some idiot pirates, playing some broken damsel in need of saving." She raised her hands to gesture to the sails. "I needed a bigger ship, and I do so love a frigate's cannon ports."

She brought her gaze back down to see his expression hadn't changed. She gently stroked his entire face with a fingertip, even caressing the edges of that strangely engrossing scar.

When she tried to lift the patch to see underneath, he thrashed his head to the side, evading her hand. After the second time she tried, she didn't do it again.

He doesn't like people seeing. That much was obvious. He kept trying to run away from her chasing finger, moving his head about, but she refused to let her captured prey escape.

"When I saw the flag, my intention was to get you to take me to your quarters, or perhaps fish me out of the water if someone didn't come for me." Rosetta gave a grand smile. "And, like most filthy pirates, when you tried to rape me, I planned to shoot you in the head with the pistol hidden beneath my skirt."

She tapped the tips of her fingers against his temple. "One shot, no more captain."

She noticed his glare deepening, even his upper lip curling back. Rosetta pursed her lips into a thoughtful pout in response.

"But then you were just so... sweet." Just when he frowned in confusion, she said, "stupid, but sweet."

He glared once more.

"How could I kill a man willing to avenge me after just moments of meeting me? I decided then that I wouldn't kill you. Instead, I would release you in Dunecaster."

He tried to speak around the gag, but it was too tight and deep in his mouth for him to make any sense. She reached around his head and untied it, slowly bringing it away from his mouth.

"Get off me, you wretched sea snake!"

She spread her arms as far at the ends of the cloth would

take her and shoved it through his teeth to shut him up once more.

"Well, that was rude."

He started bouncing her on his lap as he struggled against his bonds, trying to kick her away.

"And here I was about to invite you to dinner."

She gave him a sultry smile and he halted. She removed the cloth once more when she could see he wanted to speak.

"I'd rather drink seawater, you insidious bitch."

He was about to spew more insults as he opened his mouth again, but she grabbed his jaw and forced it shut.

Alister couldn't believe the gall of this devious, deceitful, fiendish whore who took his precious ship from him!

She tricked me! She'd played broken to get him to lower his guard to enact this treachery. This was the most shameful way his ship could have been taken from him. *I let a woman take over my ship!*

The legends around his name would fade and he'd be turned into a laughingstock. He wouldn't be able to make port again without being mocked.

Now the coy snake was coiled on his lap, stroking his face and complimenting him. He knew there was venom behind her benign words. She was up to something, and he wanted her off his lap *and* his ship before she continued to tarnish his reputation.

Without warning, she grabbed his face, hooking her index finger into the side of his mouth to inspect his damn teeth – like they had anything to do with what was going on here.

"Oh ho! Mr Smith!" she yelled with glee as she started pulling his lips to the side. "This one has all his teeth." She tilted her head back to look at the older gentleman. "You do know how much I love it when they have all their teeth!"

He tried to shake her away as she moved to the other side of his mouth. He felt like an attack dog being examined to know if it could be useful or killed to make space for a better hound.

"Oh wait, never mind. He's missing one."

Yeah, I am. He was missing a tooth at the back of his mouth, lost after being punched in the face when he was younger.

Get your fingers off me! He snapped his head forward. His eyes grew far and wide in shock when it moved to the side instead.

He couldn't believe the blistering stinging sensation he felt. She'd struck him. *Him!* Alister fucking Paine, one of the most dangerous pirates on the seven seas. Someone who had killed so many men, it bordered on *mythical*.

His blood boiled, and he turned his head back to her with his nose crinkled tightly. "You–"

She slapped the same cheek again, the pain worsening the second time. "If you try to bite me like a dog, I will punish you like one."

He brought his head back to face her. He didn't know how tight his face was screwing up, but he knew he'd never been this filled with rage before. It tightened his skin, pulsated in his muscles, clutched into his bones.

I'll kill her. He didn't harm the weak, only the strong, and he didn't care if it had a dick or pussy.

And this woman was strong in cunning, body, and emotion. *When I get free, I'll kill her dead!*

"Nngh!" A strangled noise came from him, his eyes widening once more. She was kissing him! It wasn't a gentle kiss, either; it was forceful, almost *violent*. His lips caved under hers as they demanded he take what she offered, even if he didn't want it. She was smart enough to not give him her tongue, but she gripped the back of his hair and made his head tilt back, while also keeping it still so he couldn't turn away.

She did it to make the kiss even deeper.

What the in the seven seas is going on? What game was she playing? She even made a small moan, like she enjoyed the way his lips felt. He was too stupefied to respond when she pulled back, blatantly licking her lips as if she'd enjoyed the taste of him.

The lipstick was almost gone now. He was sure she had spread it all over his face with the way her lips had moved over him. His nose crinkled with disgust. He'd just watched both his men walk out with their pants loose and lipstick on their faces.

"Haven't you had your fill of men today?" he spat though clenched teeth.

"I've never had my fill of men." Humour seemed to make her blue eyes brighten in the light. "What's one more?"

He leaned forward so he was almost nose-to-nose with her. "I'd rather be fed to the kraken."

He'd rather not take a woman taken by his men already this day. He didn't mind the prostitutes in the ports, as long as it was only him they shared their bed with that night.

"Pity," she tsked, not looking particularly upset. "I was hoping my sincere apology might mean we could become... friends."

"An apology is only sincere when you try to rectify your actions!"

"I won't be giving you back this ship." Her eyelids tipped with long dark lashes dropped into a light scowl. "Bark and yell to your heart's content, but you are just wasting your breath. Do you want to eat or not?"

"I'd rather starve."

She licked her lips once more as she twirled a few strands

of his long hair around a finger and spoke like she hadn't heard him.

"I may be willing to offer other things." He felt her hand grip his flaccid cock through his deliberately baggy breeches. "Your men will tell you just how much fun I am."

The shameless confidence on this woman was enough to make his body stir; she, thankfully, had removed her hand before she noticed. Fortunately, he was too disgusted by her harlot attitude and too angry that his ship was overrun to actually grow fully hard.

She dipped her head forward while cupping the side of his jaw. Leaning forward and slightly to the side, she grabbed his singular golden loop earring between her lips and teeth.

She tugged on it.

"Bite me, and I will do it back," she warned, since her neck lay right in front of his teeth. He sighed defeatedly, knocking the back of his head against the wooden mast.

Why is this mad woman doing this?

"Just tell me what you want so you will get the fuck off me." Now that he was acting calmly, though still seething with rage he was unable to leash, he realised she smelt sweet.

She was wearing a perfume. *How long has it been since I smelt a woman?* He expected her to smell haggard, like the brine of seawater.

Instead, there was something about the scent of her. He tried to remember where he knew it, and why it made his chest feel heavy. *Where do I know this...*

He shook his head when the memory of white gardenias sitting at his mother's bedside came to mind, little flowers blooming on a small shrub, almost a bouquet on their own.

He immediately stopped fixating on the way she smelled and barged her with his shoulder to get her to speak. "State your business so you can get your fat arse off me."

It wasn't. He'd stared at it enough with the tights she wore.

He'd been watching her all day, scheming. He'd been hoping to eventually get one of his crew to release him, but she didn't have many of them on the surface. When they happened to be up above, they were constantly watched by her own men.

"Where's the key to the safe?" She sat back and he saw the playful hint to her eyes still present.

Is that truly what she wants? If so, why pester him like this?

"Can't find it, sweetheart?" He leaned forward with a grin. "Good. That booty is mine and my crew's, and when I take my ship back and wring your neck before tossing your dead body into the sea, I expect every bit of treasure to be safe inside."

Sweetheart. It was a pet name he gave to women he felt nothing but contempt for.

She brushed her fingertip over the curve of his nose before bopping the tip of it. "Couldn't help but try."

She ruffled his cheeks with both hands like she was tousling the head of a cute puppy. She finally raised herself from his lap, smiling all the while as she went. Her body was bent, like she wanted his eyes to find her cleavage, her free, unstrapped breasts visibly swaying against her tunic as she stood up straight.

As soon as she stood, her flirtatiousness fell like the act it was. He realised he'd given her something. That, or she was merely done playing with him.

"Oh, Walter!" she shouted with a giggle to someone above.

A thin, coal-covered looking man came sliding down one of the securing ropes of a sail. He continued to hold onto it, swinging in the air as he spoke without touching the ground.

"Ye called, Captain?"

"Tomorrow, how would you like to blow something up? Something big, heavy, and full of treasure?"

"I can make something go boom?" He put his hand over

his heart. "That's worth more than any treasure!"

My poor ship! "Don't you dare!"

She ignored him, not even sparing him a final glance as she practically skipped her way to the helm, dismissing the man steering it.

It took him a long time to notice, but she'd never covered his mouth, or Pierre's either. He was too stunned, too disgusted, his mouth slightly ajar, to speak as he stared at her.

"What a woman!" Pierre sighed next to him. "I think I'm in love."

"Have *fun* did you?" Alister sneered back, regaining his composure. *Whore.* He was thinking about Pierre this time.

The man was promiscuous; a lady's man – always had been. Then again, she must have something worth offering if she'd managed to even get Derek to lower his breeches for her.

"Seems like you're the only one who had fun," he chuckled back.

He turned his head to the side, barely able to see the man in the peripheral of his good eye. "What's that supposed to mean?"

"Did she kiss you as well?" Pierre must have been speaking to Derek with how quiet his voice was. "I know you well enough to know the rest, old man." His voice grew louder when he turned back to Alister. "Looks like you're the only one she got on top of."

He opened his mouth to disagree, accusing them both, then immediately shut it. *Wait a second.*

"Neither of you actually fucked her?"

"Nay, but she seemed earnest with you! I wonder what would have happened if you'd said yes to her offer of dinner, because that's all I got." The man then gave a loud, rolling burp that echoed into the night. "Sorry, been holding that in for ages. I didn't want to disturb you two."

"I'm surprised you didn't try to convince her otherwise."

"Oh, I did; she flat out refused. Said she just wanted to make you green. Don't really know why." Alister was one more shock away from keeling over. "Anyway, I think she was probably bluffing, but she is a rather odd woman."

"Aye, you can say that again." *What's her game?*

They both quietened when one of Rosetta's men overheard them speaking and told them to shut up.

I need to figure out how to take back my ship before we arrive at Dunecaster.

CHAPTER FIVE

As much as Alister fought it, sleep had overcome him while he was watching the woman steer his ship.

He didn't know why some of his disgust had faded at hearing that neither his quartermaster nor first mate had actually lain with her, but it had. Unfortunately, he was still bubbling with anger that she had taken over his precious crew and warship to investigate the feeling further.

He had been mulling over it, scheming how to get free and take them back before he'd fallen asleep. When he woke, he hadn't expected to see her still at the helm.

The bright morning sun bore down on his face, shaking him awake, and his brows drew together when he turned his head to see her still there.

She manned the wheel the entire night?

The hands taking care of the sails had already retired and a new crew had rotated in. Only when the sun was nearing its highest point did Naeem finally come to take the wheel.

Even Alister could see her shoulders and arms immediately slump in relief as she let go. Holding onto her right shoulder with her left hand, she rounded it as though it was injured.

Mr Smith met her as her boot found the bottom step of the quarterdeck stairs.

"Take me to what loot they have that we might be able to

trade and sell at our next port."

Alister struggled against his bounds in protest. *That loot is mine!* He'd stolen it; it was his to sell and bargain for. Pirates weren't always hoarders of gold and jewels. Alister was a trader, and a bloody good one at that.

He'd got top dollar for every bit of fabric he stole, every block of soap he'd taken, and every candlestick he'd commandeered. Then, all the gold coin he won by bargaining, he'd share with his crew as their share of wages.

They'd been at sea for almost eight months. He refused to believe they'd worked so hard and tirelessly, fighting ships, losing valuable men, and spilling blood, just for some little girl to take it!

"Rosetta," Mr Smith said with a worried tone. "You must rest; you've been at the helm all night."

She shook her head, her long brown hair, knotted and tangled, swaying from side-to-side as she gave Alister her back.

"No, I will rest tonight. There is still far too much to be done in daylight, and I won't waste time just for a few hours of restless sleep." She turned to the side, allowing him to see her face as she nodded her head towards the helm. "You will be taking over at night, like usual. Naeem will do most of it today, and then tomorrow, he and I will take our normal shifts."

"You're as stubborn as an ox." He fingered his short hair, combing it back in frustration. "You never listen."

"Leave me be, John," she snapped with a dark tone. "I still need to know what firepower we have. I didn't get the chance to look yesterday, considering the late hour when we took the ship."

A bright smile took over her features, softening them from the tired and exhausted state Alister could see she was in.

"How did the men like the feast I ordered for them?"

It was obvious she worked hard – just like he did. Being a woman, he expected her to run to her bed for a much-needed nap, not continue her duties as a captain. He was watching her, gauging what kind of person she was so he could figure out how to best take her down.

Mr Smith gave a small chuckle. "You sure do know a way to a man's heart. Their bellies are full of good meat and the tension on the ship has lowered. Still, I suggest you don't go below deck on your own."

"I will go where I please on this boat." She pointed at the man's chest, deliberately poking him and causing his shoulder to dip back. "Our men will watch over me, and I will gut anyone who tries me."

"You're a new captain of this crew, Rosetta. You may not know who Alister Paine is, but I do."

Alister's head shot up at his name, then further when their gazes trailed to him. His face was screwed into a silent snarl.

Mr Smith ruffled his hair once more. "If I knew whose warship we were heading towards, I would've advised abandoning the plan."

"It's too late for that," she cut in, her eyes falling away from Alister with boredom.

She really doesn't give a shit who I am. She was a fool!

"You don't understand. The crew are used to a fierce and merciless man as their captain, one with many famous exploits under his belt. If every tale and story I've heard is true, then we have pissed off a bad man who will most likely chase after us with vengeance. He's a criminal, Rosetta, one of the worst kinds."

This brash woman had the hide to stomp over to him like a troll and kick her leg forward with her hands on her hips. She slammed the bottom of her boot dangerously close to his head.

He didn't flinch. No, he calmly looked up to her with a grin as she leaned on her bent knee closer to him.

"Got something to say to me?" he sneered.

There wasn't a shred of fear in her features as she examined him, cocking her head to the side. "Is it true? Will you come after me with revenge leading your path?"

"Oh aye, sweetheart." He wasn't sure what he would do when he got his hands on her, but he knew it would be harsh.

"Then I might burn this ship when I abandon it," she warned, her eyes squinting into a foul glare. "Don't test me."

"Abandon it?"

"Yes, Mr Paine." His upper lip curled back at being called something so common. "I have my eye on something bigger and better than your glorified rowboat."

Better? What could be better than his warship? It was in perfect condition, filled to the brim with cannons. There was no boat that could give her the freedom and speed this one could provide.

Does she not realise how hard it is to take over a frigate in the hands of pirate hunters? What he'd had to do, how much blood had been shed, to simply obtain this vessel was one of his greatest achievements.

"Once I complete my goal, there is nothing anyone in this entire world can do to make me regret what I have done." She gripped his jaw, pulling his head forward as she bent over him further. "You could rape me, flay me, burn me, gouge out my eyes. You could even tie me to the outside of the hull so that I can feel the waves crashing over me as I eventually drown, and I would take it all laughing."

"You seem determined for a foolish woman," he spat. "You will think differently when the time comes."

No one is impervious to pain.

She gave him a cruel smile. "You may be able to pierce my body, but you will never be able to pierce my soul." She threw his head back so hard, the back of his skull bounced off the mast behind him. "Until then, I doubt you will find me before I have sent this ship to sail, by itself, on these seas."

She stood back to walk away from him. "It's a large world out there. Good luck finding me."

"You'd be wise to kill me if you want to live!"

She turned her head over her shoulder to look back at him. "Your crew won't follow me if I do. They made that obvious when they didn't fight mine simply to save your life, like you *actually* matter."

Smart woman. So that's why he was still alive.

"Mr Smith, show me the rest of the stocks," she demanded, leading her quartermaster below deck.

The day passed long and slow with him stuck to the main mast pole. Alister was thankful for the shade cast by the sails when the sun finally started to drop.

Finally, after what seemed like eternity, Rosetta emerged to the surface. Both her hands held the bottom of two plates as she walked across the deck, then up the stairs to speak with Naeem at the helm. He watched the man laugh when she placed one of the plates on the table bolted down next to the wheel.

Naeem reached over and quickly shoved some of the meal into his mouth. Mr Smith followed behind her with chalices, placing one in Naeem's hand. He took a few large gulps before setting it down.

They spoke for a short while before she patted his shoulder and made her way back down the stairs. To Alister's annoyance, she came to stand in front of him yet again. He thought she would glare down at him, as he did up at her, after how their last conversation had gone.

Instead, she knelt into his lap like she had done the previous day, straddling his waist in an intimate position he didn't appreciate.

"Get off me," he growled, his lips thinning.

What is it with her and sitting on me? If his hands weren't bound, he would throw her off his lap with so much force, she would go tumbling over the railing.

"If you bite my fingers, I will ensure you choke," she threatened as she reached onto the second plate.

She grabbed a bit of smoked meat and raised it to his lips. The moment the aroma of food entered his nostrils, his stomach grumbled like a wild beast, but he turned his head in refusal.

"You missed out on chicken yesterday." She nodded her head in the direction of Pierre. "He ate most of it, though. For a skinny man, he eats like a horse."

Alister couldn't help but snort. *She's right about that.*

"Eat, Mr Paine. I will not be feeding you again."

"Don't call me that," he demanded, turning his head back to her with gritted teeth. "My name is Captain Alister."

"A person must have a ship to be a captain, and currently, you don't own one." Her smile was sweet, but her words cut with lethal venom. She pressed the meat to his lips again in offer. "Now, eat."

He bit back the string of insults on the tip of his tongue and willingly took it, chewing with disdain.

Being hand-fed like some child. Oh, the embarrassment!

"I was going to proposition you over dinner." She placed the plate onto his lap, precariously brushing his crotch with the backs of her fingers as she did. "But I knew after speaking with you yesterday that you would deny me."

She picked up the bread and dipped it in some honey. It was one of the few things that would keep for a long time if stored correctly.

"And what would you have propositioned me with? What could you possibly offer me?" He took the bread she presented with his teeth, his eyes narrowing while he waited for her answer.

"You'd be surprised what I can offer."

She watched him calmly, seeming relaxed in the position she was in, and he noted just how dark the circles under her eyes were. She looked exhausted, and her voice cracked like it was getting tired of functioning. It reminded him of the deep voice a woman would get after a night of screaming and moaning.

Just as he was contemplating these thoughts, she dipped more bread into honey, like she was mocking him and his hungry state as she stole from the very plate she'd apparently prepared for him.

She giggled at his dumbfounded expression, and he cleared his throat to regain his composure.

"Ah yes," he projected purposefully. "I do believe I got a taste of what you can offer."

"I may be seated atop your lap, but you are still treating me like a pitiful woman, rather than the person with the wit and power to steal your ship. You lack the power here to continue your condescension. I have *so* much to offer."

"Come," he chuckled. "Do let me hear your idiotic idea."

"No."

His jaw dropped a little at her defiance. She shoved the bread into his open mouth, and he chewed it with irritation.

She raised her hand behind her and Mr Smith placed the second chalice into her waiting palm. She tilted the rim of it to Alister's lips and allowed him a sip of the grog water.

They added rum to their stale water in order to make it bearable; most sailors did.

"I realised yesterday you would reject it, and that if I removed your shackles to eat by your own hands, you would try to attack me." She fed him a bite of meat with a dull expression, as if they were speaking of the weather. "Which is why we have to do it like this instead."

"So yesterday—"

"Men are stupid when angry." She threw him a smirk, one of cunning and pride. "They reveal things they shouldn't in order to hurt, without realising they've showed their intentions."

His eyes widened. "You tricked me!" *Again!*

She tossed her head back and gave a horrid, bellowing laugh. This Rosetta didn't have a feminine sweet laugh; no, she had an annoyingly deep one.

She leaned to the side to face Pierre. "I told you it would work, didn't I?"

"Marry me, please," the blond-haired man laughed back.

"Why should I? You wouldn't give up your port girls to be faithful, and most likely give me a disease in the process."

"That's not fair."

Alister could tell by his tone that Pierre was pouting. He couldn't help thinking, once again: *she's right about that.*

She turned back to Alister.

"So, if you had just shut up and behaved, I probably would have tried to speak with you over food, hoping to gain your trust so we could be of use to one other, and you would have tried to overpower me."

She attempted to give him the last of the food, but he just stared at her, realising why she had tried to tease him the previous day.

Why she had purposely let Pierre and him speak.

It was so he could see the act right after it was played without realising why. She had tried to incite jealousy, anger, any emotion that would have made him appear foolish, and she succeeded.

"You took away your chance to get at me by being foolish."

"You... You..."

He wracked his brain for the worst insult he could come up with, but all he could think of was: *you brilliant, annoying woman!* She'd pulled the wool over his eyes, and that was rare for him.

She shoved the chalice against his lips and forced him to drink before shovelling more food into his mouth. Then she stood, pointing to both he and Pierre, demanding they be gagged for the remainder of their trip. She disappeared into her chambers just as the sun finished bathing them in the last of its orange light.

The following day, he'd awoken with the sun in his eye and her already at the helm.

It wasn't long after he'd woken that he heard someone shout from the crow's nest. "Land, ho!"

For the first time in months, he heard the squawking of sea birds that only ever flew near land. It indicated they'd arrived at Dunecaster Island.

Prisoners were ushered from below and told to climb down to board the rowboat prepared for them, guns and swords pointed at them as they did.

Rosetta wasn't taking them to the port inside the inner crescent of this large island, but rather to one of the many sandy banks on the outer edges. He could see trees swaying in the distance, poking out from the hills and hiding the very few houses this far from port.

Mr Smith emerged from his chambers to take the wheel while Rosetta and Naeem called out commands to the crew.

Once everyone was in the boat except for Derek, Pierre, and himself, they were finally unstrapped from the mast and taken to the side deck railing. Swords were unsheathed as Derek was unshackled and told to climb down the side to the rowboat currently floating next to the ship.

"What about me leg? Ye think I can climb down the side of a hull with a wooden one? Are ye cruel?"

He eyed Alister as he spoke, who returned his look with a subtle nod of his head. *He's going to be a distraction.*

There was no way Rosetta, a woman kind enough to let them live, would let a crippled man do something most would consider impossible. *She will fall whim to his lie.*

Alister had to stifle the urge to grin.

Derek had been a one-legged man for over ten years. He could climb, swim, run, jump, and do everything anyone else could. He knew how to use his body to his advantage, despite such a large part of him being missing.

It made him appear weaker to those who didn't know him, since there was always a negative light cast upon a man without a leg. People judged him immediately, despite not knowing he was stronger and faster than most. He often used his arms to assist him. It was one of the reasons he was so bulky and strong.

"I don't care if you fall off my ship, just so long as you get off it." Rosetta folded her arms and tilted her nose up at him in a snubbish manner.

"What if it falls off while I'm climbin' down? I'd lose me own leg to the sea!"

"Then give it here," Naeem said, holding out his hand while stepping forward. "I'll toss it down to you."

Shit. They weren't falling for his trick.

"Nay," he grumbled, turning to the railing. "I don't trust ye lot. I'll just do me best."

He started climbing over the edge, giving Alister a glare. *You tried, old salt.*

He was still without a plan, and it was getting closer to him having to climb off his own ship. Pierre was next to be pushed forward, climbing over the railing without hesitation.

"I will miss you, my sweet, elegant rose," he called to Rosetta from the other side, reaching his hand out to her as if he wanted her to take it. "I hope our paths meet so we may wallow in our passionate sorrows when you see my beautiful face again."

She gave a laugh in return, and he began to climb down, shaking his head with humour at himself. Pierre often thought he was the funniest man on Old Gaia.

Then, Alister was left standing alone.

More men surrounded him, as though they were aware that now would be his most opportune moment to fight back.

I'm alone. As much as it pained him to admit it, he knew there was nothing he could do. *I've failed.* He hadn't come up with a single plan to escape.

"I'm sorry, but I don't trust you enough to unshackle you," Rosetta said as she loomed closer.

She emptied the coins from the bag around his waist into her palm to steal them, before pushing the key for his bindings into it. He noticed, for the first time, the differences in their height. He hadn't thought he was almost a foot taller than her.

How did such a small woman get the better of me?

She lowered his gag so he could speak.

"How the fuck am I supposed to climb down?"

The smile she gave him was haunting; she came even closer and reached up to hold both sides of his jaw.

Her lips found his, a hard pressing kiss like before, demanding and rough. He tried to retreat from her, his feet shuffling back. Within moments, the backs of his legs found the railing and her hands slipped down to his chest. She shoved him over, and he went tumbling back. His body flipped through the air before he crashed headfirst into the water.

Pierre was still climbing down and watched him fall. The man must have dived after him; after he hit the water and sank, uselessly kicking his legs since his arms were strapped behind his back, Pierre yanked him to the surface.

"Hoist the sails!" he heard her boom from the distance as he shook water from his head. "I want all hands on deck to get as far away from this wretched island as fast as the wind will take us!"

His prize warship was already on the move and Alister could do nothing. He knew she would maroon him on this island, but his jaw still clenched in anger as he watched his own ship sail away.

I bloody failed!

"That was quite the farewell," Pierre snarked as he dragged Alister towards the rowboat by the back of his jacket. He must have seen her kiss him.

"She stole my fucking ship!"

"I think she likes you." Alister turned his head so sharply and so swiftly, he felt his neck crick painfully. "I wish she would have kissed me farewell."

He huffed menacing, quick breaths. "I'll kill her for this!"

"Oh aye, I know you will, but first, let's get to shore."

Alister started kicking his legs to help, his dumbfounded state snapping away, only to be filled with determination.

"Silly woman," he laughed, almost throwing his head back as he was dragged through the water. "We'll be back on that ship by the month's end."

Pierre grinned at him knowingly, while Derek grabbed him by the shoulder of his coat and carelessly dragged him into the rowboat.

On his knees in the small, overcrowded boat with nineteen other men, he watched the stern of his ship, the Howling Death, catch the wind and fade away.

If they had been able to see the front, he would have seen the figurehead sculpture. The forefinger bone of the cloaked grim reaper would be pointing the way, its hand outstretched wide while the other held a lantern. With a howling, screaming face, its hollowed eyes would have been watching the spray.

The sculpture at the front of his boat sent fear into all who saw it, and it had been a source of pride since the day he'd obtained it.

Alister knew, deep down in his bones, he would go after that woman. He would never forget her remarkably striking face, her blue eyes filled with cunning and annoying wit. The smell she gave off reminded him of his mother's bedside table, and the way her mouth tasted...

He would also never forget what the bitch had done to him.

Once he had the handles of his wheel back in his large, calloused hands, he knew his outrage would fade.

He would make that woman pay for what she had done.

He gave a grin, surprising his crewmen staring at him -- he was sure it was an expression that appeared pure evil.

I can make her pay in so many ways.

CHAPTER SIX

Rosetta peeked up under the rim of her hat at the sails as the men worked at furling them away.

The crew worked tirelessly to yank ropes through rigging to pull them up towards their holding rods before neatly tying them securely. Not one of them feared falling, all too experienced to make such a rookie mistake.

Others were on their hands and knees, scrubbing the main deck, while more were in the lower decks, pumping out water. Even more were on the outside of the hull, suspended by ropes, scrapping off the barnacles they could reach without careening the vessel. They were also currently replacing frayed rope, dodgy rigging, and removing damaged timber slats to hammer new ones in.

As much as she thought the ship could do with a thorough cleaning by beaching it and ridding it of rot as well as the barnacles cleaving to its base, she couldn't waste that much time.

Everyone was moving, not a soul resting.

"I expect you all to keep working," she shouted. "We only have a few hours until sunset."

Then, Rosetta finally walked down the stairs to take her below. She no longer had Mr Smith on her tail constantly. After so many weeks, an assassination attempt would have revealed itself by now. It hadn't – all her new crew kept their blades and hands to themselves.

That didn't mean one or two of them hadn't gotten their throats slit at the mention or rumours of a mutiny. With the fear that her crew, truly set on having her as their captain, would hear of it, they stopped trying to have her voted out.

They didn't want to risk their own swift death.

The tension had eventually faded, and everyone worked together as one team. It helped that they'd recently attacked a bountiful trading boat. They'd stolen everything worth taking and she told the men that, once they found port, she would sell it and give them a share of the wages – just as she had done with what had been on this ship when she'd commandeered it.

She'd spent what she'd needed to in order to restock the ship, before handing out most of the spoils to the old crew. She gave a handful of her own coins as payment for helping her.

Rosetta herself had taken very little. She had bigger goals than glittering gold.

Making her way further into the bowels of the frigate, she found the room she wanted with the man she needed to see inside.

"Mr Darkley," she greeted as she entered the dimly candlelit kitchen, taking the older gentleman by surprise.

"Yer got light feet, Silver," he replied, chopping his cleaver through the head of a fish. "Yer shouldn't startle men like me. We tend to swing first, then ask questions."

He turned his large frame towards her. Mr Glen Darkley was a tall man, towering over her with a large, muscled gut and wide shoulders. He sported a well-maintained moustache that curled at the edges, as if he'd managed to gel the tips, but the rest of his face was shaved. His grey hair was over an inch long at the top, but the sides were surprisingly neat.

She couldn't find a better word than stern to explain his

features. His jaw was stern, his black eyebrows stern, and even his wide nose was masculine and stern.

His eyes were usually squinted, as though he showed little care about anything enough to open them fully. His bottom lip, the only one she could see, was always in a grumpy, downward position.

He wore a white tunic rolled up to reveal thick forearms covered in hair. It was buttoned to his collarbone, one button shy of being all the way. He wore brown breeches and a brown apron over top.

"You are just too busy in your activities to listen to anything around you," she rebuffed, taking a seat at one of the long tables available.

She placed her feet on the bench running down the length of it to make herself comfortable.

"Alister had a cleaver thrown at him once," he told her, grabbing another fish. "If I'm willing to throw one at *him*, ye better hope yer just as quick to avoid it."

She leaned back to rest on straightened arms, tilting her knees to the side in a way that spread her legs apart. She didn't care to sit in a lady-like fashion.

Mr Darkley was a calm man; strict, but calm.

He was the cook for the previous crew, and she had come to learn he was an excellent one. Since his food was better than anything her own could make, she'd placed him in charge of feeding the entire crew.

"Where's your boy?" she asked, searching around the dim kitchen and finding it empty.

Clint Darkley was a young boy, no older than fourteen. He had messy black hair that didn't know if it wanted to be long or short. He often tied it back from his face with a faded red bandana so he could see beneath the mop.

Rosetta often found him peeking at her and figured the young teenager had a crush. She was the only woman around and they were always so full of... annoying urges at that age.

"Who knows? Lad's probably off climbing the shrouds when he ought to be down here with me, helping." He nodded to a barrel. "We got fresh lettuce from that trading boat; I needed him to help me peel it."

She'd come to learn he'd opted to stay on the Howling Death because of his son. He thought it'd be safer if he stayed on rather than joining Alister on whatever journey he would be forced on because of her.

As much as she needed all the crew, the idea she could be putting the young boy into a very dangerous situation that could get him killed weighed on her. She'd tried to get them to leave when she'd stopped at Vinil, but he'd refused and she didn't press him.

It wasn't her place.

With a silent sigh, she hopped down from the table and reached into the barrel, bumping him with her hip before extracting a head of lettuce.

"We've just finished setting anchor, so we'll be staying in these shallows for the night." Rosetta grabbed another lettuce head and began to peel. She was glad the men were getting some greens; it would help to stave off sickness if they ate well. "I want to set up a big feast tonight. You'll be required to cook more than you usually do. I want it to be rather generous, a show of appreciation for everyone's hard work."

"Shall I have a plate made up to be brought to yer quarters?"

"I've decided to join."

His moustache twitched, and he turned his eyes, as dark as ink, towards her. "That'd be a sight."

Rosetta had not eaten with this new crew before; she was too apprehensive of them. His surprise didn't come as a shock.

Her gaze fell to his spices instead of responding. "You've got quite the collection."

Mr Darkley gave a huff of what she guessed was pride. "I make sure the crew collect them when they go through other ships, and I often spend my wages on them whenever we port. I keep a large stock. It helps with the tastelessness of smoked meat and dried beans."

She nodded like she understood, currently on her fifth lettuce, before he handed her a knife and told her to cut up smoked meat she'd much rather not touch. As much as she'd eat anything, it didn't particularly have the grandest smell.

"You should get nutmeg. It's sweet but can be added to almost anything."

"Don't know what that is, Silver. It sounds like something for the tastes of women."

She'd long ago realised he'd call her by her last name. She didn't mind it, conceding to let the crew call her whatever made them comfortable, depending on what it was, of course.

She clapped her hands together. "Then you, sir, will soon learn the wonders!"

"Yer seem to know much about the kitchen." He turned to place the fish he'd prepared into pots to cook. "What were ye before a no-good pirate?"

"A stupid girl," she grumbled back, turning her darkening gaze to the food in front of her. "What I was before I became a sailor is of no importance."

She peeked at him from the corners of her eyes to see he raised a dark bushy brow at her.

"Hey Pa!" a boisterous young voice shouted from outside the room. "Have ye seen Captain Rosetta? I cannot find 'er."

They turned their heads to the doorway, and Clint froze at the sight of them. A blush immediately brightened his cheeks, and she gave him a blank look in return. She wouldn't encourage a foolish young boy's desires.

"Now that you are here, Clint," she started, placing everything down on the bench and stepping away from it.

"You can do the job you are supposed to when it's time to prepare the meals."

"A-aye, Captain," he stuttered, coming forward to take over so quickly, he almost tripped.

"Ha!" Mr Darkley laughed. "He doesn't listen to me or Alister, but he'll listen to ye." He slapped the boy across the back of the head. "Yer were climbing the shrouds again, weren't ye?"

"I wasn't, I swear!"

Rosetta, with a silent laugh, left father to scorn son.

She went to check on the tasks she'd handed to the crew while they were stationary. Everything was cleaned to the best of their abilities, the stocks and supplies organised the way she'd told them to. Although everything had a place when she'd taken over, it had been messy and terribly organised.

She was just thankful everyone was adjusting to the new way she did things. They'd learnt she could be cold and harsh, but everything she did had a reason.

She would lash out when needed, but she wasn't reckless about it. *Have I gained enough of their respect though?* She thought some of them had begun to see her differently, perhaps even liked her.

It disheartened her that some refused to acknowledge her unless absolutely necessary. They refused to let go of their bitter resentment.

With another, louder sigh, she took the stairs to the surface, no longer needing to be below deck.

"How goes it, Rosetta?" Naeem greeted as she walked across the timber, giving her a large smile like usual. "You did well getting us here on schedule."

She never doubted that she would. This was a scheduled stop on their trip. She'd always planned to drop anchor and have the crew rest on these shallow shores for the night.

"Of course. The crew must rest before we head out to open

ocean." She placed her hands on her hips. "Are you doubting me, dear Naeem?"

"Not at all; it was nothing but a compliment." He placed his hands up in surrender, his smile never fading. "Jonny boy told me you were dining with the crew this evening."

"Yes, well, I want to see their reaction, since I ordered them a feast. We did well with that last trade boat, and they have worked so hard." Her eyes swept up to the sails that were rolled away, most of the men gone now that there was little to do above the surface. "And today as well."

"Good idea," Naeem commented, nodding his head as he placed his hand on his chin in thought. "I'm sure they'll appreciate it."

The only ones who remained on the surface were those relaxing. Some were sitting and speaking with each other. Others leaned against the railings on their forearms to watch the horizon as the sun exploded in colour against the sky.

She was sure they were trying to see the green flash of light that would spark when the last of the sunlight faded away. It wasn't that rare of an occurrence if one spent long months at sea, but there were many fabled myths surrounding it.

One of the men was carving into a piece of wood to create a carved statue. Many of the crew on this ship before she'd taken over used it as something to do in their downtime.

She'd come to enjoy watching them, often praising their skills. They shyly smiled at her compliment, and she figured they rarely received soft words. Rosetta knew encouragement was a good way to gain their favour.

She waved Naeem forward so he would move. "Let us speak of the next route and what is to come. Where is Mr Smith?"

"He's in his quarters, having a grandpa nap."

Rosetta wacked him in the stomach. "Stop picking on him. You know he hates it when you talk of his age."

"But Rosetta, I fear he will die of old age at helm."

The chuckle he was trying to stifle made her turn away before he realised she was smiling with humour.

One of the reasons she enjoyed Naeem's company so much was because he was a rather gay man, quick to laugh and often sharing that with others. *He's like a brother to me.*

After waking Mr Smith, all three entered her chambers, which also served as the navigation room, to speak about the rest of their trip, how and where they would sail.

They did this often, making sure they were on schedule and taking the best route possible. They rarely shared their plans with others. Her original crew knew what she was after and why, but it was protected information she didn't want to share with the new additions.

Only when it was on the horizon would she tell them what was to happen.

Before long, night fell, and a knock sounded at the door to say the feast was ready. Rosetta put an arm around each of her friends' shoulders, giving a large smile.

"I hope you're hungry, boys. I've instructed Mr Darkley to cook a feast to fill your gluttonous bellies."

Naeem and Mr Smith nodded as they made their way below deck to join the many others in the dining area. Dozens of men were seated in front of long table, while others were on the floor with their food, digging in with hungry hands.

It was a large area, but fairly cramped with the number of men inside it. Mr Darkley was serving food and taking away empty plates as he went.

"You're joinin' us, Captain?" one of the men asked, pausing with a forkful of fish and lettuce at his mouth.

A string of eyes found their way to her as she entered.

"You bet ya," she answered back. "So, move your bony arses down." She used the tip of her boot to make the men shuffle down so that she and Mr Smith could be seated at the end of the bench. Naeem took the opposing side of the table to face her.

"The chickens are all gone already, you selfish pigs!" She reached forward to grab a section of fish, some dried beans, and fresh lettuce, piling them onto her plate.

"It's fast hands down here," someone yelled down the table. "If you wanted chicken, you should have eaten in your quarters."

Her lips thinned at the prudent tone.

"I'm not bothered." She'd been joking, after all. "Eat well, boys. You deserve it after the past few weeks." She searched the table. "Now, where's the rum?"

A bottle suddenly slid down the table and she quickly caught it before it fell off the edge. The tension that thickened the air after her entry eventually settled, and the men ate comfortably as they talked amongst themselves.

Chatter was constant, the bellows of laughter frequent. The sounds of crisp food crunching, mouths chewing, and utensils clicking filled the area. Lit lanterns hung on the walls while candlesticks melted carelessly onto the wooden tables.

It was a mismatched mix of men. All ethnicities were represented, which was common with their profession. No one cared too deeply about the colour of skin when they were worried about surviving on the harsh seas or fighting for their lives.

Someone stood on the table, holding their hand out like they were gripping an invisible sword. He was telling a tale of an old fight they'd had attacking a ship. Both crews liked to tell stories of heroics from before they'd met. They were often the villains, but they spoke like swashbuckling heroes.

She didn't care that it was a story about the previous captain's endeavours, not when she could see the entire crew bright-eyed as they listened. *This is quite the tale.*

"You're forgetting how Pierre lost his sword, so he stole

the scurvy dog's peg leg when the man was on his back," one of the men butted in. Apparently, the two men had been fighting back-to-back but were overrun. The crew eventually came together to save them, but it had almost ended in defeat.

"Derek was furious with him for weeks!" another piped up. "Even tried to get the captain to nine-tails him!"

Nine-tails was a kind of whip used to achieve high levels of damage when giving lashings. She'd seen them in her quarters when she'd gone through Alister's possessions. She'd never seen one before, and she could tell this one was well used.

"Reminds me of a tale of Rosetta and me when we took our first ship," Naeem chuckled. "Minus the peg leg."

"You almost got me killed, you daft twit," she laughed, kicking him under the table.

"I was trying to save you!"

"What?" a man down the table nearly growled. "Didn't try to trick the opposing ship with your pussy?"

The words hit like a dagger, quick and sharp.

Apparently, some were still rather upset with how she'd deceived her way into taking over the Howling Death.

Mr Smith smacked the bottom of his fist on the table, a loud thud stealing everyone's attention. "She is your captain, and you will give her the respect she deserves!"

She threw up her hand to silence him before he launched into an angry ramble that would only make his face grow beet red.

"Let's be real, boys." She laughed, gesturing both her hands forward. "I use what I have available. As you saw from the last takeover, I am more than willing to pick up a sword, but my greatest skill will always be my wit."

"You say you have wit, but you don't know what's coming for you."

A sigh fell from her lips. "I am a woman, whether I want

to be seen as one or not." She let her eyes skate over the men. Silence had overcome them as they turned their gaze to her. "Only a foolish woman would believe she can outdo the brawn of a man."

She made a show of grabbing Mr Smith's meaty bicep.

"I will always use my skills to my advantage, but I am strong enough when it counts." She pointed to the man who spoke ill against her. "I'm not some weak helpless woman who sits in port, sewing needlepoint tapestry, while she waits for her Jolly Sailor Bold. I have my strengths."

"Ye say yer strong, but ye got pissy little arms," someone else chimed in. "I bet ye couldn't beat tiny Clint in an arm wrestle."

"I'll take that bet!" Clint exclaimed with a grin, raising his arm into the air like he'd won the treasure of a lifetime.

"No," she giggled. "I'd rather not steal the poor boy's coin."

"I'll pay his wager," a different man offered, throwing a silver coin onto the table. "I know I'll be reaping the reward. You're weak. You won't be able to beat a fourteen-year-old."

With narrowing eyes, she nodded for Naeem to move, and Clint took his seat.

With a childish grin, the blue-eyed boy raised his pale arm and wiggled his fingers. He was taunting her.

She took his hand with her right, and Naeem placed his hands on top of their clasped fists.

"You'll be doing double duties with your father if you lose," she told the boy, whose grin fell immediately. "I think Mr Darkley would like that."

She peeked over to the chef standing to the side.

He folded his arms across his meaty chest. "I hope she wins then."

She and Clint turned back to face each other. Naeem counted down from three and then released their hands.

Within a second, Rosetta slammed the boy's hand against the table. She knew she'd win, and cheers rung out.

"He didn't even stand a chance!" someone yelled.

Laughter followed.

"Double duties, Clint. For a week," she told the bright red-faced boy.

Naeem patted Clint on the back. "They forget she mans the helm. She has her strength."

"I'll take ye on," a voice said calmly.

She raised her brow at the large man who climbed his way to her. He brutally pushed the boy out of the way and plopped himself into the seat instead. Hitting his elbow against the table, he held his hand out.

"Unless yer afraid to pay up."

Kent was the man's name, a brown-haired, tan man who was practically a giant. He liked to keep his face clean shaven, but his hair was never the same length, as if he often sheered it precariously with a dagger.

"You're twice her size!" some yelled. "That's not a fair bet!"

"Who gives a shit?" he spat, his grey eyes squinting. "She thinks she's got something because she can overpower a little boy." He wiggled his fingers. "How 'bout ye take on a man. That'd shut yer pretty mouth up."

"No problem," she said with a smile, placing her elbow on the table again. She confidently grabbed his big fist with her smaller one. "What's the bet?"

"Ye show us yer tits."

"Rosetta..." Mr Smith warned.

Her smile grew wider. "And if I win, you will wear my lipstick every day for a week to show just how much of a big, ugly girl you are."

With a grunt and nod, they tightened their hands to curl around each other's thumb. Naeem came to place his hands on top.

"One. Two." He moved his hand. "Three!"

Just as their hands started pushing and Rosetta felt her arm starting to fall, she grabbed her fork and stabbed it into his bicep, right near the crook of his elbow. A yelp sounded and she took the opportunity to smack his fist against the table.

He shot up, slamming both his hands flat against the table. "You cheated!"

"Of course, I did!" She laughed at his snarled-up face. "I'm a pirate! We don't play fair."

"In this game, we do!"

"I used wit against brawn. That is what I do, that is how I win, and that is why I am Captain." Rosetta knew what she had to do now and stood, turning her head to the side to nod. "Clint, step out for a moment."

With a whine, the boy did as he was told, and Rosetta worked on untucking her tunic from her tights.

"What in the seven seas are ye doing?" Kent asked as he cradled his elbow.

"I cheated, so I will pay up my part of the bet."

Rosetta lifted her tunic and exposed her breasts for all to see, taking them by surprise. Some whistled at her, others bashed on the table. Of course, there was an overwhelming amount of cheering.

Her face was unbothered as she stared at the wall. *One. Two. Three. Four.* She lowered her tunic and tucked it back in again. Then, she reached into the small pouch attached to her hip to pull out her red lipstick.

"But I still won." She threw it at the man, and he skilfully grabbed it from the air. He inspected what she'd thrown at him with a shocked expression. "Every day, you will be a little girl for us all."

His mouth drew open, his flabbergasted expression so precious, she found it worth exposing herself. He was a stupid man, an arrogant one who wasn't charming.

"You may start now." When he looked unsure, she added, "Do you need me to do it for you?"

"Farkin' damnit!" He couldn't refuse her, not when she had indeed won *and* paid her debt. He applied the lipstick to his mouth, doing a terrible job of it, might she add.

"Oh Kent! Such a pretty woman," one of the men laughed. "Will you suck my dick with your bright red lips?"

More insults and teases were thrown at Kent, who grumbled as he took his seat, plopping down defeatedly. He ate in silence, huddling around his plate with shame.

"Does anyone else want to wear lipstick?"

No one answered her.

CHAPTER SEVEN

Like most nights, when Rosetta returned to her quarters to sleep, she jumped into the hammock in her tights and tunic.

She'd removed her boots and doublet coat, hanging them over one of the chairs, her hat sitting on top. Inside the hammock with her was a pillow and blanket to keep her warm throughout the cool night.

As much as she tried, it was hard not to think about the man who had once slept in her hammock. Everything smelt of him, musky and masculine.

There was the lingering tinge of salt covering every nook and cranny of the vessel, she could also smell a hint of sweet wood and bark. A scent belonging to men who were like strong, warm trees she wanted to cuddle into as they shared that intoxicating essence of sweetness with her nose.

It was heady and often made her miss being curled under a warm body.

Where are you now, Mr Paine? she asked the ceiling as she stared up at it, her hands folded behind her head.

She had one foot inside the hammock while the other swayed back and forth outside of it, making it shift side-to-side.

She could only imagine where he could be, perhaps still stranded on Dunecaster. Then again, after meeting him, he may already be trying to follow her.

Good luck, she snorted.

The ocean was vast and finding her was near impossible.

Within a month, she was hoping to have completed her goal; she doubted he'd ever find her again.

Which... was a shame.

His voice, although filled with obvious rage, had been rather a deep, husky baritone. It would have been pleasant with naughty words or soft grunts of pleasure.

She'd liked the way he looked. *Long black hair.* She twirled a strand of her own in thought before rubbing it over her lips. *Eye that looked like the sun in daylight.* She'd found it quite spellbinding and stared at it while she'd been feeding him, despite paying careful attention to their conversation.

A big wide body. He was covered in muscle; she bet he'd crush her if he laid on top of her, which, quite frankly, she adored.

He'd had black chest hair she would have enjoyed running her fingers through as she admired the bulky strong muscles beneath it. He was covered in so many scars, she doubted he'd mind if she added to them.

Strong men don't mind being clawed at.

Rosetta disliked soft men who cried if she dug her nails in too deep. *They always stop thrusting just as I'm climaxing.* It always stole the intensity of lust-making, forcing her to lie still like a virgin maiden.

She gave a small smirk. *I doubt he would've been like that.* Alister looked rough, brutal, the kind of man who could have tossed her onto the bed from the other side of the room.

It was hard not to think about him when she knew he was on her tail, and she was surrounded by his scent every night as she slept. His men also spoke of him incessantly, like heart-sick lovers.

From the moment he'd opened his big dumb mouth and chose to avenge some poor, helpless woman, she'd been attracted to him. Well, she would have been attracted to his good looks regardless, but she wouldn't be fantasising about him without the words he'd spoken to comfort her.

That strange kindness, from someone who looked like a scarred villain, tugged on one of the few heartstrings she had.

Ugh! Rosetta turned to her side to curl up. *I miss men!* Men who weren't her crew; she could never cross that boundary, *ever*.

I want to see my port boys.

A good stiff fucking would stop her fantasising about the arrogant Alister Paine just because she was sleeping in his damn hammock.

It would stop her from trailing her hand down her body and into her tights so she could caress her delicate, throbbing clit, playing with the sensitive nub at the apex of her thighs just to rid herself of her self-created ache.

Once she had what she wanted, she'd steer the ship straight to port to let her crew, and herself, finally blow off some much-needed steam.

With her plan set, once she gave herself a kind of blissful, orgasmic relief, she finally closed her eyes.

Deep into the night, Rosetta was jolted awake by the sound of a bell. *Ding. Ding. Ding.* She was immediately alert.

The warning bell. She rolled out of the hammock with skill, falling through the air before her bare feet swiftly found the floor. *We're under attack.*

She grabbed one boot and shoved it on. The other, she shoved on her other foot as she hopped around to grab her weapons belt.

Who the hell is attacking us?

They were anchored near the shore of an unoccupied island, far from any shipping routes. No one should be able to see them, surrounded by mountains on one side and open sea on the other.

"Raise the Jolly Roger," she yelled as she opened her door. "If they're pirates, let them know to back off!"

She froze when she glimpsed men climbing over the railings of the main deck. It was too late.

"Rosetta!" Naeem shouted, climbing the steps two at a time. He'd probably been asleep too, since he looked just as dishevelled as she did. "I can't see another ship."

"Then drop grenades into their row boats!" She turned and pushed him back down the stairs. "It's a sneak attack."

Of course, it was. That's why they were being invaded with the dark of night covering their approach.

"Whoever they are, they will regret trying to take my ship!" She walked to the railing of the quarterdeck to speak to her crew surfacing one-by-one, nearly ninety men ready to fight. "I want them all dead!"

How dare someone try to take over my ship! In the dead of night, no less!

Her men began to fight the enemy who had finished their climb onto the deck. It was done near-blindly, as some of her crew worked to light the lanterns so they could see their foes. Last thing they wanted to do was attack their own men in the confusion.

Someone climbed over the railings on her level, like a creepy spider emerging from the darkness. It was hard to see him in the dark of night as he held onto the shrouds. The crescent moon above was the only reason she could see him at all, casting the front of him in shadow.

She unsheathed her sword to raise it at her attacker, and her eyes nearly bulged out of her skull. *He's as big as an ogre!*

"Did ye miss me, lads?" a boisterous, booming voice chuckled out.

There was a wave of silence and pause that washed over the entire crew. Even she knew the familiar voice.

Her lips parted in disbelief. *Alister.*

His crew that had chosen to stay on the ship with her turned on them.

He stepped down seamlessly from the tall railing, like he was merely taking a normal step. At the same time, he drew his cutlass sword, glinting in the moonlight, as he stomped his way towards her.

"I told you you'd regret not killing me." There was a smugness to his tone.

Then he swung.

Rosetta deflected it, stumbling to the side from how swiftly she'd needed to protect herself. With a menacing laugh, he swung sideways.

She had to curve her body backwards to miss the tip of his blade cutting across her stomach. Her hair waved in front of her face, almost blocking her view for a moment. When he tried to slash downward, she pushed the flat edge of her long blade and held the length of it against his.

She kept him at bay, but her arms bounced downwards at the sudden force of his weight. She could feel her arms shaking. He was stronger than her, which was no surprise.

When he reached out to grab her, she ducked down and walked backwards. She couldn't take him head on like this. He was too big for her alone, too strong, too tall, too everything!

I have to run. But to where? *I just need time to think.*

"If you want me," she mocked at him, "you have to catch me."

She turned to run towards the quarterdeck railing and heard him give chase. His weapon belt jiggled around just as much as hers and their boots hitting the timber beneath their footsteps thudded hard through the night air.

Grabbing a rope to the sails, she flung herself off the edge of a rail. She flew through the air, aiming towards the rear of the boat before swinging back around.

Her boots found the main deck, right in front of the cabin where Naeem and Mr Smith slept. Without hesitation, she opened the door and locked herself inside, frantically looking for a place to hide.

She'd seen him jump from the top railing and land onto one knee when she'd entered the room. The door flew open, banging against the wall before swinging shut. She emerged then, her pistol raised at his head.

As though he knew she was there, he suddenly pushed her hand upwards before she could shoot him. She released the trigger before she accidentally wasted the one bullet she had.

He held her wrist tight. "Got you, lass."

She kneed him in the crotch with every bit of force she could muster; she knew she'd kneed him in the balls.

He grunted, loosening his grip as he keeled over a little, grabbing at his precious jewels she'd just damaged.

She lined up her pistol again. He stepped sideways and slapped her arm to the side, knocking it from her fist. Rosetta slashed forward with her sword then, and he raised his cutlass to block it.

Shit. What do I do now?

"Get off my ship!" she yelled, slicing her sword through the air once more.

"It's my ship!" he roared.

He swiped his leg out to the side and tripped her. Her sword flew out of her hand as she fell, crumbling against the timber. She stifled a wince when her elbow and hip smacked against the ground, her sword clanking against the floor and out of reach.

He grabbed her wrist to try to force her onto her stomach and into submission, but she booted him in the gut before she punched his good eye with a heavy hit.

He grabbed her other wrist so she couldn't attack him again, but that wouldn't stop him. Rearing up, she sunk her teeth into his arm, biting him like a rabid dog.

She knew she must have drawn blood, with the cooper taste that flooded her mouth.

"Give up. I've already got you, and my men will overtake yours in the next few minutes." He twisted her body so her front was against the floor, capturing both her wrists with one, large hand. "You've lost."

Even though it was useless, Rosetta kicked her legs and wiggled her body in a bid to escape. *No! No! No!*

She hadn't completed her goal yet! *How did he even find me?* It had barely been a month since she abandoned him on Dunecaster Island.

When he lowered himself against her back to keep her from moving, she snapped her head back. She felt the back of her skull collide with some part of his face and he gave a yelp of pain.

"Bloody hell!" He picked her up by her arms and shoved her back against the ground, knocking the wind from her by bashing her chest against it. "You just don't give up, do you?"

I was so close! She had been waiting years to be this close. She almost, *almost,* felt real tears welling in her eyes. They tingled in her nose, and she fought to suppress them, refusing to allow this man to see her emotions.

"So, what now?" she asked through clenched teeth, turning her head back to look at him over her shoulder. "I can only imagine what you've got planned for me."

He sat over her bottom, straddling it to keep her down. He raised the hand not holding her arms behind her back and rubbed his stubble-covered chin, looking up at the ceiling in thought.

"Not quite sure." He turned his eye down at her, a grin forming across his features. She noticed his canines were large and sharp, making his grin almost wolfish. "But I know I'm going to enjoy the hell out of it."

Alister yanked her to her feet, shoving her forward while still holding her arms behind her. He opened the door and brought them out into the open, setting the sharp edge of his cutlass at her throat.

"Got her, lads!" he yelled, his voice flying across the deck. Those closest to them paused their fighting, making those further down halt when they realised what was going on. "Drop your weapons or I'll slice her pretty throat."

The sound of swords clanking against the wooden deck sounded. No one resisted when they understood they'd lost. Their surrender was immediate.

Her eyes found Naeem's, whose eyelids curved under heavy bows. He looked disheartened. He looked disappointed for her. He even mouthed, *'I'm so sorry'*.

Rosetta shook her body from side-to-side in a last attempt to free herself, but he only pressed his blade closer on her neck. She turned her head up to avoid it, having to stretch her neck back to the point where it was almost painful.

"Tie them to the main mast and the railings," he commanded, forcing Rosetta to watch her men be bound. He pushed her forward. "And her with them."

Multiple hands grabbed her, dragging her backwards. They shoved her down to her backside to not only tie her to the mast, but also bind her hands in front of her.

Daylight began to break over the horizon as they were finally fixed to the ship and unable to escape. A lavender purple sky still twinkling with stars showed them it was going to be a beautiful, cloudless day. Such a pretty sight for such an ugly situation.

She would much have preferred the misery of rain.

They were so close to land, they could hear the sounds of seagulls squawking. It sounded as like they were mocking them and it made her mood sour further.

She was tied to the main mast, next to Naeem and Mr

Smith, others lining it they circled the wood completely. The rest of her men were tied to the deck railing supports.

She watched Alister as he stood in front of the cabin door on this level, hands on his hips, a triumphant look on his face.

"Good job, lads." His eyes swept over the men standing – his crew. "It feels good to see all your ugly faces together again."

A wave of chuckles rolled over the crowd, and even Rosetta could feel the cheerful energy that rolled from them.

She'd thought Alister looked good bound in shackles and forced into submission, but he looked irresistible with the confidence that now seeping from him. His strong chest was puffed with pride, contentment making his rugged face appear even more handsome.

Dick, she sneered in her mind.

Rosetta needed to think a way out of this, but currently, that didn't seem possible.

He paced the deck as he looked over her crew with thoughtfulness. His grin had grown smaller, but it was obvious he was in a rather good mood.

"Here's what's going to happen. You are all going to swear your loyalty to me and join my crew." He disappeared from her sight, but she could hear his heavy bootsteps as he stomped. "You will stay on my ship, under my command, and earn your wages. You will work, whether you want to or not."

He started up the other side of the long deck, walking in front of every single one of her crewmen, before coming to stand in front of her again.

"Say aye if you agree."

Rosetta narrowed her eyes when he looked at her, and she saw the twinkle of humour in his features. *He's expecting them to instantly join him.*

When silence fell over them, she watched as his humour slowly faded and realisation set in.

None of her men were willing to switch sides.

"You say aye," he warned, his smile fading into a mean sneer. "Or you die."

"We'd rather hang than abandon Captain Rosetta!" Naeem shouted, squirming in the ropes tied around them all.

One of Alister's dark brows raised in astonishment. "All of you?"

"Nay," one of her men said, before another, then another, until every single one rejected his offer.

She knew the way her pursed lips turned into a smirk looked menacing, that the way her eyes squinted with glee helped derail his happiness.

He removed his cutlass from his weapon belt and pointed the tip of it under her chin to lift her chin.

"What if I take her life? Will you still wish to swear your loyalty to a dead woman?"

"Do it and find out," a voice shouted from the other side of the mast.

"Most of us have sworn to follow her to the grave," Mr Smith finally chimed in. "If that means joining in her death now, then so be it."

"Most, but not all. I say aye," a man tied to the railing said. Her gaze fell to him, and she gave him a soft smile when he whispered, "I'm sorry Rosetta, but I value my life more than yours."

"It is fine. I harbour no ill feelings," she told him. "But you will never be allowed to join my crew again."

He seemed to wince.

A second 'aye' followed, and then a third.

Silence filled the area once more.

Three men. Three men had surrendered to Alister's will and would be spared death. The rest of her thirty-odd men remained on her side.

Staring down his cutlass at her, Alister patiently waited for more. When none came, he stepped back, shaking his head in disbelief.

"Truly? You all wish for death, including hers, rather than to join my crew?" He pulled his cutlass away from her chin. "What witchcraft have you cast over these men that they would so hopelessly follow you?"

"Freedom," Naeem cut in, making Alister's eye move his way. "We were not forced to stay as her crew; we have all chosen this path. You cannot offer us what she has."

"I am offering you more than freedom!" He cut his sword to the side, making a whooshing noise as it sailed through the air. "I am offering you treasure and the ability to leave my crew once we make port!"

"We have chosen to follow her for a reason."

"And what reason is that?" His upper lip curled back in agitation, and the glare he wore made his face seem dark and ruthless.

Even Rosetta thought he looked frightening, but she felt little fear. She couldn't, not when her goal had fizzled from her grasp and now laid as a heart-wrenching ache in her chest.

"Freedom," Mr Smith reaffirmed.

"Freedom," another said, before they all began to chant the word in unison.

Freedom. Rosetta closed her eyes as she listened. *Freedom.* She let her head rest back against the wooden pole behind her, turning up to the sky. *Sweet, sweet freedom.* She breathed in deeply through her nose before letting out a relaxed sigh. *My freedom.*

She opened her eyes once more to face Alister.

A frown crossed his features. He truly thought her men would have caved – it was obvious he couldn't comprehend why they would choose to follow a woman over him.

"What's it going to be now?" she finally asked, her men quieten. "Will you cut our throats and feed us to the fish? Will you hang us? Will you imprison us, sell us to the highest bidder? What is the punishment for stealing your precious ship, *Captain Alister?*"

I must say, I'm rather disappointed I won't finish what I set out to do.

She wouldn't have minded if death found her after she finished, but it was rather hollowing now that she was facing eternity before completing her task.

CHAPTER EIGHT

Alister had to make a choice. No, he had to make a plan, because he didn't bloody have one!

He'd honestly thought her crew would join his, considering he was a man, and she was a woman. He was the great 'Bloody Storm of the Seas' after all, and she was nobody.

What was he supposed to do now?

He mulled over his options while some of the crew who stayed behind showed him the changes she made to his ship.

Everything was neat and organised in a way that was, surprisingly, better than how he left it. He wasn't happy, but he couldn't deny it was more efficient.

Everything had been changed, from the way the cannonballs were stored to the barrels of food now in alphabetical order. Their recent loot was put away in a manner that allowed for maximum storage space for more.

Even Glen Darkley's kitchen had been rearranged and, apparently, the stubborn man was rather pleased with it. Not even Alister could get him to change his ways if he didn't want to.

He was surprised to see Clint there, already helping his father, considering the boy liked to hide in the sails if he could. He hated kitchen duty.

"What are you going to do to her?" one of his crew asked.

Alister didn't like the look in his eyes.

"What's it to you?" he snapped, grabbing him by the collar of his shirt to bring him closer. "Grown to fancy her while she was captain, did you?"

"No." Greyson rubbed the back of his brown, medium-length hair. "But she was good to us. We expected her to treat us like shit, but she didn't."

Another man came to lean against the wall in the dim hallway with his arms folded. "She was fair."

"I don't give a shit what she was. She stole my ship."

Actually, Alister *did* care how she'd treated his crew while he was gone. He cared about their well-being, not that he showed it.

Now that he was in possession of the Howling Death again, he wasn't too upset he'd lost in the first place.

He wouldn't tell them that, though.

"Aye," the one against the wall said with a nod. "But we're saying she ain't bad."

"Bitchy," another man laughed as he rounded the corner, walking past them with a small crate of rags. "She was bitchy, but she was funny."

These three men had fought with him when he'd returned but she'd somehow managed to gain their respect. *How does she do it?* Alister couldn't believe his ears. They weren't saying it, but he knew these men were asking him, in a roundabout way, to show her mercy.

How does she get men to fall to her will? They were like him, not interested in *mercy*. So, why her?

Things had changed on his ship. Already, he could see the friction between those who stayed behind and those who had jumped off at Dunecaster with him.

Those who journeyed with him were rightfully angry; they wanted payback and punishment for everything they'd suffered getting here. Those who stayed behind were relieved to have him back, but also worried for those of her crew they had started, unwittingly, building relationships with.

"She must be a siren then," he spat, pushing the man away. "Since you've all lost your bloody minds."

"Nay, just one hell of a woman."

Greyson shook his head. "I think the feast last night helped to convince us she's crazy."

Which, of course, they liked.

"Why?" Alister asked, his brows crossing.

"Where is Kent?" Greyson laughed. "We should get him to give the Captain a big, wet kiss."

A laugh sounded from them before they walked away, hoping he'd follow. Curious to know what the hell happened, Alister did.

It didn't take them long to find the man even taller than Alister in height. He was standing in his sleeping cabin, going through his personal items like he feared something had gone missing during the takeover.

"Good gods," Alister remarked. "Why is he wearing lipstick?"

"Captain!" Kent exclaimed in shame, rubbing the back of his arms across his mouth to smear it away.

"Hey!" Greyson leapt forward. "You can't remove it just because you're ashamed Alister's here."

"She's tied to the mast." He pointed his finger at Greyson. "She can't force me to follow the bet."

"Yeah, but we can!"

"Tell me what is going on!" Alister yelled, appalled that she was forcing one of his men to wear lipstick like some... some... woman! *What has she done to my men?*

"She beat him in an arm wrestle."

Alister's eyes widened. *Impossible.* Kent was almost as strong as he was.

"She stabbed me with a fork! It shouldn't count."

Greyson wagged a single finger at Kent.

"She still slammed your fist down. It doesn't matter that she used her brain to do it." He wagged it even harder as he said, "And she paid up her side of the bet because she knew she'd cheated."

Well, that made more sense.

"She bet that you wear her lipstick if you lost," Alister stated, folding his arms across his chest to hide his curiosity. He rubbed his chin. "What was your bet then?"

"We all got to see her tits." Kent grinned, cupping the air in front of his chest. "Had been dying to see her rack."

Alister gave a bellowing laugh. He couldn't believe it. "She actually paid up?"

"Oh aye," Greyson said, his smile forming. "She offered because she knew she'd cheated the rules of the game but told Kent here he still had to pay up for losing. Told him he had to be a pretty woman for a week."

"And you'll honour that bet," Alister told him with a chuckle, slapping Kent on the back when he gave a whining groan.

"Look, if you want her dead, then so be it. We will follow your lead," Greyson sighed, ruffling the back of his hair again. "We don't really care what you do with her, but we can't say we hated her in charge."

He expected Kent to disagree with him, but the man merely turned his gaze away when Alister raised his brow. *Even he agrees?*

"Your expression has been noted," Alister told them, looking away from Kent before turning from the room. "I'll think on it."

He didn't need to. He'd made up his mind a long time ago that he wouldn't kill Rosetta Silver, not if he didn't *have* to.

Actually, there was much he wanted to do to her and none of it required violence. Unfortunately, he didn't trust her.

He'd thought he'd imagined it, perhaps exaggerated her beauty from the last time he'd seen her, but he realised he was mistaken. *She's a bonnie lass.*

Other than being sleep tussled, her long brown hair had been brushed – unlike the nest of knots he'd seen last time. Her deep blue eyes twinkled with the sunlight growing on the horizon, catching his attention every time he looked at her.

Her nose was small, curving upwards. Her lips pouted with a defiant cuteness he thought she'd displayed before – rather than just appearing that way.

Those wild freckles from many years in the sun reminded him of the wild personality she'd already shown him. Her skin was light but tanned.

She hadn't been wearing her doublet coat this time, so he'd seen her in those black tights and white tunic tucked in just below her palm-sized breasts. Her body was curved, but strong.

He'd bet that tunic hid strong muscles.

Still, the lass had kicked him in the nuts, blackened his good eye, and split his upper lip. She appeared gentle, but she was anything but.

And Alister liked them feisty. A nasty piece of work who could take him when he wanted to vent his many months at sea like a rutting animal.

This woman would be able to handle him, might even enjoy it, and he couldn't do anything about it because he knew she'd most likely try to slit his throat.

So, what was he supposed to do with her?

With a grumble, he walked through the lower decks of his ship to breach the surface. His men lazed around the ship, very few of them needing to watch over their captives. Most of them were below deck, since the ship was stationary and didn't need manning.

He entered his chamber on the quarterdeck and inspected

it. There were a few of her personal items laying around. More specifically, there was a tiny chest filled with the dress she'd used to trick him, as well as other items of little importance to him: shoes, perfume, womanly things.

Then, he noticed the pillow and blanket in his hammock. Pulling on the blanket, he brought it to his nose to find it smelled like gardenias, a scent she'd worn last time.

It seemed to be a favoured smell of hers.

It was strange to think that an odd woman had been sleeping in his bedding.

He moved away from the hammock to inspect his desk and her route, wondering where she was heading and why. It looked as though she was trying to intercept a ship, but he couldn't find any information stating which one, only some diagrams of its interior.

What are you up to? Alister could only guess.

He spent the rest of the morning in his chambers, fixing it back to the way he liked.

CHAPTER NINE

Not long after Alister attended to his cabin, steaming food was brought in and placed on the dining table. He'd ordered Glen to make food not only for himself, but the men who had travelled with him. None of them had eaten well for the last few weeks.

He continued to shuffle papers, going through them carefully, while they set down plates and a bottle of grog, as well as rum.

"Bring her in," he ordered.

Alister realised he should hide her long, double-edged sword in a better location than across his desk. He'd also found her pistol and placed it on the dining table to keep in view.

Can't have her reaching for either.

A few moments later, Rosetta was shoved into the room. Her hands were already unbound, like they had no fear of her – which Alister didn't.

"What is the meaning of this?" she asked with a brash tone, folding her arms across her chest to stand in the middle of the sparsely lit room.

His were already folded while he leaned his backside against the desk. He looked over to her with a mocking sneer.

"You have quite the hide to speak like that as a captive."

She gave a defiant upturn of her head, snubbing him with

her little nose.

The sun shining through the timber gridded window was the only thing casting light into the room. Alister walked to the eating table and pulled his chair out. He sat, not pushing it back in.

After he curled his arm over the corner of the backrest of his chair, he gestured to the seat across from him with his hand. "Sit."

"What? Dinner before you kill me?"

He gave a mocking snort. "If I wanted you dead, you'd be dead." He brought his eye from the chair to her face, raising a brow. "I do believe this would be lunch, considering the hour."

With unladylike stomping, she grabbed the armrest of the seat, turning it slightly to create room. It scraped loudly against the floor as she proceeded to plop herself into it.

Alister grabbed her pistol, cocked the hammer of it, and pointed it at her head. "You and I are going to have a little chat."

She looked at the barrel of the gun with a bored expression. "Pointing a woman's own gun at her. That's a rather low move."

"Ah, but you see, I can already tell you're a devious fucking bitch." He placed his elbow on the arm of his chair while he kept the gun trained on her. "If I don't do this, you'll try to scheme a way of killing me, considering I've taken back my ship."

With a harrumph, she folded her arms once more and crossed her legs in frustration. He reached for the bottle of rum, poured a silver chalice of it, and slid it over to her.

"Drink, eat, speak with me."

He took a chug from the bottle directly, hitting the base of it with a thud against the table when he was done.

"You were pretty smart with the way you tricked me." He

saw her lips part in surprise at his compliment. Her squinting eyes trailed down his broad chest and then back up to his face with an unsure expression. "You wouldn't have taken over my ship if you hadn't done something so dishonourable."

Her arms loosened before she finally unfolded them to grab the chalice. She gave a long a sigh.

"There is no honour with pirates."

"True." He gave her a grin. "Which means you're good at it."

She cocked an eyebrow at him, taking a sip of the rum like she didn't care if he'd poisoned it or not. The feast between them wasn't fancy, but it was enough to pique her interest by the way her eyes swept over it.

"I saw you organised my ship."

"The systems you had in place were inadequate." She finally gained the courage to place an egg on her plate. "I've just made improvements to what was already there."

Alister had been surprised to see two chickens on the ship; she must have bought them when she'd taken them to port.

"I didn't realise they were so lacking until I saw the changes," he admitted.

Rosetta narrowed her eyes at him suspiciously. "You are being gracious. Why?"

Alister started piling his plate with smoked meat, dried beans, eggs, and whatever else he could grab from the bounty before him. He eventually placed the pistol down, close to his plate just in case, so he could eat.

With a knife and fork in hand, he said, "I am merely reflecting on what I have seen. I have many questions." He pointed his fork full of egg in her direction. It slipped from his fork to splatter against his plate. "I'm also rather curious how a wee lass like yourself found herself on these seas, became a pirate, got herself a loyal crew who would die for her, and then made her way to captain a ship to commandeer mine."

"I don't have to tell you jack shit about myself, Alister Paine," she practically growled.

He gave a shrug like he didn't care, looking away to focus on his food. *I missed Glen's cooking.* The crew who'd stayed with him had been terrible cooks.

He ate like a starving boar, ravishing his plate with not a shred of etiquette or care for the lady in front of him. He smacked his lips, filling his mouth with heaping, hungry bites.

She, on the other hand, took small, neat bites of her food.

When he was done, he leaned back in his chair to watch her nibble at her own plate while he took swigs from his bottle.

"I am rather curious. You sold my loot."

"What of it?"

He placed the bottle down, rolling the base edge of it. "What did you get for it?"

She pursed her lips. "Three-hundred and sixty-seven pounds."

"Ha! How did you manage that? I calculated around three-hundred and twenty."

She gave her own laugh. "Mr Smith was a hard-working businessman before I met him. He can swindle any man out of the highest price. There is none better than him."

Alister knew exactly who he was from overhearing their conversations when he'd been her captive.

"Then why is the safe so empty?"

What did she do with all of that coin? He'd expected to see a hoard of it, yet there was barely anything inside.

"A hundred and seventy of it went to your crew," she admitted, grabbing her chalice to lean back in her chair, mirroring him. "A further eighty went to mine."

Alister cocked his head to the side, his brows furrowing deeply. "Why was it unfairly shared?"

She gave a shrug, talking over the rim of her silver cup. "Your men earned it, mine didn't."

She gave more to my men because they'd been the ones to steal it. It was clever on her part.

"You only did so because they would have been upset otherwise." He gave a huffing chortle. "You did it to appease them."

"So?" She rolled her eyes at his imprudent tone. "You mock me by pretending to know me, but anyone in my position would have been a fool not to do it."

Alister pointed the rim of his bottle at her. "You're right, which is why I agree with it. I just won't let you spin webs to deceive me; you've already done enough of that."

The naughty smile of pride she gave made him wipe his mouth on the back of his hand. That smile could do twisted things to a demented man like him. He found it suggestive – even if she was trying to be malicious.

"What do you really want?" She waved her hand at the table between them. "You haven't just invited me here to eat and converse. Tell me what you want."

"In due time."

He let his eye trail over her, hoping she didn't see it for what it was: appreciation. The woman had a body men would kill to touch, and she sat in way that exuded wicked confidence.

That assertiveness gave the assumption she would be bold. Alister had to force himself to not let his wandering eye linger and return to her face. *She looks like she'd ride me well. Too bad she'll most likely try to cut it off first.*

"What did you do with the rest of my loot? Where's the rest of the coin?"

She sighed once more. "I spent it fixing and supplying the ship. The number of holes I found were pathetic and we barely had enough food and water to make it to port."

"Vinil port," he told her.

When her eyes squinted, a dark grin began to form across

his lips, curving them wide enough to reveal his teeth.

"How..." She seemed to think better of her question. "How the hell did you find us? This island is deserted; not many sail near. No one knew we were approaching it. How did you know we were here?"

Finally, she asked him the question he'd been waiting for, and he was so proud of his answer, he even started to snicker.

"You're witty, but foolish." He leaned forward, resting one of his forearms across the table. "While I was tied up and your crew weren't looking, I instructed one of my men you'd kept to find out your plan. They climbed the outer hull, crawled through the window of this room, saw your plans, then relayed that information to those you'd imprisoned. Those lads gave me that information when we were in Dunecaster."

Paling realization struck her face. Her eyes widened, her lips parted in a stupefied expression.

"Aye, lass," he chuckled, reaching over the table to point a thick finger at her. "You'd written this pit stop. Since you had to port, and we were already at one, we laid in wait for you. We saw you approaching from shore."

The small boat he'd used to get here was hiding between the mountain walls.

"But how did you even get a ship? It's barely been a month!"

Alister had to admit, he was having fun revealing his scheme to her, detailing how she'd failed.

It serves her right after what she did.

"I had a small chest of treasure buried on Dunecaster in case I ever faltered, got drunk, and gambled our supply funds away." He shook his head, finally leaning back. "Luck on my part. I don't gamble like I used to, but it meant I had the funds to buy another ship, supply it, and head straight here in less than four days. We arrived three days ago."

He'd gotten his men to row to shore when he'd taken back

his ship so they could burn the one they'd used to get here. He hoped she would ask him about it so that he could tell her he it was currently burning, because he didn't want to give her the option to somehow getting away.

"That's why you were so confident!" She bashed the bottom of her fist against the table to punctuate her words. "And here I was, thinking your arrogance was unfounded."

"My arrogance is never unfounded," he answered with humour. "I have chests buried across the seven seas, except for the south."

They were all small chests, ones that barely held much, but enough to save him if he somehow messed up.

"Why not the south?"

Alister liked the hint of curiosity in her voice, as well as the appreciative eye she gave him, even if she tried to hide it behind a sip of her rum.

He gave a shrug. "Haven't sailed it much."

"Because you're after Dustin 'The Raider's' treasure."

A scowl washed over him. "How did–?"

She gestured her hand towards his desk. "I went through every nook and cranny of this room. It wouldn't take a genius to figure out what you're after with all the crossed-out maps."

It was true. Alister was after The Raider's infamous hidden, and apparently vast, treasure. It was said to be a place rather than a hole he needed to dig, a cave filled to bursting with gold. He wanted – no, *needed* – to find it, own it, possess it.

He'd also sworn an oath to the previous captain before he died that Alister would prove it wasn't a myth. Mad Dog had been laughed at for racing after it, and Alister was set on proving he was right.

"Aye," he sighed, his eyes closing in frustration that she'd figured it out. "That's what I search for."

"Fool." She thrust the insult at him like a dagger. "Even I

know only mad men chase after it."

Alister let his usual cocky grin fill his face and leaned against the table once more. He tapped two fingers against his temple.

"Good thing I'm not right of mind, then, eh?"

He expected her to glare; instead, a smile curled her lips. She'd liked his comment, and he liked that look.

She's a tempting woman. Her words danced with his like the tango of battle, sharp like a thrust of a sword. Her posture said she cared little about her predicament, as if she was confident she could scheme her way out of it.

Her piercing blue eyes weren't afraid to hold his own, something most women shied away from. They didn't often like his external appearance, or his mean demeanour.

She was willing to go toe-to-toe with him.

"Surrender your crew to me," he said gleefully, lightly slapping his hand against the table to punctuate his demand.

"Excuse me?" Her words sounded like they'd clogged in her throat, high-pitched and dumbfounded.

"Surrender your crew to me and I'll head straight to port and let you go, alone."

He was willing to offer this pretty little snake freedom for entertaining him so well.

She blatantly laughed at him.

"No way!" Her shout was full of adorable giggles of defiance as she sipped from her chalice. "You're demented if you think I'll give up so easily."

"Between the two of us, we have lost valuable men. I won't push my crew to the bone just to fly my sails."

He was finally at why he'd called her in. Now that the formalities were over and he'd hopefully gained enough of her trust, he could be open about what he needed.

Unfortunately, it wasn't what he *wanted* from her.

"I don't care. I won't hand over my men to you." She

narrowed her eyes down her nose. "They're mine."

"I don't keep long-stay prisoners, and I don't sell men." He wouldn't waste his supplies and he didn't partake in human trafficking. "The men on my ship work for me, or they die."

There was no in-between. He wouldn't make her the exception simply because she was a beautiful woman. Alister was a pirate, a killer, a criminal.

He was never the hero in anyone's story.

"No. I won't be separated from my crew."

There was a desperate hint to the way her eyes widened for a moment, the way her brows twitched instead of frowning completely.

Her fleeting emotion faded, and she crossed her arms across her chest. It wasn't done in defiance, not with the way her face was turned to the ceiling, like she was deep in thought.

She's trying to think of a way out. He almost wanted to laugh at her.

"You have brought me to the perfect place to maroon you lot until your answer changes."

The way her eyes slowly trailed to him with shock was delicious. *She will learn that I'm cruel.* She would come to fear him, as she rightfully should.

"I don't even need to move the ship to push you into the water. Tempest Island is well-known for where we pirates maroon men." He gave her the evillest grin he could muster, hoping to scare her just a little. "Either your answer will change after five days, or their loyalty will fade with hunger and desperation. They will abandon the captain who allowed them to suffer."

She threw her hands forward. "What if we help each other?"

"Come then, let me hear it."

He made himself comfortable in his seat, wondering how

she was going to try and bend to her will. Would she resort to more trickery? He was rather excited to find out.

One of his brows raised when she rose from her seat and made her way over to him. His hand shot for her pistol, which was still cocked, and he pointed it at her. He slid his chair back so there was space to easily manoeuvre if needed.

She didn't seem to care about his defensive posture, or the gun. She picked up his empty silver plate and threw it to the floor so she could sit in front of him on the table. It clattered against the ground in a circle before finally settling with a ringing *ting*.

Her knees knocked together between his, her hands back against the table while her bottom seemed to rest on the edge.

"Watch it," he warned, turning the gun from her torso to her face. "I don't particularly trust you."

"I'll help you get more men, your own, if you help me get a particular ship."

Alister's eyes crinkled so deeply, he thought it'd begin to hurt as a laugh grew in his chest.

"I don't help charity cases, lass." He relaxed in his chair, sprawling in it like a lazy noble. He rested the elbow of the hand holding the gun on the armrest once more. "I'm not the kind of man who steals from the rich to give to the poor. I don't care who suffers in this world, as long as it's not me."

"But–"

"Nay," he answered with a scowl.

She kicked both her legs forward, the bottom of her boots hitting the corners of the armrests. Her legs were spread directly in front of him, and the way she leaned forward to rest her elbows on her knees allowed him to see directly into her opened tunic, down to her bare stomach.

It was still enough to cover her breasts, but the dip in her body meant he could see the inner parts of those mounds. They were round, pale in comparison to the tanned skin of her upper chest, just begging to be touched.

There was nothing to strap them down and they jiggled in the tunic, catching his attention as he'd tried his damn hardest not to look. He was rather envious some of his men had seen them but he hadn't.

He quickly looked back up to her face before he was caught.

"Why not?" she asked sweetly, her lips pouting more than usual.

"Why should I do anything to help you?"

Her perfume caught in his nose with how close she was: sweet smelling flowers that reflected nothing about the harsh woman in front of him. She was a devious bitch, smart enough to use wiles against stupid men, and he considered being a stupid man for a moment.

His hardening cock was begging him to.

"Is there nothing you want from me?" Slowly, like approaching a feral animal, she reached her hand out. She touched her fingertips to the dark hair of his chest revealed by his own white tunic. "I can get you another map of Dustin's treasure, one you don't have."

That was the problem with Dustin's cave of loot. There were many fake maps, and he'd been chasing them all down, going to each location just to find it had been another empty lead.

"You cannot promise things you don't have."

Her touch was surprisingly gentle, her fingertips trailing up his chest until she was brushing them over the side of his neck.

"But I know they are on the ship I want."

"Pretty lies," he huffed, his voice almost cutting off when she brushed over his jugular – not because he was worried she'd injure somewhere so vital, but because the tickling sensation made his breath catch.

He pressed the barrel of the pistol under her chin in a

blatant threat. She seemed to understand he didn't mind her touch; he just didn't want her to attack him.

Her hand came back down to finger the thin silver chain around the base of his neck. She followed it until she found the pendant high on his sternum. He felt the metal go from warm to cool as she flipped it to look at the other side.

When she lifted it carefully to inspect the writing on it, his free hand shot forward to wrap around her wrist.

She gave him a small smile, her blue eyes holding his singular one as she moved her hand away. "Surely you wouldn't strand a poor, helpless woman on an island with only men."

"Maroon," he nearly gasped when she slipped her hand inside his tunic to palm his chest, precariously brushing one of his nipples. When it happened again, he knew she was doing it on purpose.

"And aye," he said with more confidence, his momentary stutter fading. "I would."

"What if they hurt me?"

She was trying to convince him he was putting her in harm's way when indeed she was the danger. She wasn't a helpless woman and they both knew it.

"Then you don't truly trust your men, do you?" He cocked his brow at her mockingly. "Surrender them to me if they are so terrible. I do like them rotten."

He needed her to. He needed her to cave, to have her men take his command. They would obviously fight to the death in protest unless she told them not to. He could kill them, but then sailing this large ship would be a struggle not even Alister could handle with the number of men he had left. It was all because of *her*.

Her hand reached up to brush fallen strands of his long jet-black hair from his forehead and cheeks. There was something in the expression she wore; a sensual sweep over his face, an almost enthusiastic gaze as she drank him in. He refused to believe she was doing this for anything more than deceiving him. His eye moved to her chest as though he was drawn to it, only to find her nipples had visibly hardened against the thin material barely clothing them.

Was she actually becoming aroused?

No, she was just trying to dupe him. He wouldn't fall prey to her again, wouldn't be swayed by this woman who was obviously, and outrageously, teasing him. She wasn't even trying to hide it.

"Alister."

His eyes shot up, realising he'd been caught trying to find those rosy peaks if he looked hard enough inside her shirt.

She leaned her body forward, her free hand coming to rest on his forearm while her other caressed his cheek, sifting her fingers through his long stubble.

"Surely there is something I can to get you to help me."

Her lips found the side of his neck before she suggestively stroked the tip of her tongue across his jaw.

Alister grabbed her thigh and tipped her forward, forcing her to fall back as her arse found his lap, and she gave a small yelp of surprise.

Her legs were spread around his torso, the back of her thighs on the arms of the chair. Her upper back leaned against the edge of the table as he forced her down and away from him.

He placed his forearm across her stomach while he bounced the pistol against the corner of her jaw.

"You're playing a dangerous game, lass."

His lips thinned into agitated lines – not because he was irritated, but because she was toying with him. He'd grown an erection long before she'd started playing this game.

Alister knew he shouldn't cave to his desire.

He was angry at his own body for not staying in control,

and the moment he gave that away, she would use the knowledge to manipulate him. He realised he'd only made it worse by having her closer to him, sitting on his lap.

"There is nothing you can say or do to convince me otherwise." Alister knew it was the truth. "Give up."

"Nothing?" She started to sit up and he let her, hoping she'd get off him now that her antics had failed.

"Aye, nothing. So don't start something you won't want to finish."

The way she sat up and stared at his face, only a few inches between them, was enough to derail him. He refused to show it, even when she subtly licked at the seam of her lips.

If she rolled her hips any further forward, he knew she'd feel his erection press against her in those thin tights. He just hoped she didn't.

"I'm a stubborn man. You won't win." Not like this, not in this situation. Rosetta could offer him anything and he'd still say no. "You're better off trying to think of a better offer than whatever it is you currently think will work."

She didn't falter. Her lips curled into a small, provocative smile, a defiant one. He wanted nothing more than to remove it with his own mouth.

Then she grabbed the sides of his head and crashed her lips against his, tilting her body forward and sitting against his hardened cock.

Alister curled his arm around her shoulder and gripped it, pulling her back to separate them.

"What do you think you're—"

She cut him off by pulling his face towards her and kissing him a second time. With gritted teeth, he grabbed the back of her nape with his large hand and pulled her back.

"Oi, lass. It isn't going to work!"

Once again, Rosetta shot her head forward and crashed her lips against his. She giggled against them, making his shaft twitch. She rolled her hips against him as best as she could with how her legs stretched on the armrests. That stroke was enough to pain him.

Screw it. She may not be giving him what he needed, but damnit if he didn't take what he wanted. He'd been wanting to fuck the absolute hell out of her since she'd pushed him off his own warship and sailed away with it.

She was offering, and Alister was going to show her why she should have heeded his warning. He picked her up, still holding the pistol while getting to his feet. With his free hand, he pushed everything within his reach from the table.

He slammed her back against it with force.

She let out a gasp of surprise at how hard he'd slammed her down, giving him the perfect chance to slip his tongue between her lips. He forcibly licked the inside of her mouth, feeling her tongue slip against his.

For the first time, Alister kissed this treacherous woman back, and he did so with earnest.

He thrust his cock between her legs, showing her exactly where this was going to go now. Just to make sure she understood, he slipped his hand under her arse, lifting her to grind his hips harder against hers.

Her mouth tasted like a mingle of food, rum, and sweet woman. He devoured the taste of her, the feel of her lips, with rough, demanding, and forceful kisses.

Alister was surprised by the small mew she gave when he tilted his head and deepened the kiss further. She even reached one of her hands up to tangle it in the loose half of his long hair, pulling him in like she *wanted* him as he worked on the ties of her black tights.

I'm going to make her regret this. Alister was set on breaking her. He was going to rail her body and he wanted her to absolutely hate herself with how much she enjoyed it. Because right then, he was a tangled mess of emotions, and it was all her fault.

Instead of killing her, he was near desperate to feel her glove his cock. Instead of punishing her, he wanted to take her, have her pining for him when he was done with her. Instead of hating her for her devious, tricky, dishonest nature, he desired her for it. He needed to see how she'd unfold at the mercy of his hips – and he was unwilling to be benevolent.

"I told you not to start this game with me," he growled as he broke the kiss. He leaned his head to the side and drew his tongue across the fast-beating pulse of her throat. She tasted of sweat and salt, and he sucked on her pulse-point, taking more of her in. "Now you can't be upset when I play it."

He wouldn't let her get away. *She better fucking want it.*

She gave a rolling, quivering breath when he pushed his hand into her tights and palmed down her flat stomach, feeling it dip under his palm. His middle finger slipped between her folds as he cupped her between her legs.

She's wet. Her pussy was slicker than he thought it'd be. He angled his head down, like he'd be able to see despite their bodies being meshed together.

Could it be she actually wants to fuck me? Could it be more than just using her body to get her way, to deceive him? He doubted he'd ever find out the truth from a liar like her.

He circled his fingertip against her clit as she rolled her hips against him. He realised she wanted him to go lower. It was almost like she was impatient when he was just trying to be courteous.

The tip of his finger found a deep pool of wetness when he reached her entrance, and he pushed inside. He stopped when he felt she'd taken him all the way to the thick, ruby-set, golden ring on his middle finger.

He felt her tense around the intrusion and his brows creased together as he explored the deepest part of her.

"You're surprisingly small."

cock. She was *so* very tempted to.

Only when she fastened the ties around her waist did his eye finally look up to her face.

He cocked a brow at her, a grin forming across his features. *And there is that smug face,* the one she had been expecting.

Rosetta returned it.

She knew he'd enjoyed this and would want more, just as she already did. She could use that to her advantage, although that wasn't why she'd done it.

She had just wanted to satisfy the fantasy she'd had for so long, to take him and soothe the burning need that had been building in her since she'd first started sleeping in his room. Surrounded by his scent. Surrounding by his things.

Rosetta had used him for her own selfish need.

"I'm still marooning you on that island, lass."

Her smile grew and she moved forward, being careful not to knee his still exposed monster, to straddle his lap. With light touches, her hands came up to caress the sides of his neck before they went to his nape.

"And I still don't care." The breathless groan he gave was wonderful as she pressed her lips to his jugular. She felt that rod of his tap against her thigh like he'd pulsated. "I won't surrender my crew."

Then she pulled back and tucked her tunic into her tights to right herself.

He rolled his eyes in a dull expression. "So be it."

He tucked his cock away, not caring to fully do up the buttons of his breeches. He grabbed her hips and lifted her off him as he stood.

She had to stop herself from giggling as he carried her out of the room by carting her at his side, but she did kick her legs in excitement. He threw her through the doorway and into bright sunlight.

"Aye lads, looks like she's chosen to be difficult."

CHAPTER TEN

Rosetta stumbled out onto the quarterdeck before he grabbed her hands and held both her wrists behind her with one, giant fist.

Alister walked her down the stairs and her eyes found Naeem. She noted his angry stare as he watched her man-handled and she knew, without a doubt, she'd been heard.

Her tit hurt and the sensitive bits between her legs weren't fairing much better. She gave him a grin, and his face grew into a bright smile of humour.

"Looks like she got what she wanted, boys!" Naeem shouted with a laugh.

There was a slight pause when they were almost to the bottom of those steps, like Alister was dumbfounded by his statement. She turned her head back to see he'd frowned before shaking it off.

"It was adequate enough," she chuckled when she looked back to her bound crew. He shook her like he knew what she said was an understatement. "Looks like we're being marooned, boys."

"Five days should teach you all enough of a lesson," Alister added with a dark tone, but she could hear the hint of malevolence in it.

"I say we eat Harvey tonight," Naeem suggested, turning his head to look at one of the men tied to the railing.

"Hey!" Harvey shouted from the other side. He bounced on his arse while jutting his chin towards another man. "Eat Carter, he's got more meat on his bones."

A string of laughter followed.

"You've got a strange crew," Alister said to her.

"Strange crew for a crazed woman," Naeem answered.

"I'll give you crazy, you piece of shark shit," Rosetta bit back, kicking her leg out at the man – not that she could reach him with Alister holding her back.

More laughter came and she noticed Alister's men gave each other confused looks.

Not wanting to waste time, Alister told his men to start untying hers one-by-one.

"Last chance," he offered when the first one was taken to the side and told to stand on the railing. She was apparently going to have to watch them all jump.

"Are you going to jump, Mr Smith?" she asked the older gentleman. "Or should I push you myself?"

With a brash confidence, he didn't jump but simply fell backwards, his arms outstretched. He twisted his body at the last moment so he could dive in hands first.

They all jumped in without hesitation, and Rosetta watched with her hands held behind her back with a bored expression. She heard the crash of bodies hit the water and eventually saw a string of men swimming towards the shore.

When it was her turn, she was shoved forward towards the railing. She was finally let go, the last of her crew on the ship.

"You'll miss me when I'm gone," she said to Alister, turning to him instead of stepping onto the railing. "You'll come for me before tomorrow ends."

He folded his arms across his broad chest, giving a short chuckle, like he truly found her words humorous. "I think not, lass. I'll see you in five days when you're ready to stop this foolishness."

Her eyes found the pretty Pierre standing next to him. She blew the blond-haired man a kiss, gave Alister her middle finger, then ran for the side of the ship.

With a perfect swan dive, she jumped over the railing and headed straight for the sea. She crashed into it, feeling coldness rush over her skin, causing goosebumps to prickle all over. The moment she broke from the water's glittering surface, she started swimming, not looking back to see if she was being watched.

Her boots were waterlogged, and her clothing was soaking wet as she waded in knee-deep water near the shore. Her hair slapped against her cheeks and wrapped around her neck as she swiped it out of her face. The salt of the sea dripping into her eyes burned them and she tasted her salty tears upon her lips.

Naeem came to get her, grabbing her arm like she needed help walking out of the water by herself. She didn't, but she appreciated the caring gesture regardless.

The sand made a squeaking sound with every footfall. Even though the water in her boots made it hard to walk, she didn't empty them until she was no longer walking through messy sand.

Her eyes scanned over the island they were on, placing her hands on her hips. It was a small mountain, as though the earth had jutted a spike of land through the water with violence to create it. There were minimal palm trees, and it obviously wasn't habitable. Still, that meant there was shade.

At least the coconuts will hydrate us. It was a hope of survival to not die from thirst so they could all suffer through hunger. That was why this island was cruel to be marooned on. Desperate to live, marooned men would drink to extend their suffering.

"So, what now, Rosetta?" Naeem asked while her crew greeted her all together. "I know you haven't left us on this island without a plan."

"Are you a betting man, Naeem?"

Without a care in the world, she shoved her hand inside the front of her tights, fishing around.

"You know I am," he laughed.

She finally pulled what she wanted from her pants. "What's the bet that Captain Alister Paine is actually a mamma's boy?"

She started to twirl something around her index finger, being careful not to fling it away.

"One silver he's not." Naeem's smile died, his eyes growing wide. "That's your gamble? Rosetta, I will truly eat Harvey if you've really gotten us stranded on this island for five days."

She turned to stare at the sea and the ship that stayed where it was, as though it had no intention of leaving. *He's going to taunt us.* He might be expecting her men to swim to him when they couldn't take starving anymore.

"Then I bet you two silvers," she said with a confident gleam. "He'll be here before tomorrow morning." She held what she'd stolen in her hand. "If not, we can eat Carter."

"Hey!"

Alister was resting a forearms on the railing of his ship, watching Rosetta and her men swim to shore.

His was relaxed, thankfully sated, with humour curling his lips. She'd gotten him off and he felt far clearer headed because of it.

"What's your plan here, Alister?" Pierre asked, coming up beside him to watch as well.

He placed both arms on the railing, bending forward to lean

against it while Alister turned to the side, one knee bent in front of the other.

"Some of her men will cave," he told him. "I don't need her entire crew. If at least half agree to my command, we'll have enough to sail." It'd be better if they all did, though. The more hands Alister had, the more he could share the workload.

His eyes turned up to the sails that had been neatly tied away. It took at least thirty men just to get this ship going comfortably and, although he had that many, it took even more to maintain it.

They couldn't drop anchor in the middle of the sea, and this ship needed around the clock work.

There were other departments that still needed to function as well; the cleaners, the repairers, the stock hands, those that helped Glen Darkley cook. With their combined crews, they had just over eighty good men. Of his own, she'd managed to drop his sixty-six men down to the fifties.

He'd help man the sails if he needed to, wasn't shy to make repairs and get his hands dirty. He'd just much rather he didn't have to.

"What do you plan to do if she agrees to give up her men?"

"Take her to port," he admitted. "Last thing we need is a woman on our ship inciting jealousy."

Pierre raised his brow and Alister returned it with a colourless expression.

"I can do what I want with her in the meantime." He turned his head back to see she'd reached shore. "I have a lot of anger I'd like to take out on her."

A lot of lust, too.

Pierre gave a snort, nodding his head like he understood. "She did steal your ship. That's a feat in and of itself."

"Brilliant bitch," he sneered, but the words didn't hold any real menace. "She's a cunning piece of work and it's obvious she'll do anything to win."

Even let me fuck her.

He knew there must be a reason other than desire that she'd let him. He may have caved, but he wasn't a fool to believe there wasn't evil intent behind her actions.

"Sounds like you."

Aye, it does sound like me. But Alister had used his brawn and cutthroat lack of morals to get his way.

"She's more dangerous." This time, both Pierre's brows raised in disbelief that Alister would admit it. "She's the kind of woman who will kiss you while slitting your throat."

He rubbed his chin, remembering how she'd held the gun to his jaw. He thought she'd may have shot his head off if she hadn't been about to reach orgasm.

"The crew have told me everything she's done since she dropped us off at Dunecaster," Pierre said. "I think I might have to agree with you. At every turn, even when taking down a trading ship, she used her wit to her advantage. She managed to turn most of those who stayed behind to like her."

"I know." Alister felt a soft breeze cut through his clothes, making it bubble away from his body as his hair crawled across his shoulders. "Greyson asked me to show her mercy."

"Considering what you're doing now, I'm guessing I don't need to ask for it on their behalf, then."

He nodded, but he wasn't pleased Pierre had been told to ask for mercy. It furthered Alister's belief that she may be some kind of wicked enchantress.

"Aye, I decided on the way here I wouldn't kill her." Even though she wasn't some meek woman, the idea of harming one still didn't sit too well with Alister. He'd kill a woman if she tried to kill him, wouldn't be the first time, but he didn't want the blood of women or children on his hands if he didn't have to. "I don't mind if she suffers a bit in the meantime, though."

"Five days is a long time."

"They'll signal when they're ready." Alister slapped him on the back before gripping his shoulder. "I want crew in the crow's nest watching the shore until that happens. I give them three days before they come to their senses."

"I'll let the men know what to expect."

"Good. Now, have you eaten?"

"Aye." Pierre gave him a satisfied grin while patting his stomach. "Glen gave us our meals while you were busy."

"Did you leave any food for anyone else?" Alister laughed at the grumpy face he received. "You're a pig, lad. Have some decorum."

They turned away from the railing and Pierre followed as he walked up the stairs to the helm. He didn't need to be here, the ship stationary, but he couldn't stop from placing his hands on the wheel. Gently, he turned it from side-to-side, relieved to feel the polished timber under his calloused palms.

It was the only thing he truly cared to maintain.

I missed you, you old boy. He leaned between the handles, unwilling to depart yet from his favourite part of his much-loved warship.

"So, lads!" Alister yelled, catching the attention of most above the surface. "Who wants to drink and play dice?"

What else were they going to do for the next few days other than laze around and get up to drunken foolery? Before long, crates were brought up for men to play on, either crouching around them or sitting on the deck. Some found their musical instruments and started playing while they sang sea shanties.

With a bottle of rum in his hand, and a cigar between his teeth, Alister watched his men. The sun wasn't far from turning into a sunset and he was rather pleased with the shouts, yells, laughter, and the occasional punches from his crew.

They were a violent bunch, but they rarely held grudges.

"Come here, pretty boy." One of his men patted his thigh while whistling at Kent.

Kent, with bright red lipstick, proceeded to punch who whistled at him so hard, the man was knocked to the ground, unconscious, in one go.

"How's that for pretty?" He spat on the ground near his feet. "Dickhead."

"Kent!" Alister shouted, walking to a barrel and patting the top. He placed his elbow on it and wiggled his fingers. "I'll make you a bet. If you beat me, I'll wear the lass' lipstick, and if I win, you have to wear her dress."

The man pointed his finger at him. "Ye can't stab me with nothin'."

"Nay, lad. I can beat you with nothing but my arm." He wiggled his fingers in a taunt once more.

"Then I'll take that bet!"

On the odd occasion, Kent had beaten Alister in an arm wrestle, mainly when he'd drunk too much or manned the helm after a difficult storm.

He was feeling rather confident he'd win today, though.

"I think the lads would like to see you in a dress."

He received a growl as Kent slammed his elbow on the table and grasped his hand. Crewmen surrounded them, excitement filling the air at watching their captain participate in their revelry.

Cigar still in his mouth, Alister placed the bottle of rum down to grab his good luck charm. Before any fight, any takeover – anything that required a gamble – Alister would grab the locket around his neck to kiss it.

It was a ritual of his, and one he never missed doing.

He'd carried it with him since he'd been a young boy and considered it a good luck charm. It was his most precious keepsake.

Yet, when he felt around his neck and sternum, he felt nothing. He turned his head down, expecting to find it and couldn't.

The cigar fell carelessly from his mouth. He released Kent's mighty fist to search inside his tunic, patting his body.

It's gone!

How the hell had he lost it? He knew he'd been wearing it last night when he'd kissed it before crawling over the side of the hull.

He'd been wearing it for seventeen years! Not once had the chain broken, not once had he needed to repair it, not once, even when polishing it, had he ever taken it off!

"Yer too scared now, Captain?" Kent gave a laugh, waving his hand towards the crew to get them to laugh as well.

Alister leaned across the barrel, grabbed the man by the cuff of his collar, and pulled him in. Kent put his hands up in surrender, no doubt unsure of him with the way his face was screwed up into angry lines of seething rage.

His eyes widened. *The lass...* The last time he remembered wearing the locket was when she'd touched it to look at it.

He released Kent and stood to look over at the shore.

"Get me a boat!" Alister roared. He started pushing confused and startled men out of the way. "Get me on that island. Now!"

He should have known she was up to no good. *She tricked me! Again!* She'd stolen his most priceless possession straight from around his damn neck. He shouldn't be surprised, but could his bruised ego take much more of her trickery?

"Alister, what's wrong?" Derek asked, rushing to his side while Alister was helping his men hoist a rowboat down the side of the hull.

He was trying to pick up their drunken and sluggish pace.

"She stole my locket!"

Derek winced. He knew how much that necklace meant to him. He said nothing, for there was nothing he could say.

"Oh aye! She's going to get it when I get my hands on her."

His ship he could replace, his crew, his loot, but his

necklace? He couldn't get another without telling the person who gave it to him in the first place, wouldn't have the precious memories it came with. He'd rather not see the disappointment on their face when he told them that he'd lost it.

A few moments later, Alister was crouched down at the head of the boat, holding on to the bow so he didn't fall out. Watching the shore come closer as men rowed behind him, his hand clenched into a tight fist.

They only just hit the sandbank when he jumped out and started running for land. Water sloshed around his knees as his men followed behind him.

He was glad he'd noticed before the sun had gone down; otherwise, he'd have to look for her in the dark. Alister headed for the trees, knowing they were most likely taking shelter within them. He came over the rise of a small hill and that's when he saw them clustered together.

He heard a shout in the distance and they turned their heads to him and the men he had following behind. Rosetta sat up against the trunk of a coconut tree.

"You owe me a silver, Naeem!" He heard her yell as she rushed to her feet.

Alister grabbed his pistol from its holster. She made an ear-piercing, squealing noise while ducking as he shot at her. The bullet hit right behind her, the bark of a tree flinging off in a mini-explosion.

He'd wasted his single bullet, and wouldn't waste time reloading his gun, as she'd started running for it. He was too busy chasing after her.

None of her men followed, not when they were trying to get in the way of his own men. He managed to duck past them before they could stop him.

He had a feeling they let him.

"Get back here, lass!" The yell he gave was laced with

fury, guttural and dangerous.

Sand shot from behind their feet as he gained on her.

"I have a name you know!"

"You won't need it when you're dead."

She took them to the shore; however, it wasn't sand under their feet, but a cliff of rocks. Waves crashed against them, spraying foam around as the ocean pushed and pulled.

He took out his cutlass when she turned to him, but he halted when she held her hand out to the side of her body. He could see the locket dangling from her fist precariously over the rocky edge. If she dropped it, it'd be lost to the sea forever.

"Stay where you are, or I'll toss it." Her eyes narrowed on him, squinting with determination. Looking at her face, he knew without a doubt that she'd do it.

"Give it here." He put his cutlass away and held his hand out. "I'll forgive you if you give it back."

He was unsure if those words were a lie or not.

She punched her hand to the side, making the locket swing. "No."

"If you drop it, Rosetta, you'll regret it."

She gave him a cruel smile. "Ah, so you *do* know my name."

"Aye, I know your name." He waved his fingers, silently telling her to toss it to him. "Now, give me the locket."

Slowly, she brought it away from where he'd permanently lose it and started to inspect it. Although she wasn't looking at him, he didn't dare move.

"Alister." She said his name while she read the front of it, then turned it. "Mum." His lips thinned in agitation as she used her thumb nails to pry open the locket. "Always be safe."

"I know what it says!" He took a step forward in a stomp against the grass and dirt and her head shot up.

"Well, Captain Alister Paine, it seems I have something to offer that you dearly want."

She closed the locket with one hand, holding it in a fist as the rest of the chain dangled. She played with the length of it, her cruel pout and squinted eyes trained on him.

"My own necklace doesn't count."

"Sure it does." She punched her hand sideways through the air and it hung over the water once more. "You can hurt me however you like, but you'll never get it back once it's gone."

He let a glare fill his features.

"I don't trust you," he freely admitted. "You want a ship, but I won't wait that long to have it back." He didn't trust she wouldn't lose it in the time her goal took.

"That's not the price for it."

It's not? "Then what in the seven seas do you want?"

"For you to actually *listen* to my offer. That's the price for your locket."

His brows crinkled together, then he rubbed his hand down his face with a weathered look. He guessed he'd never actually listened to what she had been trying to say back in his cabin. He folded his arms across his chest, but his feet stood in a stance that would have told her he was defensive.

"Fine, speak it."

"I want a ship, a particular one. I want you, your boat, and your men to help me get it."

He quirked a brow. "What would I get in return?"

"Maps. Uncharted maps you don't have, maps to not only The Raider's treasure, but many others too."

He snorted at her confidence. "You have no idea if your maps lead to anything real."

"No," she admitted, and he watched her eyes trail to the side in thought, with a hint of sadness he wasn't sure was real. "But I know they are ones you don't have. I've seen them; I've been on the ship before."

He shook his head. "It's not enough, not with the amount of time and coin I'd have to invest. I told you I don't help charity cases."

"I can get you men." Her eyes came to him once more. "There are more than enough prisoners on board to fill both our crews. They will be thieves, murderers, or pirates. They will agree to freedom – anything is better than the noose."

Alister's eyes widened, his lips parting ever so slightly. "You're talking about Queen Mary Anne's head fleet ship! That's a bloody suicide mission."

She brought her fist away from over the water to cup her hand, holding the locket with the other one, as she gave a mocking snort.

"I thought you were one of the most notorious pirates on the seven seas of Old Gaia. Didn't know you'd be afraid of just one ship."

He looked at her with an incredulous glare. "One ship? It travels in three! The Laughing Siren alone has over a hundred and forty soldiers on board."

There was a reason Alister had never attacked it.

She didn't seem phased. "The other two won't attack the head ship once we're on it, and once Commodore Theodore Briggs and his first mate Samuel Lester are dead, the crew will falter and surrender if we overpower them."

"You seem to know a lot about it." His eyes squinted suspiciously.

She shouldn't know this much about the commanders of such an important royal vessel. It was protected information and, now he knew the schematics on his desk applied to this one.

"Like I said, I've been on the Laughing Siren before." She paused, considering her words. "My father was a soldier on it."

"Can't it be a different ship?" Was he really considering helping her? "The other fleet ships will have prisoners."

She shook her head. "It won't have the maps, and it has to

be that one. Since I set sail on these seas, I knew it was the one I wanted. I know its ins and outs, where it is weakest and the easiest way to take it. The prisoners mean I already have hands to hoist the sails, and there will be enough for you to choose the ones you want. You'd have a full crew, nearly twice the amount you have now."

A full crew of more than willing men was actually a pretty good deal.

"It'd also have coin on it," he mumbled while placing a hand over his lips and chin in thought.

"You can have it all. The guns, the swords, the clothing, whatever stock they have." He raised his brow at the idea that she'd let him have whatever he wanted from the cargo bay. "But you'll leave us enough to survive until we can resupply."

The Laughing Siren was a Galleon ship, one of the largest sailing. It was slow but strong, always manned with cannons.

My frigate is one of the only ships that can take it on.

"I could end up sinking it if we try," he told her, making sure she understood what could happen. "And I won't let my own ship perish just to get you yours."

She gave a shrug. "Either I have it, or it's at the bottom of the ocean. I'll be happy with either one."

She's truly set on it. This new development made him look at her in slightly different light.

She was selfish enough to have it in her possession or in nobody's. He'd thought the same thing about the Howling Death when he saw it for the first time.

He started to rub the long stubble on his cheek as he contemplated her offer. *It's not a bad deal.*

"The loot we'd gain would be enough to appease my crew." It would be their biggest payday yet, and he wouldn't have to share it with the prisoners, since they'd only have just joined him.

"Until we take the Laughing Siren, my crew and I will help

you sail." She folded her arms across her chest, turning her head to the side with an upturn of her chin. "And we, including myself, will follow your command."

Alister raised his brow at that. "You'll listen to my orders?"

"Yes." She released her arms to point at him. "But I won't scrub the deck. You won't have me bending over on my hands and knees for men to stare at my arse."

He couldn't help chuckle. *Well, that's a fair request.*

"You will still have to work."

"Put me in the kitchen with Mr Darkley. I don't mind helping him cook and I'm good at it. I can also hoist the sails."

His head fell back as he gave a bellowing laugh to the sky. "You won't be manning the sails, lass. I've got strong men for that."

"I'm just as fit as your injured men!" she shouted.

A guttural noise of irritation sounded from his nose.

"Are you judging a man simply because he's missing a leg, or a few fingers, or an eye?" He pointed at his own eyepatch. "Every one of my men are able-bodied, regardless of the parts missing. I wouldn't change my crew for any other, even if they had all their parts!"

Her head reared back, her eyes going stark. It was obvious Rosetta realised she'd offended him, very deeply. He was a formidable captain, and he was half-blind, for pity's sake.

"Stop treating me like a woman," she huffed, stomping her foot in a tantrum.

"You were screaming like one earlier!"

His eyelids flickered rapidly at the hint of redness he caught in her cheeks, but it quickly faded.

"I am still just as capable as a man."

"And you will work where I put you," he told her, shaking his head in disbelief. "You said you'd follow my orders, but you're showing me you will be incapable of doing so."

"Fine," she huffed, once more folding her arms, this time with a defeated slump. "Do we have a deal, then? We will work for you while you help us get the Laughing Siren, and then you can raid it for whatever you want, as long as I can still sail it."

"Nay."

"But–"

He put up a hand to stop her. "I have to ask my men first. I can't make a decision like this without their approval."

A bright smile filled her beautiful face, catching his attention as the wash of the sunset bloomed behind her. The sky was still a day blue, but the clouds had turned flame orange with purple shadows. It was a wonderful sight with her in front of it, near to stealing his breath from him.

He didn't like the reaction that he got by looking at her – not when he was still rightfully angry.

The things I can take from that ship would be worth more than I can raid in a year. With so many men at his disposal, it *could* actually be possible.

"But you will ask them?"

Why did smiles like that from pretty women do strange things to the insides of men?

"Aye, I will." Alister wasn't stupid enough to pass up such an opportunity.

She suddenly threw the locket at him, and he caught it in his right fist. He stared down at the silver locket in his big palm, surprised she wasn't going to hold onto it as collateral.

She gave it back.

CHAPTER ELEVEN

Rosetta walked next to Alister as they made their way back to their crews, which she hoped would become one for a short while.

She had an extra spring in her step, thankful that her plan thus far had worked in her favour.

He shot at me. She peeked at him from under her lashes. He'd almost killed her! The shot had been less than a foot away from her head.

He must have been truly furious I stole his mother's locket. Her eyes fell to it already hanging around his neck, bouncing against his sternum with each footfall.

He seemed to be deep in thought, and she figured he was mulling over the deal.

She thought he might be interested once he listened to what he could gain from helping her. He'd been too arrogant before, refusing her without letting her explain.

He eventually broke the silence. "What's the deal if they say nay?"

"You will take us straight to a port where you know I can get new hands, and you will let us go." She placed her hands behind her back, giving a shrug. "I can find a new ship."

"You won't get the Laughing Siren on your own. It'll take years to get a ship that can take it and a sizeable crew that can over run it."

"I know," she answered with a dejected tone. "I had everything I needed when I took your ship."

Rosetta's hopes had been dashed, and she didn't often get her hopes up for this reason.

Silence fell upon them once more.

There was a defined line that seemed to have been drawn in the dirt between their men when they found them. Neither would attack each other, but they all had their weapons raised. They were patiently waiting for them to return to see the results.

"Captain," multiple men from both crews greeted them in unison.

A giggle fell from her when they both answered in reply. He gave her a strange scowl before turning back to them.

"She's coming with us. The rest of her crew are staying behind."

"For now," she added, to calm her men who looked concerned.

Then they nodded – they'd known what she'd planned to ask, and now they understood she'd managed to convince him to at least consider it.

Alister nodded his head towards the beach. "Get in the boat."

"Rosetta," Naeem started, before flicking something at her.

She caught what he'd tossed her with one hand and noticed Alister watching her palm as she opened it. She had a silver in her palm. She held it up to the last of the sunlight with two fingers, like she was examining to see if it was real, despite knowing it was.

With a small smile of triumph, she headed towards the rowboat, clunking down the beach to hop inside. Alister and his men followed suit and began rowing towards his ship.

Alister had his arms folded, sitting on the bench across from her. He tapped his bicep with his head turned, refusing to look at her.

"What was the bet?" His tone was dark, as though she should be worried about her answer.

"That you're a mamma's boy."

She heard someone behind her nearly choke on their own spit as they tried to stifle a laugh. His head shot to the offensive sound with such a deep glare, she thought it might set the man on fire.

"I honestly thought it would take you longer to realise," she admitted. "Is she dead?"

She figured that was the reason he was so protective of the locket.

"What she is is none of your fucking business."

"And here I thought we were getting along." She sighed, but it didn't hold any real emotion.

"We are. You'd be dead if we weren't."

"You can say that again," someone rowing the oars said. "We're all surprised you're not."

"That's because you dogs asked for mercy on her behalf."

Rosetta slanted her head to the side, her brows furrowing. "They did?"

Alister finally turned his eye towards her but, by the way he looked at her, it seemed he was set in his sour mood. "Aye, seems some of my men took a fancy to you while you were captain."

She wondered if that was the whole truth. "How's Kent?"

She noticed the edges of his lips turn up, even though he battled against it. "Getting groped and whistled at."

"He looks better as a woman than I do."

"True," he blatantly lied, that smile of humour growing to full force. "Was about to make him wear your dress before I noticed you'd taken my locket."

She slapped her knee with glee. "That I have to see!"

"Maybe you will," Alister answered with a tone she

thought may have sounded hopeful when the side of the boat hit against the ship's hull.

Metal, staple-shaped handles were permanently fitted to the side so they could climb up it. She was the first to do so and she had a feeling Alister was staring at her arse while he climbed behind her.

Alister leaned one of his boots against the railing of the quarter deck and stood before the people below him. Everyone was on the surface since he needed to address them all.

He'd already relayed the offer she had given him, and the kinds of things they'd get in return, if they helped her procure the Laughing Siren.

Now came the vote.

"It'll be to the majority vote. All those in favour, raise a hand." Just over three quarters of his crew raised their hands in the air in agreeance.

"Then I will accept her offer and we will work together. I want some of you to row to shore and pick up her men. The rest of you, make room for them in the cabins below and rearrange yourselves how you see fit."

There were many sleeping cabins below deck, but it was usually filled with two or three men each. That would now be more crowded with the new arrivals. The rare, obnoxious snorers, sometimes lucky enough to get their own cabins, would surely now be banished to some dank corner of the ship to suffer together.

Once they were moving, he lowered his leg and turned to her. Her hands were on her hips, but there was no mistaking the cheerful expression she swore.

"There you have it. I'll have Pierre and Derek vacate the

cabin below so you may sleep in it."

She shook her head. "No, don't make a distinction between me and the men. I'd rather not deal with the backlash."

"Then where else are you going to sleep?" he asked with a tone of uncertainty. "I won't be giving you mine, lass."

She rolled her eyes at him. "Just give me a cabin with Naeem and Mr Smith. I'll be comfortable sharing with them."

She's happy to sleep with men present? Just how comfortable was she with them?

"Fine." He pointed his index finger at her. "Don't sleep with the crew while you're on my ship."

The way she scrunched up her nose with a strange smirk made him wonder just what the hell kind of thought she'd had to make such a strange face.

"Why not?" She batted her eyelids, her smirk turning into a pout like she was trying to hide her taunt.

It didn't take a genius to figure it out. *She thinks I'd be jealous.*

"If you sleep with one of them, you'll have to sleep with all of them." He swayed his hand to the side, as if he was referencing a vast number. He also wouldn't take her again if she did, but he wouldn't tell her that.

"Excuse me?" She sounded the words deliberately, her mouth staying open once she was done.

"My men share everything. Food, coin, women." He brought his hand back but tilted his head forward to be more level with her. "If you take one of them, they will treat you like every other woman they meet: a prostitute. Unless you want hands grabbing at you constantly, which I have no interest in getting in the middle of, don't give them a reason to treat you that way."

"Then shouldn't I be doing it anyway, then?"

His brow creased in confusion. "Why do you say that?"

From what he'd discovered earlier, she hadn't bedded any

of them. She'd been far too small for that, since she'd taken a while to adjust to him.

"Are you not a part of your own crew?"

He gave a curt laugh. "Aye, but I'm different and they know that. I can do what I want with you."

Both her brows raised. "If I let you."

He was the one to roll his eyes this time, turning away from her to head below deck. "And stay away from Pierre. If he tries, he always manages to succeed. He's got a way with women. Just a fair warning."

"What am I supposed to do now?"

He gave a shrug, holding the handrail as he walked down the steps.

"Wait for the rest of *my* new crew to board. I have shit to do." He turned his head back with the smuggest grin he thought he'd ever worn. "Since I am the captain and all."

Her scrunched up nose of annoyance was delightful to him.

He had to speak with Glen about her helping him in the kitchen, cooking and cleaning. He may not like her encroaching on his area.

He would also choose the most suitable cabin for her, one she wouldn't have to pass many men to get to.

This better not bite me in the arse.

Even if it did, tomorrow when the sun rose, he'd finally be able to set sail.

CHAPTER TWELVE

The following morning, Alister searched his ship for Rosetta and found her sitting on one of the eating benches in the kitchen, talking with Glen.

She was peeling potatoes, the skins falling into an empty barrel, while he was frying up meat.

"I'm surprised you're already up," Alister commented, since he'd first gone to her cabin to wake her. He'd found Naeem and Mr Smith in their hammocks, but not her. Since she wasn't there, he'd gone to search for her, untrusting and worried about what she was up to.

He wasn't expecting to find her already doing chores.

"Thought Mr Darkley would need help making the boys breakfast."

Sure, but someone needs to be awake *to have a thought.*

"Come, he can take care of the rest for now. We have much to discuss."

He walked out of the kitchen area and down the long hallways. Eventually, he heard her footsteps tapping behind him to catch up, right as he was reaching the stairs to the surface.

He led her to his chambers. Sitting behind his desk, he gestured to the maps she'd organised when he been gone.

"Explain your plan because right now, I can't see it."

He'd gone through what was on the desk by lantern

throughout the night, but he couldn't understand a thing.

What he *did* notice was a rough diagram of a ship that looked drawn by someone who'd been inside it: roughly how many levels it had, what kinds of rooms there were. Information like that was invaluable and would help them greatly.

From the other side of his desk, she stood to pick up the smaller maps and random assorted papers.

"That's because you've made a mess of it!"

Revealing the map of the northern hemisphere below everything, she pointed to Tempest Island, their current location. She explained the route they were taking while placing smaller maps of the locations they'd be passing close, so they had a better gauge of the surroundings.

She showed the route she'd originally set up, then the information she'd picked up on the Laughing Siren's sailing route – from its original port for its current voyage, all of its stops, and to where it was currently heading.

To have such updated and new information meant she must have paid a pretty penny for it and been in contact with someone who could get it for her.

"I was hoping to intercept it here." She pointed to a small collection of islands. "We were going to lay in wait for when they passed and surprise them so they couldn't run."

He looked over everything with a careful gaze. "You've put the Howling Death in a position of destruction with your plan."

Which is probably why he hadn't understood it.

Alister reached into one of the drawers and pulled out his measuring compass and a ruler. He changed the length between the two needles and started walking the route of the Laughing Siren and the places they could intercept it.

"I hadn't particularly cared for the state of this ship once I abandoned it."

"Duly noted, but not something I will allow," he answered, eyeing her for a second with a disgruntled expression. "The two accompanying ships will attack mine and try to sink it. I want to avoid that possibility as much as possible."

Placing his elbow on the table so he could fold his arm and cup his chin while he walked the points of the compass, his brows furrowed in concentration. She leaned over closer in front of him to watch what he was doing.

"We'll have to figure out how to approach it oncoming rather than from the sides or rear." He nodded his head to gesture outside the door. "I have front cannons, they won't."

"Try not to put too many holes in it." He heard the grimace in her tone and tried to look up to her. He didn't make it that far with the way she was bending forward.

His eye found the gaping opening of her tunic; he had a near perfect view down it. He turned his head down to the table before she noticed where his gaze had trailed.

The woman's got a sinful body.

The way she wore her clothing left extraordinarily little to the imagination. Her tights hugged her all the way up past her navel. They revealed every curve she had, every outline of bones and taut, toned leg muscle. Her tunic was always precariously unbuttoned, so low that he'd often caught peeks of those round mounds as he towered over her.

Even when he'd been trying to shoot her yesterday, he'd still found her tantalising.

He'd been hoping that nailing her would ease some of his desires, but unfortunately, he'd enjoyed it so much, he found himself constantly fantasising about doing it again.

"You don't have a map of the Kou Pelin Islands." He tapped his finger against a place directly on the fleet's path that would be perfect. "We can direct the fleet and cut the Laughing Siren off from assistance for a short while. By then, it will be too late, and we hopefully will have boarded enough men that the Howling Death can back off while we take over."

The Kou Pelin Islands weren't accessible because they were nothing more than cutting rock formations hundreds of feet tall. From a distance, a sailor could see the tops of its trees and greenery, but the rocks couldn't be climbed.

Alister grabbed a blank piece of paper and opened the square, glass ink bottle. Dipping his quill, he started drawing a rough sketch of what the four islands looked like; two sections of four towers connected with an archway.

"If we come around from the topmost island, we might be able to push the Laughing Siren through the middle of them, which means the other two would have to back off to go behind it or around the other towers."

Rosetta came around the table to get a better look at his drawing so she didn't have to look at it upside down. He felt one of her knees knock against his own.

"Wouldn't that mean we'd have to go around as well?"

Alister shook his head at her thoughtful face before looking back to his sketch. "My ship has a shallower hull and is narrower. I can go through the gaps of the two islands clustered closer together, whereas the fleet ships will have to go all the way around to avoid the sand banks if they don't go through the middle."

He looked to her once more, unable to stop his eye from roaming over her as she bent over the table, giving a side view of her.

Shit... Why does she have to smell so good? He slyly covered the bottom of his face and nose to hide from her aroma. He cleared his throat to bring himself back to their conversation.

"There is a much wider gap between the two outer islands. Commodore Briggs will probably try to go through the very centre to flee, since it will be deep enough for his ship. We will be coming at him in a way that would force a collision if he doesn't. He won't sink his ship that way."

"He also wouldn't be able to turn the ship sharply enough with them so close."

"Exactly, he either has to go through them or could get stuck on the banks turning next to them."

She tapped her fingers against her lips in a thoughtful gesture, before trailing her finger over the route of the galleon ship she wanted.

"If we fail there, there's no other opportunity to commandeer it before it makes port in Oklay."

Oklay was a city in Banksia, where the prisoners were taken. They would be given a trial and hung in front of the Queen and her consort.

Queen Mary Anne was a powerful and stony-hearted ruler. Alister admired her for it, while also wanting absolutely nothing to do with her. He knew she'd hang him for his crimes before he even opened his mouth.

"We can't attack it on its way back; it'll have no prisoners for us to take." Her brows knotted together once more, this time in concern. "I also don't know how long it'll be before embarking on a similar voyage. It's usually carting cargo for the Queen or being used for trading."

She really does know a lot about the ship. She knew where it was going, the places it might go, why it might go there.

"It doesn't matter if that's the last spot to commandeer it." Her eyes slowly trailed to him at his stern tone. "It's the spot we'll most likely succeed. Like I said, this is a suicide mission, but it doesn't *have* to be. I'm not really interested in courting my own death."

"I might be though," she whispered, low enough that he'd barely even heard it.

"Here then." He handed her the compass and grabbed her arse by squeezing the side of his hand between her cheeks to turn her. She gave a small yelp of surprise at his touch. "You figure out a better spot."

He folded his arms with irritation as he leaned back in his chair, slumping in it. She immediately dropped the compass to the table like it was a hot metal rod sitting in fire.

"No."

"Nay?" He gave a mocking laugh. "Don't be defiant just because you aren't getting your way. Have a look and tell me a better option."

He gestured to it with an aggressive shove of his hand.

"I'm saying I can't." He noted that her gaze flickered everywhere but his face, almost like she was avoiding meeting his eyes. "I understand the use of the compass, but..."

There was only one reason why she couldn't do it.

His arms loosened but didn't unfold. "You can't count."

"Mr Smith does it for me. I'm a woman; I was never taught how to do complicated math. I can do small amounts but the use of a compass and the spaces in between need to be accurate. If I'm even slightly off, it could put us off course."

He gave a sigh, suddenly feeling terrible for making her feel awkward. He ran his hand over the top of his hair, pulling on the loose half-bun at the back.

He should have known better than to think a commoner woman could count in this day and age.

"I'm not surprised. The fact that you can even read is a miracle."

It was only a hundred years ago or so they'd stopped burning women on the stake when they'd learned that they could read, claiming they were witches. Even though things were changing, and women were encouraged to learn, only those who'd received a higher education were taught. Some commoner women were as well, but it was rare and generally taught by a mother or friend who knew how.

He figured Rosetta was one of these rare women. She obviously wasn't a noblewoman.

"Here." Alister opened the compass so it would reflect three miles. "That's how far we can see through a spyglass. That's the distance our hiding spot needs to be so we can see the fleet. You've chosen the Dotoro Islands because they're within that range, but other than flat sandy islands that won't hide us, the Kou Pelin Islands is the only other location."

Now that he'd simplified it, she took the compass from his hand and started walking it over the map.

Once more, he leaned back in the chair. He knew she'd argue with him if she didn't see it for herself. *She's stubborn.*

She pulled out smaller maps that showed the shape and topography of the islands before placing them back down with a shake of her head.

Then Alister realised he'd done himself a favour.

His teeth were revealed by a wide grin, his eye dragging over the curve of her backside as she leaned over in front of him. If he wanted to, which he very much did, he could reach out and touch it with ease. It was large, round, and hugged so tightly by her pants that he knew its exact shape.

"What about the Flinagan shores?" She turned her head to look at him over her shoulder.

His sight darted to her quickly. "Same problem as your original location. It leaves us open for attack."

She gave him an irritated huff before squinting her eyes at his face. "Are you laughing at me?"

He shook his head. "Not at all. I'm merely thinking about all the booty I plan to acquire."

Her booty. Particularly, how many times he might be able to get that backside of hers hitting against his hips as he rammed into her before they made it to the Laughing Siren.

He was getting hard at the prospect.

It would take them three weeks to make it to his chosen location and, if sex between them was as good as the first time, he might want it constantly.

She threw the compass down on the table, making him wince for his poor tool. "Okay. So, maybe you're right."

"Careful, lass. These tools are important and fragile." He reached for it, checking to make sure it wasn't damaged from her brutality. "Good. Now, let's talk strategy."

She turned to lean that thought-stealing arse against his desk to face him. He kicked his leg forward so it would be between her calves, trapping her where she sat.

Her eyes slid over him as he started to talk about the multiple ideas he'd already come up with while his own eyes did the same.

As he'd noticed the last time they'd been alone in this room, the sunlight coming from behind him brightened the blue of her eyes and made her skin shine.

He leaned forward to point at the diagram of the ship, discovering she was the one who'd drawn it. It showed each level, what it generally held, and where the prisoners might be. The one he was really interested in, though, was the main deck.

His men needed to know where the hatch was so they could stop re-enforcements from getting to the surface and where all the best vantage points were. He also liked that he knew how high the cannon ports were. It would do less damage to the hull of his ship below the water, where it could sink them. They could stick around for longer than he originally thought.

She stayed leaning against the desk, but she twisted her upper body to look at the scrolls, almost lying on it.

It put her even closer to him and he couldn't keep from being distracted by their proximity, the amazing way she smelled; he was getting more aroused by the second. Maybe it was because he was excited about what he stood to gain if all this went well.

He turned his head to her, putting his face a short distance from hers. He was surprised she'd remained silent while he was talking, allowing him to create the plan he thought best. Considering she'd been hunting this thing, he thought she would have had more to say.

"So, you agree with me? This will be the best way to attack."

She gave him a crooked smile, and he watched her eyes drift over his face as it grew. "Sure."

He poked the table, then the maps. "You're not going to fight me on this?"

He'd essentially told her what was going to happen, and that she'd have very little part in it. *She'll just get in the way if she tries to help.*

"You're the expert."

She's up to something. He could tell by her tone, and the fact she'd given in so easily, but he didn't seem to care when her eyes stopping moving to stay fixed on his mouth.

She's got some kind of hold over me. He shouldn't be this drawn to her. Like a siren calling unwitting seamen to their deaths, he was utterly entranced by her charms. He knew it was happening, so why did he still want to let her drown him?

It worsened when she seemed to inch closer.

His hand shot forward to grip her around the nape of her neck as he pulled her in. Her hair brushed the back of his knuckles like silk against his skin.

She gave a subtle moan that he returned as their mouths met. Soft lips greeted his own, and he couldn't control his urge to deepen it. Leaning back so they were both more comfortable, Alister tilted his head to do just that.

His hand squeezed her nape when her tongue slipped forward at the same time his did to meet in a wet clash; the intricate dance made his body pulsate in response.

He felt her hands palm his chest before little nails dug in through his tunic as she fisted it. He could feel warmth building between them, could taste the way they mingled.

When he placed one of his palms on her thigh to caress up the length of it, though, she tried to pull away, separating their kiss.

Alister yanked her back in to steal her lips again. *Nay, I'm not done yet.* There was a momentary pause where she accepted it, before she pulled back once more.

"Sit on me," he demanded as he reached down to pry a boot from her.

"No."

Her leg shot forward to kick against the edge of his chair. He jumped when she almost kicked him in the groin.

She licked her lips before wiping her mouth with back of her hand. "The first time was free," she told him with breathless pants. "The rest must be earned."

He ran both his hands up the calf of her leg. "I'm getting you a ship, lass." He couldn't believe what he was hearing! "What more could you want?"

She was the one who had been teasing him, and yet now she was pulling back? He couldn't help noticing her nipples had hardened under the tunic, her eyes softer in expression. Even her cheeks were a little pink, like she may be warm with desire.

"That's not what I mean by earned."

What's that supposed to mean?

She leaned forward to cup his jaw with one hand in such a forceful grip, it caved in his cheeks. She gave him a quick kiss on his stupefied mouth.

"But you have a pretty face, which helps."

Pretty was the last word people used to describe his features; his face had long ago stopped being his fortune. Harsh, roguish, scary – those were words people used now. Women even sneered or turned their noses up at his scars until they discovered how fat his coin pouch could be.

Irritation bubbled up inside him when he realised she was

intending to reject him, even as a grin formed.

"Aye, but you want me, Rosetta." It wasn't a question but a statement, one that gave him self-assurance.

She tilted her foot so she could press the tip of her boot gently against his erection, like she knew he had one.

"I think you're the one who wants me right now."

There was a flirtatious hint to her eyes, one that only increased his desire to flip her over and slam into her. *Saucy lass.* She could say what she wanted, but Alister had a feeling that, if he slipped his fingers inside her, he'd find her slick and warm.

"Oh aye," he admitted, grabbing her by the back of the knee and pulling her into his lap. "And you'll let me have you again by the time we reach the Laughing Siren."

I give her three days before she lets me take her, he thought confidently, a mischievous grin forming across his face.

Then he took her mouth in an unyielding, passionate kiss, one she couldn't escape from and one he wouldn't relinquish until he was done feasting.

CHAPTER THIRTEEN

Alister had been wrong in his estimation of getting Rosetta beneath him again.

Five days they had been sailing and every day, he brought her into his quarters with the excuse he needed to discuss their plans.

For five days, he'd needed to give himself release after their meetings because he'd manage to steal her mouth, which she was happy to supply, but nothing more.

He wanted the woman, but he refused to allow her to get him pent up. That's what he'd told himself, at least.

Alister knew he needed to release some of the tension growing inside him. That's why, when he heard the man in the crow's nest shout 'Sail ho!', Alister had grinned.

Killing someone is just what I need. Looting and slitting throats was exactly what would raise his spirits after receiving bruising kicks to his ego from her rejections.

"What kind of ship have we got?" he yelled back, moving away from the helm for a moment to grab his nautical spyglass.

"It's a frigate, Cap'in!"

Hmm. He leaned against the wheel to keep it steady as he raised the lens to his good eye; to see another frigate was never a good sign.

When he finally found it, inspecting it for what details he

could make with the distance, Alister's lips drew tightly together. It worsened when he heard the clomping bootsteps of what sounded like a bear coming up the stairs.

"Is it a trading boat?" Rosetta asked him.

She must have heard the commotion from below deck and came to investigate.

"Nay," he answered sourly, lowering his lens. "Pirate hunters." Alister immediately began turning his ship the other way.

"You're turning away from it?" She gave him a mocking, snide laugh. "And here I thought you were supposed to be some great killer who didn't run from anyone."

He turned to her with a foul face, pointing his index and middle fingers of one hand at her.

"And whose fault do you think that is?"

She quickly frowned, her head shaking in confusion.

"We made a deal, lass," he bit, straightening the wheel. "It's your fault I can't go after it."

As much as he knew he could take it on, the amount of damage his ship would obtain could put them at a disadvantage if they wanted to capture the Laughing Siren. He wanted to sink it just because of its existence, but he'd made a deal with Rosetta, and he intended to keep it.

"Oh." Her gaze shied away from him in embarrassment.

"Go back to your station," he demanded.

"I've already done my duties!"

"Then go do something else!" His mood had soured further, and if she wasn't going to give him what he wanted, he needed to ride out this terrible mood on his own.

"But–"

"Cap'in!" Keat in the crow's nest shouted. "They're turning to us!"

Shit. "I need all hands on deck!" he yelled. "They know who we are."

They must have seen his ship's figurehead before he managed to turn. Pierre and Derrek gave orders while he kept his focus on measuring how far the pirate hunters were by eye. He was diverting the way he'd turned to try and keep them relatively on course. It did little to help; they were going the opposite way.

"Here, let me help," Rosetta offered, stepping forward with arms raised. "I can man the helm or watch the ship."

He thwarted her reaching hands out of the way. "Touch the wheel of my ship, lass, and you'll regret it."

This was his position, and he refused anyone's help when he didn't need it. The only ones he would ever trust to touch his ship were Pierre and Derek.

The way her face tightened into a spiteful look raised his hackles.

"Aye! Now get below deck and stay there, where you are safe." When her look darkened, he pointed at her again. "The last thing I need is a woman getting in the way!"

"I've fought against pirate hunters myself!"

"I don't give a shit." He grabbed her shoulder to turn her by force, shoving her towards the deck stairs.

She stomped down them, and he looked through his lens once more.

She'd distracted him for long enough that the ship had jumped in size through his magnifying telescope. *They're gaining on us.*

The ship was smaller than his, lighter, and they had the wind on their side. Before long, they'd be upon them.

"Change of plans, lads!" he yelled, turning the wheel of his ship the other way. "Ready the cannons and prepare yourselves for war."

If Alister couldn't run, then he would fight, despite the position it put them in for getting her ship.

When they were in range of the Howling Death's front

cannons, he knew there was no point in raising his black flag. They knew they were coming, that they would fight to the death.

"Fire the front cannons!" The command echoed throughout the ship, voices deep and loud as it travelled until he could no longer hear it.

Two bangs sounded as the front cannons shot. One hit the front of the other ship while the other hit the water with a giant, spraying splash.

"Again!"

When that same side was hit once more, and they didn't receive fire back, Alister knew two things.

One, this frigate didn't have as many cannons as they did, to the point where it didn't even have a front cannon. Secondly, it was moving down the left side of his ship.

"Ready the port side cannons!" Alister turned his wheel to the right to help stop the potential collision. "Derek!"

"Aye, Cap'in!" He came bounding up the stairs, taking the wheel from him without another word, as though he already knew what he wanted.

Derek would protect the helm better than anyone and would be better at defending than attacking if the need arose. That peg leg didn't make him steady for crossing ships, but he would if they were desperate.

Alister withdrew his cutlass, readying himself for battle.

"Fire!" Once the command started echoing, he also yelled, "Move across!"

His men swung to the other ship while the crew of the other did the same. Alister gutted a man before he even had the chance to land, then he stole his rope and swung his way over.

He booted someone in the chest as he landed, letting go of the rope so he could hold his cutlass with two hands and shove it into the enemy's head.

There was no point in finding the captain. If he knew who

Alister was, he'd probably eventually try to greet him.

Metal rang as swords crossed. The sound of the occasional gun fired as men wasted their singular bullets.

He felt a swift but shallow slice across his shoulders. If he hadn't been moving forward, it would have been deeper. Alister turned and blindly swung, hacking into someone's side with his longer reach. The bearded man gave a gargle that worsened as he yanked his sword back to remove it.

He quickly raised his cutlass to the side when he saw someone barrelling towards him on his good side. He blocked the attacker and thrust his hand forward, grabbing him by the throat and lifting him off the ground. He let go of his sword so he could attempt to pry his hand off him, just as Alister pulled his sword back and stabbed it through his torso.

Blood quickly covered him as he took life after life with little care. The ground beneath his feet shook each time his cannons hit their ship, but he knew his own was receiving fire as well.

His men were already going below deck to kill the gunmen, slowly overtaking the meagre crew.

Alister hadn't wielded a crew this large before, so he was sure the sheer number of them had come as a surprise.

Just as he was turning to find another target, someone cut the throat of an enemy next to him. A heavy burst of blood sprayed over the side of his body, hitting him in the face and covering his eyepatch.

His tunic was covered in blood that was not his own. Unfortunately, some had gotten in his good eye, temporarily blurring his vision. He went to rub it away.

"Watch out!" He knew that voice. It wasn't hard to distinguish a woman's voice.

Just as he wiped the worst of the blood from his face, he watched Rosetta land on top of a man about to cleave Alister's head off.

She rolled forward to get away; she had done enough to protect him so Alister could kill the man himself. She quickly pulled her gun from its holster and shot a man in the back of the head. Pulling her sword from its sheath, she turned to Alister. She must have thought he was an enemy because she went to swing and then immediately halted.

"What the hell are you doing on this ship?" he roared, so loudly he knew a few heads turned.

He was even more furious when he had to quickly pull her forward to stop someone from cutting her from behind.

"Helping!" she shouted back, running down the deck and out of his reach.

She leapt, shoving her sword into the back of someone who had been overpowering one of their men.

It wasn't hard to tell who was their crew and who were pirate hunters, since their clothing weren't rags like their crew. Pirates typically didn't care about the way they looked.

Fuck! He didn't have time to watch out for her when he had men coming at all sides. When he realised it, he knew they knew who he was.

His face was known. He had dozens of wanted posters with sketches of his face; Alister couldn't touch land without someone recognising him.

He lost her in the fray. Rage and fury coursed through his entire being, so hard that it felt like it hardened his muscles into stone.

As he fought, barely gaining a scratch, men joined the fray, helping to take those down those encircling him. He kept them at bay, knowing he couldn't get kills in unless he was lucky, not with this many around him, not when he was this overrun.

He constantly had to duck blades, thankful no one held a loaded pistol.

Just as he was about to swing a deathblow down on one of two left, a sword protruded through his enemy's chest, nearly stabbing into Alister. He jumped back and quickly aimed for the other, cleaving him in two.

The holder of the sword was Rosetta.

She didn't pay him any notice. She just removed her sword and turned back to the rest of the ship to assist others. Alister couldn't ignore the fact she'd watched his back, twice now. *I was saved by a bloody woman!*

Once the men around him were dead, the only ones left to fight were stragglers. They were deposed of quickly, considering they were being overrun. They couldn't trust a single soul on board to join their crew; they'd slit their throats in their sleep.

Once everyone was dead, Alister quickly swung back to his ship when it turned back around to pick them up. The pirate hunting ship was both on fire and sinking to the bottom of the ocean. There was no point in staying on it, unless they wanted to join its ugly fate.

They had been victorious, but they had lost quite a few good men. He knew the hull of his ship had suffered massive amounts of damage, and he wasn't sure if he had the supplies to repair it properly.

It was littered with caved in sections from impact and occasional holes from where cannonballs had hit the same area twice.

"All those not hurt, start working on repairing the holes closest to the water," he said as he stood on the prow of the main deck. "Make sure the ship is safe to sail before going higher."

He knew they must be taking in water.

He wiped away the blood he could feel trickling down the side of his face; he was covered in it. They would need to use some of the seawater seeping in so they could bathe.

All he knew was that he still held a clump of anger in his chest. It was nestled so deep, he could feel his nose crinkled and his teeth bared as his eyes searched those of his crew staring at him.

They'd gained nothing from today. No loot. No supplies. No crewmembers. This fight had been about nothing but survival.

Bloody pirate hunters. They were the last thing Alister wanted to see on the horizon.

If it weren't for the fact that everyone was mostly silent, he wouldn't have heard someone speak up quietly from the back.

"Are you okay Rosetta?" Naeem asked, grabbing her arm to check her.

"Sure am," she laughed quietly, pulling from him. "You owe me for saving your life, yet again."

The only reason Alister had seen this interaction was because he'd started stomping his way through the crowd that parted for him. They wouldn't dare get in his way.

"But you're hurt."

"It's okay." She brushed her tunic down to hide a cut. "I'll fix it la–"

Before she could finish, Alister grabbed her wrist and started pulling her through the crowd.

"Hey!" She yanked on her arm, bashing her fist against his hold. "Let me go, you manhandling bastard."

He didn't care if he was making a scene. His men all turned their gazes away to go back to their duties. They knew he was furious. He had every right to be.

Dragging her up the stairs of the quarterdeck, he opened the door to his cabin and threw her inside.

"What's the meaning of this?" she asked, stumbling forward before she quickly righted her footing. She spun around to him just as he slammed the door shut.

"I told you to get below deck!"

"No!" she yelled back. "I will not sit on your ship like some fragile, scared, helpless woman!"

He stalked her, pointing the index and middle fingers at her. His eyes were so narrowed, his eyelashes impaired his vision while his teeth gnashed together so tightly, he feared he'd shattered them.

"You gave me your word that you would do as you're told!"

Her eyes widened as she backed up. She threw her hands forward beseechingly, but she didn't look afraid. She looked cautious. It looked like she was ready to defend herself.

Alister didn't like that look. It was defiant, insubordinate, and downright rebellious. He wanted her afraid. Some of his own *men* were more afraid of him than this silly woman.

"I saved your life!" she yelled, making him halt for a moment. "If it wasn't for me, you'd be dead!" *I bloody know!* "When I saw you couldn't see, that's when I swung across."

He stepped forward once more. "So, you were still above deck when we had enemies swinging over?"

Her lips pursed together, but she stood her ground. She even had the audacity to fold her arms across her chest and turn her head to the side dismissively.

"I didn't have to save you," she said with a bored tone, refusing to turn her face to him when he was right in front of her. She was treating him like he was insignificant, like this conversation was pointless. "It would have been better for me if you'd died."

"What's that supposed to fucking mean?"

"I could have gotten your ship and your crew for free!" She stomped her foot like a child having a tantrum, even her cheeks puffed out. "I would have been the new captain. You would have been out of the picture without me having to do a thing. They couldn't blame me for it!"

Alister's jaw dropped slightly. *She's right.* It would have been beneficial for her if she'd let him die. That did nothing to settle his anger, though. No, it worsened as she dropped her arms so she could push at his chest, her hands slipping over him due to the sticky, crimson liquid covering him. A wet, metallic smell tangled in his nose.

"I would have if I'd known you were going to yell at me for it!" She shoved him again. "I don't need this shit from you."

Alister needed to rein in his fury before he did something careless and stupid. Despite it, his body was pumping blood violently through his body, in places where it shouldn't.

He didn't know what was coming over him. Perhaps it was because he'd never had a woman around right after he'd fought, but his anger was shifting into something else entirely.

She was injured, covered in blood, and he couldn't help but find her so sexy because of it. She looked wild, fierce. Rosetta looked like a murderer, and he felt his stomach clench in want.

His body was thrumming with aggression.

The need to release the pent-up desire inside him had only grown. The way she looked with copper liquid clumping in her hair, splattered across her face, reddening the white of her tunic did strange things to him.

He nearly wanted to groan when he saw her sodden top was so damp, it stuck to her skin, moulding around her breasts and clinging to them. It highlighted her nipples to the point that he could perfectly see their shape.

He grabbed her face and forced her head up, making sure she couldn't face away from him.

"You're a distraction," he bit, letting his eye flicker between both of hers. "You may have saved my life, but you almost got me killed. I was surrounded because of you!"

She pushed against his chest in an attempt to get him away. "Then keep your eyes on your enemy instead of being an idiot!"

"You will do as you're told, Rosetta!"

"Go to hell!" She landed a particularly hard blow to his

shins. "I won't let you push me down the ranks and make me a useless woman!"

It was because she was a woman that he was concerned! It didn't escape his notice that she'd never taken anyone head on. She'd only assisted in fighting, and he could only imagine what would have happened if she'd been cornered.

It was because she was a woman that they were in this position, one where he was shouting when he'd much rather do something else, like kiss her.

When kicking him obviously wasn't working, she screamed in his face, "Fuck you Alister!"

Everything built at once. *Gladly.*

Alister shoved her so hard against the wall, the wind knocked out of her, and she let out a tight gasp. He crushed her lips beneath his, needing to kiss her, needing to smudge the blood of different men across each other's faces.

He lifted her leg and thrust his already hardened shaft against her.

For five days, he'd wanted this woman, who had teased him, kissed him, given him nothing but an ache rather than release. It felt like she was trying to make him desperate for it. Was it another trick? A way to control him?

He should be furious. He should be threatening her with his nine-tail whip for disobeying him, like he would have with any other crewmember. Instead, all he wanted to punish her with his cock.

Her lips were moving underneath his, despite her slapping at his shoulders, making him grab her wrists with his hand to pin them above her head. He thrust against her again, right against the centre of her body, her leg at his hip, spreading her. She gave a sharp exhale; he let out a small groan.

She bloody wants it. If she didn't, she wouldn't be reciprocating, wouldn't be kissing him back, wouldn't be bucking her hips against him like she was seeking his dick.

She was confusing him, and he had no idea how to handle the whiplash of emotions.

One minute, he was close to being inside her, the next, she was leaving him with a painful erection. One minute she was sitting on his lap with her tongue halfway down his throat, the next, she was trying to get away.

She instigated it almost as much as he did, yet she was always the one to pull away. She was fucking with him. Alister didn't appreciate being fucked with. He pulled on the ties of her tights and shoved his hand inside the tight space.

"Wait!" she gasped, managing to get her mouth free before he controlled her back into the kiss. She gave a mew when he shoved his hand between her thighs further and touched her.

I want inside her. His want for it grew when two of his fingers rubbed over her entrance and found a little wet pool waiting for him.

"Nuh-uh," she murmured against his crushing mouth, making it hard to understand her.

Then she kneed his side.

His anger spiked higher, and he quickly shoved both his hands to her arse to lift her before slamming her back against the wall. She couldn't kick him if she was pinned, her legs spread for him in the air. She needed to hold onto him if she didn't want to risk falling.

"You have been teasing me, lass," Alister sneered. "I told you I don't playing games." He kissed down her neck, shoving himself against her again, just so her body would stroke his. Anything to make himself feel better.

"S-Stop," she muttered quietly, but her voice broke on a moan when he slipped his hips over hers, right against that sensitive nub of her clit.

When he heard her moan, he made sure to press harder.

"You don't do what you're told. You won't go where I tell you to. You come into my cabin and kiss me – only to deny me moments later."

She was turning him into a tangled mess, and he didn't like it. *She almost got me killed!* She also saved him. What was he supposed to do with the hate-filled lust that was clinging to him? Especially when he could feel her legs tightening around his waist.

I'm going to fuck her. He wanted to take all his anger and frustration out on her. He wanted to feel that wetness around his shaft again. Hell, Alister just wanted to hear her moan. He was going to take all of today's anger, blood-lust, and frustration out on her.

He bit her neck simply because he wanted to hurt her, bruise her, just as she had with his ego. Thrusting against her again, his eyes narrowed at the wall.

Why does punishing her sound like a stupendous idea?

He started pulling at her tights, putting her in a position that had her knees buckling in as the fabric slipped over her arse. The only thing supporting her was one of his hands and her arms around his neck.

"Please," she said quietly, her head falling forward to rest against his shoulder. "Stop..."

It sounded like a bloody defeat. There was a shaky kind of tone to her voice, one Alister hadn't heard from her before, one he thought he would never hear. His hand stopped.

What the hell am I doing?

Just because she wanted him, that he could feel she did, was clinging to him, didn't necessarily mean she was *willing*.

Shit. She had him so messed up he'd almost thrown his morals out the window. *She'd asked me to stop three times.*

He'd almost taken someone when he shouldn't. Alister had been moments away from slamming into her.

He felt like a monster.

Dropping her feet to the floor, he shoved her tights up her legs to right her and hide her body from his sight. She gasped as she bounced on her feet from how harshly he yanked them up. He threw her to the side and watched her stumble in his peripheral.

"Get out," he said with a dark quietness, keeping his focus on the wall in front of him. Leaning against it with both hands, he tried to take back control, tried to right his mind. *Shit. I need to calm down.*

"You..."

"I said get out!" He felt like a freaking bastard. "I'm pissed off and I'm not thinking straight."

He didn't understand why she was still here, talking to him, when he'd been touching her without her consent. He had been undressing her, thrusting up against her like a crazed madman. Most other women would have run out crying.

She came to tentatively touch his shoulder. "What about your back? You've been hurt."

Did she understand that he immediately regretted what he'd been doing and was trying to soothe him?

I don't need her pity! It was her fault for taunting him to this state to begin with!

He reached out and grabbed her neck in his hand. Turning, he faced her. He expected her to look afraid, but instead she looked up at him with a steely glare.

"You want me to treat you like a man? The next time you don't do as you're told under the command of my ship, I'll put the nine-tails to you like anyone else, got it?"

He couldn't use his cock to punish her just because he was horny for her. He needed to treat her like everyone else if she wouldn't take him.

She rolled her eyes at him. "Fine, I'll go. Take care of your own wounds for all I care."

Good. He let her go, pushing her away. "Go be annoying elsewhere."

She immediately turned from his cabin and left him by

himself so he could vanquish his anger, lust, and regret in solitude.

With her gone, his mind didn't feel so muddled.

CHAPTER FOURTEEN

After that terrible day, Alister expected her to stop coming to him.

He knew he'd gone too far and had almost realised it too late. Yet, she continued to stand near him. She spoke to him at the helm, asked him how his back was healing. Annoyingly, she even tried to check it by pulling his tunic up until he wiggled away before she could see.

Instead of getting Clint to bring him food or grog water, she continued to do it.

She didn't seem upset or bothered by what had transpired between them. She glared at him, smiled at him, acted exactly how she had before.

She even came to look over his shoulder when he was in the navigation room, watching what he was doing so she knew where they were in the world. Not seeming to mind that she was alone with him in a confined space, she inspected the maps so close to him, he could feel her shoulder brushing his.

He'd been apprehensive of her at first, closed off, considering his actions. Then, despite everything, she was the one who instigated a kiss, like she couldn't help herself from tasting him.

Rosetta, with one draw of her silky pouted lips, sent him hurtling right back to desperation for her.

They were playing cat and mouse once more.

A game where, if she wasn't with him in his chambers, he would corner her somewhere below deck just to tease her, hoping the more he tried to touch her, the more likely she was to falter. Sometimes, it left him cursing his own stupidity, as he'd often leave with an ache in his groin, but he couldn't help grinning when he walked away from her panting form.

Unfortunately, that was until a nasty rumour started, something he wasn't particularly pleased with hearing.

"Aye, Alister. She's sleeping with her crew," Pierre told him while Alister was manning the helm.

He was supporting himself against the wheel, speaking with Pierre about the state of his ship. He wanted a full report every day to make sure there weren't any complications with the repairs. They were uncertain about the state of the hull since it still had holes and leaks.

"*My* crew," he corrected with a hostile bite to his tone. That wasn't why he was angry, though. "How do you know this?"

"Rumours have spread that she was seen in the hammock with Naeem the last few nights." Pierre looked down at his filthy nails before biting into one. "Apparently, the other cabins heard some odd noises."

"Why should I care?" Alister gritted out, gripping the handles tighter.

"We know you're keen on her." His eyes drew over Alister knowingly, one of his blond brows raised. "We were just wondering if that was still the case."

"I don't give a shit what you do with her."

Aye, lass. I told you if you sleep with one of them, you sleep with all of them. Except him.

He didn't like that she'd been seeking his mouth, teasing him and denying him, when she may have been with another.

The grin that formed on Pierre's face soured Alister's mood further. He'd thought the relationship between herself and Naeem was a little strange. It was a little too close.

Naeem had stomped his way into Alister's quarters the first day they'd set sail, demanding to speak with him.

Apparently, he and the rest of her crew were worried her safety wouldn't be a top priority. There had been a threat that, if she got hurt in any way, they'd turn on him with a vengeance.

It was one of the reasons he hadn't liked her on the pirate hunting vessel. She could have been injured or killed and her men may have turned on him, despite the fact it was her own fault, that she'd gone against his orders.

He needed them to sail, especially now with the amount of work that was needed below deck. It was around the clock work.

Alister had mocked him, but he'd still thought it was odd he was chancing that kind of threat. It was as though he feared for her more than Alister's reaction.

His eyes narrowed as he glared at the front of his ship after hearing this terrible news from Pierre. *Perhaps they're in love with each other.* For whatever reason, they'd been denying it until now.

It might be because they were forced to occupy the same sleeping space, forced in close proximity with each other.

He didn't like this.

He had to make certain of the rumours. So, Alister stood outside her cabin with his back to the wall. He folded his arms and listened in.

Hearing Mr Smith shouting for them to shut up so he could sleep while a giggling Rosetta laughed at Naeem who told him he was just jealous she was in his hammock tonight, confirmed what he'd been told. He hadn't stuck around to hear any more.

Out of curiosity, he'd changed the shift arrangements. He put Naeem on night duty to see what she would do – only to find out she'd been seen in Mr Smith's hammock.

Alister couldn't believe the update he'd received the next day. The man must be twice her age and she'd still brazenly hopped into bed with him.

Since he'd heard of her lying with Naeem, Alister hadn't spoken to her unless absolutely necessary. Although he was still attracted to her, his desire had fizzled away near instantly.

She was now just becoming an annoyance, one that was starting to upset the men. Once the rumours began, he'd started receiving reports of men receiving a slap for trying to bed her as well.

He wasn't interested in getting in the middle of it. That was, until she stormed her way into his quarters without knocking while he'd been asleep in his hammock. The door slammed against the frame loudly, shocking him awake. He moved his arm to cover half his face, hiding the scar as if he was merely hiding from the sunlight filtering in.

Then he raised his head from where it rested to face her. "Oi, sweetheart. It's too early for that kind of noise," he groaned with a dull tone.

"Get your men to keep their bloody hands to themselves!" she screeched at him with such an unladylike, gremlin voice that he grimaced at its ugliness.

With a sigh and a roll of his eyes, he dug into the creases of his hammock, knowing his eyepatch was somewhere in it.

"I told you what would happen if you slept with one of the crew," he said, refusing to play dumb to her coy actions, putting his eyepatch on to cover his blind eye. He adjusted it until it sat right. "Doesn't matter if they were your own."

He watched her eyes widen and her mouth fall open. She reached behind her and slammed the door shut. "Excuse me? I haven't fucked anyone."

He rested his head back, kicking the leg outside his hanging bed so he could make it swing from side-to-side. He closed his eyes, more interested in sleep than this conversation.

The sun is only just rising. Why am I dealing with this shit now?

"That's not what I've heard. You've been caught in bed with both Naeem and Mr Smith."

"To go to sleep!"

"Pardon?" He lifted his head once more to look at her. "You expect me to believe that nonsense? What kind of woman crawls into a man's bed but does nothing?"

She'd taken him easily enough, a stranger, someone who'd raised a weapon to her, threatened her.

The audacity of this woman with her lies. He and his men weren't idiots, and the cabin walls were only thin timber.

"A cold one!"

"There are blankets, sweetheart," he chuckled darkly.

"They are itchy," she rebuffed. "My skin is sensitive, and they still aren't enough to keep the cold at bay."

"You had no issues before; why now all of a sudden?"

"Because my coat was enough to keep me warm! The hull currently has holes in it."

His brows furrowed. *Well, that is true.*

"It is damp below deck and the wind coming through makes it freezing down there." She folded her arms across her chest, narrowing her eyes into a deep, icy glare. "I can't sleep when I'm cold, or itchy, or uncomfortable."

He leaned up on one elbow, balancing himself with years of skill. "Why didn't you tell me then? Hm?"

He shook his head; he had no reason to believe her.

"And what am I supposed to do? Complain to you I'm cold when there is very little you can do about it? I'd rather not be mocked. I've already been just for owning a pair of tits."

His lips thinned at the truth of her words. He would have laughed at her for it, poking at her for her gender since men could handle the temperatures below deck, no matter the state of the ship. Men were resilient, women less so.

"Do you think it's comfortable lying next to Naeem or Mr Smith? Naeem is a wriggler in his sleep and Mr Smith snores like an ogre, but they are warm."

Alister's gaze turned towards the bed below him, one he rarely used unless he was too drunk to make it into his hammock.

She'd slept with the blanket and pillow.

He'd seen them both inside his hammock when he'd taken his ship back, and his were made of higher quality material than the grey blankets the crew had.

His eye turned back to her to see her visibly cringe.

"And the idea I'd sleep with Mr Smith is ridiculous. He reminds me of my father."

"And Naeem?" he questioned, trying to keep the curiosity from his voice.

"He is my friend and has been for many years. They are the only people I trust; they are family to me."

Is that why she was comfortable with sharing a cabin with them? Alister thought for long moments.

"I can't have you sleeping with men for warmth because the ship has been damaged."

"What else am I supposed to do? Freeze to death?" She tapped her toe impatiently. "Those that catch a sickness on the seas are a liability and are prone to catching worse illnesses."

If one person gets sick, the chances are others will as well. Now *that* was something Alister couldn't have.

He gave a sigh at her dramatics before rubbing at the hair on his cheek as he contemplated his solution. With the dampness and the wind, he doubted even if he gave her his blanket that it would be enough.

I can't put her with Pierre and Derek. She'd been right that if he gave her that cabin to herself, he'd have to deal with an upset crew. He was already giving her special attention; any more would be an inconvenience that could cause tension he didn't need.

"Alright, lass," he finally sighed. He couldn't believe he was about to say this. "Bring your hammock in here."

"What?" Her head reared back while her face twisted into a wide-eyed glare of disbelief. "Sleep in this room... with you?"

"Aye. You were able to sleep comfortably in here before." *It also means I can keep an eye on her.* "The men will back off once I explain."

"I don't want to sleep near you." She eyed him suspiciously in his hammock. "I don't think I trust you."

"Hurtful." Alister placed his hand over his heart like she'd wounded him. "I wouldn't harass a lass while she slept."

He might before that, though.

Her lips pursed into a cute pout of annoyance, her foot tapping harder while her head turned to the side in thought.

"Can I have the blanket and pillow?"

He let his arm fall from his hammock so he could gesture to them below. "Does it look like I need them?"

"Fine," she huffed. "I'm already sick of almost falling to the floor because Naeem tried to roll over."

A light chortle escaped him. *Now, wouldn't that be funny.*

Rosetta slammed the door on her way out and Alister folded his arms behind his head, grinning at the ceiling.

She'd just given him a ticket to an easier way between her legs. Now that he knew the actual truth of what had been happening, perhaps the damage to the hull, and finding out about these rumours, had been a good thing.

She hadn't denied his offer, showing she truly had just been cold, rather than promiscuous.

She can't escape me if she shares my room.

CHAPTER FIFTEEN

Rosetta's life on the Howling Death had fallen into a routine over the last few weeks she'd been onboard.

Each morning, she rose before most to help Mr Darkley and his son in the kitchen. She'd follow his instruction, giving her own ideas as she went—which he mostly shot down. He was a stubborn man who liked to do things his way.

She'd help place food on the dining benches so the crew could grab their grub before they went about their jobs. Those who were about to go to bed would come to have their morning meal before sleep.

Then she'd help clean the kitchen.

She'd have free time between meals, and she'd mingle with the men, talking to those who also on breaks.

She spent some of her time above, on the deck. Standing in the warm sunlight, Rosetta would lean against the railing and watch the horizon. Some would find it boring to watch the wide and desolate ocean pass by, but she didn't. Not when every minute, she was sailing closer and closer to what she wanted. She often thought of her future, what she would do once met her goal.

Obsessed. That was the word many used to describe her hunt for the Laughing Siren. Foolish was the word others chose, thinking she'd never obtain it.

I'll prove them all wrong.

Her eyes would often stray to the man steering her to potential victory. With the wind blowing his long, black hair any way it may, he stood over them behind the helm like a god of the seas.

Pierre would speak to him, and she could tell they were discussing their current position by the fact that he would go over scrolls of parchment with Alister.

Others also came to talk to him in the times she was above, most of which were casual conversations to appease and entertain him.

There were times he was so focused on their direction, it didn't seem like he knew she was watching.

Then there were times when she'd look from the horizon to find his gaze was already on her. There was a dark glint to his eyes some moments, one that made her lick at the seam of her lips. She returned the fierce look with one of her own.

Rosetta liked to approach him with a certain swing to her hips, a certain crossing leg walk. She would even skim her fingertips against the railing when she walked up the stairs.

It was always followed with a lie that she was just checking to see if he needed food, or water, or something else, when really, she just wanted to annoy him with her presence.

She often got the reaction she wanted; to string him high and dry since he couldn't leave his station, or openly try to touch her without wanting to insight jealousy from the others.

Before anything could be said or done, she would return to the kitchen to help Mr Darkley prepare the feast for the night.

Men would eat their dinner before lazing around the ship to drink and sleep, while others rose for their night duties.

Then, once again, she'd help clean, as she did with the other meals.

It kept her busy, and she was thankful that the in between times were no longer accompanied by groping hands. She'd been irritated that the moment anyone got a sniff that she might be having sex with someone, everyone had turned on her like uncontrollable, grunting pigs. All those except her original crew – who apparently had never heard the rumours. Otherwise, they would have shut them down.

Men had started to grab at her thighs or arse while trying to talk to her, brush their hands against her face, get close to her. Even slapping a few of them hadn't worked until she blatantly grabbed her pistol and threatened one whose unruly behaviour turned to anger.

It died down the moment she moved her sleeping hammock to Alister's quarters.

He hadn't been joking when he said they'd turn to me like a harlot. She couldn't blame men for being men when they were probably used to being around women who liked being shared because it got them more coin.

That was a lie; she totally could, but she didn't see the point in holding onto that particular grudge when there was nothing she could do about it.

After three days, she'd been overwhelmed.

The groping hadn't really stopped, but at least it was now only one set of hands. She also often groped back before she came to her senses.

There was something about Captain Alister Paine that got her all hot, bothered, and stupid. And even forgiving.

She'd met many men like him in the past, and they'd all given her the same reaction. She'd never spent this much time with one, though.

There was something about his carefree, nonchalant personality that drew her in. Quick to laugh, but also to anger; he was a man of muscle and steel.

Every time he cornered her, as if their paths just kept meeting when they really shouldn't, his mouth was like a raging storm. Like a tiny boat, she got swept up in it and lost.

The number of times she'd almost caved was disastrous.

He still hadn't earned her yet.

Rosetta rarely slept with the same man twice, unless he paid her for it. She wasn't a prostitute, but there were a few port boys she allowed to think she was so she could get paid for something she already wanted.

She cheated them out of money they didn't really need to lose because she wasn't hungry for coin. She usually had plenty. *It's their fault for being so stupid.*

She wouldn't tell Alister that. She wouldn't allow him to think of her as a prostitute or treat her like one.

She knew she was drawing a very definitive line with all the rejections she'd handed out over the past two weeks. What impressed her, though, was that he didn't have a tantrum when he was rejected, not like so many other men.

She'd forgiven him for the day he went too far simply because of the way he'd looked afterwards.

His face had been crinkled into a mess of emotions, a few of them confused and apologetic. He looked troubled. Without needing to say anything, she could see he'd realised his mistake.

They never spoke about it, and she initiated contact again to show him it was forgiven. It was also because she had just wanted to satisfy her hungry hands and mouth that had been itching to touch him. Rosetta was selfish.

Afterwards, when she continued to reject him, he didn't seem to care that he wasn't getting what he wanted. He'd tease her, trying to get further and further each time. Before he could go too far, she'd stop him, and he'd call her out on the fact that he knew she wanted it.

The last time he'd said it, he'd slapped her on the arse and walked away while whistling like a deviant.

Arrogant bastard, she'd thought with a smile of humour at his back.

So yes, over the course of the last two weeks, Rosetta's life had settled into a routine, but she didn't think she'd ever had this much fun on a ship before.

She'd go to sleep before him, and she woke before him. Today, she'd woken earlier than usual and had since been sitting on the steps of the quarterdeck, deep in thought.

It wasn't long before someone troublesome came to bother her. With calculating thought, she knew exactly how to bother him back.

"Ow! Ow! OW!" the person sitting between her legs shouted like a five-year-old. "You're as bad as my mother!"

"Then stop struggling so much!" she yelled with exasperation, like she couldn't understand why he was so upset when she knew exactly why.

She was the one purposely torturing him, after all.

"But you're hurting me!"

"That's because you don't know how to sit still!"

"Because you're bloody hurting me!"

It was a struggle to stifle the evil, maniacal laugh that threatened to escape.

"Why are you complaining so loudly first thing in the morning?" Alister grumbled from behind them, coming out of his cabin sooner than he usually did.

The sun was only just rising; he usually didn't appear on deck until it was finished. He would take over from Derek, who had been steering the ship throughout the night.

"I've been tryin' to shut 'em up, but they just won't listen to me," Derek shouted. He was probably also one of the reasons Alister had woken up.

"She's torturing me, Captain," Pierre whined, reaching his hand back like he needed saving. Rosetta yanked the hairbrush though the man's long golden locks.

"He said he dearly missed it when women in port brushed his beautiful and glossy hair." She tilted her head back to look at Alister. "So, he told me I should do it for him."

Pierre had seen her brushing her own, something she did when she remembered. Since she'd woken up at such an early hour, she decided to untangle the knots from her own hair.

Without looking, not taking her eyes from Alister, she continued to forcibly yank the brush through Pierre's knots.

She noted the way Alister looked at his own long hair, then at her with a strange expression. She couldn't believe it. It almost looked as though he wanted her to pay him such attention, regardless of Pierre's whining.

"But you don't have to be a brute while doing it!"

Rosetta gave Alister a smirk, then a wink, which made his expression turn into a laughing smirk.

"Sure, I do. It's just so knotty, Pierre. You did tell me it would be an honour if I did it."

She could be gentler, starting from the ends, but instead, she was choosing to rake the brush from the scalp down.

"Rosie, please," he cried, trying to reach behind him to stop her, since she had him trapped by a fist full of hair.

Rosie...

Rosetta visibly shuddered, a deep roll of nausea rolling through her to the point she felt bile rising. She almost wanted to run to the side of the ship and be sick.

She let him go to wrap an arm around his throat while pulling her pistol from its holster.

"Don't *ever* call me that again," she hissed through gritted teeth, putting the barrel of the gun to his head. "Nobody is allowed to call me that."

"Oi!" Alister warned as he stepped forward.

She turned her head back to give him a glare. "You either." She could see his upper lip curled back in a show of irritation. "You can call me whatever you want except that, got it?"

They could call her bitch, slut, idiot, sweetheart, whatever name they wanted, as long as it wasn't *that*.

"Okay, we got it, lass." Alister lifted both his hands to wave them down. "Now, put the gun away."

Rosetta spun the gun on her finger before she shoved it into its holster. Booting Pierre in the back, he stumbled as he found his footing. She threw the brush at him so hard, his stomach caved like he'd been pelted with a fist.

"You can brush your own damn hair."

Then she got to her own feet to storm towards the kitchen. *I have duties anyway.*

A hand grabbed her before she even made it halfway across the deck.

"What was that about?" Alister pulled on her arm to turn her around. "You can't go around threatening my crew just because you're in a bad mood."

"I'm not." She ripped her arm away. "It's none of your business!"

"Are you on your monthlies or something?"

The heat on her face had nothing to do with embarrassment and everything to do with rage. "How dare you say something so rude, you absolute prick!"

It may be true that Rosetta was feeling the twang and pain of receiving her monthly waterfall of suffering, but that had nothing to do with her foul mood. She'd finished it anyway, but she always had a slight twinge the following day afterwards.

"Then you need to calm the hell down." His words insinuated he may have been more understanding, but she refused to let him think this had anything to do with her womanly makeup.

"I *am* calm!" she yelled at the top of her lungs, almost a screech. "I don't have to justify why I'm upset, but if it's so damn important, I just don't like being called Rosie!"

He opened his mouth to argue but a shout sounded from above, stealing everyone's attention. "Sail, ho!"

They turned their heads up to the crow's nest, their meaningless argument forgotten.

"What kind of ship?" Alister yelled, turning to walk back up the stairs to the table next to the helm.

Rosetta's captain instincts kicked in and she followed. Watching him pick up his nautical spyglass to look over the horizon, she tried to see without one.

"A colourful one, Captain!"

When he found it, she watched him smile with those big, even, white teeth.

"Looks like we've got ourselves a trading boat." *That means...* He put his fingers to his lips and sounded off an ear-piercing whistle. "I want all hands on deck! We're about to get the supplies we need to repair our ship."

He turned to Derek, who looked tired and weathered.

"Sorry old salt, but it looks like you're going to bed late."

"Aye, Cap'in, don't ye concern yerself for me." He reached out to pat Alister on the shoulder with hard slaps. "I'll hold yer ship for ye."

Derek kicked his peg leg back to brace himself. With bulging muscles, he turned the ship so they could chase the trading boat.

As much as she wanted to call out commands, witnessing Alister take control of his men was something she'd come to enjoy experiencing. It was exhilarating and made her blood pump harder.

The way he yelled out to his men, harsh commands that demanded they be obeyed, his strength as a captain. The laughter and glee behind them only riled the men up further.

Once one man started singing a hard-working sea shanty, the ship came alive with power. Violent energy poured from them until she thought it might become something tangible.

"Man the sails." He pointed when his feet met the main deck. "Ready the cannons, gunmen." He swiped his arm to the side. "I want you all bloodthirsty!"

She didn't think he'd noticed she was shadowing him until he turned around and almost ran into her.

"And you." He grabbed her shoulder and pushed her behind him. "Get below deck."

Excuse me? The pirate hunters she understood; they'd focus on her as a hostage, but this was a trading ship!

"I'm a pirate, Alister." She pulled her sword from its sheath around her hips. "I'm not some starry-eyed damsel who needs protecting. Stop treating me like one!"

"I don't give a shit what you are." He pointed his finger at her sternum. "You are not stepping foot off this ship until we have all those men bound. If you want to help so badly, protect my ship if one of them tries to jump across."

"But–"

"You gave me your word that you would follow my orders. I won't have you disobeying them again." He leaned forward to be level with her with a dangerous glint in his eye. "And I'm giving you one, savvy?"

She blew a curl of hair from her face with a huff, resigned to following his order to stay on the ship after what had happened last time.

She just wouldn't go below deck.

Alister removed his black doublet coat and carelessly threw it into his quarters, like he thought it'd get in the way. His sleeves were already rolled up past his forearms, showing off his dark hair and the scars he had underneath them.

Rosetta had never seen him without his tunic on, but she'd known from the first time she'd seen his face that this man was covered in scars. She was curious to see just how much of them peppered his skin.

When the jolly roger was raised, the ever famous black flag with a white skull and two swords crossing underneath it, the trading boat turned to flee.

"She's a clipper, Cap'in," Derek yelled from the quarterdeck.

"Aye, but we're faster."

Before long, the Howling Death came into range of the boat and Rosetta went to the railing to watch them uselessly trying to flee.

"Run a shot across the bow!" Alister yelled, and she heard two cannons boom. Cannonballs fired from the front, crashing into the water.

"They're striking their colours," the man in the crow's nest told them with a cheer, but she'd already known that, could see they were lowering their coat of arms.

"They're surrendering, lads." Rosetta turned back to stare at Alister just as he grinned with triumph. "Get ready to board."

That's a Western trading ship! She tapped the railing with excitement as they came up beside it. She'd been hoping they would come across one before she had to part ways from this ship and its crew.

Multiple men sailed from ropes to the larger ship. Others laid long planks of wood between their railings to stumble across.

It was hard to hear in the distance, but she figured Alister had told the men to tie the traders up since they weren't killing them. No one had drawn their swords.

The moment Rosetta saw their crew starting to bring over raided supplies was the moment she swung across. He did say she could cross once they were bound.

She didn't spare anyone a glance as she headed below deck. There was only one thing she wanted on this boat, and it wasn't loot or treasure.

There weren't many men below deck, but she had to duck under the arms of occasional men carrying heavy crates while jumping over cups and items carelessly been thrown from rooms into the hallways. She peeked her head inside to see men digging through items to find anything worth stealing.

Excitement that filled her lungs as she giggled. Raiding a ship was one of her favourite activities.

She'd almost tripped a few times because she was running. She needed to get where she wanted before the men ransacked and trashed it. It would be the last place they'd raid.

That's why she hadn't wasted any time in crossing over the moment they started. *I hope they have what I want!*

She couldn't contain her hopeful grin.

Alister was watching his men finish dragging up the last trader they'd found and tied him up when someone caught his attention.

He watched Rosetta land on her feet on the boat he was currently standing on and immediately head below deck. *Damnit! That woman just doesn't listen.*

He gave his final orders before chasing after her. *I told her to stay behind!*

There were more men closer to the surface, but the deeper he went, trying to find her, the less of his crew he saw. He checked inside every room he passed, trying to find a trace of her.

The urge to throw her over his shoulder, cart her back to his ship, and berate her grew nigh overwhelming with every minute that ticked by. All she had to do was follow his damn order. He was furious he had to do this when there were other, more pressing things that should be taking priority.

Anger bubbled but he knew he needed to snuff the worse of it. *Does she* want *me to nine-tails her?*

He never thought when he'd threatened her that she'd

actually do something deserving of it!

He found her in the place he, strangely, figured she'd go. She was standing in the kitchen, smiling at a tin of something. Then she went to put it into the pocket of her coat.

Fuck! Alister ran forward and pushed her out of the way. He grunted, and she went crashing against the wooden benches before tumbling to the ground.

Alister turned while pulling his pistol from its holster to point it at the man who had just sliced his cleaver through the air. He shot him in the head. A loud bang sounded before the cook stumbled back, hitting pans hanging from a rack. They made loud, clunking noises as his lifeless corpse hit the ground.

Holding his side, he made sure the area was clear, walking around to check every shadow, every spot a man could hide.

"Alister!" Rosetta shouted, coming up to grab his hand. "You're hurt."

He elbowed her hands out of the way to keep pressure on the wound to his side. "I told you to stay on the ship!"

He wrapped his large hand around her throat and pulled her in. He wasn't choking her, but damn did he want to. He may have even squeezed a little tighter than usual.

"You said I could come across once the men were bound."

"*And* we had checked that we hadn't missed anyone!"

"I was fine on my own."

"Really?" He gave a laugh, but it didn't hold a single shred of humour. He released her and pushed her back. "Because I just stopped you from getting hit by a cleaver."

The man had been slowly sneaking up behind her with it raised. Alister had intercepted him just in time so he sliced sideways instead which got him in the torso.

Hissing in a breath, he looked down, thankful the injury was on the side he could see and moved his hand away. He pressed it back when he saw how quickly he was bleeding.

If he'd had his cutlass in his hand, he might have been able to deflect the attack, but he'd been too busy trying to find her to hold it.

"I knew he was there." She narrowed her eyes on him. "I was just reaching for my pistol when you pushed me."

He didn't care if it was a lie or the truth. That wouldn't change the fact she'd disobeyed his order and he needed serious medical attention. He turned away from her, walking down the hallway so he could find the surface.

"Let me help you," she offered, coming beside him as he placed his hand on the wall to steady himself.

He wasn't weakening, he was just bracing himself through the sharp throbbing pain that came with every footfall on that side of his body.

She tried to put his arm around her shoulders, but he nudged her out of the way.

"I don't need anyone's help, Rosetta," he barked. "Never have, never will."

"Captain..." one of his men gasped when he made his way into sunlight.

"Aye," he nodded with a disgruntled tone. "Blame the lass."

He grabbed one of the ropes still connecting to his ship and used it to steady himself as he walked across a plank.

The entire time, he knew Rosetta was following him and he really wished she wouldn't. He didn't need some woman fawning and cooing at him because he was injured.

At least she's getting off the trading boat. He wouldn't have to think about her while tending to his wound. He wanted to be angry, but he was too concerned about himself to care. He'd deal with her later.

"Do you have a doctor on board?"

He guessed her question meant she didn't.

"Nay. You killed him when you took over my ship." He

turned his head to the closest man available and found Clint staring at him, wide-eyed. "Boy."

The fourteen-year-old came running over, his tousled hair held back from his face with a bandana. "Y-Yes, Captain?"

"Bring a clean cloth, a bowl of grog, and a large bottle of rum to my quarters."

Clint went running, as if the backs of his heels were on fire, to quickly disappear below deck.

Alister headed for his quarters. Just when he went to close the door behind him, he felt resistance. "Leave me alone, lass."

This wasn't for the faint of heart and he didn't want to deal with someone who might faint. Heading deeper inside, he grabbed a clean eating knife. He also grabbed a small candlestick and the flint and tender he'd need to light it.

Once it was lit by setting wood shavings on fire and using that to light the wick, with one blood-covered hand, Alister removed his shirt. He fell into one of the dining chairs and started heating the blade of the knife.

He could see in his peripheral she had ignored him and was kneeling at the small chest of her personal items. She'd already removed her coat and rolled up her sleeves, which he'd never seen her do before.

"Do you never listen?" His voice was quiet from pain, but there was a bite to it. "I told you to get out. You've already screwed up enough today by not following orders."

She didn't stop what she was doing, nor did she answer him. Clint burst through the door, running forward to place everything he'd asked for on the table before leaving.

Alister threw the cloth into the grog water to soak with his free hand. Then he grabbed the bottle of rum, ripped the cork out with his back teeth, and spat it across the room.

He chugged half the bottle in one go, trying to numb himself by drowning in it. It wouldn't be enough. He'd need at least three bottles before he'd be even tipsy – if he was lucky. Rum barely did anything for him these days.

"You shouldn't drink; it'll make you bleed more."

He pointed one of the fingers holding the bottle at her.

"You don't get to tell me what to do." Then she knelt in front of him, between his legs, reaching to grab the cloth. "Oi, what do you think you're doing?"

"I have tended to every wound of my crew." Her voice was small, her expression grim, but she looked surprisingly composed. "As well as my own. I have a little bit of medical knowledge."

She's got scars? He knew she'd hurt the back of her arm the day of the pirate hunters, but he thought that might have been her first. It hadn't looked deep.

"Is that why you followed me in here?"

"Yes." Her eyes came up to his face, and he noted a hint of softness he'd never seen before. Soft was not something he usually thought of her expressions. "Let me help you so you don't have to do it yourself."

His lips pursed into a thin line before he turned his head away. "Fine. You'll need to cauterize the vein first."

"I know that." She twisted the cloth to wring it out, and then made him jump when she wiped it over his side. "Will you be able to handle being stitched or should I expect you to wriggle like some?"

"Stitch me? Lass, you ain't coming anywhere near me with a needle and thread. Just stop the bleeding, I can heal the rest."

She was silent for a few moments. When he looked to her, he could see she was inspecting his wound.

"No," she sighed, patting his wound again with the soaked cloth. "You'll definitely need a few stitches."

"Nay." He shoved the burning hot knife towards her.

"It'll help stop you from getting an infection."

"I've healed through every injury I've ever gotten the same

way."

She gave a shrug. "And today you'll get a new way."

Alister slammed the bottom of his fist against the table. "You're one stubborn bitch, you know that? I'm telling you nay."

She pushed the tip of the blade into his wound, and he gave a yelp he tried to not let out. *It's worse when someone else does it!*

"You got hurt because of me," she said once she was done cauterizing his wound to stop the bleeding. "Let me tend to you properly. It's my way of showing I'm sorry."

"Ha!" he chuckled darkly, feeling the corners of his eyelids crinkle while taking a swig of rum. "Can't believe my ears. The lass is apologising."

He took another swig, glaring up at the ceiling in thought. *She'll keep pestering me.*

"Exactly, so let me help."

Knew it.

CHAPTER SIXTEEN

When Rosetta first entered the room behind Alister, she'd taken her sewing instruments from the small chest of her personal items. She came to kneel in front of him, using the cloth to clean his wound as best as she could.

She'd used the flame to burn the tip of her needle before she cleaned it as best as she could, and then she'd gotten to work sewing him up. The injury was just below his ribcage on his right side. It wasn't too large or deep, but it was enough to concern her.

She could tell by the scars on his torso that he had cauterized every wound he'd ever gotten and never tended to them properly. He had shallow, white streaks all over his chest, stomach, shoulders, and arms.

The way she was doing it would cause less scarring.

Every time she pushed the needle in, he would take a swig of rum, as though he was trying to drink courage. He didn't move, but she did hear him hiss out a breath through clenched teeth.

She tied the last knot and used the knife to separate the needle from the thread.

"There, was that so bad?" she asked, placing them on the table.

"Aye, can't say I'm partial to how that felt," he answered,

pulling on his skin to better examine the stitched wound.

"You'll heal quicker like this. So even if it hurts now, it'll hurt for less time."

He looked at her, still kneeling between his knees, giving her a grimace. "Is that even true?"

A quiet laugh fell from her by accident.

"Yes." She brushed the backs of her fingers over a scar that ran from his sternum all the way to his navel. "You also won't have such a deep scar."

He has so many of them. She'd never seen a body this riddled.

"Don't give a damn if I've got scars, lass." He went to take a drink, looked at the bottle, then tipped it upside down. He placed the empty bottle on the table carelessly. It fell to its side and rolled. "Doesn't hurt so bad anymore, either."

She fingered a scar across his chest and the pectoral muscle beneath it seemed to leap to her touch.

This was the first time she'd seen him without a shirt on and she was able to see his torso in all its strength and glory. She quietly admitted to herself that she was enjoying the view. Rosetta didn't mind the stain of blood still on him, either.

His chest was covered in black, curling hair that made his tanned skin seem pale in comparison. There was even a goodie trail of it running down his navel to fade into his breeches. His stomach was made of defined muscles, his torso thick with them.

"Why didn't you stay on my ship?" His tone wasn't as sharp as it was before. She thought perhaps her touch was easing his anger.

She sifted her fingers through the hair on his chest, letting her eyes drink him in without a care in the world if he wanted her to stop.

"It was a Western trading ship. I knew they'd have nutmeg and I told Mr Darkley about the wonders of it. Wanted to see if they had some before your men ransacked the kitchen and made it impossible to find anything."

Things often got lost in raids once everything got piled into the cargo bay. What one man thought was treasure, another thought was trash. Seeing this man half-naked, for example, his chest and torso on show for her, was a treat she wanted nothing more than to savour. Another woman with a soft and fragile heart may have found him unsightly.

She couldn't stop touching him even if she tried.

"You disregarded my orders... for a spice?" His voice held disbelief and her eyes darted up to look at his confused expression.

They came back down to watch her hand as she deliberately brushed over his chest to almost knead him, flicking one of his nipples along the way. Both his hands twitched, like they wanted to turn into fists.

"I thought it was safe and that you'd rounded up all the traders." She gave a shrug, bringing her hand back over the sensitive little point to see his hands clench. "Didn't mean to disregard it."

Her hand started trailing over the scar that ran down his side and over his hip. It brought her hand dangerously low on his stomach. She even fingered one of the deep V lines that ran diagonally down his hips.

"You're giving me ideas here, Rosetta." Her eyes darted back up to his face to see him searching hers. He didn't often call her by her name, but it made the corners of her lips curl upwards every time. "Not really in a magnanimous mood at the moment."

When she looked down, she could see the bulge of something slowly, but visibly, growing in his breeches.

"I guess you *were* trying to save my life."

She brought both her hands to the waistband of his pants and scratched her nails up his hips lightly. His stomach dipped, clenching, and that bulge suddenly got bigger.

"And I am already on my knees." She placed her hands on the buttons of his breeches, then paused when her gaze found his wound. "Are you alright?"

"Oh, aye," he said with a hint of humour, the anger in his eyes fading into something much more dangerous. "It'll fix me right up. Call it an addition to your healing penance."

Rosetta raised up on her knees to press her lips to his stomach while her hands worked on undoing the buttons holding his breeches closed.

Her body reacted swiftly to her own actions as she stroked across one of his scars with her tongue. She brought it over his nipple like she had with her fingers and the exhale he gave made her belly clench low with a shuddering flip of desire.

She was growing more excited by the minute at the idea of touching him. She'd given herself an excuse to do so, to give him a reward for protecting her, like she'd needed something to convince *herself* she could.

Just as she was about to dip her hand inside his breeches and pull out what she had wanted to taste for so long, a knock sounded at the door.

Both their heads turned.

"Alister," Pierre said from the other side, the handle of the door starting to turn. "Are you alright? Heard you were–"

Alister shot forward and grabbed the empty bottle to throw it at the door that was slowly beginning to open. She was thankful it was opening in the direction away from them.

Glass shattered across it, and it suddenly shut.

He turned his head back to her. "You were saying?"

She stifled the urge to giggle and slipped her hand inside. She gave his hardened shaft a stroke as she freed it, making it jut up from between his hips.

Her eyes went heavy as she stared, licking at her lips. She didn't know where she wanted to start. Everywhere seemed to call for attention. The pink, broad head with the little slit at the top and its flared rim. The two thick veins on either side of it. Even the ridge underneath seemed to beg for her to cup it with her tongue.

"You look hungry there, lass."

She was. She was *giddy* at the prospect of what she could do to him.

She cupped the side of his cock, barely able to fit her hand around it, as she leaned in to press her lips to the other side. She kissed it, rubbing her lips over it as she travelled from the base all the way to the rim of his cockhead before going back down the other side.

Using his fingers to comb through her hair, he grabbed a fistful as she pressed feather light kisses sporadically over him. Only when he let out another deep sigh, his cock pulsating in her palm, did she swipe her tongue across the tip. Then she gloved it with her mouth, sucking on the head with tight suction.

She twirled her tongue around it at the same time and his head fell back against the chair. She met his eye with her own and curled her lips up into a smile at his look of bliss.

She slid her mouth down further, and his nose crinkled as he groaned.

When the tip of his cock pressed against the back of her throat, she drew up, only to push back down. Every time she brought her mouth away, she cupped her tongue back and slipped it forward as she pushed on.

She was slow at first, but the faster she went, the harder his hand gripped the armrest of the chair. His other hand fisted her hair tighter, pulling harder on the strands. His abdomen dipped.

Placing her arms onto his lap for better purchase, she stroked the base of him as she moved her mouth. His hips started to twitch, almost as though he was absentmindedly thrusting his hips. Rosetta got her first hint of salt.

When she did, she pulled away to trail her tongue over him, letting her teeth catch on the head to add a different sensation. He let out a puff of breath, almost like a pent-up sigh from her taking her mouth away, as if he'd needed a moment of relief.

"Fuck, Rosetta. Were you a whore before you were a pirate?" he asked, before she derailed his thoughts by dragging her tongue over one side of his sac.

She took his words for what they were, a compliment, and brought one of those little orbs into her mouth to suckle on it.

Watching this masculine, arrogant man shudder, his muscles jerking all, made her grin up at him.

Ho! Ho! I'm really enjoying this.

She moved onto the other, rolling her tongue this time to feel it move, and he bounced his leg like he couldn't stop it from quaking.

She started to stroke him as she flicked her tongue back and forth, and his face crinkled up into a furrow like she was torturing him... and loving it.

Without warning, he pulled on her hair to release his sac from her tight suction. She trailed kisses back up the side of his thick, throbbing shaft instead. It was warm to the touch and so engorged; she knew it must ache terribly. She could feel it pounding in her palm with deep pumps of his heart.

"You know," she said between kisses with a hint of humour in her voice, making sure to look up at him. "You're pretty sensitive."

"Oh, aye. That might be because you're playing with my cock." He made it seem like what she was doing was different to what he was used to.

She wondered if Alister was used to women who were focused on the end rather than the journey.

She, on the other hand, rarely did this; only when she really wanted to, when she intended to make the man she was sucking lose his grip on reality and only focus on her mouth.

Impatient, he yanked her head and forced her lips to the tip of him. "Now, suck me like before."

She knew exactly what he meant, and if she didn't comply, he'd make her do it. He looked desperate for it, so twisted up with need that it practically radiated from him. After teasing him for two weeks, she didn't doubt Alister was desperate for her to make him come.

What he didn't know was that she'd been teasing herself at the same time. Her pussy throbbed to replace her mouth around him and grind herself into bliss. Every stroke of her mouth made her body jealous.

Rosetta brought her mouth up and down over him in rapid goes, twirling her tongue all the while to give him exactly what he wanted. She'd give in today simply because he'd been a good boy and saved her – even though she hadn't needed saving.

"Haa." His head tilted back, his sight turning to the ceiling as his eye rolled into the back of his head. Alister let out a deep, long groan that resonated in her ears, his mouth falling open wide.

His hand gripped her hair even tighter, while the other came to hold her around her nape, almost like he was afraid she'd try to back away before he achieved release. He gave another groan and gave her another hint of salt to taste.

"Aye, just like that."

His grip on her started to tighten, his hips rocking more. He even subtly moved her up and down just a little faster while she licked him at the same time. Her tongue was a never ceasing limb, constantly moving, slipping over his delicious cock.

Then he shoved her head down further and held her still.

She felt the first burst of liquid fill her mouth just as he gave a deep, groaning exhale, his cock pulsating between her lips and under her palm as he came.

She stroked him with her hand and slipped her tongue side-to-side, which made his body shake more,

She waited for his orgasm to end, for him to release her, before she pulled her mouth away to swallow down the salty taste of him.

He fell back and sprawled across the chair, his chest heaving as he caught his breath. His gaze fixed on her, moving across her body almost like he was inspecting her, he huffed.

With surprisingly quick speed, he launched forward and grabbed one cheek of her arse while wrapping his arm around her shoulders. He lifted her, slipping her over his legs until she was seated around his hips with her knees on either side.

"Alister!" she gasped, trying to back away from him.

His arm held her still as he brought his mouth to her throat. She didn't realise he'd loosened her tights until he shoved his entire forearm down the front of them, cupping the sensitive flesh between her thighs.

"W-wait," she gasped, a shiver rolling through her when he drew his firm tongue across the sensitive spot of her jugular. "You're injured. I don't want to pull your stitches out."

His breaths were hot and panting as he spoke, giving her harsh nips with his teeth.

"I have been waiting nearly two weeks to feel your pussy again." He gave a small noise of appreciation as he circled her clit. "Tell me to stop, Rosetta. Otherwise, I'm going to shove my fingers inside you."

Her breath hitched at his words, and she squirmed in his lap, her body bucking into his hand to get him to go lower.

When she didn't say anything, he speared her core with a thick finger, making her yelp from the quick intrusion. He added a second and she let out another gasp, feeling her body stretch for him.

"I knew you'd be fucking wet. I bet the sea would be drier than you are right now."

He pulled his elbow back, forcing her pants down until they were past her hips and bundling under the curve of her arse, creating room for him to pump his fingers inside her.

She felt just how easy the glide of his fingers were, how slick her core was for him. She let out a pant, her body growing lax and surrendering to his touch.

"Ohh," Rosetta moaned, her hips twitching into his palm as his fingertips brushed over just the right spot.

A shiver of goosebumps washed over her entire body. She dug her nails deeply into his forearm, needing to hold onto *something*.

"You're small, lass." He rotated his fingers, as if to punctuate his point. "If I'm not inside you soon, it'll hurt again when I enter you."

She almost said yes, she needed to say no, but what fell from her neither. "Please."

She was already too close, and she was desperate to be thrown overboard to crash into waves of bliss. She hadn't been able to give herself release, since she'd been sharing a sleeping area with others. Rosetta wouldn't dare do it in this room, where he could have caught her in the act.

Her cries were soft, but the ache of her swollen pussy was growing strong. Rosetta was building, and the higher the climb, she knew the harder she'd fall.

He tipped her back so her shoulders could rest against the table in front of him. She got a moment of reprieve from his mouth when he pulled his head back to look at her twisted, needy face.

Alister had freed his other hand so he could lift her tunic up until it was bundled around her throat. Her exposed breasts jiggled every time her hips spasmed, every time her stomach dipped when she tried to roll her hips, every time a quiver of breath racked through her chest.

"I have been dying to see these tits."

He palmed her side from her thigh all the way up until her breast. His thumb flicked over an aching, hardened bud as his hand caressed up to her neck, then back down to squeeze her entire breast.

Alister leaned over her body, his fingers pumping faster as he did. He licked across the scar that travelled from her hip diagonally up her body, and then enclosed the nipple next to it in his mouth.

One of her hands shot up to grab his long hair as she moaned, palming his head to push him deeper against her chest. He twirled his tongue around her nipple and she saw stars.

The second twirl had her head tilting back against the table, a roll of desire flipping low in her belly. The third time was accompanied by a hard suck and Rosetta was gone.

His mouth followed her breast as her back arched, her core spasming around his thick, rough fingers as she came, her body pulled tight like a rope pulled from both sides. Rosetta let out a near sobbing cry as she orgasmed, waves of it crashing over her.

The moment it stopped, Alister used the hand between her legs to push deeper and lift her at the same time until she was lying on the table.

Then, everything got rougher.

He curled his free arm around her head as he sucked her breast harder, a wonderful tight suction, while his tongue danced over her. His fingers moved faster, the sound of her wetness permeating the air.

Rosetta wanted to spread her thighs more as he used his thumb to circle her clit, but her pants wouldn't let her. He was focusing all his attention on just the right spots, and she hurtled towards the edge she'd just finished falling from.

Locking her arms around his head to hug him to her, she dug her nails into his back as moan after moan fell from her lips. Everything was spasming; her thighs, her biceps, strange muscles in her back she didn't know she had.

Her nipple had started to go numb, almost painfully so. She yanked his hair to get him to move away. He went to the other one so he could torment it as well. It was like he was unwilling to move away from her chest, licking at it, sucking, even giving the mound of her breast little nips.

She could feel his stubble poking her skin, soft sandpaper- that had her wanting him to caress her with just his cheek and chin. He tongued her nipple before he brought it into his mouth, just as he stopped pumping his fingers and instead stayed deep to rub the tips against her swollen ridge.

The different sensation threw her to the clouds again.

Without warning, Rosetta climaxed around his wiggling digits, her mind going blank. Little sparks flashed behind her eyelids, even as she came down into his warm embrace. He left his fingers inside her so she could adjust slowly back to normal and let her body flutter around them.

Finally, he removed them to place his arm around her head, tapping kisses up her chest, neck, and jaw. His breaths were heavy and laboured, making her skin prickle as they rolled across it.

Her back arched a little when he slipped the entire length of his cock against her, rubbing over her soaked entrance and clit.

"I need to fuck you, lass."

Yes! By the great sea gods, yes. Rosetta wanted that more than anything.

His mouth found hers before she could reply to force her into a deep, hungry kiss. She felt him tilt his hips again, the tip of his cock finding her entrance.

Part of her wanted to pry her legs apart so he'd actually slip inside, rather than just running over her like a cruel tease, but another part had her breaking away from the kiss, tilting her head back.

"N-no."

He may have saved her, and she may be desperate for him, but he still hadn't earned it – even if she didn't know how he was supposed to. If she did, she'd tell him, just so she could have him pumping inside her again. Fuck, she wanted it.

She wanted the bulging muscles of his arms trapping her while he crushed her under the heavy weight of his sweaty, blood-stained body. She wanted to hear him grunt while he ravished her with heavy thrusts that made her feel like she was in heat. She wanted that thick cock to stretch her pussy so far, it burned.

Right now, she wanted it more than she wanted to breathe.

Her core ached for it, dripped for it, clenched in pathetic emptiness for it. She was so sensitive that she knew it'd feel like she was floating the moment he entered her.

She was so turned on by everything they had just done, she could barely take it anymore.

"Bloody hell."

He leaned back on straightened arms to stare down at her.

Her hands fell to rest against her chest, feeling them rise and fall with her panting breaths. He pulled his hips back so he could remove the kiss of their bodies and instead grind his shaft over her clit again.

"What more could you want from me?"

Fuck. Her tunic was around her throat, her tights almost at her knees. She was completely exposed, and if Alister wanted to, he could take her anyway.

She should be afraid. She knew he'd almost done it last time. Yet, she wasn't. She felt remarkably calm looking up at this man with a merciless and violent streak. She'd seen it, witnessed it first-hand.

She was panting, watching him as his eye trailed over her body. The way his lids grew heavy told her he liked what he saw.

"Damnit woman," he bit, shaking his head. "You look like you want it more than I do."

He started to pull back, making himself stand while allowing her to sit up.

"You're still going to have to help me get rid of this," he told her, his hand reaching down to stroke his shaft.

She winced when she looked at it. It looked more engorged than before, the veins throbbing wildly. It made her wonder just how hard his heart was pumping.

"But I've already sucked you."

"Aye, and you can do it again for every time you put that needle in me."

"That's like nine times!"

Although Rosetta didn't mind tasting him again, the idea of all that work made her jaw ache.

"It was seven." He gave her a grin, placing his hand around the back of her head to draw it down to his cock. "And maybe I'll let you off after this time if you let me do it. If you pleasure me well, I may even fuck you again with my fingers until you're satisfied."

She squinted her eyes up at him in a glare. However, the idea that he might give her another orgasm, or a few, had her nibbing her bottom lip in contemplation.

Rosetta parted her lips.

Alister pushed in as far as he could and then ground his cock against the back of her throat. "Now that's a good lass."

CHAPTER SEVENTEEN

Alister held a cigar between his fingers, leaning against the railing of the quarterdeck, staring down at his crew. He held a near-empty bottle of rum in the other hand, gently tapping it against the railing in time with the music. Men were singing, playing instruments, or tapping on barrels to add their own drumming.

Night had fallen, and everyone was drinking, relaxing, and merrily partying. A grin was fixed on his features, watching them carouse on the main deck.

Men were gambling. Laughter was constant. The sails were furled away, the anchor dropped to keep them near shore.

They had made it to the Kou Pelin Islands two days earlier than planned, the winds favourable, and were currently celebrating.

Alister watched Pierre forcefully take Rosetta's hand to make her dance. She leapt at the opportunity. It didn't take long for Pierre to realise that his chosen dancing partner was rowdy, and Alister knew she was stepping on his toes on purpose. Her squealing laughter was a dead giveaway.

Rosetta liked to pick on the man who thought his usual charm would work on her. It bit the man in the arse every time. It was often the highlight of Alister's day to watch her mess with him.

Since they'd arrived at Kou Pelin Islands, however, he'd

noticed her behaviour had changed. A smile rarely left her face. She was excited.

She really wants that ship.

Alister thought, *hoped*, he might be able to get it.

The cannons were ready, the men prepared and told of the plan. A week ago, they raided the trader's boat and completely refilled his own with the supplies procured.

Even though all the holes in the hull had been fixed, neither one of them had spoken about her sleeping arrangements. Currently, Rosetta still slept in his cabin in her own hammock. He thought she had grown comfortable and didn't want to relocate again. Alister had no issue letting her stay.

Unfortunately, it did very little to assist him in bedding her. They were rarely awake in it at the same time.

She's gone before I wake. He often missed his opportunity to catch her crawling into her hammock because he was busy. He manned the helm for most of the day, but afterwards, he still had work to do as captain: checking the stocks and cargo, speaking with his crew about any issues.

That's why tonight was a surprise. Rosetta was still awake, far past sundown.

"The woman's got spirit," Pierre said with a disgruntled laugh, making his way up the steps after escaping her. "I think she's broken my toes."

"You'll be right," Alister told him, ashing his cigar before taking a deep draw of it.

"How is it you're able to fuck her but I can barely get close to her without getting hurt?"

The issue was: Alister wasn't.

She won't give in. He knew the lass wanted him, but other than the day she'd gotten him sliced with a cleaver, he hadn't gotten into her pants again.

No matter what he did, said, or tried, no matter how aroused he got her that she'd be literally grinding her body against his, she wouldn't cave.

His time was almost up.

Alister wondered if getting her the Laughing Siren was the price. *That's a big ask, lass.* He almost thought it could be worth it.

He could only imagine the reward, when saving her from the cleaver had gotten her to suck him with her annoying, naughty mouth.

For the past week, he'd been reflecting on that day.

For the rest of his life, he didn't think he'd ever get the sight of her out of his head. Her tunic bundled around her neck and her tights down her thighs, lying back against the table while she looked up at him. Her hands had been curled just above her exposed breasts, her thighs wet from his touch.

There had been an innocence about her, a softness in her blue eyes.

Her brown hair had haloed around her head, those freckles across her nose pinkened in obvious arousal, eyes fixed on him. Her huffs of breath had been quiet, but they fell from wet and swollen lips, even though he'd never kissed them.The contrast of that look when she usually looked either devious or bitchy had been mind-achingly haunting. Even now, it made his body shudder in desire.

Alister thought he could've drunk in the sight of her like that for eternity.

"That's 'cause yer an annoying lil shit, Pierre," Derek said from beside Alister – who had been standing there silently the entire time.

"You're joking, right? I'm way easier to handle than him." Pierre hiked his thumb at Alister. "Don't know why she picked him over me."

Because she's a smart lass. Alister probably wouldn't have been as interested in getting her the Laughing Siren if she hadn't tried to catch his attention.

"She's liked our cap'in from the start," Derek rebuffed. "And she knows ye'd probably give her a disease."

"She doesn't like me," Alister cut in, ashing his cigar again before letting it burn. She may like the idea of his dick, but he knew she held no feelings for him. "She argues too much with me."

They bickered constantly. She wouldn't follow orders, and Alister would yell at her for it. Some men cowered at the brutal tone of his voice sometimes, but Rosetta? Rosetta would either glare or laugh at him for it.

She's got a spark in her. An irritating one he found daring.

"That's because she's crazy!" Pierre yelled, shaking his head while taking a swig of his own bottle of rum.

"Men call women like that crazy because they don't have the skills to handle them," Alister told him with a chuckle. "The lass' mind is perfectly sound, she's just strange tempered."

"It's only crazy men who would marry a woman like her," Derek added.

"Good luck to the man who marries her," Alister snorted. "Only a fool would take her on, and if he didn't start out mad, she'd drive him there."

"Hear, hear!" Pierre cheered in agreeance. He stared down at his rum bottle, turning it from side-to-side to read its partially wet and destroyed label. "Still, she's fun to have around. Oh! And the food. That woman sure knows how to cook."

Alister knew everyone had enjoyed their meals the day she'd introduced them to nutmeg. Even Glen Darkley had been impressed – and the older man was hard to stir emotion from.

From their position on the quarterdeck, peering above the rest of the ship, they watched Clint try and steal a dance with her. She quickly flung him away after a few spins. She stole

Naeem to swing with instead, and he seemed eager to let her.

"Still don't understand the relationship between those two," Derek muttered with a dark tone.

Neither did Alister.

They seemed closer than what was normal and he'd noticed Naeem watch over her carefully when he wasn't busy in the sails. Alister got a lot of chances to spy on people from the wheel of his ship.

"She's just as close to that Mr Smith," Alister added in her defence. "She's found people she trusts on these seas; that's rare to find."

He had the same inkling about the two beside him. Pierre and Derek were the men he kept closest, which is why he'd placed them in their respective positions. He'd convinced his crew to vote them in.

Speaking of Mr Smith, Rosetta eventually grabbed the unwilling older gentleman and forced him to skip with her.

Watching them, Alister realised he didn't know anything about her, or her relationship with those men, or how she'd come to be on his warship.

How did she come to be the captain of a crew? A crew that would die for her. Hell, Alister didn't even know where she'd come from.

Hmm. He raised the hand with the cigar to brush a rogue hair off his cheek. *Drunk women tend to be loose.*

If he couldn't manage to sleep with her tonight, perhaps he could get her to reveal her past, her secrets.

Who are you really, Rosetta Silver? Who was this tantalising woman in Alister's sights?

Her dancing eventually stopped. She fell with her back against the railing, towards the back of the ship that led to a small platform. She sat between Naeem and Mr Smith, placing an arm around each of their shoulders.

A horrible laugh sounded over the distance as she stomped

both her feet. He shook his head. *Woman laughs like a squealing pig.* It was high-pitched and cringeworthy.

Alister chugged the remainder of his booze and carelessly threw the bottle down to the ocean.

"Alright lads, looks like I need another drink," he told them, taking a last draw of his cigar before flicking that away as well.

He just really needed to leave.

Even though Rosetta was often distracted by those she danced with, her eyes instead found Alister towering above all on the quarterdeck.

He seemed to be in a good mood, with a grin plastered on his face, a cigar in one hand and a bottle in the other.

After she spent some time trying to get Pierre to leave her alone, she'd peeked up to the three men talking. She'd spoken very few words to Derek in the three weeks she'd been on the ship, but she didn't mind the older man. He usually answered her in grunts when she handed him his food.

Pierre was too friendly and familiar for her to ever be comfortable with. She enjoyed picking on him and hurting him for her own entertainment. He'd never asked her to brush his hair again, and she doubted he'd ever ask her to dance again either.

One lesson at a time.

But ever since she sat down between Naeem and Mr Smith, her attention had been solely on them.

Naeem's chest heaved with heavy breath, still trying to calm his heart from dancing with her. "Damn Rosetta, you know how to make a man trip over his own feet."

"Agreed," Mr Smith chuckled. "You're not graceful."

"I am a wonderful dancer!" She kicked her legs forward before taking a swig of her drink with a laugh. She knew it was the truth. "I'm also a wonderful singer."

She opened her mouth to start, and they clapped their hands over her face to stop her. Her laughter grew, muffled by their palms.

"You only sing when you're drunk." Mr Smith looked at her, much like how a father would in disappointment or worry at a daughter. His lips drew into a thin line, his bushy brows furrowing. His eyes squinted at her, as though inspecting her current state. "You should slow down."

"Perhaps I am a little intoxicated." She gave a shrug before swinging them from side-to-side in the embrace she'd forced them into. "I'm just excited."

"We've almost got the Laughing Siren," Naeem cheered, taking the bottle of rum from her hand to raise it in the air like a cheer before drinking from it. Apparently, she was sharing. "How long have we been waiting for this day?"

"Over three years," Rosetta smiled, turning her head up to the stars with joy. "For three years we've been hunting her."

"About bloody time," Mr Smith added in.

"I thought you'd die of old age before we got her."

"Little shit." Mr Smith reached around Rosetta to slap Naeem in the back of the head.

"You still could. The night's still young." This time, Rosetta heard the slap Mr Smith delivered and even she winced.

"Quit it, old Johnny boy!"

"Stop it!" she yelled with a stomp of her foot before they could get into some sort of brawl. It wouldn't be the first time Mr Smith had chased Naeem with a sword or gun, threating to cut or blow his head off.

"I can't wait to hold her wheel in my hands," she said to them, clenching and unclenching her hands. "To weigh the anchor and see the wind fill her sails." She huddled them in closer until they were almost face to face to hush their conversation. "And to finally..."

A set of boots stopping directly in front of her cut off her words.

"First, we have to procure her," Alister said down to them – like he wanted to cut in on their fun. She hadn't even realised he'd moved from the quarterdeck. He'd even managed to get a new bottle. "Like I said, we could sink it. You'd be smart not to get too excited."

She pulled Naeem and Mr Smith so they were no longer huddled together. With her back against the railing, she took his eye with her own, a bright grin filling her features.

"And I've already told you. If I can't have it, I want it at the bottom of the ocean."

"I'll drink to that!" Naeem shouted with glee, chugging from her bottle. He handed it to her, leaving her barely a sip's worth.

"Why do you always do this?" She shoved him, forcing him forward while she delivered a heavy slap to his back. "Go get me another, you selfish prick."

Naeem crawled forward for a moment before getting to his feet. He tripped, knocking into Alister by barging into his shoulder.

"Wassup, *Captain?*" His tone had a sneer to it; he didn't see him as his true captain.

Alister grabbed the man's shoulder and shoved him away. "Go get her a bottle, lad."

All three of them watched him stumble away.

He knocked into multiple people and almost fell against men throwing dice. They stood with their fists raised in anger for disturbing them, before realising it was an accident of a clearly disorientated drunk man.

"You know he isn't coming back, right?" Mr Smith asked

with sincerity, his fluffy brows furrowing with concern.

He rubbed his hand through his full-fledged but neatly shaped beard, before knocking the rim of his glasses so they sat better on his face.

"He'll find a place to pass out," Rosetta confirmed, nodding her head in his direction. "He's useless when he's like this."

"Damn that boy," Mr Smith sighed, rising to his feet. "I better help him, otherwise we'll be fishing him from the water again."

There had been an odd occasion of Naeem walking on the deck of a ship with drunken legs, before he stumbled sideways and over the railing. It'd taken them some time to realise he was floating away asleep. That was quite a night.

She watched Mr Smith chase after him before her eyes turned to Alister.

"Well?" She raised a brow at him, leaning back against the railing to appear calm and collected. "Are you going to sit or are you going to keep standing there like a big, tall idiot?"

She knew he must have come to speak with her. Alister rolled his eyes and had the audacity to sigh like *she* was bothering *him*.

He took a seat on the steps, sprawling his body against them. His elbow leaned behind him, one leg straight while the other was bent. She couldn't help feeling he looked remarkably self-important with how he'd positioned himself. After a few minutes, she scooched down the railing to the very bottom of the steps so she'd be able to hear him better.

Up went the bottle as he took a drink.

"Yes!" She raised her hand out. "Hand it over."

"Nay." He swiped it to the side, out of her reach. "Get your own."

She gave a pout. "If I get up, I'm not coming back."

She could see he wanted to deny her, was mulling it over

heavily. He eventually sighed defeatedly and placed the base of the bottle in her outstretched hand. The glass was cold in her warm palm. She took it, drank deeply, then handed it back.

"You've a strange relationship with those two," Alister commented, nodding his head towards the direction they'd gone. His face was dull, as if he didn't really care, but she'd noticed he often pretended to be disinterested. Alister liked if everyone believed nothing much bothered him. "Been curious as to how you met them."

Rosetta pursed her lips, her eyes squinting in suspicion. "Are you trying to get to know me, Alister?"

He gave her a grin that told her he was fine with being caught so quickly. "Aye."

"Why should I tell you anything? You haven't shared anything of yourself."

He rubbed at his cheek, turning his head to look at the water. "Guess that's true. What do you want to know?"

"Really?" she asked with a note of surprise. A spark of curiosity came to life inside her. "You'll really answer?"

He gave a shrug. "Depends on what it is."

"Why are you searching for this treasure when most don't think it exists?" She brought her knees up so she could hug them, making herself comfortable.

"I promised the previous captain that I would search for it and prove he wasn't insane," he admitted, his gaze returning to her.

"Like on his death bed?"

Alister gave a deep chuckle. "Kind of. Do you know of the pirate Cole 'Mad Dog' McCarthy?'"

"A little." Rosetta gave a small shrug. "He searched all his life, sailed over every part of the world, to find the Raider's treasure trove and never found it. He's the reason everyone thinks it's a myth."

"When he got too sick to carry out his duties as captain, he told the crew to vote for a new one, pushing my name forward." Alister took a swig of his bottle, turning his head to look at the tall tower of rock they were docked beside. "The men were happy to have me as their captain, and I promised him I would search for the treasure trove in his stead."

Wait... That's how he became Captain? That was such a simple story! She expected some sort of grand, epic tale.

"Do you know what he died of?"

"A bullet to the head."

Rosetta reared her head back. "I thought he was sick."

"Aye, he was. Could barely stand." Alister looked down at the bottle, a dark expression falling over him. "So, he placed his pistol in my hand, stood on the railing of his ship, and told me to shoot."

Her eyes widened, her mouth falling open in disbelief. "And you did?"

"Aye. Shot him right between the eyes." His gaze swept over her grimace. "He loved the sea, refused to die on land to get treatment. He wanted to be with the water, and he knew he was a hindrance. He was a sick man on a ship. He was in the way, and he knew it."

"And here I thought you had a heart," she laughed, trying to hide that she was balking at his tale.

He folded his arms across his chest defensively.

"That's why I did it. He asked for the mercy of a quick death, and I gave it to him." Alister gave a huff, running his hand over the top of his head. "How did you become a captain then?"

"Ughhhhh." Rosetta groaned so loudly she was sure the nearest port heard her. "That is such a lengthy answer. Much has happened over the years. We will be here all night."

"I've got much time."

Rosetta shook her head. "I'm usually asleep at this hour."

"Fine," he chuckled, realising she had no intention of

answering. "How did you meet Naeem? Like I said, your relationship with him is odd. The crew have noticed as well."

Rosetta turned her head up to the stars to look for encouragement. *How do I answer that?*

"I have known Naeem since I was fifteen," she told him, not pulling her face from the sky.

Alister's dark brows creased deeply. "You knew him before you become a pirate?"

"Distantly, yes." She ran the pad of her thumb over the edge of her nails absentmindedly, a minor distraction. "I only befriended him right before we decided to run away together."

"Like lovers?" Once more, his face was dull, but she thought she heard a hint of an emotion in his voice.

Rosetta gave a bellowing laugh. "Not at all! We just decided we should run away and become pirates together. He helped me do that."

"Is that the truth?" She could tell Alister didn't like her answer by his narrowing gaze. "Because that sounds like some made up fantasy story of a girl."

"That's exactly what we did. We both decided we didn't want to be where we were anymore, and we used each other to get away. Because I was a woman, Naeem was the man I needed when my voice was meaningless. If I wasn't pretending to be a man, that is."

"You pretended to be a man?" There was a crinkle of humour in the corner of his eyelids. "You're a bonnie lass. Did it even work?"

Rosetta's lashes flickered in surprise at his compliment. It had been delivered so smoothly, but he'd never directly commented on her features before. The sound of waves lapping at the sides of the hull filled the silence.

"Kind of." She pouted, placing her chin on her knees. "I had to pretend I was a young boy. They kind of look like girls."

Alister laughed loudly, pointing his finger at her to wag it, like he'd already summarised that's what she had to do before she'd said it. Then he took a swig of his drink, wiping his mouth on his forearm.

"Alright. What about Mr Smith?"

Rosetta shoved her hand out, refusing to answer until he handed her the bottle. She swallowed a fifth of it in one go before she handed it back.

"About a year after Naeem and I set off, we managed to sneak our way into a port. Naeem was Captain for me at the time and we'd collected a very small crew, pickpocketed and worked for enough coin to buy our first boat."

Rosetta nibbled at the corner of her lips, not liking this part of her history. The next part wasn't really her story to tell, but she thought there might not be any harm in telling Alister.

She couldn't help sweeping her eyes to the furled away sails, inspecting them to hide the swell of emotions she felt.

"Mr Smith was going to be hanged for murdering the man who killed his wife. The man wanted to steal his daughter to force her into marriage once they were out of the picture and no longer supporting her. He wanted her, and the inheritance she would have obtained from their deaths."

"What does that have to do with anything?" Alister cut in.

Rosetta rolled her eyes, continuing on. "We were watching the public trial. Nobody believed he'd killed the man for that reason, instead thinking he'd killed his wife and the man she'd been having an affair with. Even though his daughter swore it was true, no one believed them."

Rosetta gave a small laugh, shaking her head in disbelief at the memory. After knowing him for as long as she did, she knew it was true.

Mr Smith had loved his wife and daughter more than anything in the world. Being apart from them, knowing his wife was gone and his daughter was all alone in the world, made him sad.

"His wife had just been murdered at the hands of this arsehole and suddenly, he was put to trial in his stead. I could see he was telling the truth. Since there weren't many soldiers, I convinced Naeem and the men to help me save him."

"You stopped his trial?"

"Oh no, the trial had ended. They were about to hang him. We saved him from his death." A solemn smile filled her face, and she hugged her legs a little tighter. "Mr Smith reminds me of my father, except braver."

"You said your father was a sailor for the Laughing Siren, which is why you've been on it. That means you've met him?"

"Of course." She scrunched her nose at him in confusion. "I grew up with him and my mother."

"I half-expected you to tell me you were born from a prostitute, lass. I'm only guessing with what I've learned."

Rosetta gave a mocking snort of laughter.

"I'm not born from a shameful birthing." Her head tilted a little in confusion from the scowl Alister made. "No, my father was a faithful, hardworking man, and my parents loved me dearly. They were caring and made sure I was happy to the best of their abilities."

"Then what were you running away from?"

Rosetta pursed her lips.

"I don't have a tortured past, Alister." Her eyes turned to him with a glare. "I was just a girl who decided she wanted to become a pirate and did so."

"I find that hard to believe." He narrowed his eye at her in return, squinting as he took a swig of his drink. "You're a proven liar."

She saw the last of the liquid sloshing in the bottle when he placed it against his stomach to rest.

"I don't know what you want me to tell you." She leaned back from hugging her knees and folded her arms across her chest. "Why do I have to have a terrible past to become a pirate? Perhaps I like the idea of glittering gold and pretty riches."

"Nay, Rosetta Silver," he said with a strangely stern tone. "You're just a funny woman, and most funny women have experienced terrible things."

She puffed her cheeks in agitation, slowly blowing out a pent-up breath. Then, she reached her hand out again. He handed her the bottle and instead of taking a drink of it, she got to her feet.

His eye followed her. "Oi, where are you going?"

"I'm tired. I'm going to sleep."

Only once she was steady on her feet, and a safe distance away from him did she finally down the last of it. She handed the empty bottle back and he tipped it upside down in horror.

He surprised her by grinning. "Do you need help getting into bed?"

She didn't trust the devilish hint to his expression. The way his lips were curled. The way his eye perused her from her head all the way to her feet, and then back up.

"Nay, lad," she said mockingly, placing her hands on her hips and leaning forward slightly. "Me thinks I can get meself ta ma own hammock."

"Nay, lass," he said back, not giving a damn that she'd mocked the way he spoke. His grin widened and changed into something slyer. "You look like you need help getting naked."

Rosetta's irritation faded so quickly, she almost giggled. She hid it behind a tiny cough. Just when it looked as though he was about to rise to his feet, she ran.

She was far too tipsy, too excited with the prospect of finally reaching her goal, to be alone with him right now.

Especially since the entire time they'd talked, she'd wanted to straddle his lap and kiss his stupidly handsome, arrogant face.

CHAPTER EIGHTEEN

Rosetta climbed the stairwell and burst onto the main deck.

With how warm and muggy the air was today near shore, she was only wearing black tights, white tunic, and boots. Her hat and coat were hanging inside her sleeping quarters.

She could hear Alister shouting before she even emerged, and the moment she did, she saw dozens of men hot on their feet, running around at top pace. He pointed to the thick iron chain needed to bring the anchor from the water.

"Weigh the anchor!"

He walked across the main deck, his head turning in every direction. His black doublet coat swayed with each movement while his brown boots made loud stomping noises with his quick steps. He threw his arm forward, his voice a deep bellow.

"Faster! I want those sails hoisted!" His head was raised as he yelled his demands.

The men were busy in the air, running across beams and climbing the shrouds. The sails had already been released and were now being fixed to catch the wind.

"Pierre!" Pierre turned to Alister while pulling on a rope, moving it through metal rigs. "Make sure the gunmen are ready and the cannons loaded on all sides."

Rosetta moved out of his way so Pierre could follow orders

as he went to descend below, then she started chasing after Alister who was climbing the quarterdeck stairs.

Derek was already holding the helm to keep the ship steady. He shooed him out of the way and took the wheel in his large hands.

"I want all spare hands on deck!"

He turned the wheel as the ship crept forward for the first time in two days. Rosetta finally made it to the top of the steps and ran forward to stand next to him. He never took his eyes off the horizon.

"There's your ship, lass."

She followed his head to see a speck of white miles in the distance. It was hard to distinguish with just the naked eye.

Rosetta had been helping Mr Darkley clean the kitchen for the morning meals when heavy footsteps began to rattle the ship. Clint came through the doorway, his chest heaving from exertion, panting that the Laughing Siren had been spotted.

Without caring to look back or finish her duties, she'd abandoned Mr Darkley to come to the surface.

She didn't care if she couldn't tell what it was in the distance. She knew Alister wouldn't have started moving the ship if he wasn't sure.

He'd told her he'd often seen it on the seas and turned the other way when he realised what it was. This was the first time he'd ever turned his warship towards it.

The wheel made clanking noises as it spun, the ship turning on a sharp angle to emerge from their hiding spot behind the topmost island. The Howling Death was sailing at a cross section to them; any moment now, Alister would turn the ship again to head towards it fully.

The biggest smile Rosetta had ever worn filled her face.

I'm almost there. Today, she would have it; today, it would be hers. *Today, I will get what I have longed for.*

"You will do as you're told today, aye?" he asked, turning

his head to eye her.

Her gaze searched over his eyepatch; the light of the bright sky made it look like he held the yellow sun in his good eye.

"I can't have you in the way. Stick to the plan."

She knew what he was insinuating: the fleet wouldn't hesitate to use her as a hostage. A woman alone on a ship was generally coveted by someone important. They wouldn't have her there if that wasn't the case. Her life would be considered a priority, and, therefore, could be used against them.

He started to turn to ship again, and the three enemy ships became easier to see as they got closer.

"Yes, I'll follow the plan."

The plan. Alister's idea that she remain on the Howling Death and let the men slaughter their way through the ship.

"Good," he said with a curt nod, setting his attention on the rest of the ship. "Raise the flag, lads! She's almost in range of our cannons."

Their black flag began to rise.

She watched as Alister reached up to grab the locket around his neck and kissed it, not seeming to care that he'd done it in front of her. *Does he always do that?*

Then there it was, the Laughing Siren in all of its beautiful sails, timber, and glory. The vessel's trims were painted blue while its timber was a sandy oak.

They couldn't see it yet, but Rosetta knew there was a carved statue of a mermaid on the bow. Her arms reached forward with her hands cupped together but open, like she was trying to catch something. Her tail fins were curled and stretched behind her, and her mouth was open, almost like she was laughing in a ghastly sort of way.

The galleon was larger, stronger in the hull than the Howling Death, but it was slower.

What will the support ships do?

"Warning cannons!" Alister yelled, and men echoed his

commands over the main deck and below.

Booms sounded before two cannonballs launched from the bow. They hit the water, nowhere near the oncoming ships.

It was done on purpose.

They were currently next to the Kou Pelin Islands. On the port side of Alister's ship, and the starboard side of the fleet, were shallow banks of sand and the massive, towering islands.

The Howling Death was coming at them from a diagonal, trying to force the Laughing Siren between the gap between the islands. Otherwise, they would run aground and beach themselves.

With the way they were heading towards the islands, if they tried to go towards the open ocean, their ships would collide.

"Again!"

Another two booms sounded.

One of the fleet ships was forced to back off from the Laughing Siren as she started to turn towards that very gap. The other was running up the side to take them on.

"It's working," she gasped.

"I told you they'd go through the middle to get away."

Turning the wheel again, Alister began leading the ship between a different but far narrower gap. His frigate was shallower and narrower in the hull and could sail through it. They were turning away before the other vessel could even find them. The Laughing Siren was on a path that could no longer be changed.

The fleet ships would have to go around the Kou Pelin Islands, since they were large ships that would be easily banked. Otherwise, they'd have to wait to follow their head ship, since the gap wasn't wide enough to allow them to pass at the same time.

Her heartbeat was a deafening drum in her ears, the thrill and excitement making it pump so hard, it resonated throughout her entire body. It pounded through her veins, even making her fingertips throb.

"I'm hoping one of them is stupid enough to follow us," Alister commented when the Laughing Siren and the Howling Death were out of sight of each other due to a tower of rock. "If they get stuck, we might be able to raid them after we take your ship."

Rosetta grabbed the arm of his tunic and swung her arms with glee, yanking him around. "I can't believe it worked!"

He gave a deep, loud laugh. "I may not look smart, lass, but I know how to take down ships."

"Smart? You're absolutely bloody brilliant!"

Her stomach clenched at the grin he gave as a reward.

"Alright, here we go!" Alister shouted, just as they started emerging through the gap. Since his ship was faster, they were coming out at the same time as the galleon.

There were dozens of men on the main deck, waiting until they got close enough to swing over. Four cannons sounded, all coming from the Laughing Siren. They missed them, but barely.

He turned the wheel once they were clear of the shore and started to creep closer.

"Prepare yourselves!"

Another boom sounded and a cannon ball hit the hull of their ship. The impact rattled the entire vessel, nearly making her teeth clatter.

So close. They were almost there.

"Starboard side cannons, fire! Port to the surface!"

His demand echoed down the line. Just when she thought it was too early, his cannons fired, targeting the cannon ports of the Laughing Siren.

"Derek," he said to the man standing behind him. "Take the helm."

His Derek's peg leg tapped against the ground as he took

over so that Alister could release the wheel.

"Now!"

Men swung across to the Laughing Siren, while others twirled grappling hooks attached to ropes and flung them across to hook onto her railing.

Rosetta followed behind Alister as he went to the railing to stand, holding to a rope to swing across. He pulled his cutlass from his belt, and, without caring to look at her, he swung from the quarterdeck without a word.

A gust of wind pushed her hair over her shoulders as she watched the chaos on the ship Rosetta wanted more than anything. *It's there, right in front of me.*

She wanted to reach out, to touch it as though that was the answer to obtaining it. To place her hand on its timber, to feel it beneath her fingertips... just once. Just once, in case it sank to the bottom of the ocean.

It was out of reach as she remained on the Howling Death, watching everything unfold.

The sound of firing cannons rang in her ears, wood splintering, men yelling. Eventually, the clang of swords made everything roar; its energy resonated as she searched for the Laughing Siren's captain, knowing Alister was going to head straight for him.

Someone is fighting for me. She knew he was really fighting for himself, for his own selfish gain, but it meant Rosetta might achieve her long-awaited goal, something she had been dreaming of for years.

He brought me here. Without Alister's help, if he had taken back his own ship and left her to rot in a cell, or an island, or even to drown in the ocean, Rosetta wouldn't be here.

She wouldn't be about to have everything she'd set out to do all those years ago. *I want this ship, and its captain and crew dead.*

It was hers. She wanted it. It belonged to her. If she

couldn't have it, she didn't want anyone to possess it, least of all, Queen Mary Anne's Commodore.

The Howling Death was sailing away, getting out of the way of Laughing Siren's cannons. Everyone who had needed to cross over had already left. It would circle back when they gave the signal and she would be able to cross.

There was minimal crew left, barely ten men who would maintain the sails. If Alister failed, the Howling Death wouldn't have enough men to sail properly. For now, it could gently glide across the ocean for a short while with no problems.

I hope he doesn't die. Rosetta was rather fond of Alister, and desired him like an ache. It would be terrible if he was to be killed because of an act of heroism and greed. *Unless he gets in my way.*

CHAPTER NINETEEN

Alister landed in a clash of fighting men.

Rifles belonging to Queen Mary Anne's soldiers were lined up to shoot his men on the deck. That was, until more of his men came up behind them and cut the soldiers down before they could shoot.

The smell of fire and gunpowder littered the air.

There were more soldiers on the main deck than pirates, but he knew his men would have already blocked the hatch, stopping those below deck from coming up. For now, they only needed to concentrate on those on the surface.

Alister didn't engage those around him unless they targeted him. He could cut them down with brutal strength of his sword.

After killing a soldier, his sight returned to the tall, thin man protecting the helm. This was the first time Alister had ever seen Theodore Briggs, but he knew by the fancy light blue and white uniform he wore that he was the man he needed to take down.

He wore a white, curly wig to signal his status, emblems pinned to his professional jacket.

Alister made his way to him, slowly climbing the stairs and fighting off those trying to fight him on his rise. A few of his men were protecting his back while also moving to the other staircase to stop low ranking soldiers from climbing.

"Argh!" Theodore grunted when Alister swung down on him, which he had to quickly block.

The force had been heavy enough that the man crumbled and stepped back, giving Alister the chance to cut the man at the helm in the back. He fell against the wheel before collapsing to the ground. Alister raised his sword to block Theodore's second attack, and the clash of their swords rang in his ears.

They pushed off from each other, beginning a complicated dance with the tips of their swords. One would step forward to swing while the other raised his sword to block and step back.

Considering the dark eyebrows above his eyes, he knew Theodore must have brown hair underneath that white curly wig. He had a neat but full beard covering his face except for just his rounded, bald chin. His cheeks, upper lip, and the sides next to his ears were covered in thick, bushy hair. He was just as tall as Alister, but he could tell the man was a few years older than him.

"I know who you are," Theodore sneered while pointing the tip of his thin sword at him. "Captain Alister 'One Eye' Paine. Bloody Storm of the Seas."

"Aye, know my own name."

He swung his sword downwards and forced the man to redirect his swing rather than block it.

"You're a wanted man."

Theodore swung sideways, forcing Alister to jump back so he didn't get cut across the gut.

"Know that too."

He swung down again, and Theodore skilfully stepped to the side to avoid it. They were circling each other, moving around the small platform.

He's good. Alister had to give him that. Theodore had obvious earned his title as Commodore, because even Alister was having a difficult time with him. *I'm still better.*

"You're one of the most notorious pirates on the seven seas." Alister hid behind the mizzenmast to dodge a swing as Theodore spoke. "I'm sure the Queen will be pleased to hang you if I don't kill you."

Alister came around the other side of the mast quickly to sneak up behind him. Theodore spun around and blocked his attack just in time.

"You're a little cocky." Alister let his fist fly, punching the man across the face. He stumbled back with a slightly disorientated wobble. "And a bit slow."

He pushed his sword forward in a stabbing motion, slicing the man's arm. He dropped his sword with a hiss of a breath, and Alister kicked it away with a grin.

"You also have no weapon."

"Not quite." Theodore quickly reached into his coat to pull out his own pistol hidden beneath it.

Alister's eyes widened. *Shit.*

The gun was kicked out of the man's hand by someone swinging onto the deck to join them. Theodore gave a grunt and Alister raised his sword while the man was distracted.

He knew the interloper was one of his own. Theodore went wide-eyed at Alister, putting his arms up to deflect the attack with his own body.

A sword blocked his swing, the metal blade tinging but slinking to the side. A glaring Rosetta had stopped his attack, her blue eyes narrowed on Alister.

She stopped my sword?

"Hey, lass!" he yelled in bewilderment. "What the hell do you thinking you're doing? You were supposed to stay on the ship!"

"Stay out of this Alister," she snapped before swinging her sword... at him!

Alister narrowly blocked it while stepping back, his brows

creasing.

"This wasn't the plan!"

Hell, she was attacking *him*. He always knew there was a chance she'd come onto the ship, but never in his mind had he thought he would have to *fight* her!

"I have my own plan," she told him with a determined glint to her eyes before she kicked him in the side – right where she'd only a week ago sewed him up.

Alister keeled forward, his free hand coming up to his side at the sharp sting. A gasp tore through him as agony spread across his torso. He was still far from being fully healed.

"Hello, Theodore," he heard her say, just as Alister turned his head up to her back.

"Rosetta?" Theodore's brows furrowed as he looked at her.

Theodore's head shook from side-to-side, as if he was trying to clear his vision. He couldn't believe what he was seeing, couldn't believe she was there in front of him.

They know each other?

Alister wanted to jump in, but she was currently in his way.

"I have waited three years to see you again." She pointed her sword at him with her shoulders rolled back tight. "Did you miss me?"

"This is where you've been?" His face turned into a twisted face of fury, flushing red. His yellow stained teeth gritted as his expression bunched into an ugly snarl. "You ran off to become a fucking pirate?!"

"Yes," she freely admitted, the bored tone and expression she wore around Alister set in her features. Then it faded into a scrunched-up nose and twisted mouth. "Just so I could one day find you and cut your damn head off!"

She swung her sword forward with a scream and the man dived to the side. "Let's talk about this."

He started backing away from her, worry and concern etched on his face. She gave a guttural shout every time she swung her sword. They were starting to circle the mast and Alister was too stunned watching them to move, especially since he'd already tried to and she'd swung at him!

"You don't want to make me do anything I would regret," Theodore warned in a dark tone.

"Oh, I'm sure you would try."

He eyed his weapon on the ground and Alister swiftly shot forward to kick it behind him, far across the deck and away from Theodore as possible. His eyes shot to Alister, giving him a glare before turning his gaze back to Rosetta when she screamed and ran forward, her sword raised, causing him to retreat.

One problem solved, now he just had to get Rosetta out of the fucking way. Right now, she was a liability, foolishly chasing him without thought.

"You don't want to do this, Rosie." Theodore had his hands raised, pushing them downwards, as if he was trying to coax her to lower her sword.

Rosie? His brows knotted together. Alister vaguely remembered her shouting at Pierre about calling her that.

She swung her sword and Theodore dodged it. It lodged into the mizzenmast instead, sticking firmly. As she was trying to tug it free, Theodore raised his fist and punched her in the face. The hit was so hard, spittle flung from her mouth.

Alister stepped forward to catch her, careful of his cutlass, but she only stumbled a step before she righted herself. Unfortunately, her sword was gone, still embedded in the mast.

She wiped the blood from her mouth with the back of her hand before spitting a glob of it to the ground.

"I've learned to stay on my feet, Theo."

"What the hell is going on?" Alister finally shouted, disgusted by watching this pathetic fight. It could barely be called a fight at all with the way Theodore was easily dodging and Rosetta was losing. She was completely at a disadvantage in skill and strength.

Now that Rosetta no longer had a sword in her hand, Theodore's worry once more turned into anger. His eyes turned to Alister with a sneer, his nose crinkling so tight, it made him appear older and uglier.

"You better not have fucked this pirate, Rosetta."

"I can do what I want," she answered, turning her nose up at him. "And you can bet I did. He wasn't the only one, either."

Theodore's eyes widened at her brash words.

"You are my wife!" He swung his arm to the side, stomping his foot forward with a loud thud.

Alister almost dropped his cutlass. *His wife...*

"You're married?"

She turned her head back to give him a dull, bored expression. "Aye, lad," she said mockingly.

He was too speechless to realise Theodore had moved.

He backhanded Rosetta so hard, she fell against the wheel of the helm. She put the back of her wrist against her mouth when she pushed off it to unsteadily get to her feet. She checked the back of her wrist to find blood before pressing against it again.

"I must say, I haven't missed that."

He hit her... Alister had seen him do it twice now, and her words only furthered his belief in the words that came from him next. He stepped forward, reaching out to grab the front of Theodore's uniform to yank him closer.

"You hit your wife?"

Alister hated men like this. Noblemen who married noblewomen, and then abused them.

'No matter what you do in your life, Alister, fight the strong and protect the weak.' His mother's words echoed in his mind.

Alister may never had met Theodore Briggs, but he knew

of the Commodore of the Laughing Siren and the two ships that usually sailed behind her.

He was a duke. He'd spent time with the Queen, sat at her table, was one of her noble servants.

That meant Rosetta had once been a tea drinking, dress wearing, high society woman who would never have fought back.

Could never have fought back.

He was almost twice her age, stronger than her, bigger than her. Alister could only imagine the kind of damage this man had done to her.

Theodore uselessly threw his hands up in surrender with a terrified expression as Alister raised his cutlass, preparing to cut the man down with a growl in the back of his throat. He wanted to enact revenge for a woman who couldn't have done it herself.

There may have been another emotion pushing him... one envious of everything this man ever possessed and he never had. Power, wealth, freedom, Rosetta.

The barrel of a gun pressed to his temple.

"I told you to stay out of this," Rosetta said, pulling back the hammer of her pistol.

He heard it clicking back in his left eardrum, but he couldn't see her; she was standing on his blind side.

Alister's gaze narrowed on Theodore who gave him a smirk. He slowly released the collar of his shirt.

She saved him.

Rosetta had protected her husband from *him*.

Alister took two steps back, and she turned it to Theodore's smirking face, which instantly fell.

"I have waited three years for this, Theodore."

Once more, the man threw his hands up in surrender. "Whatever you've done, Rosie, I'll forgive you. Just put the gun down before you accidentally hurt someone."

A snort of laughter came from her. "No."

"We'll get you the help you need," he offered, gesturing a hand towards her in hopes she would take it. "Please, dove."

"What? Like some loony house for women?" She stamped her foot, her lips turning into an irritated pout. "I don't need any help! I'm not fucking crazy!"

"I know things were hard for you after you lost our child."

The things Alister was learning this day were just becoming more and more damning.

"I didn't lose it!" She stamped her foot again, but this time, her face screwed up into a terrible expression of anguish. "You hit me so hard I fell down the stairs! You killed our baby!"

"I did no such thing! I only shoved you a little, but you've never been steady on your feet."

Not once in the three weeks that Alister had known Rosetta had he ever seen her trip or fall, even when drunk, or when the sea was turning with violent waves.

"You still can't admit to it." Her hand was beginning to shake, her gun quaking in the air. "You believe your own stupid lies."

It took him longer than it should have to realise her face had turned bright red with tears. Real tears.

She won't kill him. Alister almost wanted to laugh. *And she told me she didn't have a tortured past.*

This had never been about procuring the Laughing Siren.

This whole endeavour had been about a wife trying to get her husband to change, to apologise, to get her own version of revenge.

I was used as a tool. To get her here, to cheat on this man, to hurt him. Alister knew, at the end of this day, she would go back to her husband, just as she was supposed to.

He and his men, *her* men, were like cattle to the slaughter. She would defend her husband's life; had already done so twice. She was going to get them all hung.

What should I care what he does with her? By law, she was his property. He could do what he wanted. Take her without her consent. Beat her. Put her in a looney house. Keep her locked up for the rest of her life.

It was cruel, but that was the society in which they lived.

Rosetta was no longer a weak woman, and he was sure she would teach Theodore Briggs to keep his hands to himself.

Rosetta Briggs. Alister's upper lip curled back a little into a hateful sneer as he stared at the crying woman. She had deceived him, tricked him, lied to him in so many ways, and he was no longer interested. *She won't shoot him.*

He would leave her to her chosen fate.

He couldn't find it in himself to hurt her for deceiving him when he really should, but he wouldn't stick around to be captured for her.

He turned away from them, quickly heading down the stairs of the quarterdeck without even wanting to look back.

"Pierre!" Alister yelled, seeing the man at the bottom of the steps. "Get us the fuck off this ship."

"What about Rosetta?" he asked, his green eyes darting to her. "I saw she was with you."

Pierre raised his sword to deflect an enemy before someone else killed the holder while he was distracted.

"We've been duped. I'll explain later." He threw his arm forward. "Call the Howling Death before it's too late–"

A loud bang sounded off behind him. He ducked, thinking the bullet was aimed for him. A moment later, a bone-crushing thud filled his ears.

His head turned to find the body of Theodore Briggs lying on the ground, a bullet hole replacing his right eye socket.

With widening eyes, he turned his head further to look up at Rosetta, still holding the pistol with smoke coming from the barrel.

She shot him. He couldn't believe it.

"Commodore Theodore Briggs is dead!" she shouted from above. "Lower your weapons or you'll join him."

Alister's gaze fell onto the main deck. Already, his men had started to turn the tide, spraying the blood of more soldiers than their own. There weren't many left to protect the Laughing Siren above the surface. With her shout, they began to drop their weapons, seeing they weren't going to be able to win.

"I am now the captain of this ship." Her eyes trailed over the ship, over every person standing. "Bring everyone below deck to the surface. If they fight, kill them."

A stunned Alister was shoved out of the way by Mr Smith who bolted up the stairs to join her. Naeem was helping the men rally up the soldiers.

What did this mean for him?

His gaze found Theodore dead on the ground. How was he supposed to feel now he knew she'd killed this man? That she'd been determined to take his life for everything he'd done to her? That she'd truly wanted the Laughing Siren and was planning on sailing it.

It meant her truths had been shadowed with hidden things rather than complete lies. He hadn't been completely deceived... again, by her. Alister had his own secrets, surely not as damning as this, but still secrets he'd rather not share.

"Mr Smith, get us out of here," she told the man.

He ran to the helm to take control of the ship before she'd even finished speaking.

When Alister turned on the staircase to confront her, she started to walk to the one on the other side. Her heavy stomps thudded against the timber as she stepped down them.

She was avoiding him.

"What do you want us to do with them?" one of the men of her original crew asked when she reached the bottom.

After walking over to Theodore's body, she started casually digging into his pockets to pull out a ring of keys. She jiggled them in her hands while she thought for long moments until she stood up straight, her stare fierce as she looked at them.

"Dead men tell no tales." She made her way to the door of the main cabin.

One man scrambled forward, his shoulders swaying from side-to-side as he struggled against his bindings and the men pulling him back. He was most likely Samuel Lester, the first officer.

He fell to his knees when he tripped. "Rosetta, you can't do this!"

She paused, turning back with a such a bored expression, it almost appeared sinister and mean. "Why not?"

"Because I'm your brother!"

The cold look she gave the man with light brown hair, blue eyes, and freckles across his face just like hers was bone chilling.

"Rosetta Silver doesn't have any family." She turned her back on him and leaned closer to Naeem as she went to open the door. "Make sure this ship gets out of here and that they're all dead."

She slammed the door behind her.

"Rosetta!" Samuel yelled at the closed door. "Wait, please!"

Naeem stomped forward and grabbed the man by the collar. The one holding him let him go, but his hands were bound behind his back with rope.

"You don't get to ask for mercy." The man struggled in Naeem's grip, his eyes stark with fear for his life. "You knew what was happening and you did nothing about it!"

"She was his wife, and he was my commanding officer. What was I supposed to do?"

"Not nothing! You saw everything and you still kept quiet." Naeem pulled his fist back and punched the man across the face. His head twisted to the side as spittle flung from his mouth. "Do you know the kind of lashings I received for trying to help her, a slave of their household who touched a noblewoman?" He punched him again. "You did nothing to save her, so why should she save you?"

"I know." Her brother's eyes crinkled into sad bows. "I've regretted it ever since she went missing."

"Missing?" Naeem released a dark laugh, letting go of his coat to stand back. "She was never lost, mate." He pulled his sword from its sheath and pressed it to Samuel's throat. "We planned before we ever left the mansion that we would come back and kill him. We were never lost, Sammy. We've always been on course to this future." The smile Naeem gave was one of the biggest Alister had ever seen. "Freedom, lad. That's all she's ever asked of us, and that's what we all now have."

Freedom. Alister remembered her men had chanted that singular word when he'd told them to abandon her and join his crew. They started chanting it now, confusing his own men and the soldiers tied up.

Without warning, Naeem slit her brother's throat, pouring a waterfall of blood down his own torso.

They'd all known. They'd all known what Rosetta had planned, why she planned it. They had all agreed to help her.

Alister turned from the chanting men and headed for the cabin. It felt like there was a fire in his stomach, burning higher with every second that passed. It threatened to scald him further with everything new he learned.

He opened the door and slammed it behind him with so much force, even he tensed at the sound. She didn't flinch as she stood at an opened safe, going through papers she'd pulled out. He could see the ring of keys dangling from the lock.

"Have your men raid the ship but leave everything I'd need

to repair it behind." She started shuffling the papers, turning them over to double check them. "Leave me enough supplies so I don't have to go to port straight away."

"Why didn't you tell me the truth?" he bit, finally putting his cutlass away and standing near the doorway. His stance was defensive, as well as aggressive.

"There wasn't as much money in the safe as I thought there'd be, but I shouldn't be surprised, considering they're ferrying prisoners," she said, blatantly ignoring his question. She was treating him as though his words were of little importance. "I know I said I'd give you half, but then I won't have enough to resupply."

Then she went to a cupboard and pulled a fancy knapsack from it, as if she knew it would be in there. She started putting some of those papers inside it, filling it to the brim.

"I'm not the kind of person to mess around with another man's wife, Rosetta."

Her calm face turned up from her task to give him a scowl.

"I have not been that man's wife for three years." She shoved the bag at him so hard, it felt like a punch to the gut. "Here are the maps I promised you."

He was forced to take it when she let it go before he'd even grabbed it. He looked down, holding it in his fist to dangle beside him as he turned his attention back to her.

"It doesn't matter what you say. You were still bound to him whether you wanted to be or not. He was still your legal husband the entire time!"

He'd bedded her, touched her, had wanted her like a damn ache, and she'd been married the entire time!

"And now he's dead." The cruel, broken smile she gave revealed just how happy she was about that.

Alister paused. *She's right.* She'd been the one to do it.

She had wanted to be the one to kill him. That's why she had gotten in the way.

His eyes swept over the wall of the office in thought, noticing the polished oak timber and the large map of the world painted on the wall. There were small ceramic tubs of paint on a small table next to it, like someone updated it when they discovered something new.

The floor was timber with a dark navy, circular carpet in the centre, while the walls were painted white with a light blue trim. The interior matched the exterior of the ship perfectly. Everything was bright and neat in comparison to his own.

The gridded windows were fancy, with swirling patterns on the outer edges of the glass. They were clean, not a single speck of grime on them. His thoughts continued to turn as he took in all these rich and elegant details.

Rosetta had hated Theodore to where she'd gone out of her way to not only get revenge, but to take his life. *Why should she have remained faithful?* Especially with what Alister had discovered he'd done to her.

"You still should have told me what I was walking into today!" He pointed to the door. "You were supposed to follow the plan; you could have gotten killed."

She gave a shrug, not seeming to care he was shouting at her. Sometimes, she frustrated him because he liked using fear to get his way and the reactions he wanted. He hated that she never fell prey to it.

"I couldn't tell you the truth. I couldn't risk you not helping me." She turned her eyes to meet his gaze. "Don't lie to me. You know you wouldn't have helped me if I'd told you. That, or you would have tried to get in the way, what I had planned, to do things *your* way."

Alister's lips thinned.

She was right, he probably wouldn't have helped her. He would have shunned her attention had he learned she was legally tied to another man. He definitely wouldn't have let her face Theodore the way she did.

She did what she had set out to do. In the same way, Alister was set on finding the Raider's treasure trove. He wouldn't let anyone get in the way until he found it.

"I won't let you ruin how I'm feeling, Alister. I have waited three years to put a bullet in that man's skull, and even longer to be free of him." Rosetta walked to the desk at the back of the room, flipping open a tiny chest to go through letters. "You can either fuck me or get the fuck off my ship."

She read the envelope of the first letter before shuffling it to the back. Her expression turned blank once more, like she didn't care which option he took.

Alister's jaw dropped at her suggestion.

Now she wants me? He'd known if he got her Laughing Siren, she might let him, but he hadn't known it would come with all this baggage. He'd been hoping, but now he was too conflicted to know what to do.

Prostitutes were prostitutes, their ties and pasts didn't matter to him. Somehow, Rosetta felt different, and he felt betrayed because of it, despite all the reasons why she couldn't have told him the truth.

His lips thinned, and his sight moved along the ground once more. *She still tricked me.* His nose crinkled in distaste, and he turned away from her, walking to the door. He placed his hand on the doorknob and turned it to leave.

But her desire had been real. There was no way she could have pretended or faked what he'd seen of her, felt from her, experienced himself.

He halted when it was just slightly cracked open.

The way she had been laying back against the table after his fingers had delved inside her, staring up at him with that sense of innocence, cheeks pink with deep arousal, still plagued his mind. To see this bitchy woman compliant for the first time had been damning to his senses.

She had wanted him, just as he did her.

There had been a side of him that hoped, once he left after getting her the Laughing Siren, he'd see her sails in the horizon in the future. That she'd take him, and then would drop anchor next to his ship so they could rekindle the obvious passion between them, entangle themselves in one night of bliss before fading away.

Alister knew he would have constantly had his eye on the horizon, quietly and secretly hoping to find her ship dancing along it, like a beacon in the night.

She'd tainted that dream for him.

He opened the door further, before pausing once more.

Or did she?

Rosetta no longer had any ties; she'd severed them herself this day. She was a free woman. A widow.

If I leave now... He knew if she ever saw his frigate, she'd direct her galleon the other way, two passing ships on the sea that would never meet.

If I leave now, she'll never take me again.

Damnit, he *wanted* her. He wanted this more than he was willing to admit.She was like the sea, dangerous, chaotic, wild, and not once had he ever turned his back on it. Not once had he ever not wanted to ride it, just like he ached to ride her.

CHAPTER TWENTY

Rosetta turned her back to the door and dropped the handful of boring envelopes she'd been absentmindedly scanning over, placing her hands flat against the desk. She stared at the cushioned chair neatly tucked in on the other side.

She couldn't help feeling disappointed that Alister had turned away, and she refused to watch him leave. The reason Rosetta had finally made the offer to him…it had never been about him earning it.

It had been about *her* earning it. She'd realised it the moment she'd killed Theodore and a swell of emotion hit her.

The first time she could tell herself it had been spur of the moment, but to take the same man again felt like a betrayal. She couldn't handle the guilt.

Not for Theodore, she couldn't give a shit about his feelings, but about the person she was sleeping with.

For a night, they both could pretend they were giving themselves to each other, but Rosetta always felt hopelessness afterwards. They thought she was giving herself to them, not just once, but twice, a third time, maybe more, but she never could, not with her tie to Theodore.

To have to look at the same person again, to face the guilt that they thought they were sharing something with her, made her feel hollow.

Alister was different.

He wasn't the first man she'd wanted to be intimate with, but she'd never been able to do it again. She'd always abandoned them with a hollow ache in her chest.

There was a spark between them, one she hadn't wanted to deny but needed to. Rosetta took in a shaky breath. *I'm free.* Free to feel whatever she wanted. To do whatever she wanted. To become whoever she wanted.

She no longer needed to murder the person whose fist had been clenched so tightly around the shackled chain attached to her throat; it was a chain that had extended thousands of miles, been weighing on her for years.

It felt like it spanned time and space, reaching across the entire universe just to drag her down into darkness.

I finally did it. She hadn't taken a full breath until this very moment.

She could finally live, and she wanted to share this newfound freedom with the person who helped her get there.

I want him. But what did it matter? She wouldn't blame Alister for walking away.

This was why she'd never shared herself twice with the same man. Alister was angry, and he had every right to be. She was sure he was disgusted, and she knew she deserved that too.

Once could be called an accident, any more and she was just being cruel. She had toed the line of what she could accept the day she'd toyed with him with her mouth.

He must feel like I betrayed him. That wasn't something she'd ever set out to do.

But I'm free now. She wouldn't have to face the way she felt now, ever again. It would taint the way she looked back on this day, but this was the day that Rosetta Silver truly got to come to life.

Rosetta Briggs was dead, alongside her husband. The

person she was now had no bond to anyone but her crew, and had no home except for the seas. Mr Smith was her father, Naeem her brother. A woman far away in a port was like dear mother to her. They were her family.

She heard the door close behind her and her head dipped forward. *He's gone.*

She'd been bracing herself for it and she finally relaxed, letting the emotions she'd been holding back roll over her.

Tears prickled the corners of her eyelids, collecting on her lashes. She tried to blink them away even though they were tears of relief, of joy. Disappointment mingled with a sense of achievement.

Wait, I hear footsteps.

Before Rosetta could turn around, a large hand grasped the back of her neck and spun her. Another hand cupped the side of her face as lips pressed firmly against her own.

With her eyes open wide in surprise, she could see Alister had his clenched tightly shut. His forehead was crinkled into deep lines, his brows knotted tightly. She could see the confusion in his features, the uncertainty.

Yet he was still here, kissing her.

Rosetta didn't care why.

A warm breath glided from her lips as she tilted her head to deepen the kiss, bringing her arms to wrap around his neck, forcing her onto the tips of her toes.

She arched into him as he slid his lips over hers. Her mind fizzled when his firm tongue pressed inside her mouth to lick against her tongue.

The moment she made even the smallest moan, his kiss became more heated. Alister started moving his lips faster, gorging on hers, eating at them feverishly. Her hands slipped down to undo the buttons of his tunic, rushing before he changed his mind. Her eyes closed as she focused on kissing him and removing his clothes at the same time.

He kept his hand on the nape of her neck, but the other slid over her shoulder to press her body more firmly against his. He was holding her to him, even when she stepped back.

He followed. When she stepped again, he tried to pull her tighter against him.

"Where the hell do you think you're going?" he asked against her lips, his words biting despite how heavy they sounded.

She pushed his tunic from him, his coat along with it, and they almost tripped when she continued to back them up. "A bed."

Suddenly, Alister was pushing her in the direction she'd been trying to lead them. Her back slammed against the wall, and he kissed her so hard, their teeth clacked together upon impact. Her lips caved under his, wetness spreading over them as their tongues danced.

Rosetta tried her hardest to match his heat as she felt behind her, tapping at the wood. Finally, she found the doorknob. The door caved underneath her, allowing them into the small room, a cabin that only held a bed, a side table, and a mounted cabinet.

There were two rooms connected to the navigation room. One for the captain and one for the first officer so they were close by. She knew the one she'd been leading them to was the one the first officer had used. Rosetta would never enter Theodore's sleeping cabin.

She started pulling on the ties of her pants while Alister worked on pulling her tunic. In a moment, it was gone. He pulled it up and off her, too impatient to undo the buttons.

Alister picked her up by the backs of her thighs, forcing her legs around his hips. She could feel his shaft hard against her, and she tried to grind her centre against it, digging her fingertips in his bare, muscled back covered in scars.

She felt him lowering them to the single bed by kneeling

onto it, before throwing her back against it. He wasted no time, breaking from the kiss to grab her leg and rip her boot off. He made short work of the other one.

Rosetta watched him, his face filled with hungry intent. His black hair carelessly slipped over his shoulders, his breaths laboured as he grabbed at the waistband of her tights, caressing up the sides of her legs with large, calloused hands.

She thought he'd be slow, teasing himself by revealing her at a snail's pace. Instead, the brute tore them from her limbs so quickly, it made her gasp.

Kneeling, he leaned over her on a straightened arm and ran his palm over her waist. His sight followed the same path with a subtle lick at the seam of his lips.

"Fuck, lass. You've got a sinful body on you."

His meaty paw closed around a breast, his thumb flicking over the tightened point of her nipple. Then he lowered his head to bring it into his mouth, sucking on it like a cherry dripped in sweet wine.

She could say the same thing about him. With exploring fingertips, she brushed her palms over his back, feeling his strong muscles, the scars decorating him.

A small raspy moan broke from her throat when his suction tightened, his tongue flicking back and forth over the sensitive bud. That wonderful pressure was taken away too soon as his lips kissed up her chest, over her collar bone, until they were moving over her neck.

She slipped her hands over his chest, running her fingers through the dark hair. She palmed every muscle she could reach in appreciation, digging her fingertips in, as she made a quick path down his torso. She was marvelling at this strong body, and she wanted him to know just how much she adored it.

Rosetta unbuttoned his breeches, dipping inside to pull his cock from it. *I want it so much.* She squeezed her hand around

Then she ground her hips against his softening erection. He almost chuckled against her lips. *Horny lass wants it again.*

The fact it was softening at all meant he'd come so hard, he'd emptied himself completely onto her stomach. *I've never come so hard my balls hurt afterwards.*

He couldn't believe he'd almost missed this, had almost walked away. He hadn't because he'd known he would have regretted it with every passing day. Despite how he'd been feeling at the time, the part of him that wanted this woman was stronger than his uncertainty.

He'd known it would have felt like this, that it would have derailed his mind so completely, he'd feel like he was drowning in her, in what was being shared between them.

But this moment afterwards? Now this he hadn't been expecting. This hard and bitchy woman who was difficult to please, he never thought she would ever be this sweet. He didn't think he'd ever had a woman be this gentle with him.

Her fingertips were dipping over the indents of his spine, like she was trying to calm him as he collected his thoughts. Her embrace was tight but intimate, and it felt like she was holding him everywhere.

Her mouth was eager and allowed him to go at his own pace, but there was something in their kiss, something that tugged on him.

This was their goodbye.

He knew it. She knew it.

She had the Laughing Siren. Once she had fully taken control of it and they divvied up everything on it, they would sail in opposite directions.

That was the plan.

It was what they had spoken about, what they had both agreed to wholeheartedly. So why didn't Alister like the way this kiss tasted in comparison to the one they'd shared a minute ago?

I will search for her sails on the horizon... But the world was a big place and the sea even bigger.

What happened if he never saw them?

CHAPTER TWENTY-ONE

Rosetta kissed Alister, moving her lips over his each time to return it. It was heated, rushed like they were trying to get in as many as they could before they pulled away.

She refused to. Rosetta refused to be the one to break from the kisses they shared, refused to be the one to separate, because she knew there would be a final one.

With his chest pressed so tightly against her own, she could feel his heartbeat starting to calm, his breaths becoming steadier.

And there it was.

She felt his head pulling back and she drew her lips over his one last time, following his mouth before she let him separate them. The arm still firmly gripping her backside released, and he had to yank it from underneath her.

She expected him to get off her, to roll away like many men.

All Alister did was take the worst of his weight from her as he placed his hand around her head, the other still supporting him under her shoulders.

She dropped her legs so they were bent, her feet flat against the bed, cradling him. She was giving him the freedom to leave whenever he was ready. Slipping her arms from his back, she placed them against the sides of his neck and jaw, searching his face.

His lips were pursed, a serious look across his features as his eye glided over her. They were only a breath away from each other, and there was a moment of silence, of pause.

Rosetta gave him a warm smile.

"Thank you." She let the sincerity of those words fill every part of her expression; in her lips, her eyes, in the way she looked at him.

Thank you for this. For this moment and what had led to it. For everything he had done, for helping her achieve her goal.

This is the happiest moment of my life. For so long, she had been hurting. She was relieved to feel the first moment of contentment she ever had.

As she stroked the short hair on his jaw, she expected Alister to chuckle, to let his arrogant and self-important personality shine. Instead, his brows furrowed deeply, his lips pursing harder together. She didn't know what it meant, but she hoped the way his eye swiftly darted over her face wasn't regret.

"Are you alright?" she asked when his gaze boring into hers became too much.

"Sail with me," he said, his tone sharp and steady.

"Excuse me?" Her voice broke an octave as she tried to sit up.

He refused to let her move, taking his arm out from behind her head to hold the side of it.

"Help me find the Raider's trove."

"You're joking, right?" She let out an awkward laugh, her eyes looking elsewhere.

He's only saying this to get a rise out of me. Alister couldn't be serious, and Rosetta hated the way her heart nearly leapt at the idea of his cruel joke.

"Nay, lass."

He moved her head until she was forced to bring her

averted gaze back to him. Her brows crinkled in confusion.

"I thought the plan was to part ways." Then she quietly said, "That this was goodbye."

"Aye, me too." His dark face suddenly turned brighter as a grin plastered across his face. "But I'm asking you anyway."

"Why? Don't get me wrong, it sounds fun, but you don't seem like the kind of man who wants a woman trailing after him. Most men go to the sea to *avoid* women clinging to them."

His grin grew wider, mischievous even. "Aye, that's true. But I don't mind the idea of good pussy trailing behind me... on her own damn ship."

She paused, her head tilting to the side with a frown.

"Wait, you just want sex?" That made much more sense.

"Why not?" He lowered his head and buried it between the crook of her shoulder and neck. He swept his tongue over it, making her tense beneath him. "Think of all the good fucking we can do while we search and, at the end, I might even share the booty with you."

Hot sex and the potential of riches beyond imagination? Now that sparked Rosetta's interest.

"That's if we find it. I still don't think it exists."

He gave a shrug before grinding his soft shaft against her clit. The muscles in her abdomen twitched in reaction. "If we find it, we're both infinitely richer. If not, one of us will get bored and sail the other way."

"That could get complicated."

He pulled his head back to see a dark look on her face. He let out another chuckle. "Nay, you are too smart to fall for someone like me."

"Maybe it was your poor heart I was worried about breaking."

His eyes crinkled with humour as an outright laugh fell from his mouth. He leaned back to kneel upright, grabbing both her thighs to bring them around his hips.

His heated gaze was body tingling. He looked over her, from her head, down her chest, all the way to her exposed folds. He used the pad of one of his thumbs to pull the lips of her pussy apart, softly thrusting against her once more. The throb that lanced her almost caused her to moan.

"My cock just isn't ready to give up the way you feel around it."

Rosetta's eyes squinted, her lips thinning. She thought her body might be thinking the same thing. "But I don't care to find the Raider's treasure. I want to take down fleet ships."

"That's your goal?" he asked incredulously. "That's how you get Queen Mary Anne to hunt you. Do you have a death wish?"

Rosetta shrugged. "Not if there are no survivors to say who's been sending her ships to Davy Jones' Locker."

"You've got some big goals there, lass." He thumbed her clit, circling it, making her hands clench, before palming his hand up and over her stomach, not caring about the sweat and his seed on it. "I'll help you sink whatever ships your heart desires."

Then he thumbed a nipple, grasping her breast in his calloused palm. She wondered if he noticed her thighs twitch around him in response as he started to pluck at it.

"Think of just how easy it will be when you point at a ship you want gone, and you've got my warship and its cannons backing you up."

"You're talking about starting a fleet, Alister."

"One of pirates." His gaze fell to the ceiling, that grin never leaving his face. "Your strength with my speed. My firepower with your cargo space." He looked down to her, excitement thrumming from him. "I may never need to dock again."

The idea of never touching land again seemed to be what threw his mind over the edge, as she felt his cock harden.

He's serious. Alister was truly asking her to sail with him... for fun?

"I don't know if I can," she sighed. "I have to ask my crew."

"Nay, you don't." He raised his brow at her, a glint to his eye. His lips even pursed together. His face said he was suspicious of her words, like they might be lies to get out of it. "Your crew will follow you anywhere, will do whatever you want. They've already proven that."

"I've only asked them to follow me until I got the Laughing Siren." *He's right, though.* She knew they would probably agree to it. "What about yours? You're asking me, but I'm sure you haven't asked them."

"I don't give a shit what they want. I've never told my crew to follow my command simply because I want it. They can put up with it for once. Plus, they will enjoy having the extra supplies you can carry." He looked around at the walls with a chuckle. "You can ferry more livestock for better eating, more booze to drink. They will appreciate that."

"Talking about crews..." Her eyes fell to the door. "They're both waiting for us."

"I'm not leaving this room until I have your answer, lass."

She brought her eyes back to see his grin had fallen and he once more looked serious.

"If you say nay, they are going to have to wait until I'm done fucking the absolute hell out of you, since I don't know if I'm ever going to get the chance again."

Rosetta looked down to the hardened shaft jutting between his hips and laying over her stomach. "And if I say yes?"

"They can wait one more round."

"And what if I say yes to your offer and no to... that?"

She didn't take her eyes off his cock, trying to suppress the urge to lick the seam of her lips in want. She even rolled her hips so that he would slip against her stomach, wet with his seed.

"You're going to help me get rid of it either way. I'm not using my hand like I have been." Her eyes widened and darted up to his face. "Oh aye, Rosetta. I've been craving you that bad."

The sheepish smile that grew on her lips made him frown.

"I have never trusted that face."

Rosetta leaned up and pressed a kiss to one of his cheeks. "I used to touch myself in your hammock before you took back your ship."

"You fucked yourself in my bed?" His nose crinkled on one side, his erection noticeably pulsating against her.

"Pictured you while doing it."

Alister's teeth gritted as he pulled back his hips and slammed his cock inside her, eliciting a sharp gasp from her. He shook his head as he moved inside her, his long hair falling over his shoulders to hang above her like a dark curtain.

"Shit, screw it." Then he groaned, his nose crinkling as his mouth fell open, his grip on her thighs tight. "Give me your answer afterwards."

CHAPTER TWENTY-TWO

Alister followed that fine piece of ass he just railed as they left the navigation room after finding their tunics, noticing the slight limp in her step. *I may have overdone it.*

The second time had been just as intense and heated as the first. Regardless, she finally gave him her answer, and he was pleased it had been a yes.

Now, Alister was going to have his fun with her across the seas. Until he grew bored of her, of course, which he knew he would. What he was feeling wouldn't last. But for now, it would give him deep entertainment and satisfaction.

She opened the door and they stepped into bright sunlight. None of the soldiers were left on the ship. He knew their crews must have slit their throats and pushed them into the water.

What surprised him was that Theodore Briggs' body was still where it had fallen.

A horrible squeal of happiness came from Rosetta, surprising them all, especially Alister, who had copped an earful directly. She ran straight into Naeem's arms, who picked her up in an embrace and spun her.

"We did it, Rosetta," the man laughed as her legs lifted off the ground.

Alister might have been concerned by watching them do this before, but not now. He shook his head at the two of them.

He had seen it all, had helped her escape. Now that Alister knew Naeem had been freed by Rosetta's will, and he'd saved her from horrible man, he couldn't blame them for their closeness. *They bonded through their pain.*

Naeem put her down and she reached for Mr Smith who embraced her tightly. She even hugged men he didn't know the names of, had never cared to since it would have been a waste of his time.

Pierre came up to him, patting him on the shoulder once before holding it.

He stared at Rosetta as he said, "Got that out of your system, did you?"

"Nay." He folded his arms across his chest, still staring at her arse like he couldn't stop himself. "She's staying with us for a little longer."

With a frown, Pierre pulled away from him. He faced Alister with a look of confusion. "What do you mean?"

He nodded his head at her. "Asked her to help us find the Raider's treasure."

"You did, did you?" His head shot back to her, a grin forming across his face. His green eyes twinkled with a mischievous glint. "That'll be fun."

He knew this wouldn't be an issue with Pierre or Derek, and he hoped he got a ring of acceptance from everyone else.

However, Alister did narrow his eye on the man. "I am telling you now to stay away from her."

His green eyes widened, slowly coming back to Alister. "You're saying she's off limits?"

"Aye. Don't touch her." *She's mine.*

He wouldn't have Pierre, or his crew, hankering away at her until she caved. Alister was going to have fun with this woman until *he* decided he was done, not because it had been decided for him.

Unless she chooses to. Then again, Alister fairly doubted she'd be the one who grew bored first.

"What do we know about the support ships?" Alister asked.

He could see his warship sailing next to the Laughing Siren and he hadn't been paying attention to know if they'd fought them. Cannons could have been firing and Alister would have been too distracted by Rosetta beneath him to notice.

"Some of the men went below deck and shot one of them down when they tried to give chase," Pierre answered, crossing his arms across his chest. He tilted his head towards Alister with a dull look. "The Howling Death couldn't assist, but we managed to get them to back off while you were busy."

He placed one of his hands over his chin in thought. So, they had indeed been in the middle of a fight, and he'd not once noticed. Thankfully it was alright, but that was still a little alarming.

"Good." It was a shame they'd sunk one and couldn't raid it before it went to the bottom of the ocean. "I doubt the other will follow. It'll probably go straight to the Queen."

"This will put a target on our heads."

"We're already wanted men," Alister chuckled. "The Queen can only increase her bounties."

"It's your ship though, and I'm sure the fleet vessel will know that. This could have her sending more hunters after us." He nodded his head towards Rosetta. "She'll have a while before they discover who's really the captain of this ship now, then there will be a bounty out on her too."

"That's true." He brushed his hand through the hair on his face. "I'm sure that's why she didn't want any survivors. They probably would have tried to kill us in our sleep had we forced them to join our crews."

"Are you sure about bringing her along? It'll be easier to see us on the horizon with two ships."

"Aye, but they'll be more wary about attacking."

That reminded him.

He reached into the knapsack from where he'd dropped it on the floor, and finally looked at the maps she'd given him. *She actually delivered on this promise.*

He'd already been to one location and knew the booty wasn't there. Three others were maps he'd never seen before. One in the east, not too far away from their current location. One in the north that looked more promising. A final one was in the south, deep into seas he wasn't familiar with.

I don't know if the Raider ever went south. He'd never had a map lead that way. The bag was filled to the brim with maps, treasure maps to other potential chests. Some were of places he wasn't familiar with, but he wanted to know the seas better than anyone, and one day he hoped he would travel over all of them.

That was a goal after the Raider's trove, though.

Rosetta was finally released from the men congratulating her and she turned to point at Theodore's lifeless corpse. "What is he still doing here?"

Alister had been wondering that too.

Naeem stepped forward with an awkward laugh, rubbing his short, curly hair.

"I didn't know if you still wanted to hang his body up and wack him with a stick until you saw what came out of him like a pinata."

She really hated that man. He snorted a quiet laugh. He wouldn't get in the way of whatever she wanted to do; it wasn't his place.

"I was drunk when I said that!" she shouted with a laugh. "You daft twit!"

"How was I supposed to know you weren't serious?"

She stood in front of the body with her feet apart, her hand over her chin in thought. Whatever she was contemplating pulled her face tight into a thoughtful expression.

Her cheeks puffed as she dropped her arm, reared her foot

back, and proceeded to kick him so hard in the nuts that multiple men, including himself, winced and covered their precious groins.

"Shit, I hope she's never kicked a man that hard in the balls while they've been alive," Pierre whined.

"She kneed me the day we took back my ship." *I still haven't gotten her back for that.*

"You poor soul."

She slapped her hands together like she was brushing them of dirt.

"I'm good. You can toss him now. Oh! Wait!" She reached down and lifted a flap of his officer uniform. Pulling a small coin bag from his belt, she tossed it into the air before catching it. "Now, I'm done with him."

She threw it at Alister, and he caught the weighty bag.

"Like I said, the safe didn't have much gold, but that's at least something. Prick always carried a heavy coin pouch to flaunt his wealth."

She gave him a bright smile after he looked inside and nodded his head with approval. *This is almost a silver coin each for my men.* They'd be pleased with that, at least.

"Alright, let's get those prisoners to the surface."

"Nay," Alister cut in. "I need to speak to my men first."

The prisoners could be divvied up afterwards. His crew came a little closer, just under fifty men, ready to listen. A sea of eyes found him, and her crew listened in out of curiosity.

"I've asked Rosetta to sail her ship with ours while we look for the Raider's trove." He folded his arms to show his unwillingness to budge in this decision. "I've already decided, she has already agreed, and I won't be putting it to a vote."

"What do we get out of it?" one of his men shouted, patting his chest once. "You're just doing this for yourself."

A few nodded their heads, agreeing with the question. Alister noticed Rosetta's men started to circle her, speaking in hushed whispers in comparison to his boisterous crew. They were a rowdy lot in everything they did.

"Aye. For once, I'm making a decision as Captain and I'm not asking for permission." He narrowed his eyes into a glare, letting his good eye trail over them. "Her ship has many benefits, like her cargo space. She can hold more livestock so we can eat better. Just think of the meat, eggs, and milk we can have, instead of the shit we've been eating. She can also hold more grog, as well as booze. Then there is the vast amount of room for other cargo so that we can ferry all the good stuff."

Like the gold and loot they will steal, which Alister would demand stay on his ship. They'd get a share of the loot, but he was an untrusting man who wouldn't let her sail away with it.

"What about the loot on this ship promised to us?" Kent pointed his finger at Alister. "I was promised a new sword!"

"Then get yourself a new sword; the armoury will be full. We can still go through this ship and take the things we want, but..." He unfurled one hand to lift a single finger. "Keep in mind that it still needs to function and will be whole with our own. If they need it back, they can take it."

The fact they could still go through the ship, and the Laughing Siren could be seen as a supply carrier for them, appeased his men. Then he was asked a question he hadn't thought of.

"Who is in command?" Pierre asked with a frown, his arms folded but more to be comfortable rather than in arrogance.

"I am," Alister snorted with a laugh. "Obviously."

"She doesn't really listen to you, or anyone, for that matter."

Hmm. Pierre was right. *She is argumentative and hot-headed.*

"No, I will follow his lead," Rosetta finally piped in, her men following behind her.

Alister realised she'd already spoken to them and gotten their approval. "Now that I've got the Laughing Siren, I don't care where we go, as long as I can sink ships." She turned her gaze to Alister with squinted eyes. "And as long as my voice is heard. I am a captain as much as he is. Therefore, I rank above everyone but him."

She turned to Pierre with her trademark dull look.

"If you're on my ship, you follow my command. If you're on his, you follow his. If I am on his ship, only he can tell me what to do. No more of this 'get me a bottle of rum, barmaid' bullshit you've all been pulling."

A few of his men chortled, most likely the perpetrators.

Alister hiked his thumb at her.

"See, lass agrees that I'm in charge." He knew that's all his men really cared about. Then he refolded his arms. "I wouldn't have made the decision if it didn't benefit you lads in some way."

His words seemed to placate them, because they gave a ring of approval, mostly. He could see there were a few that still weren't sold but they didn't care enough to come forward.

The prisoners were all brought to the surface while Alister, Rosetta, Pierre, Naeem, and Mr Smith stood on the quarterdeck to look over them. Unfortunately, Derek couldn't join them, since he was steering the Howling Death.

"How many are there, Mr Smith?" she asked quietly as they brought their eyes to the confused men standing in neat rows and columns. They were about a foot apart from each other, as directed by Rosetta, who wanted to see them properly.

Just as Alister was doing a rough count, Mr Smith said, "There's ninety-six."

She placed her hand over her lips to whisper, "I thought there'd be more." Then her gaze travelled over Alister standing next to her. "How many do you need?"

"At least thirty." He was being generous. He wanted more, but if he asked, she'd struggle to fly her ship.

Thirty should bring my numbers to just under eighty. He'd lost men today, more than Rosetta's crew, who all seemed to be accounted for except for one or two.

"What would that leave us with?" she quietly asked Mr Smith, showing she really couldn't count the simple number. The way she awkwardly asked the question showed she was more embarrassed than she'd originally let on.

Should I teach her? She'd said she knew simple math, but this was very simple. *Then again, I'm sure Mr Smith has been teaching her.*

He had little interest getting in the middle of her business if it was already taken care of.

"We would gain sixty-six, bringing our numbers up to one hundred, including ourselves."

Rosetta ran her fingers through her hair in obvious frustration. "This ship requires at least a hundred and twenty men to function properly."

Alister eyed the four masts on this fully rigged galleon. It required more men to sail this vessel compared to his medium-sized ship with its three masts.

"Not really," Alister butted in, bringing their eyes to him. "You need at least fifty men to hoist the sails in the day and the same at night, but that's if we are changing course often or have heavy winds. The rest of the time, it's just maintaining it and that doesn't require as much effort. You won't tire your men out much if you bring that number down to forty. The rest you can have doing the other tasks."

"I can also help to man the sails when I'm not taking the helm at night," Mr Smith offered.

"No you can't, old salt," Naeem chuckled. "You'll break a hip."

"Naeem, you're quicker than everyone else anyway,"

Rosetta sighed. "You've got speed in that stupid body of yours. We'll all have to help. Mr Smith and I will take longer shifts at the helm so you can take a position throughout the day in the sails."

"Was going to do that anyway," Naeem said, his dark eyes falling over the prisoners. "I won't leave you unprotected with them."

His comment made Alister's brows furrow. *She'd be left alone with unknown criminals.* He hadn't thought about this obstacle.

Rosetta rolled her eyes with a loud gruff of annoyance at them, who all suddenly looked at her with concern. She stepped forward to take the stage.

"My name is Rosetta Silver, and I am now the captain of this ship. We have killed Queen Mary Anne's soldiers, those who set sail to have you hung for whatever crimes you have committed. We are your saviours. You are all to be converted into the fine art of piracy, for that is the price of your freedom. You will work on our ships, or you will join the soldiers currently sinking to the bottom of the sea. Do I have any naysayers?"

Silence fell over the entire ship. No one said a word, no one even dared to cough, in case it was taken as a rejection.

"Perfect!" she exclaimed, clapping her hands together in a single slap. "You will be divvied up between myself and–"

Alister stepped forward and grabbed Rosetta by the shoulder to put her behind him. *Very sweet. My turn.*

"I am Alister 'One-Eye' Paine, the Bloody Storm of the Seas, and Captain of the Howling Death." He leaned his foot against the railing, placing his forearm across his knee. "I'm sure many of you have heard of me."

A sense of restlessness fell over them. Some shifted in their positions, eyes going wide.

"Aye lads," he said. They should be afraid.

He turned his head back to give Rosetta a grin of pride, only to find she was pissed at him for pushing her out of the way. With a shrug, he turned his head forward again.

"Here's what's going to happen. This ship is currently under my protection while it flies next to my sails. If we so much as hear a single wind of the possibility of a mutiny or uprising, we will do the Queen a favour and hang you ourselves. I don't keep prisoners and I don't like betrayers. Some of you will find yourselves on my ship, and if you do, be prepared to not leave my employment unless I find a replacement for you. You are already dead men, and I have no problem with making you deader."

Rosetta came up beside him with her arms folded, tapped the toe of her boot, and glared at him. Alister conceded. He'd done what he wanted, delivered his threat.

He backed away so she could come forward again.

"Those of you who have sailed before, move to the starboard side of the ship." Alister estimated that forty men moved to the right, and the others shuffled to get out of the way. "Good. You are now under my command."

"Oi, lass," Alister said with a bite to his tone. He quickly grabbed her shoulder. "You can't take all the sailors!"

"I need experienced men who know how to hoist a sail, Alister. Your crew already know how to do that and can teach those who don't. You can't expect me to sail with inexperienced men who don't even know what a rig is."

Damnit. Unfortunately for him, she was right.

"Fine," he snapped, before stepping forward. "Those of you who have committed murder, to the port side." When no one moved, he rolled his eyes. "That's the left side of the ship!"

If he couldn't have sailors, he'd at least have men who weren't afraid to kill. If they were serial murderers, then they would get along splendidly.

Almost thirty uncertain men moved to the left side of the ship.

"You are under my command. My crew will show you how to get to my ship and will instruct you on your duties." He waved his hand to the blond man next to him. "I know he looks like a woman, but Pierre is my first mate, and you will listen if he gives you a command. You will find Derek already at the helm – he is the quartermaster. If you don't listen to them, you will find yourself beaten with the cat o' nine tails, got it, lads?"

Cat o' nine tails was a short whip with nine ends, knotted at the tips for maximum damage. It was a severe punishment, and just one lashing would be enough to teach any man a lesson.

A string of 'I', 'ayes', and 'yesses' came from them.

"Take 'em away lads!" His crew started rounding them up and moving them over. He turned to Rosetta. "The rest are yours. You can keep your thieves and beggars."

But Alister was certain she'd taken all those who had been arrested for piracy. They had been the men he'd originally wanted.

Once more, Rosetta stepped forward.

"Okay boys. I'm going to make this simple. I don't give a shit what you've done, if you're innocent or not, why you did it, or who you did it to. You are dead men, so feel free to reinvent yourselves. You can't go back to your families, or you'll be arrested. You have no homes, no friends. You're all nobodies, just like us. So, let me make this as monosyllabic as possible..."

She paused for effect.

That's a big word, Alister thought to himself with a shake of his head. *Noble people with their vast vocabulary.* She was speaking to most likely commoners. They wouldn't understand.

"That means clear, boys," Naeem cut in with a laugh

before Alister could say anything.

"I may have tits, but I will cut off your hands if you touch me. I will cut out your tongue if you holler at me in any inappropriate way or call me anything other than Captain. Naeem is my first officer." She gestured her hand to him. "Comment on the colour of his skin, and I will flay yours." She gestured to the other man standing with them. "This is Mr Smith, my quartermaster. Comment on his age, and I will make sure you never get the pleasure of reaching it. Savvy?"

There was a ring of agreeance.

Alister raised his brow. He was impressed by her much-needed threats. *Tough woman.*

She stood up straight and stared at them. There was a pause where no one said or did anything, waiting for what she would say next. Even Alister was puzzled by it.

"Well?" she yelled, feinting a physical taunt by stepping forward with a stomp. "Get to work, you scurvy dogs!"

Men moved to rush around in confusion, nearly bumping into each other in frantic steps. Her crew, with faces of humour, quickly stepped in to take charge and direct them. Even Mr Smith and Naeem stepped down to assist, leaving Alister alone with Rosetta.

He got to watch her take in the reality that this ship was hers now.

She turned and walked to the helm, brushing her fingertips over the well-polished wheel. Then she clutched two of the eight handles firmly, squeezing them so tightly, he thought she was trying to break them.

"I have waited so long for this day," she murmured.

He wasn't sure if it was to herself or to him. "Your father was never a sailor on this ship, was he?"

She shook her head. "No. My brother was."

"That wasn't enough for you to know this ship inside and out. You knew this ship because Theodore brought you on it."

"Partially," she admitted, slowly bringing her eyes away from the wheel to his face. "My father was a businessman like Mr Smith. He designed this boat."

"Your father helped build it?"

"No, Alister. He designed it." A small, sad smile filled her features as she stared forward. "*I* am the Laughing Siren."

Her eyes strolled over the railings, the sails, just as he did the same with an unnerved hint to his gaze.

"He told me when he had it made that I was the inspiration. When he had the mermaid carved at the front of the ship, it was because he loved the way I laughed when I was truly happy. He said I had a wonderful laugh."

Alister snorted. "Your laugh is terrible, lass."

"I know," she sighed, her sad smile not falling as she hugged the wheel in longing. "Theodore hated it, told me I sounded like a screeching monkey. He would often tell me to shut up."

He suddenly wished he could eat his own words.

Although her laugh was something terrible, he'd come to find it quite adorable for such a small woman to produce such a boisterous noise.

She seemed to sense his disquiet.

"This ship has always been mine. When Theodore discovered I was the inspiration for it, he'd told the Queen this was the ship he wanted to sail. I hated the idea of him having it." Then she muttered, "He didn't deserve anything that represented me."

"It's a beautiful boat." Just like its inspiration.

He couldn't stop his eye from falling over the pretty woman who was truly a brute inside, a sensual, bitchy woman who tied him up in knots.

"You lied to me," he told her.

"I did that a lot." She brought her gaze to him. "You're going to have to be a bit more specific."

"You told me you didn't have a tormented past, but what I discovered today is pretty twisted."

"It's a complicated past."

"*I* have a complicated past, Rosetta," he laughed darkly. "Yours is tormented."

She narrowed her gaze at him.

"I refused to wear it. I am no longer that person, and I will never allow someone to treat me that way ever again."

"So, you're from Luxor." She thinned her lips that he knew where she was from. He rolled his eyes. "It's where *he's* from. Even I knew that."

"I wasn't born there. My family is from Showater City, just a few ports down."

That made Alister frown. "Then how did you end up marrying him?"

She gave a groan, lying over the wheel in dismay. "Why do you even care? I'd much rather not talk about it."

"I'm curious." He gave a shrug before crossing his arms, raising his brow when she pouted. "If you weren't from the same city, how did you end up in his sights?"

"My brother," she sighed. "My father used his ship making business to get my brother employed. He first saw me when I was nine, there to congratulate my brother for joining his crew."

Alister came forward to lean on the wheel, curling his arm around the handles. Leaning back, he crossed one foot in front of the other. He was trying to get her to stop using it to hide.

"From that day, he visited my father to look over his ships under the pretence he was looking for more vessels for the Queen's fleet. He would visit my brother, got him promoted quickly. It was all a guise so he could check on me. When I turned twelve, he told my father he wanted my hand in marriage, to arrange it for when I was old enough."

"So you had an arranged marriage."

"No," Rosetta said with a shake of her head. "He denied him. He wanted me to choose my husband when I was old enough."

Alister frowned once more. "Then how did you end up marrying him anyway?"

Rosetta gave a laugh, and yet it bitterly held very little humour in it. "Theodore tried to ruin my father's business. He made sure he couldn't sell as many ships, did everything to make sure he lost his income to the point where we were, so poor we had to start selling items."

"Your father actually agreed to give you to this man because of this?" Alister couldn't believe it! They had willingly handed her over to someone obviously bad and corrupt.

"I didn't know until after I married him – when it was too late." She pressed her chin again the wheel, right near the crook of his elbow. "He got drunk a lot. He told me what he'd done one night when he was too drunk to remember. So, when I turned fifteen, when he demanded my hand in marriage, and my father was so desperate that he agreed to it."

"Fifteen? Lass, that isn't legal."

"It is if your parents agree to it," she muttered. "My father didn't want to, but he had no choice."

She trailed her eyes to him.

"And you agreed to this?"

She squinted at him, seeing he wanted her to wear some the blame. *If she agreed to it...*

"He promised to save my father's business, and he paid for me rather than my parents needing to give a dowry." She turned her eyes away. "I did it to save my family, not knowing what I was truly walking into. I was a teenager, thinking I was to be married to a duke. How was I supposed to know he would start beating me?"

She has a fair point.

"So, you were an underage bride sold to a man set on destroying your family just to have you."

"Aye, lad," she mocked. "He sought after me hard, apparently because I was this beautiful thing, and he hurt me. He at least delivered on his promise to promote my brother again and save my father's business. He'd bought the Laughing Siren before all this, though."

"You noble people are so complicated."

She gave a snort of laughter. "You can say that again."

"If you wanted him dead, why go through all this trouble? Why not just poison him?"

"Because I wanted to be free." She leaned back to palm the handles again, glaring at them. "If it was discovered I'd murdered him, I would have been sent to prison. The day he killed our child was the day I decided to escape, become a pirate, and steal this ship by putting a bullet in his head."

"What did you say to piss him off?" Her lips thinned and he let out a laugh. "Don't get me wrong, lass, I'm not the kind of man to hit a defenceless woman, but I do believe I shot at you. You've got a bold personality; I can only imagine how much he hated that."

A smile pestered her lips. "He was expecting some quiet woman," she agreed. "Instead, he got me." She gave a deep sigh, turning her head up to the sky, as if to pull strength from it. "He was so drunk that he told me if our child wasn't a boy, he'd tell the woman he'd gotten pregnant that he'd take that child and make me raise him. I didn't know he'd been unfaithful to me, so when he told me that, I told him if he continued to have port girls, I would sleep with other men while he was away at sea."

Alister cleared his throat of the lump in it, stepping away from the wheel. It seemed his movements caught her attention because she looked to him. She rolled his eyes like she could read his thoughts.

"I understand it now," she laughed. "Women can't swim across the sea and tell each other. It's easy to have other girls." She turned the wheel from side-to-side with a smile. "It's lonely at sea. I had to sail it to understand what it's like. Still, you would have thought he would have kept his dick to himself."

She leaned her elbow on the wheel, resting against it. It didn't seem like she was willing to let it go now.

"I was a good wife. I did what I was told, did my wifely duties without complaint. I held teas, parties, showed off his wealth to make him happy. Unfortunately, any mistake, no matter how large or small, was punished. I looked forward to when he would piss off to sea."

It didn't take Alister much to realise it. "You never wanted him to come back."

"Nope. I wanted him good and dead long before I set out on doing it myself. Even though I hated it at the time, I'm glad it led to this." She gave Alister a brighter smile, her blue eyes catching the sunlight and making them look like shallow water. "I think I was born to be a pirate. I hated sitting around like some stupid, brainless woman. He never shut up about the sea; it's all he would talk about. He told me about being in command of a ship and crew, and I used that information to become a captain. He had old books on sailing, which I studied before I left. The moment he left for duty, I ran, since he wasn't around to stop me."

She fell back, stretching her arms out while she held onto the handles and bowed her back. It was like she wanted to turn upside down, the tips of her mud-coloured hair almost brushing the timber floor.

"There is no truer freedom than being a captain of the seas."

Alister shook his head with a deep chuckle. "Well, ain't that the truth."

CHAPTER TWENTY-THREE

Rosetta brushed her fingertips over the blue railing of *her* ship, a small smile fixed upon on her features.

Alister had already gone back to the Howling Death and was currently leading the way. She could see the back of him manning the helm from the short distance between them.

But she wasn't walking the length of her ship to look at him. She was doing it to admire what she was currently standing on. Unlike the Howling Death's grey and aged sails, the Laughing Siren had crisp white ones. The sandy oak timber was polished, sanded, cleaned, then finished with wax. Not a rope was frayed, not a single metal rig rusted.

It was beautiful.

She walked her way to the very front and held onto a rope to lean over and look at the wooden mermaid sculpture with a far too jolly face. Its hands were forward, like it was reaching for something, its tail curled down before its fins spread behind it.

"When you told me this ship was glorious, you weren't kidding," Mr Smith said as he came up the short rise of steps.

Rosetta reached her hand out to the mermaid, wanting to touch her but unable to.

"It is, isn't it?" She finally stood back and turned to him.

His eyes moved over her, much like a proud parent. "And

it's yours now."

Hearing him say those words, with that look in his eye, that caring and proud expression, made tears she didn't even know she'd been holding in come to the surface. Mr Smith had never seen Rosetta cry before, but he didn't look at her with shock. It was almost as if he was expecting it.

He closed the space between them and brought her in for a tight hug. He placed an arm around her shoulders while he wrapped the other around her head. A quiet sob fell from her as she reached around and grabbed the back of his brown tunic so that it was bundled in tight fists as she buried her face against his chest.

He turned them so his back was to the rest of the ship, hiding her from the crew as she wept.

How did he know? How did John know Rosetta had been holding this in?

She didn't know if they were tears of pain or tears of joy, but they overtook her so violently, she shuddered as she took in his comforting warmth and embrace.

Was I waiting for Alister to leave before I did this?

She didn't think she would've had the courage to cry in front of him. Rosetta didn't want him to know just how deeply she'd buried the hurt of her past.

She knew it had happened when she'd been facing Theodore, but that was different. That was in the moment. It wasn't the yawning depth lingering afterwards that was far worse by comparison. Only Naeem and Mr Smith knew just how much Rosetta had been hurting.

"I've waited so long for this," she cried, shaking her head to nuzzle her face against him. She was probably getting tears and snot all over him, but he didn't seem to mind. "Why did it have to take so long?"

Three years she'd been holding this in. Not once had she ever cried about it, not once had she let it ache her heart this heavily.

"Shh." He patted the back of her head in a soothing manner, tenderly brushing over the length of her matted hair. "All that matters is that it's done, that he's dead."

Her fists clenched tighter, pulling on his tunic.

"He couldn't even admit to it." A hiccup of breath clogged her chest. "He still tried to tell me it was my fault, John."

"It wasn't Rosetta." He held her tighter. "You know that. Don't listen to the words of a bad man."

"I wanted that child," she finally admitted, for the first time to another person. Not even Naeem knew. "I wanted something to love, something to care for. I wanted to cherish something the way I wanted to be cherished."

John was a father; she knew he would understand.

Rosetta had wanted to grow a daughter who would never be forced to make the decision she'd made, or a son who was nothing like his horrible father. It was her hope for a life she thought she could bare when she'd been married, to focus all the love and attention she had onto a child.

She hated Theodore, hated him from the moment he revealed how he'd tried to destroy her family. She'd even accepted the occasional slap until then, but then she'd turned spiteful, which earned her harder and harsher punishments.

"Why did it have to be me?"

"Because no other woman would have had the courage to do what you did today."

A louder cry fell from her at his words. She knew he was right. No other woman would have had the will, the smarts, the strength to do every terrible thing she had done to get to this ship.

But it shouldn't have had to be anyone!

"The things I've done, John..." Some of them were unbearable in her memories.

"I know I wasn't there for the beginning," he said with a

comforting whisper, tilting his head to place his cheek on her hair. "But we're all here to make sure you don't have to do those things again, unless you want to."

She gave an awkward laugh. "You wouldn't say that to your daughter."

"No," he laughed back. "I would never approve of her doing those things, but that's because it wouldn't have made her happy. You're different to her; she was soft and precious."

"I-I'm totally precious too."

His chest rumbled as he squeezed her tighter and laughed a little louder. "Yeah, but you're as soft as a rock, my dear."

"Thank you," she sighed when her sobbing subsided, finally releasing him. "I needed to let that out."

"I figured today would be the day you would finally give in."

She looked over the railing to stare at the sails of the Howling Death to peek at the horizon, only to notice Alister could see her approaching the rail. She quickly turned away. With her back to him, and the rest of the ship, she quickly wiped at her face.

Shit, hopefully he didn't see. At least he wouldn't have heard it, but she was sure her face was a terrible, tear-shed pink.

"Are you sure about this?" Mr Smith asked with a tone of concern.

She saw in her peripheral that he was staring at Alister with his hands folded behind his back.

She waved her hand up and down at him dismissingly. "Stop being so overprotective."

"Is this what you want to do, though? You told me you wanted to sail away from the east, but that's currently our heading."

"There's a map leading that way he wants to follow while we're in these parts."

He turned to give her a frown. "That's not what I meant, and you know it. *He* is leading us that way; are you sure that's what you want?"

"No," she laughed.

She came to the railing to stare at Alister, leaning against it with one arm folded while she rested her chin in her palm. He was looking away once more, the blistering heat had faded from her cheeks enough to know her colour was returning to normal.

"I don't know what I want. I just want to follow what feels good for once."

"He's a pirate," he said with far too much bite, and her eyes trailed back to him.

"So am I," she rebuffed.

"Yes, I know, but he may end up being just like Theodore. This could all be a façade to get goodness knows what from you."

"Then I will put a bullet in his head too." She turned back to look at Alister, who once more had his head turned to her. She gave him a wave by twinkling her fingers at him. "I'm sure he will irritate the shit out of me soon enough and we will sail away with any treasure we gain along the way."

"You're using him?" Mr Smith leaned his backside against the railing with his arms folded. "That sounds more like you."

Her answer was slow to come.

"In many ways. This means I don't have to choose our heading – since I have no idea where I want to take us. As much as I dreamed about today, I didn't really have a plan otherwise." She gave a sigh at his raised brow, like he didn't truly believe her. "I just want to feel like a real woman for once. Is that so much to ask for?"

He gave a warm, welcoming chuckle. "Not at all. I'm just making sure *you* made this decision and not coerced into it."

She gave a warm smile. "I'll never allow a man to force

me to do anything again. You should know that by now, John."

She childishly poked her tongue out at Alister, who was eight years older than her twenty-one. He just shook his head like he was disappointed in her before turning his head forward once more.

"Come, I want to see the interior of the ship and the damage his crew made to our stocks."

She moved away from the railing so she could wander below deck and take in the heart of this ship.

"I would have advised against this," Derek said to Alister while he was manning the helm.

The winds are steady today. He didn't have to put much effort into steering his ship other than keeping it on track.

"Aye, I know." He took his eye away from the horizon to peek slightly behind him at Rosetta, only to find she'd moved away from the railing of her ship. He shrugged and turned away. "I've made my decision."

"Ye know Mad Dog would never have approved of this."

"Nay, but he isn't the captain anymore."

Derek had been Captain Mad Dog's quartermaster and his first mate for most of his command. He knew the man better than anyone, even Alister.

"What happens when yer done with her? Women don't like ta be scorned, turn spiteful when they do."

Alister didn't think Rosetta would care that much when he told her he was done with her. Still, he said, "As long as she doesn't point her cannons at us, I don't care how she feels."

"What if she does?"

Alister gave a snort of laughter. "Her hull may be stronger

than ours, but we have more cannons."

He'd fight fire with fire and then hightail it away.

"What if she tries to follow?"

A strong grimace almost made him shudder with disgust. He couldn't think of anything worse!

"She won't. She's not stupid."

Derek raked his fingers over his long, scraggly beard. "The crew is worried yer going to turn soft."

With a snarl on his face, Alister grabbed Derek by the scruff of his shirt and yanked him closer. They were almost nose-to-nose as he lifted the man to the tips of his toes while his peg leg scratched at the ground.

"Then you tell those lads that they've got another thing coming. No woman will have the power to make me any less of a killer. I'm not called 'the Bloody Storm of the Seas' for nothing, and they best remember that or I'll gut them."

He tossed the man back, almost making him trip because of his unsteadiness on his wooden leg when it slipped. He couldn't believe what he was hearing about his own men!

"I'm not some land loving man," he spat, every ounce of hatred he had settling onto his features. "I have no interest in buying some house, starting a family with a woman, and living my days in peace. I plan to die with my sword in my hand and covered in another man's blood. If I so happen to look like I'm going that way, I'll put a bullet in my own head."

Derek nodded his head as if he already knew that.

"The lads want to know how long we should be expecting this arrangement, then?" Derek folded his meaty arms across his chest, familiar with Alister's angry outbursts. "They want to take advantage of this."

"Who knows?" Alister admitted. "A month? Maybe six?" He shook his head with a laugh. "I doubt it'll be longer than a year."

"What if we find the Raider's trove?" Derek gestured his

chin towards the Laughing Siren. "Do you plan to share it with them?"

He shrugged. "A small portion of it as compensation for holding supplies for us. That treasure is ours, and I won't let anyone else's greedy hands have more than I'm willing to part with." Then a wide, evil grin spread across his features. "I'm hoping we've split ways before we find it."

"Are ye actually taking us towards those maps she gave us then?"

"Oh, aye. I'm not waiting to find it. I'm just hoping she draws the short straw with the maps I choose to go to first."

"Yer a devil as always," Derek laughed with a deep bellow, stroking his beard with humour. "I didn't think we had nothin' to worry about."

"Nay, so make sure the rest of the men know that."

Alister didn't think his men would ever turn on him, but he didn't need mistrust birthing on his ship. He needed their faith in him, their loyalty.

He needed them to care for his back more than their own, and if that meant plucking out a few weeds who may be trying to birth insane ideas like he was going soft, then so be it.

I may be sweet on the lass, but I'd never give up my crew for her. His gaze spanned over it. *This is my home.*

He'd be damned if anyone took it away from him.

CHAPTER TWENTY-FOUR

It had only been nearly a month of Alister sailing next to Rosetta and the Laughing Siren, and already he was growing irritated with the woman – but for all the wrong reasons.

His men had discovered she was just as ruthless as he could be, as she kept taking them off course.

It hadn't taken them more than five days to sail to the eastern map she'd given him to find nothing there; another false lead of promises of wealth. A freaking goose chase for mad men like him to go after.

Alister often wondered if maps like these were created so pirates would be away from frequently used trading routes. So many times he had come across them, maps that led to nowhere, nothing. It meant he had seen much of the world, but it often left him frustrated, impatient.

Currently, they were heading towards the most northern lands to the location he thought looked more promising.

Rosetta turning them off-course by suddenly steering her ship often got under his skin, but the reason she was doing it wasn't what bothered him.

Her crow's nest was higher, and they were able to see a ship in the horizon better than his. A bell would be rung from her ship, the only real communication they had, and she would steer her ship towards what she wanted. She didn't care if it was a trading boat stocked with items they could raid, or if it was a fleet ship. Rosetta would turn to it and hunt it. Sometimes, Alister let ships pass when he was getting close to a location. She didn't. She had gone after two ships, but it hadn't been a waste of their time. It had just made getting to the north take a few days longer.

Both had been trading boats.

They'd raided them and left the men alive. Neither needed more crew and once they were done, they abandoned them on their nearly empty vessels.

Because of her, they'd gained enough supplies that they wouldn't have to dock into a port for quite some time. It had also gotten them some worthwhile loot they could sell once they finally did. He held all of it.

Today, though, had been different. The ship she'd headed for was a lone Queen Mary Anne fleet vessel – a large one that almost rivalled her own.

When he'd fought to raid it before it sunk, he hadn't liked seeing her walking in his peripheral, not when he was still swinging his sword to kill the last of the soldiers on board.

He watched her shoot a man in the head before she disappeared into the small navigation room. With an aggravated sigh, he cut the man in front of him from nose to navel before carefully to follow her.

She'd partially withdrawn her sword while turning to him, thinking it might have been an enemy. It wasn't the first time they'd crossed swords because they'd spooked each other. When she saw it was him, she pushed it back into its scabbard and turned back to what she was doing.

After he closed the door and walked to the desk, noticing she'd opened the drawers, he grabbed the chair behind it.

"Why is it you never stay on your ship when I tell you to?" he asked while shoving the chair under the handle of the door to prop it closed so they wouldn't be disturbed.

"Because unless I'm on your ship, you have no command over where I go." Her voice was strained as she tried to turn the wheel of the black metal safe she wanted.

It was pushed into the corner and hidden away behind cupboard doors. He could see the key already in the lock. *She must have found it in the drawer.*

She continued to make soft groaning noises as she pushed all her energy and strength into unlocking the mechanism. It looked a little old and well-used.

"I'm still a captain, and a pirate, and I won't stay on my ship to watch like some woman."Alister, with a huff, came up behind her. He grabbed the locking wheel of the safe she'd been struggling with and turned it for her with little effort. It released and she pulled it open.

"You're never on my ship for me to tell you where to go!"

Damnit! Rosetta had not once stepped foot on his ship since they set sail, refusing to leave the Laughing Siren unless they were raiding.

That was why he was growing irritated.

It was obvious he wasn't bored with her, since he often found himself climbing her hull to creep onto her ship. Like a man searching for water in the desert, he constantly sought her out to drown in her.

She never comes to me.

Yet she was happy to come here – where there were swords, guns, and the potential of being harmed. Apparently, coming to Alister's bed was too much of a task.

"I like my ship," she mumbled. "Why would I leave it?"

Not seeming to realise the danger she currently had pressed behind her or his bubbling frustration, she dipped her body into the large safe to inspect inside it.

It left her bent over, her arse pointing towards his groin. Alister placed his hands on the rim of the safe edges to lock her in instead of on her hips to pull her against him.

There was a hefty pouch of obvious coins, but other than that, there wasn't much else to loot besides papers she started going through. Most of them found their way to the floor, deemed uninteresting.

What is wrong with me? He was angry with her, found her lack of reciprocation in effort as a rejection, but the moment he was in her presence, it all faded away.

Even now, he was furious she had put herself in harm's way, but he couldn't stop himself from leaning closer to breathe in the sweet smell of her when she stood back up.

He smelt the side of her neck and her hair to take in her perfume of little white flowers. There was the scent of Rosetta behind it that seemed just as damning to him.

She smelt sweet. She smelt of woman. Sensual. Arousing. Heady in comparison to the salt of the water that constantly sloshed around them.

Maybe it was because when he did come to her, she would accept him without hesitation. There was never any reluctance or barrier to sly his way through.

If he came to her cabin to corner her, coming up with any excuse he could to be near her – whether it was to talk to her, fuck her, berate her about something – she'd be the one to suddenly bring him in for a kiss before he could utter a single word. She'd wrap her legs around his waist as if she wanted to climb him like a tree, forcing him to catch her.

She'd grip his hair and tug until his neck was strained, forcing him into deep kisses that would cause him to lose his focus just so he could get lost in her.

Why can't I get her out of my head? He didn't understand why he hadn't sailed the other way yet, considering the way she was making him feel.

He often found himself eyeing her ship to look for her. He'd grin if he found her watching him going about his duties. She often did this, go to the railing to see what he was doing.

If he turned his attention to her fully, she'd give him this twinkling wave that often made him want to abandon the helm so he could climb up the side of her ship like a desperate madman. It was like an invitation, like she was trying to tease him from afar.

His mood would sour if he couldn't see her. He didn't like it when she wasn't in his sight, like his eye was starving to get a glimpse.

With his breath fanning so close to her skin, too easy to drink in the smell of her, he said with a rumble, "You will have to come to my ship eventually."

Because Alister wanted a night of her in *his* bed, especially since he'd never had the pleasure of having her in it or waking next to her.

No, instead he had to make his way back to his ship in the middle of the night or she'd be up when the sun rose and left him alone in hers. He hated that, waking up in her bed to find it empty. It almost felt like he had to do a walk of shame to his own damn ship!

It was worse when he made eye contact with their crews along the way.

"When I'm ready," she answered absentmindedly.

She was still shuffling the papers, as though they were more important than the man currently caging her in.

"What's wrong with my ship, lass?" he asked quietly, moving a hand so he could brush her hair to the side and expose the pale skin of her neck to his attention.

"It's dark and musty, and I know that bed isn't as soft as mine."

He pressed his lips to her skin, needing to taste her almost as badly as he needed to take his next breath. She seemed to understand where his mind had gone and lowered her hands. A delighted shiver moved down her shoulders.

"Alister," she warned, but he was no longer listening.

He didn't care what she was warning him about.

I came in here to yell at her. Hell, she was arguing with him, and yet, his body couldn't seem to get enough of her.

He wanted to lash out at her, but he suddenly couldn't remember why. Why did it matter when she was here in front of him now?

It's been four days since I've touched her.

Alister had refused to go to her ship in an attempt to force her to his. He hadn't done it gracefully and often, his men received the backlash of it. Lucky for him, they didn't know the difference – he was often aggressive and rude.

For four days, he'd been holding back every single urge, every single ounce of want growing steadily by the minute. The more he turned his sight from her ship in order to reject his own ambition of climbing to her, the more frustrated he grew.

"You and I both know you only sleep in your bed if I'm in it with you."

He drew his lips over the side of her neck with another deep breath to take her in. He even nipped her. His hand came forward to slip over her shoulder and inside her tunic to grasp a breast, the other leaning against the safe.

"You sleep in that hammock." She had one strung up inside the room above her bed like he had. "Come sleep in mine if you don't like my bed."

"We can't both fit in it." Her voice was growing smaller, like her hard personality was fading to the soft one she only shared with him when he touched her just right.

He thumbed her nipple just to make her twitch in his arms.

"Sure we can." He pinched it between his thumb and index finger, letting the rest of his splayed fingertips caress the underside of her soft, creamy mound. "We'll figure it out."

She always responds to me.

He knew it, too. He knew she was overcome by whatever

had hooked inside them when she was in his presence as much as he was. Even now, he could feel her nipple had hardened under his attention. Her breathing was shaking, heavy. She even leaned against him, like her back sought his body against hers, the warmth he emitted.

So, if she still wanted him, why wouldn't she come to him?

"I don't want to leave my ship."

She broke the trance he was becoming undone by as she turned and folded her arms across her chest. She was escaping his hand that had slipped inside her tights so he could run his palm against her stomach to go lower.

He didn't know if she'd done it to be defiant or to hide those taut little nipples that were easy to see stabbing against her tunic. His sight often slipped to them, his hands itching to touch them like a beckoning call.

"Then stay on it," he bit, his nose crinkling as he placed his hand back against the safe to cage her in again. "Don't come onto the ships we raid."

"You're starting to piss me off with this, Alister." He noted the glare she gave him behind cold eyes. "Stop making me feel like I'm not worthy to help."

"And you're pissing me off by coming to this ship but not mine!" He gripped the edge of the safe with such strength, he feared he'd crush the metal under his fists.

"Why do you even care?"

"Because you could get hurt, Rosetta! You could be targeted and–"

"That's not what I mean!" She stamped her foot like she was ready to have a childish tantrum. "I already know that. I mean, why do you care which ship we're on?"

"Because you're making me feel like you don't want me, lass!" He ran one of his hands over the top of his head to brush his hair back in frustration. He couldn't believe he was admitting this. "You're making me chase you like you don't give a shit."

Alister didn't chase any woman.

They flock to me in ports! Hungry to have him. Maybe his coin too, but regardless! All he had to do was crook his finger at a woman and she would be in his lap.

But Rosetta wasn't fawning to him, nearly tripping over her feet just to have him.

He watched her brows twitch, her folded arms loosening. "But it's obvious that I do."

He freaking knew that each time he was with her. The way her hands would explore him made tremors roll through his body like he'd never been touched before, was starving for the attention. She'd place them everywhere, his chest, his arms, every scar on his body like she enjoyed the feeling of them. She'd cup his face, stroke his hair, make him feel handsome when most others made him feel like a hideous villain.

She'd grip his hair like she wanted to forever get tangled into it – she even asked him if he would let her plait it, like she wanted to play with it.

None of this stopped him from feeling the way he did when he was away from her, on his ship, alone, hoping she might come to him, as if she might *ache* for him like he did for her.

Then she didn't.

He felt like he was the only one who needed it, rather than just wanting it.

"Do I?" he sneered, grabbing her around the neck with one hand so she couldn't look away from the intensity of his gaze. He wasn't gripping her tightly, but his aggression was there, a reaction to the way he felt prodded. "Because I don't know what you truly want, what you're after."

When she squinted her eyes with suspicion at his words, he pulled her closer, so they were just a breath's distance away. He didn't appreciate that his mind immediately dropped to her puffy lips, like he wanted to take them with his own now that they were just a short distance apart.

The only reason he didn't lean in was because of the spiteful expression on her face. His thumb seemed to have a mind of its own, though, as it brushed her jawline in a caress.

"Don't look at me like that. You've lied to me and deceived me more times than I know. How am I to know the truth?"

What was her truth? Did she want him like it seemed she did when he was touching her, or didn't she by the fact she never sought him out for more? He'd once wanted her pining for it, so why was it him instead?

She's got my sail ropes in knots.

Her lips thinned into worried lines, and her eyes averted from him. His own widened.

I knew it... He didn't like the way his chest swirled with a dark emotion. *She's been lying to me.*

What about, he didn't know, and he wasn't sure if he wanted to know. His mind seized on the fact she'd been sailing with him for a month and may not have truly wanted him, but something else he had.

Is it the Raider's trove? Was she planning on trying to steal it from him all along? He released the intimate hold he had on her throat, surprised she trusted him enough to let him, and dropped his arm.

"Fine, Rosetta." He gave a dark chuckle to mask the darker emotions he felt. "You stay on your ship while you point it the other way, because I'm not changing my course."

Not with how close he was to what could be the goal he'd been seeking for years. How quickly he'd come to this decision didn't surprise him. He was just disappointed because he wasn't done, but at least it was on his terms.

"Alister, wait." She reached forward to grab his wrist gently in both hands.

He gave her a grin to show her just how little it bothered

him that he'd part from her.

Seeing his expression, and the fact he was pulling his arm away from her as he backed up, she gave a sigh. She folded her arms and turned her head to the side to dismiss him.

He reached around her to grab the pouch of coins from the safe, his chest brushing up against the backs of her arms. It brought him closer to her, and he took in once again the smell of gardenia flowers. He hated to admit that it would be one of the many things he might miss about her.

When he held the pouch, he stepped back from her. He turned while tossing it in the air, waiting for her to tell him they were supposed to split it, and then he would unfortunately have to tell her he didn't care.

"I'm afraid to leave my ship," she muttered quietly.

Well, that was unexpected.

He halted but didn't turn to the door he was only a step away from. "You say that, and yet, here you are."

"Have you not noticed it's never my original crew that helps to raid?"

His brow crinkled in a frown of thought. No, he'd never noticed that, but that's because he didn't truly care about her crew. They were her responsibility.

He looked at her from the corner of his good eye over his shoulder. "What do you mean?"

"I only ever send the men who were prisoners off my ship. I'm afraid that if we move too many of those I trust, they will try to take over my ship while we're gone, and your men are too distracted on the boat we're raiding to help."

He finally turned around and realised her dismissive posture had never been dismissive to begin with. It was defensive, as though she felt vulnerable telling him and didn't like it. It was more obvious as she spoke, her shoulders turning inward.

"I don't trust them yet, and there are too many of them to

get to know quickly. Over two-thirds of my men are people I don't know, Alister. That's why I've never come to you."

He'd like to believe her but... "Why didn't you tell me this sooner?"

"When have you asked?" She folded her arms tighter and refused to look at him, her eyes narrowing at the floor. "What happens on my ship is none of your concern, nor is it your issue. My fears could be unfounded, and I might have nothing to worry about, but currently, I have them. I haven't told anyone this; I don't want people to think I'm paranoid or crazy. I get enough of that bullshit already."

Her fears were justifiable. Her new crew were all criminals, and she had no idea the crimes they'd committed, or how terrible they could be.

"You know I'll assist you if they try."

He looked down to the pouch in his hand with uncertainty. Did she truly have such little faith in him to think he wouldn't? Did Rosetta think he was that much of a dick to the woman he was sleeping with?

"And sink the Laughing Siren at the same time?" She brought her eyes to him so he could see they were crinkled with something he'd never seen from her: fear. "I know I said I'd rather see her at the bottom of the ocean, but that was before I sailed her. I don't want to give her up now I have her." She started nibbling on the inner corner of her lips, more so the bottom one. "I'm also worried they'll kill us before we even get the chance to take it back from them."

"If you're so afraid to leave, why are you here now?"

"I know you want to keep me safe for some stupid reason, but if I do that, they will see it as a sign of weakness. They'll think I'm incapable of being a captain willing to cut throats." She narrowed her eyes and held his with a fierce gaze. "Do you know what it's like for a crew to tell you you're too 'soft' to be Captain? Do you know how many throats I've had to cut to stop that word from spreading, not because it has nothing to do with my capabilities but because I'm a woman?"

No, because Alister had never been soft. However, he didn't like the possibility of it being mentioned. Derek just telling him there was a possibility of it had him clutching him by the scruff of his tunic.

Alister finally came towards her with his brows furrowed further, his lips pressed tight together. "That's why you do it? You've been doing this even when you were on the Howling Death." *More lies?*

She lifted her finger to point at him.

"No, I didn't. After the pirate hunters, I stayed on your ship like you told me to until I thought the fighting was done." She poked him in the chest. "I didn't mean for you to get sliced that day."

"And yet, I still got cut," he chuckled, his anger lessening with every word out of her pretty little mouth.

She'd been afraid and just didn't want him to know. He'd gained her trust in many ways, but apparently, nothing deep within her mind. She'd never sought comfort from him, and he'd never tried to give it to her. Why should she have told him the truth?

"Do you think I want to get hurt? There was a reason I tricked my way onto your ship, Alister."

Once more, she folded her arms and turned her head to the side like she was dismissing him, and he now saw it for what it really was: someone trying to hide that they felt vulnerable.

How many times has she done this in front of me? So many he couldn't count, and yet he'd always fallen for the trick and dismissed her in return, rather than reaching out to her.

"I can't fight men like you. Men bigger and better than me," she admitted with shame, her shoulders slumping forward. He almost took it as a compliment.

"Aye, you're right, Rosetta." He could tell she didn't

appreciate him agreeing with her by her hands tightening into fists, but he was already opening his mouth. "You're too smart to fight a battle you know you can't win."

She brought her gaze to him, just as he carelessly dropped the pouch of coins from his hand. He heard it open and spill against the ground.

"Instead, you wrap your finger around men like me to get your way."

He crossed the small space between them and reached down to grab her by the backs of her thighs. She let out a strange, adorable squeak when he forced her to hold onto his shoulders when he picked her up.

He held her legs around his waist. She was above him, and he looked up at her with that sense-stealing breath of distance between them.

"You're far more dangerous, lass."

His words were rewarded with a small smile, her hair curtained around his face as she leaned over him. "At least you have the brains to realise that."

Apparently, he was an idiot in other ways, though.

She reached her hands up to hold the sides of his jaw and crashed her lips down onto his.

Shit. I almost walked away from her... again.

And what for? Because she wouldn't come to his ship? Because he was too unseeing to realise she'd been afraid?

He held her to him as he kissed her, allowing her to remain above him since she locked her ankles around his torso. It seemed she enjoyed towering over his massive frame for once.

"Don't think you're going to get away with the shit you just pulled," she said between kisses.

Alister winced. He could only imagine what that meant. "Then don't leave me in the dark."

She pulled her face away from his to give him an obvious glare. There wasn't any real sharpness to it, though. "Has anyone ever told you you're mighty arrogant? You could at least say you're sorry."

"That word isn't in my vocabulary."

Her glare deepened and he grinned. He stepped forward until his legs found a desk. He threw her back to it, its contents slipping off to hit the timber floor. He lay over her, bringing his lips to her throat to roughly nip it with his teeth, tongue trailing over it.

"Wait!" she half-giggled, half-yelled. "We can't do this here."

"Oh aye, we are." He started turning her over when she released her legs to get between them. She was trying to force them apart. Alister laid her front against the desk. "Just like that first time."

When he'd had her over his dinner table: the time that had started all this.

Because I still want her as much as I did then.

"And if you continue to come onto the ships we raid," he told her, his lip drawing a sensual line over the crook of her shoulder and neck. The way her skin prickled with goosebumps made him grin.

Then he shoved one hand up to grab a fistful of long hair to yank her head back. The other pulled on the ties of her tights so he could slide them down to the middle of her thighs.

"Then this is what is going to happen every time."

When she did exactly what she did last time, grinding her hips back against him, Alister let out a chuckle. *Impatient wench.*

"Would you like a knife to stab me with?" Alister asked while reaching down to unbutton his breeches as raw excitement thrummed through him. "Or would you prefer your pistol again?"

CHAPTER TWENTY-FIVE

Rosetta sat in one of the rowboats as men rowed with large oars. She turned her head back to see Alister had already reached the shore they were approaching, helping his men to pull their boat out of the water.

She had to give him that – he wasn't afraid to assist when he had to. She'd seen him heave the ropes of his sails to help if one of his men was on duty at the helm. He lifted stock if he was rearranging it to accommodate newly raided supplies.

He wasn't afraid to get his hands dirty or wet.

He rarely stopped moving.

He was always watching his crew work to make sure it was done right, would give advice to newcomers if they were unsure rather than punishing them if they did it wrong.

With a sigh, she admitted, *he's a good captain.*

Turning her head back to look in front of her, she eyed the men in front of her. Other than Naeem, she didn't know any of them. She'd done this on purpose. These were the ones who avoided her, or those she had the least interaction with.

In the five weeks since he discovered the truth she hadn't wanted to particularly share, Alister's presence on her ship had increased.

She didn't know if it was a good thing or not.

He didn't do much. He just leaned against the railing and watched her crew work like he did his own. He explained it was easy to see if someone had the idea of turning on the captain if you knew what to look for.

Apparently, there was some stray gaze to be wary of, but she'd never experienced a mutiny before, nor had a crew she didn't trust fully.

He also worked closely with Mr Smith so the prisoners were never left alone as a group without one of her original crew present. She knew he was intelligent when it came to taking down ships, but she hadn't thought he could be strategic in other ways as well.

Rosetta was working on bonding with her new crew slowly. She was speaking with her men as much as she could, despite her hesitation.

So, when they had finally reached the northern map's location, she organised to bring these ones with her in a show of faith. They wouldn't know Alister had brought his most trusted men to watch over them in case something went astray.

They'd discussed the plan before they'd gotten into their boats. She knew being cautious was the smartest thing she could do, but she had begun to see a shift over time.

The tension she'd been able to feel on her ship had lessoned as people got used to their roles and her command . Some were becoming friendly with her, and she was starting to feel more comfortable on her own ship.

Things are settling.

She didn't think she needed Alister's help, but she appreciated he'd at least tried, even though sometimes, the way he looked standing there on her ship, his arms folded, with a deadly look as he watched the men, had been a little unnerving.

He always wore this strange expression, like he was ready to reach for his pistol and shoot a man for simply sneezing. He was an ominous presence.

At times, Rosetta found him scary, especially when he was

angry. There was something about a towering, muscular man shadowing all light with each step closer, one who exuded strength and brutality, coming at her with a snarled-up face.

Sometimes, she laughed at him to hide her uncertainty, or that she was ready to reach for her own sword. Other times, she'd take his mouth with her own, which seemed to be the easiest way to melt that expression.

It really depended on where they were and what they were arguing about.

She often wondered how other men saw him, since her opinion was skewed by their relationship with each other. She'd seen men avoid him without question, refusing to be in his sight, like it could put a target on their backs.

There had been whispers circulating about the unease of sailing next to the Captain of the Howling Death. Apparently, his name was more widespread than she'd originally thought.

Then there were the rumours about her.

She'd nearly laughed her boots off and given herself a stomach-ache when one of her men told her some of the others didn't trust a woman who allowed someone like Alister to touch her. They were afraid of her because she had somehow 'tamed' him.

I hope he doesn't get wind of that. Rosetta hadn't tamed him at all. She didn't think any woman could tame Captain Alister Paine.

Still, she'd take it and wear it like a shroud of protection, since it secured her position. If they thought she was fearsome for merely opening her legs to him, then they must think she was ruthless in some way.

Despite all of this, she still refused to leave her ship unless she absolutely had to. He didn't seem to mind so much now that he'd discovered the truth and understood why.

Unfortunately, she didn't think her body could keep up with this brute's constant taking. She wished she hadn't told him so she could finally get a break for a night.

Then again, I may not be here now. She hadn't gotten him back for almost walking away. *Stupid bastard.* Not that she had ever really complained about his constant attention, since she enjoyed it every time.

She twirled a clump of hair in thought. *That man has got something over me.* Something that had her gripping him almost every night in earnest. Something that had her nails digging into him so he couldn't escape before she was ready for him to return to his ship. Something that had her waiting for him if he hadn't come to her throughout the day.

Rosetta refused to let him know just how badly she craved him. She wouldn't reveal she had an appetite that perhaps her body couldn't keep up with, that she just never seemed to be satisfied, to the point where she wondered if she just wanted him to break her beyond repair.

He was arrogant, mean, overbearing. Sometimes, he gripped her body so hard it hurt; sometimes, he grabbed her throat possessively that she struggled to breathe, and yet her body thrummed more because of it rather than being hateful.

He was always rough, and it allowed her to be as feral as she wanted. She bit him, scratched him, tugged on his hair as hard as he did hers, and not once had he told her to stop.

I should end this. Before he became permanently imprinted on her body.

The last thing Rosetta needed was to one day end things and ache for him to the point where she couldn't be satisfied by another.

I won't let any man have that kind of power over me.

Still, she hadn't liked when he tried to walk away. She didn't like the way it felt, how her hands had reached for him without her consent. She had reached for him like some woman begging for a man not to leave her! How pathetic!

She thought perhaps it was because of the reason why he

was walking away.

Rosetta, for some stupid reason, hadn't wanted him to think she didn't desire him. She didn't want her inability to tell him the truth to be the reason this ended too soon.

It should be because one of us is done with the other. She had a feeling it would be him first.

She pretended she didn't care, but she couldn't deny to herself the way things between them clutched at her. Which meant Rosetta needed to start drawing away, to prepare herself. Her heart was already closed off, she'd made certain of it, but she needed her body to get over him before it had to.

Then again, I can just use port boys to forget. She almost laughed to herself. Now didn't that just sound like a stupendous idea.

When the bow of the rowboat hit the bank of sand, it broke her out of her thoughts. They hopped out to lift and carry it away, their feet sinking in the wet sand as water kicked up around their feet.

Once it was secure so it wouldn't float away, she turned around to find that Alister had already started to walk ahead. He was leaving her behind! *Arsehole, we're supposed to be doing this together!*

Rosetta chased after Alister with Naeem in tow.

The rest of the men stayed behind with the rowboats next to Alister's men. They weren't ranked highly enough to be a part of this.

The small cape of shore they landed on was surrounded by unclimbable cliffs that towered above them in a semi-circle. This was a small area covered in trees, grass, overgrown shrubs, and sand – always sand. It rolled onto a large mass of land part of the large country of Polytuik.

They had been hesitant about coming here, since it wasn't a safe place for criminals like themselves and had a strong alliance with Banksia, Queen Mary Anne's country.

The only reason they did is because they could tell it was cut off from the rest. The cliff edge meant the likelihood of encountering anyone was low. It was a coastal area, completely secluded.

She could see a small waterfall sprinkling water down, probably to a river or lake that would eventually wash out to the sea.

"Hey! You could have waited for us."

Alister didn't greet her, like he didn't care or hadn't heard her, too fixated on his task. He was searching for a particular tree, looking for a special marking.

When he found it, he started taking large, long steps with a face that told them not to disturb his deep train of thought. He was most likely counting how many steps he was taking and making sure they were in the right direction. He was calculating everything.

Pierre and Derek were holding two shovels each. She thought that was strange, considering the Raider's trove was apparently a cave, no digging required.

She was surprised Derek's peg leg wasn't sinking into the soft ground with every heavy stomp he took.

Blowing a curl of her hair out of her face in agitation – Rosetta hated running – she leaned closer to Pierre. "Why do you have shovels?"

He leaned closer to her to talk back just as quietly, likely worried about disturbing Alister. "Usually when we don't find it, we sometimes find something else. Nothing worse than having to row back to the ship for a shovel to dig."

Rosetta placed her hand over her chin and lips in thought, nodding her head to say she understood. "Do you think there is something here?"

They ventured further through the brush and tall trees with no branches except high above to umbrella them. Seagulls and other coastal birds squawked and chirped while bugs made screaming buzzing sounds. This was the perfect damp yet warm environment for mosquitos, and she had her hand ready to strike if they came to drink from her.

"Oh aye," Pierre answered, a grand smile spreading. "There're markings. If someone else hasn't found it, then there will be something for us."

He put his arm around her shoulders and pointed to Alister in front, leading them. He annoyingly placed most of his weight on her. "And he wouldn't look so serious if he didn't feel it deep in his bones. You can see it, can't you? He knows there's something here."

Rosetta let her eyes drift over him in a more assessing way than before.

His pace was slow, like he was taking extra care to be certain of where they went and how far his steps were. His eyes were narrowed while his dark brows knotted tightly with concentration. His lips were thinned and slightly pursed, his good eye fixed only on what was in front of him. He didn't even brush strands of his messy hair from his face when the wind blew them astray.

One of his hands was rubbing the long stubble on his face. She even thought his thumb was brushing over the bottom of the scar that ran under his eyepatch.

He does look rather determined.

Her gaze stayed fixed on his eyepatch. Rosetta had never seen under it.

On the odd occasion she would try to reach up so she could lift it, he would, what he thought was sneakily, evade her.

He never took it off in her presence, not when they were being intimate, not when he fell asleep next to her – she couldn't even lift it then, because he'd awaken if she touched his face.

What is under there he is so concerned about me seeing?

It made her more curious by the day. She wondered if she

would ever find out.

Alister stopped, looked at the map in his hand, and started to search around a group of trees. When he found another marking, he took them in a different direction.

"This isn't the Raider's trove," Alister finally concluded, pulling the map away from his sight and shoving it in his pocket.

Now that he was willing to talk, Rosetta came up beside him. "How can you tell?"

He pointed at the cliff wall to their left. "It doesn't lead to there, to a cave." Then he shouted to those behind him by dipping his head back. "Looks like you'll be digging, lads."

"Aye, Cap'in," Derek answered, while Pierre just groaned.

Alister's intuition was spot on. Not even five minutes later, they stopped in front of a small boulder etched with a cross.

Pierre threw one of the shovels at Naeem, who hadn't been paying attention and got smacked in the torso. He let out a surprised grunt.

"You'll be helping."

"Ah yes, get the black man to do labour," Naeem chuckled. "Sounds about right."

"Then you should be good at it," Pierre winked back.

Rosetta scrunched her nose at Pierre's comment. She'd gutted men for less. She didn't like anyone being discriminatory to Naeem, her dearest companion, in the same way Naeem had beaten men who had made cruel comments about Rosetta being a woman.

"Shut up, you pissy dick white boy." Naeem reached forward and patted the man on the shoulder as they walked closer to the boulder. "You've got a pretty face, but I bet women are more satisfied after me."

"Ho ho! Then whip it out, laddie, and we can compare."

Laughter rang from them both as Derek silently walked with them.

Rosetta had noticed the two men, in their mid-twenties, had somehow bonded over the months. It'd started when she was still on the Howling Death, hunting for the Laughing Siren.

They were forced to interact, considering they were their first men.

They often picked on each other for things they would punch another person for commenting on. It was a common trait between them, jostling and harassing people for things they couldn't change or help.

They were both terrible bullies.

It was generally done in jest, but most didn't appreciate having parts of themselves commented upon, like their weight, their height, their skin colour, their age, especially with Alister's men missing parts of themselves.

They started digging while Derek handed Alister the last shovel, and then all four of them were throwing dirt to the side. It flung around carelessly.

She looked down at her empty hands.

"What do you want me to do then? You only brought four."

Alister looked up at her, frowning a little in confusion, as though the answer should have been obvious. "Stand there and look elegant. Let us do the digging."

With an irritated huff, she folded her arms over her chest and stepped out of the way of flinging dirt.

"I'm never elegant."

A chuckle fell from all of them.

"Aye, I know that, lass."

"Sing us a tune, my sweet Rose," Pierre said with extended notes, like he might start singing a ballad. He put a hand over his heart while lifting the other forward.

Although he still made charming remarks like this, she'd realised long ago that he and Alister's men no longer tried to get into her pants. Pierre was the only one who still did it in jest, but even she knew that's what it was – a joke.

"You don't want her to do that," Naeem commented with a shake of his head. "You'll regret it."

"Why?" Pierre asked with much sincerity. "I bet she has a lovely voice."

"Dig, you lazy dog!" Derek yelled at Pierre, since he'd stopped completely.

To assist, Naeem backhanded the blond across the back of the head. Pierre winced.

"She sounds like a drowning cat," Naeem finally said. Then he frowned after flinging a spade full of dirt behind him, deep in thought. "Actually, I think a drowning cat would sound more pleasurable."

It might be because Rosetta had never sung softly. She often belted out lyrics on purpose to sound like she wanted to kill men with nothing but her voice.

"Is there anything she can do well?" Pierre asked. "I still think she broke my toes while dancing."

"Cooking," Naeem answered.

Alister's gaze turned up to her with a mischievous smirk. She rolled her eyes at him, and where his obvious thoughts were.

Horny bastard.

"How does a noblewoman learn how to cook?" Derek threw in. "Doesn't sound normal to me."

Her narrowed gaze fell to Alister, who was paying too much attention to the knee-deep hole to notice. She wasn't particularly angry at him; she just resented more people knowing about her history than she was comfortable with.

He'd obviously told Derek and Pierre about her past without her consent. She wasn't pleased about that.

"One who had nothing else to do in a mansion but be bored. I used to help in the kitchen when I was child, since my mother cooked, and then I helped the maids when I was older."

Pierre opened his mouth with his head turned to her,

probably to ask her more questions.

Alister quickly cut in. "Enough talk. Dig," he demanded.

She wondered if he'd saved her from being bombarded by questions on purpose. Then his eye darted up to her face for a second with a serious look, showing he had. She gave him an appreciative smile, and he looked back down once more.

When they were nearly hip height into the hole, one of them slammed their shovel in and a subtle boom echoed. They dug around what they found.

Naeem and Derek climbed out of the hole to reach for the medium-sized, wooden chest as Alister and Pierre started to lift it out. They placed it next to the hole.

Covered in dirt, like it had been sitting beneath the earth for over fifty years, the chest was medium in size, no larger than a man's torso. Rosetta had been hoping it was bigger.

But at least it isn't small.

Rosetta came forward to watch Pierre bash repeatedly at the rusted lock with his shovel. Each hit shook off a little more dirt from the chest, revealing more of its design. The lock eventually broke, and he stepped out of the way so Alister could kneel and slowly open it.

They all peeked over his shoulders to see what would be revealed.

Inside were coins of silver, bronze, and gold, with an occasional piece of jewellery, like a necklace or bracelet.

"Aye. How's that for booty, lass?" The grin Alister gave her was smug. "Glad you stuck with me now?"

"I don't stay around men for coin, Alister. Otherwise, I would have never left Luxor." She gave him a dull expression. "The duchy treasury was massive compared to this."

Her lips curled at the scowl he gave. *But it's the truth.*

Theodore may have been a cruel man, but he had so much wealth, she could have asked for anything, and he could have provided it. Any whim, any request. A gold-plated horse carriage, a thousand doves.

Rosetta had tried to play a game of what ridiculous thing could she ask for before he said it was impossible. He never did, but he often told her no simply because it was ridiculous.

"You sure know how to make a man who just became rich feel poor." He shook his head, digging his fingers into the coins like he wanted to make sure they were real. "The crew will be pleased to finally have some wages."

"Aye, they will," Derek confirmed.

"Both crews," she said, crouching down to reach inside and grab a handful of coins.

There were more silvers than anything else, which took her by surprise. *I thought most chests were filled with gold.*

Alister gave her a strange look, one that screamed greed. It was obvious the idea of sharing it wasn't favourable to him.

Still, he said, very slowly like the words were forced from him, "Half each."

"My crew is bigger!" she exclaimed. "I have more men to pay."

"Half, Rosetta." The deep tone he gave told her he wouldn't budge.

She threw the coins back in the chest. "Fine."

They closed the lid. Naeem and Pierre were the ones instructed to carry the heavy thing back to the beach. While they struggled, Derek walked behind them with two shovels in each hand, watching them closely, as though he wanted to make sure they did a proper job of it.

Rosetta had long ago realised Derek was judgemental and liked to berate Pierre for even the slightest wrongdoing. Considering it was those two together though, they probably would find a way to mess up carrying a simple, yet weighty, chest.

She fell back to walk beside Alister who was also holding two shovels as well.

"Thank you," she muttered quietly, watching where she was going instead of looking towards him. She had her hands clasped behind her back. "I don't like sharing my history."

"Aye." In the corner of her eye, she could see he was nodding. "It's none of their business."

She pursed her lips into an irritated pout. "Then why did you tell them?"

She watched as Pierre and Naeem started pulling the chest in opposite directions to make each other trip in jest. Derek rose the shovels above his head and threatened to beat them to death if they didn't stop.

"It was better if they knew some of the truth." When he turned his head to her, she turned hers slightly towards him to make sure he understood he had her attention. "I trust them. They're good men. They won't share that information, nor will they truly care what you've done. They only care about what you do now."

"Calling a criminal a good man is an oxymoron, Alister," she laughed lightly.

He returned it just as soft. "Aye, but they're good to my crew... and yours now."

"And what about you?" She already knew the answer; she just wanted to know what he thought about himself.

He looked ahead and away, his expression turning stern and thoughtful.

"Hmm. When I must." His response made it seem like he didn't always want to be a good man – even to his own men. "I value my crew. I treat those who earn it with the respect they deserve."

He lifted his hand so he could grab a few locks of her hair as they walked. He started tangling them around his digits, as if he wanted to become ensnared.

"I am neither a good man, nor a bad man. I take what I want, I steal what I want, and I kill who I want. There are those

I do not feel the need to needlessly kill, those smart enough to surrender to me. It is never mercy, since I've often stolen all the supplies they need to survive, but it means I give them the chance. It's often because I just don't see the point."

Gently, he eventually lifted his hand to his face to take a quiet, yet sweet, sniff of her hair. Feeling the strands lifted, hearing him want to take in the smell of her, as though he couldn't help himself, made her stomach clench.

Her skin even prickled on her neck.

How could one simple gesture have her eyes searching for the perfect place to hide, or a boulder at hip level so he could bend her over it?

"Then I am neither a good woman, nor a bad one," she stated back, turning her face to the side to give him an impish smile. "I kill because I have to, not because I want to."

"Aye, that I know of," he chuckled, releasing her hair and giving her a wicked grin. "You're just like me, lass. Cold-blooded."

Even though they were almost shoulder to shoulder and walking rather intimately next to each other, he didn't step away from her when they saw their men.

Cheers rung out from them all, sitting around in the sand, when they came into view. Alister pointed at four of her eight men.

"You lot – you're riding back with my men." He pointed at her rowboat. "Put the chest in her boat."

Everyone shared a look of uncertainty between each other before doing as he commanded.

"I don't understand." She came up beside him when he started to help her men push her boat into the water.

"You want half? You're going to work for it."

He hopped inside, and she realised he was intending to go with it, and her, to the Laughing Siren.

CHAPTER TWENTY-SIX

Rosetta was forced to turn her back to the men in the boat when Alister sat at the very head. He folded his arms and leaned into the corner, eyeing her and the chest between them.

She was sure he was carefully watching her back, too. He was pleased by today's spoils, but he didn't wear a smug smile.

"I think I've worked enough for it." She patted the top of the dirty chest. "I'm the reason you had the map."

"You're going to help me count it."

He squinted his eye at her when her lips pursed into thin lines of irritation.

She leaned as far forward as she could so the men behind her wouldn't hear her whisper. "You know I can't."

"Oh aye, and I know why."

She gulped. She didn't like the sound of that. Rosetta mulled over what it could possibly mean as they slowly rowed to her ship.

They climbed up the rope ladder rolled down the side of the hull while men pulled the boat, the chest sitting inside, to the main deck. The bustle of excitement was instant the moment all eyes fell on their booty.

"Move," Alister demanded to the crowd as he took one handle while Naeem took the other. "You'll get your spoils once we've gone through it."

They carried it up to the navigation room. He dropped it in the middle of the circular blue rug in the centre and told Naeem to leave. He started going through the drawers of her desk before pilfering the many cabinets and draws fixed to the walls.

"I knew there'd be one of these in here." He pulled a magnifying glass and a jewellery loupe – a small magnifying piece that sat in the socket of a person's eye – and placed them on the desk.

Her navigation room was brightly lit, since the back wall was almost completely covered in windows. The room was semi-circular in shape, with two doors on either side that led to sleeping cabins; hers, and one unoccupied since it had belonged to Theodore – she still hadn't stepped inside.

"Why are you doing this here?" she asked when he dragged the chest next to the desk and took the seat behind it.

It dragged across the floor with a sharp scraping noise that made her wince. *My poor flooring.*

"Because you don't like being off your ship for long periods of time." He opened the chest and pulled a jewelled necklace from it. "And we're going to be here a while."

He placed the jewellery loupe to his good eye and started checking the quality of the stones, lifting the magnifying glass up to further check when he needed to.

Knowing he was right, Rosetta grabbed a chair from a different, smaller desk that would have belonged to the first officer and brought it to the wrong side of the desk than she should be at. *He's in my bloody seat.*

She plopped herself down, put one knee on top of the other, folded her arms, and watched him.

He has many skills. Not once had she seen Alister be presented with a task he couldn't complete. He was smart in his own way. Not cunning like she was, but if Alister wanted something, whether it was a ship or a task done, he always knew the best way to go about getting it.

Except for her.

Sometimes, he was exactly how he needed to be to make her melt into a useless puddle. He was never gentle, but his large hands could turn her body into putty. His words, his deep, gruff, growly-like voice, set her spirit alight to the point she wanted to burn him with the flames he ignited.

Other times, he was so off the mark, she thought he was the biggest idiot to ever be born into the cosmos.

This moment was one of those times.

"Well?" he asked, never lowering the loupe.

She didn't know how he could see she wasn't doing anything. He was blind in one eye and probably couldn't see she wasn't doing anything because of the tool in the other.

Her voice raised an octave in pure, unimaginable disbelief at his stupidity. "You know I can't count!"

"Because you refuse to learn."

"That's not true." She kicked her foot up and down, making it sway. "Mr Smith has been teaching me."

"Trying. You refuse to learn from him."

He put down the necklace and blindly reached into the chest to feel for a different piece of jewellery. Once he had one, he started inspecting it as well.

"That's not true," she rebuffed once more.

He gave a dark laugh. "Don't lie to me, lass. I've spoken with him, and he's told me you refuse to listen."

"What does it matter if I don't want to?" She turned her head to the side. "I have him to do the math for me."

It was all just so... boring, numbers and counting. Rosetta couldn't think of anything worse. She could count to twenty, but then she got lost and confused, embarrassed every time she got it wrong.

"He won't be around forever. You need to be able to do this if you want to be a good captain."

"Naeem can count." He couldn't read too well, but he'd learned enough math from Mr Smith to take over his duties.

"And what if they are both gone?"

A spike lanced her chest and twisted her gut.

"I–I'll, uh, find someone else."

"Someone you can trust with all the information?" He turned his head up, looking at her through the eye tool. "Or would you prefer to leave yourself open to getting robbed literally right in front of your very own eyes and not know it?"

"You're such a bastard sometimes." Her voice was disappointed and defeated.

"That I am. I didn't get my reputation by being kind."

With a sigh, Rosetta took herself from the chair and knelt next to the chest. "What do you want me to do?"

"You can start by going through all the coins and separating them into groups. I noticed there were different kinds from different countries. They're all worth different amounts depending on where they're from because of their purity and their size. The bronze all seems to be the same."

Sitting on the floor since it would have the most amount of space, Rosetta started doing just that.

Since there wasn't a lot of jewellery, Alister eventually joined her, helping her go through it all. By the end, they had separated everything into six different piles: two of bronze, three of silvers, and one of gold.

"You can do the silvers; I'll do the rest."

Rosetta sat with her legs spread with piles between them and on either side of her. Alister moved to make himself comfortable by laying on his side, starting by counting the smaller bronze coins.

"H-how am I supposed to do that?" The number of silvers seemed daunting to her.

"Put them into stacks of ten, and then put those stacks into groups of ten."

She tightened her lips inwardly. "Well, that doesn't seem so hard."

Alister looked up to her with a grin. "Aye, it's not. You've gotta have a little more faith in me, lass. I wouldn't make you do something I didn't think you were capable of doing."

Some of her apprehension lessened and she gave him a half-hearted smile. She started doing as she was told. He made sure she knew how to count to ten first by making her do it out loud the first time. He was done long before her, and eventually started to help.

Then came the hard part. She had to calculate how many silvers they had by their large groups of stacks of tens, in groups of tens.

Her eyes fell to him as he explained it. He didn't seem bothered he was doing this for her, that she kept making mistakes – especially when they starting bringing the total worth together. Not once did he wear a look of humour or snort with laughter.

She half-expected Alister to make fun of her. Instead, he made sure she understood the math before moving onto the next puzzle. He often pointed to the piles between them and circled his finger around them.

Eventually, everything had been halved, despite the occasional odd number of coins. He placed his half back into the chest to take to his ship later. Hers remained on the floor so she could eventually put it in the safe.

He held her gaze with a knowing stare when they were done, one side of his lips curled upwards in a smirk. "There. Now you can't say I stole more for myself."

"Wait." She looked around at her piles. "So, it wasn't just to make me learn?"

"Nay," he chuckled. "Didn't trust that you wouldn't say I tried to cheat you out of some of it."

Then He started pouring a handful of coins from one hand

into the palm of the other, making them clink together. Once the hand above was empty, he grabbed what he'd dropped to do it again.

Well shit, Alister knew her well enough to know she would have done exactly that.

"Plus, counting chest loot is fun. I don't get to do it often, but it's one of my favourite activities." He looked at the coins in his hands instead of her, almost like he couldn't meet her eyes, as he murmured, "Wanted to watch you do it with me."

A slight feeling of warmth spread across her cheeks, and she chose to believe it was because of a sudden hit of arousal rather than a small blush of tenderness from his words.

He'd never said anything that sweet to her before.

What is it with this man and the way he makes me feel?!

He was being... considerate, *nice*, more so than usual. It was getting her body in all kinds of disarray.

Rosetta almost launched herself, crawling above him to straddle his waist. She brought her lips to his, needing to shut this bastard up with her tongue before he said something even sweeter.

"Oi," he chuckled beneath her lips, half-kissing her back, half-trying to talk. "We're going to have to count those again so we can get it to your men."

"Okay," she answered, a tiny moan following it, clutching the scruff of his tunic to keep him to her. She pulled on it to the point she thought she may rip it in her swelling need. "Sounds good. Whatever you want."

She didn't care what she had to do, not when right then, in that moment, she needed this big, annoying brute inside her more than anything.

Alister turned them over, spreading more of the neatly placed coins around as he carelessly laid her down. Cold coins pressed into her bare back when he yanked her tunic from her tights and off her body to reveal her breasts, making her back arch away from the floor, precariously into him.

She could even feel her hair getting tangled in the coins around her head when he pressed his hips between her spread thighs and gave a deep thrust. They clinked and clanked against each other as the pile slipped more around her. She thought it sounded how she always imagined glitter would sound like, almost sparkling.

Then his lips and tongue were on hers with such force and heat, Rosetta thought she might turn into a puddle beneath him.

I've never been taken over a pile of money before. She knew that was what was about to happen. A grin crossed her kissing lips, unable to stop herself from curling them. He leant to the side on one elbow to keep his weight off her.

Because of his hungry kisses, Rosetta hadn't realised that Alister had undone the ties to her tights until she felt his warm hand dipping into them. Her stomach dipped beneath his calloused, caressing palm, knowing exactly where the descending touch was going.

Her hands shot forward, grabbing the rim of his tunic to pull it up and off his body. A spark of pleasure shot through her when his fingers found her folds and the tips of them pressed against the nub of her aching clit.

But there was a place her body wanted to be touched more, and when she realised he intended to circle his fingers and tease her, Rosetta bucked her hips forward. She wanted them lower.

He wouldn't.

When she bucked her hips a second time, she noticed his hand followed her movements. He stayed with her clit, slipping over it and using the wetness of her arousal to play with it. A soft moan fell from her because it felt wonderful, but it only increased her need.

Warm chuckles came from him as he parted from their kiss

to brush the side of her face and down her neck with his stubble. She felt his breath roll over her scalp near her ear, sending a shiver of goosebumps crawling over her skin, making the hairs stand on end.

"You're wetter than usual, lass." He spoke softly with his lips against the curl of her ear, humour rumbling from him. "What's got you all riled up?"

The flush of her arousal hid the heat of embarrassment that rose underneath her skin. She would never admit to Alister it was because of his stupid, sweet words that may not have been intended to be so in the first place.

"Just shut up and put your fingers in me." She wished she could eat her own words with how heavy and husky her voice sounded. It gave away completely that Rosetta was aching for him to touch her.

Her hands clung to his back when he finally drew them down, her nails already digging into his skin. *Yes!* Her mind screamed when he prodded her entrance, when she noticed herself just how wet that pool was.

"In here?" He pressed the tips of two fingers inside.

A broken mew came from her in answer, and she tried to spread her thighs wider for him, that small amount of pressure already perfect.

He pulled them away with a chuckle, pressing against her clit again, and her lips parted in disbelief.

Screw this. Two can play at this game.

Rosetta's hands shot forward to undo the buttons of his breeches. If he was going to tease her, then she would do it back.

She pulled his cock from its confines, and her pussy immediately clenched when she felt how hard he was, like warm stone under her palm. That pool at her core grew she used all her restraint to stop from squirming. Now that she was holding it, her body was literally *weeping* for it.

"It seems like you need my cock, Rosetta."

Her body shivered for a moment underneath him when he stroked his tongue just below her ear, especially when it was accompanied by his words and his fingers swirling her throbbing nub.

"N–No."

"Why do you always lie?" he chuckled, slipping his fingers down just enough to take some of her wetness and push it up her folds, showing he had proof. "You're wetter than you were before."

She didn't answer him, couldn't answer him, when she looked down and stroked her hand over his cock. The girth of it was calling to her body, begging for him to spread her, stretch her.

Her inner walls wanted to take its velvety texture and glove it in wetness. It desperately wanted that wide, broad, and flared head prodding so deep, she knew she'd feel it later, once she'd finished screaming.

She stroked her hand, gripping tighter around the head when she pushed down. She received a small, breathy groan in return, but she wanted Alister shuddering, to get him back for playing with her, denying her.

"It's not going to work," he said, spreading his fingers around her folds. "Your hand doesn't feel as good as your pussy does."

A gasp broke from her when he suddenly slipped his fingers down to push two inside her. Her core clamped around them when she felt his rings at her entrance, almost as if it was trying to suck them in deeper, when she could feel he was as deep as he could get them.

The question of why he pushed them inside her when he said her teasing wasn't going to work was answered when he started moving them.

"Do you want me to fuck you, Rosetta?" Her hand slipped

"Now, open your mouth." He started drawing her closer to his flaccid cock. "You're going to make me hard again and then I'm going to fill your mouth with my seed." He twisted his head, his grin growing mischievous and malevolent at the same time. "And this time, you're going to drink it."

With no way to escape, her eyes turned to his cock, covered in her multiple orgasms.

Oh shit, what have I done?

CHAPTER
TWENTY-SEVEN

Alister wiped the water dripping from his face with his hand, blinking rapidly to disperse it from his eye so he could see where his ship was heading. His long hair was stuck to his skin, drenched and heavy as it wrapped around his neck and face. With a steady stance, his well-worn boots slipped back an inch whenever he tried to brace himself to steer.

He knew calling out commands from his position was near pointless. He doubted anyone would be able to hear him. He would just have to have faith Pierre was leading the crew while he was otherwise occupied with a more dangerous and turmoil battle.

For three days, the drenching rain had poured on them.

Below deck, men were trying to pour out the water that had gotten in. They used mops and buckets and whatever else they could find to carry it to the surface and dump it back into the sea where it belonged.

Others were making sure all the stock and cargo was still where it was supposed to be by strapping it down, working to make sure everything that needed to remain dry was covered and up off the ground.

The Laughing Siren was still next to his ship. Although the rain had been constant, the winds had mostly been light – meaning they could remain close by.

The occasional harsh wind would cut through his sails and rock his ship to the side but, other than having to turn the wheel to right it occasionally, things had been easy. It was nothing he and his men couldn't handle. They were experienced sailors and had flown across the waters in storms worse than this.

That was until this afternoon.

A gale of wind blew, right before the first large wave hit the side of the hull and tried to knock him towards the Laughing Siren.

"The storm is worsening!" Alister yelled over the roar of the rain hitting the timber of his deck, doubtful anyone was able to hear him.

His ship was lighter and therefore slowed down when wind tried to push them back. Rosetta's started to creep up beside him, heavier and able to take the harsh winds and waves better.

He peeked back to see Naeem at the helm, trying to control the growing storm. He couldn't see Rosetta.

Good, she's inside. She was the last thing he needed to worry about right now. He had other problems on his mind. He didn't need her making him think she was truly insane by trying to brave the terrible and dangerous weather.

"Cap'in, we need to start moving away from the Laughing Siren."

"Get inside, man!" Alister yelled, swiping his arm to the side at Derek, who was running up the stairs.

As much as the old salt was one of his best men, his peg leg made him near useless in the rain. It didn't have enough grip and he'd seen Derek slip too many times in the past. The man was destined to die with a sword through his belly, not because he slipped and washed into the ocean.

When it didn't seem like he was going to do as he commanded, Alister yelled, "NOW!"

He wasn't going to lose anyone simply because they wanted to fight a storm when they couldn't. He wouldn't waste his time with foolishness.

I know we need to move away. But they needed to communicate with it first.

"Pierre!" When the man couldn't hear him, he yelled as loudly as his lungs would allow him on a bellow, "PIERRE!"

Alister saw him turn to face his call from below deck, managing to hear his voice. He was heaving on a sail rope with multiple others.

Someone took over what he was doing so he could run up the stairs, nearly barrelling into Derek, who was trying to climb down them.

"Go to the Laughing Siren," he said when he was next to the helm, holding onto the railing of this deck to stay steady. "Tell them to meet us at the Kannas Islands."

He knew from the last time he'd looked at a map that they weren't too far from those islands. There was a cape they could use to shelter from the worst of the storm. As much as he wanted to keep moving forward, it seemed they needed to wait this out.

Currently, they were heading west and had been for two weeks. Not wanting to go south yet to follow the last map he had, he was going to the other map locations he'd been given that weren't of the famous loot he was after.

"She won't listen to me, Alister," Pierre said with a shake of his head.

"Aye, she will." He righted the wheel when a wave tried to steer his course. They weren't too bad yet; they still had time to deliver the message. "She's already inside. She knows how bad this is getting."

She's smart. She would have to know she can't help.

"No, she's not."

That made his eyes widen. He snapped his head to the side

to see her pushing Naeem out of the way and taking the wheel.

"She can't!"

Even Alister knew he was going to struggle through this storm, and he had three times the muscle as her! He could see how bad it was going to get; it wasn't his first storm like this. It was going to be a strain even on him.

She pointed forward, telling Naeem to do something. He was just as shocked to see him falling away from the wheel and doing what she commanded. The man abandoned her to take care of the helm by herself.

Every curse Alister knew fell from his mouth.

He hopelessly looked at the wheel in his hands, the way he was gripping the handles with tanned knuckles threatening to turn white. *Damn her to hell!*

"Take the helm!" He waited for Pierre to take it from his hands before letting go. "Steer it closer."

It has to be me. She won't listen to anyone else.

Hell, she barely fucking listened to him, but hopefully, he could knock some sense into her for once.

"What do you want me to do if you can't make it back?"

"Kannas Islands. Wait for me there." He started making his way to the steps. "But I'll be back." He wouldn't abandon his ship when it needed him the most.

Alister started climbing the shrouds so he could get up to the top level of his sailings. One wrong foot and he could find himself crashing into the waves.

He found the rope he needed, waited for the perfect moment, and swung over. The wet rope slipped through his calloused hands as he slid down when he knew he'd swung far enough.

Alister's feet found the main deck of the Laughing Siren, and he immediately started sprinting for her.

Just in time, too.

A large wave knocked into the side of the hull and the

wheel gave a punch of a turn, knocking her off her feet. She went sliding to the floor as the wheel began to spin out of control. Alister grabbed the handles and righted it before any real damage could be done to their course. Thankfully, it had been heading away from the Howling Death rather than towards it.

Rosetta got to her feet and tried to barge him out of the way with her shoulder.

"Move!" she exclaimed, trying to take the handles from him with her smaller hands.

"Get below deck!" When he wouldn't move, she pushed him hard, just as the boat swayed and he was forced to back off. "Do as you're told for once! You can't man through this."

"I don't need your help!" He watched her struggle to fight the wheel but managed to hold it straight. Her face was tight with tension. "I know what I'm doing."

When it started to win in its tug of war with her, and a long-winded grunt of effort came from her, Alister reached forward to help her steady it.

"Nay. You don't." If she did, she wouldn't be here trying to do this when it was obvious that she couldn't.

"I'm getting real sick of your shit, Alister." She turned her head to him with her teeth clenched tight. "Go back to your own ship and get it the hell away from mine before we get tangled!"

Every second that passed brought stronger and stronger winds, bigger and bigger waves. Alister was running out of time to return before Pierre was forced to steer away. He shouldn't be wasting his time arguing with a stubborn woman! He didn't want to be doing this.

"Where is Mr Smith?" *Why isn't he here to talk some sense into her?*

Alister was aware Naeem did whatever she told him to without considering anything else. Without question, he followed her so obediently that it was prideful, but Mr Smith didn't. He often advised her to take different choices. Smarter ones. Safer ones.

"He's in his cabin. He can't help through this, he's too old."

She had the intelligence to know that, and yet she was still out here in the rain like a madwoman.

"Rosetta," he started with a warning in his tone, but she turned her head to him so sharply with a spiteful frown of her brows, it quietened him.

It didn't stop him from returning her glare, though.

"I get that you want to help but I know what I'm doing. I don't want your help, Alister." She stepped forward, closer to him so she could scream only a few inches from his face. "I was a captain before I met you, and I'll be one long after you're gone from my life!"

The way she yelled those words at him, with the face she wore, made something lance his gut.

"Move!" someone yelled next to him, yanking on his shoulder to get him out of the way.

The shock he felt because of what she'd said to him was the only reason he stumbled back. Naeem got between them and started hooking something around her waist.

Are those... cannon grenades?

Rosetta looked down to what he'd clipped around her waist and threw her head back to bellow out a laugh. "Are you trying to blow me up?"

"I couldn't find it!" he shouted with panic. "Had to improvise."

"It'll have to bloody do then, won't it?"

Alister watched Naeem take over the helm as Rosetta fell away. She leaned down and picked up a length of rope that was wrapped around the support and tied it around Naeem's waist for him.

"I want you stuck to this helm, got it?"

"Aye, captain."

She ran to the quarterdeck railing.

"Abrasive actions, boys! Secure your lifelines! If I find out even one of you fell into the ocean, I'll hunt you down and drown you myself!"

Like they hadn't realised they could need it, men started running towards the main mast of the ship to tie rope around their waists to secure themselves.

"Bury the hatchet! Anyone below deck is stuck down there for now."

She started stomping past Alister with the intention to walk down the stairs to the main deck, but he grabbed her arm to stop her.

"Head to the Kannas Islands. We're going to seek shelter from the storm."

She turned to him, ripped her arm from his grasp, and stepped forward to be closer. "My ship can't go that way! She's too deep. Go to the Grutten Valley."

The Grutten Valley was similar but wider; it wouldn't shelter them as well. Kannas Islands had taller rock formations in its crescent moon shape, which would give them as much calm as they could get with this kind of storm. *Why would she choose to go to-* It clicked with Alister.

"The shallows," he said with a gasp of realisation. He hadn't thought about them because it wasn't an issue for his shallow hull boat.

"Aye, lad," she sneered. "The shallows. Your ship can navigate through that cape in a storm like this, mine can't. Now go back to your own ship!"

Rosetta sprinted away before he could say anything else.

She tied a lifeline to her waist and started shouting orders from the main deck to her men. Her voice reached them all, even with all the noise of the storm.

A large gust of wind hit so strongly, even he had to brace himself and step back. He expected to see her go flying with her light weight, but she remained fixed on her feet where she was. His eyes found the six cannon grenades around her waist.

They're weights to keep her on her feet. Rosetta had increased her weight so she didn't get thrown around like a rag doll by the wind. No doubt this was her idea. *She's brilliant.* He'd bet she usually had a proper weight belt, but Naeem had been unable to find it.

Alister found his feet stuck where they were as he watched her direct men with such finesse that even he was awed.

"You're realising it, aren't you?" Naeem shouted to him over the storm, water running rivulets down his face. "Why we follow her, why we do what she tells us to."

He was. Alister was finally looking at her as a captain who could be equal to him rather than a woman playing pretend. *I've always looked down on her.* He hadn't realised it until this very moment.

A lightning strike above them flashed a hot, bright light, illuminating her. The thunder that immediately followed sounded as though it was trying to tell him something.

"She's never needed your help." Alister turned his gaze to Naeem as he spoke. "She knows she's too weak to hold the helm of her own ship through a storm like this. She knows she's too light to climb the shrouds right now. She knows she's not going to be of much use, but she won't sit by idly and watch her ship struggle while she's warm and cosy in her cabin."

Rosetta started checking the lifelines of her crew, pressing her boot to the mast as she tugged on the ropes with all her strength. She was making sure they were all tight and she wouldn't lose any of them.

"She knows what she has to do to survive." The face Naeem wore was so full of pride and full of faith, it almost shined from him. "She's always been like that.

"Aye," Alister finally said. "I see it."

He ran down the steps to go to her and caught her right before she tripped back, having to catch his own footing since he almost did as well. He didn't do it because she needed him to save her, but because he was intending to grab her anyway. Holding her around the nape of her neck so they wouldn't get pushed apart by the waves and wind tossing her ship around, he stared down at her.

Their hair blew over their shoulders, wet but no match for the wind. It was like they wanted to become tangled.

"You've got this, lass," he said, truly believing it.

She frowned at him; no doubt puzzled by the words he would have to explain later.

The blue of her eyes had never looked this dark. They were the exact same colour as the inky navy of the storm waves behind her.

"Grutten Valley, four days."

She rolled her eyes. "The Laughing Siren can take a storm like this; better hope it's not your ship that sinks."

True. The Howling Death was smaller and had a larger chance of being barrel rolled over. Thinking of his warship, Alister let her go without another word. He grabbed a rope and ran for his ship before it was too late. He flew through the air with his feet out in front of him.

Alister landed on the quarterdeck deck next to Pierre.

"You're lucky!" he shouted. "Was just about to turn away."

Taking the wheel, Alister, without hesitation, started steering his ship away to a safe distance.

Not once did he look back for the Laughing Siren to make sure it was following, safe, or nearby. Not once did he let his eye stray from what was in front of him as he navigated his ship through flat sections of water between the growing waves. The waves that did manage to hit the hull made the Howling Death rock violently side-to-side. It was a struggle just to hold onto the wheel of the helm.

Alister often had to right his footing and brace himself. Everyone was working their hardest to control the sails while the winds blew. Frothing water sloshed over the main deck to wash out over the other side. Anyone caught in that current was swept off their feet and barrelled into the railing.

Darkness came long before the sun was gone, but when it was, the only thing lighting the way were the crackling strikes of lightning. They occasionally struck against a wave in the distance.

The navy-blue sea eventually turned the blackest colour, as if God himself had poured ink beneath the crashing surface to create a nightmarish vastness to its yawning abyss.

Thick, dark, grey colours blanketed the sky, not a star in sight to guide the way. The sky looked like it was falling, ready to crash down upon them. The clouds were rolling, as if they would eventually wash them into the next life.

The Howling Death was in that limbo place where the sky and the sea touched.

The only reason he knew which way to go was the compass necklace he hung around his neck. Alister fought against an element that could sink him with just one towering wave. Every hour brought worse and worse conditions as he fought against the tidal swirls.

Pierre and himself took shifts steering. One would rest for a few hours, trusting the other to be in control enough to sleep, before the other would take over.

When he slept, the raging and violent sea swung his hammock from side-to-side, rocking him like it was a mother trying to aid a newborn babe to sleep.

For almost two days, it never let up, never gave them reprieve. He barely ate; it was near impossible for Glen to cook with the state of the ship.

Alister saw the large mass of volcanic land like an unlit lighthouse out at the sea. It wasn't active, but it was easy to see from a far distance. *She picked a good island to track.*

It could be seen from miles away, even with the dark clouds that hid the sunlight. He'd been going in circles for the last day trying to find it.

Staying a safe distance from it while he tried to figure out which way the low, wide crescent cape was, the storm continued.

"I thought they would have beaten us," Pierre said, coming up beside him since he'd gotten one of the men to wake him.

Alister was attempting to safely move through the points of the wide cape while the waves pushed to change his direction.

The moment he passed them, he almost sagged with relief as the intensity of the water immediately dropped. The wind still knocked them around, but he no longer had two different elements fighting against him.

Inside the Grutten Valley's storm breaking rocks that circled them, everything seemed calm, a place of serenity and peace surrounded by violence. Mostly.

The harsh rain never stopped falling.

Alister brows drew into a deep frown. "Me, too."

The Laughing Siren wasn't here.

It should have beaten them, since the Howling Death would have been thrown off course more. The size and lightness of his ship was perfect for fighting and chasing others, but storms often got the better of them.

"She'll be here," Alister answered with certainty.

He still told his men to drop both anchors and hunker down through the weather. They secured the sails, making sure they were neatly furled away. There was an air of tension throughout his ship as he walked below deck.

At first, he thought it had just been him, but it seemed all of them were worried for the Laughing Siren when it didn't show over the course of the next two days the storm raged.

Silence fell on them as they ate. They drank, but his men did it with long, sullen looks on their faces that only deepened when they turned their gazes to him.

Alister always returned them with a plain expression, like he didn't care, but as every hour creeped on and Rosetta didn't come, he couldn't stop his brows from being permanently crinkled together.

On the fifth day, the sun finally greeted them shyly behind heavy clouds.

"Do you think it's a break or should we expect more weather?" one of his crewmen asked him.

They all spoke to him periodically while they sailed, if he was steering the ship or merely walking through its dark halls. Alister scanned his eye over the horizon to see the clouds moving further and further away, growing softer and lighter by the hour.

"We should have clear skies for a few days." Whether the storm would return, he didn't know. "Check the sails; I know some of them have tears."

His ship had seen better days and they would use this chance to repair all the damage they could.

I gave her four days. It should have been more than enough time. *We made it here in two.*

After another two days of sunshine passed, seven days in total since he'd last seen the Laughing Siren, Alister was now ready to set sail again.

The winds were calm, the sky clear, the waves gentle. Even sea loving birds squawked, telling all that even the animals were confident enough to emerge from their hiding spots.

"It's been a week, Alister," Pierre said, heavy concern in his voice.

He'd come into Alister's chambers to speak with him while he sat at his desk, mapping where they had come from to this island. He was mapping the course they'd probably taken.

It would have only taken a day to sail here with calm seas. Seven days she'd had to make it here, almost half of which had been calm.

Which meant Alister knew the truth now.

"Do you think her ship sunk?" He could tell Pierre was afraid to ask by the tone in his voice. The worry in it was unnerving and made his nose crinkle when he realised it was *undeserving.*

Alister threw his measuring compass against the large map against his deck. He didn't care if he'd damaged it, not with the anger that suddenly burned up inside him like a hot, fiery tornado.

"Nay," he snapped with a lethal tone. "Her ship is fine. The bitch just ain't coming here."

Rosetta, for whatever reason, wasn't coming.

He turned his gaze up from the desk to glower towards Pierre. He knew it was the truth. She would be here otherwise.

"Tell the men we're leaving in an hour."

When he left Alister alone to brood by himself, he removed his eyepatch and threw it at the table. His face itched incessantly because he wore it constantly. He'd usually sleep without it but had refused to in Rosetta's bed.

He was furious, but most importantly, he couldn't stop himself from feeling disappointed. Possibly rejected?

I wasn't done with her. But apparently, she was.

Five days of storms he could have said they were lost at sea and couldn't find their way, but it had been two days of sunshine and her ship still hadn't dropped anchor next to his.

She told me she was getting sick of my shit. He picked up his measuring compass again to place one point of it against the desk. He spun it between his forefinger and the table, watching it twirl. *She said that she would be a captain long after I was gone from her life.*

He gave a chuckle. *Had she been planning to use the storm as an escape the entire time?*

He didn't understand why she would have needed to. She could have just told him. *Why would she direct us here then?*

Wait... The tool fell from his hand. *She's got most of our supplies!*

He wasn't so stupid to have her carry everything, but she still had most of the grog water, rum, and food.

His eye fell on the door of his cabin, realising they were going to need to find the nearest port if they wanted to eat in a week.

She stole from me! He slammed his fist against the desk, making everything on it bounce or rattle. *Again!*

CHAPTER TWENTY-EIGHT

With the storm raging on, Rosetta walked up the steps of the quarterdeck with Mr Smith hot on her heels.

They both went to the helm and grabbed the wheel together. They steadied it, allowing Naeem to fall away.

"Go rest," she told him. "We'll take over."

He nodded, untying the rope from his waist to put it around hers. Then, he worked on getting a second rope around Mr Smith, securing him to the support of the wheel as well. Together, they had the strength to hold the wheel and steer it.

For nearly an entire day, this is how they had been navigating a storm she could see wasn't going to calm any time soon. Mr Smith and she would take the helm while Naeem took the time to sleep – just so he could come back and be at it again.

They couldn't be trusted alone; neither one had the strength by themselves.

Nobody seemed to have noticed she hadn't rested much herself, and she'd much prefer to keep it that way.

Rosetta was tired, but she hadn't been able to think about anything other than making sure her ship and crew were fine. She was worried. She didn't think she'd sailed through a storm this difficult before.

She knew they were encroaching on the second night when

Naeem came back to take it again. The sky was black, and she couldn't see a wave coming unless a strike of lightning forked its light across the sky.

"Go sleep, John." She needed him off the deck.

She only allowed him to leave his cabin when she needed his help at the helm. The rest of the time she commanded him to stay inside.

He nodded, leaving them.

"We can't see where we're going," Rosetta said to Naeem, standing beside him while he steered. "Do you know where we are?"

She looked down at the compass that said they were heading in the right direction, before placing it around his neck for him. He checked it as well.

"No. Hopefully, we find it soon." He turned his head to her for a moment. "Did you see the Howling Death at all?"

She shook her head. "No, it's gone."

Naeem was staring at her as a flash of lightening lit up her face. He inched closer, like it would help him to see her better.

"Bloody hell, Rosetta. When was the last time you slept?"

Shit. Just when she thought she'd been getting away with it. "I slept earlier."

"When? Because you didn't sleep when I was last at the helm, and you couldn't have with John." The fact he hadn't called him Johnny boy meant he was serious.

"I'll sleep soon. Let me check everyone's lifelines first."

Her legs were tired, as though they were filled with lead, her arms ached, but she knew she wouldn't be able to sleep with so many men who could potentially have an unsecured rope. She didn't want them spiralling off the ship and out to sea.

Rosetta ran down the steps and started grabbing the ends of ropes, making sure they were tight against the mast bulbs jutting out from where they were connected.

Just as she checked the last one and was about to let go, a sudden big wave crashed into the side of the hull.

Falling, she tried to hold onto the rope, but it was too wet. It slipped from her fingers, somehow managing to burn her palms in the process, despite its soaked texture. Rosetta went flying backwards, heading towards the railing as the ship gave a heavy dip like it might tip.

Water came rushing over through the other side, pushing her faster and further than she would have if it didn't.

I don't have a lifeline!

"No!" she heard someone yell. "Save her!"

As she flipped backwards and was about to roll over the railing, she managed to grab the edge of it.

Holding on for dear life, her body dangled on the *wrong* side of the railing. She could feel her hands slipping and she knew she was digging the tips of her fingertips in so hard, they were turning white. Coldness from the storm made them ache terribly with her fearful grip. She kicked her boots against the outer hull, trying to find purchase so she could climb over.

A gurgling, roaring, near-sucking sound came from behind, one that sent fear and terror through her and chilled her all the way down to her bones. She thought her heart might have stopped in her chest.

She looked to the side to see a wave coming right for her. Her eyes went stark as she realised she was about to be washed away.

Oh gods! Oh no! Shit! She kicked harder, desperately trying to get purchase before it was too late. *I need to get over!*

There was nothing else in the world that could make her realise how insignificant she was than seeing a towering wave almost the size of her ship coming towards her, curling with froth like the mouth of a rabid, disease-ridden dog.

A set of hands grabbed one of her wrists and she looked up at one of her crewmen just as the wave hit.

Rosetta was flung to the side, but the person holding her managed to use the momentum to swing her back onto the ship. They held onto her with her between their legs as they both went sliding around the deck. She tried to snuff the scream that was trying to lock in her throat.

"Are you alright, Captain?" the man who had saved her asked once they settled. She looked up at someone she didn't know well, one of the prisoners she'd released.

"Yes," she said as he helped her to her feet after he got to his own. "Thank you."

She told him to go back to his position in the sails before she bolted for the quarterdeck.

Her eyes fell on Naeem, who looked pale with fright, as he watched her climb to the top of the stairs. His eyes were near bulging out of his skull; she was almost certain he'd been the one to call out.

With a nod to him, Rosetta entered her cabin. Closing the door, she fell to her knees.

I almost died.

If that prisoner hadn't grabbed her, she would have been washed out to sea. She would have been pushed so far underwater, she doubted she would've been able to reach the surface before she drowned.

She felt weak as she shakily got up and stumbled to her sleeping cabin connected to the navigation room. Getting into her hammock was a struggle with her exhaustion and the intense rocking, but she eventually managed.

Her sleep was restless as she swayed around, but she did get a few hours in. Mr Smith was the one to wake her, realising she hadn't come to him for far too long. The worry that lanced her chest caused her to almost fall out of her hammock.

"How long was I asleep?!"

"Eight hours."

Poor Naeem! They ran outside to find the storm just as

dangerous and unrelentless as when she'd left it. It seemed never ending, like it would continue for the rest of eternity.

She put her hand on his shoulder and he turned his head to her.

"Finally! I can't feel my fucking arms anymore." He let go so they could take over. He patted John on the shoulder as he said, "Watch her; she almost went into the sea."

The look Mr Smith gave her behind his rain dotted glasses was enough to make her cringe. They both had to steady the wheel when it tried to turn.

"It's fine. I—"

A bright flash of light blinded them.

A horrible, heart-wrenching, cracking and fizzing noise sounded alongside an ear-splitting *boom*.

No! No! Nooooo! Rosetta bounced on the spot, biting her bottom lip with her brows crinkled tightly together as she stomped her foot.

The main mast to the Laughing Siren was hit with a powerful lightning strike.

Once the eye piercing, sight blinding light vanished, fire gave them enough light to watch it slowly break in half and topple against the deck. Men dived out of the way from below, while those who had been in the air were tossed from it.

Thankfully, their lifelines stopped them from falling into the water, but she was sure one or two of her men had either died from the impact or had been electrocuted.

The odds of this happening were so rare. Rosetta felt her heart drop to her stomach as her eyes bowed heavily.

We can't sail without it. The storm was now going to take them on an adventure she wouldn't be able to control.

All of their jaws dropped, their eyes wide at what they'd just witnessed. Nobody could believe their terrible luck.

"There's nothing you can do, Naeem," she told him, seeing he was stuck where he stood. "Go sleep."

There was nothing *any* of them could do.

She and Mr Smith would have to hold the wheel, since they still needed to stop the ship from toppling over. If they let go, they would spin in circles until they tilted or a wave pushed their ship under.

Unfortunately, holding it would do little to help where they were taken. The rest of the sails would help direct them, but without a fully working main mast, the waves would be stronger and would heave them around.

"Rosetta..." Mr Smith said once Naeem was gone.

"She won't sink, John," she reassured. She had too much faith in the Laughing Siren for it to do that to her. "We have to keep pointing east."

Rosetta flipped open her navigation compass to see they were pointing the wrong way. Mr Smith helped her to turn the wheel.

"If your will could be ridden, girl, we could make it anywhere." He gave her a grin so wide his teeth, with the occasional missing one, showed. It was something he rarely did. "If you say we'll make it through the storm, then we will."

She didn't know if he said it to lift his own spirits, or hers. She appreciated the gesture regardless. "You've never doubted me, have you?"

"No." He shook his head, pushing up on the handles as they tried to ride through a flat part of the sea between two waves. "I hope my daughter turns out as strong as you at your age."

"I've told you that we're going to go back to Port Douglas once we've checked this next map's location."

Mr Smith came from the mainland islands of the western countries, and that's where Rosetta had found him in her first year of being a captain. They were heading in that general direction because of Alister.

"No. If the guards see me, they will take me in."

As much as her heart was broken for her ship, Rosetta gave

a bellowing laugh. She needed to keep herself focused; she couldn't wallow in sadness just yet. There was still too much to do. If she showed her crew uncertainty and fear when they needed her to be strong, what kind of captain was she?

"I'd like to see them try." They turned the wheel once more, but it did little to help as they rode across the base of a wave rather than beside it. "I told you I'd take you back to your daughter once I had this ship. I've got her now, and I always deliver on my promises."

The look he gave her was the same one he'd given her when she'd first made this promise. It looked like his eyes were filling with hopeful tears.

Rosetta knew this man before her was a great father. He'd taken her under his wing, sheltered her, protected her, cared for her more than he'd needed to. He was not bound to her by blood, and yet he cherished her like she was his own child.

She could only imagine how much he loved his daughter. How much he had tended to her, provided for her, by giving Rosetta just a partial amount of the tenderness he must have for his own blood related child.

He deserved to have her in his arms once more.

She may even come with us. Rosetta would allow his daughter onto her ship so they could be together once more.

"First though, let's make it through this."

"Aye, Captain!" he cheered with a gruff voice, making her smile.

CHAPTER TWENTY-NINE

On the fourth night, the storm finally let up enough to get a small break in the clouds to see the night sky.

Rosetta read the stars alongside Naeem and Mr Smith, and they discovered they'd been blown far off course.

With the sorry state of her poor, damaged ship, it would take Rosetta another full day and night to get to her and Alister's meeting location with her mangled sail.

That's if the weather continued to clear.

When the morning came and they were showered in bright sunlight, Mr Smith stayed with Rosetta while she steered by herself.

Only once Naeem had rested did she finally allow the hatch to the lower deck to be opened permanently and let the crew come to the surface. They'd rotated shifts during the storm, but she was now allowing them all to greet the sun.

What she thought would be a celebration of success, considering they were all still alive, swiftly turned into something nasty.

"I thought we were going to be joining the Howling Death during the storm," one of the people asked from the crowd of nearly a hundred men.

"We are. That's currently our heading," she answered from the above deck. "We're about a day away with our sails like this."

The top half that had split apart had long ago rolled into the sea, taking part of her railing with it. She still had the bottom sails, but the top was completely gone.

Men stood around what was left of the main mast and she could see the look of concern on their faces. "You couldn't even captain us through a storm without almost sinking us!"

"Mr Smith had to help you hold the helm!" another yelled. "What kind of captain can't even steer their own ship?"

"Men died because of you!"

Rosetta's heart nearly seized in her chest at their words, especially when men agreed with those who had spoken.

A large group of them began to make their way forward, pushing others out of their way to the point they almost fell to the ground. She could only guess the number coming forward. It appeared to be at least a fifth of her crew.

"A woman shouldn't be on the seas, let alone commanding over men," one of them said, pointing a finger in her direction. "You almost got us all killed. Hell, three men did die!"

She gripped the handles of the wheel, refusing to step away from it. It was her ship, and it would always be hers.

"I also got us through that storm with a damaged ship! I would like to see anyone else do better." *I worked tirelessly! I barely rested and they want to blame me?* "I can't control where lightening will strike. Their deaths aren't my fault. I'm not a god!"

"But the gods of the seas bless good sailors and ruin those who aren't! The destroyed mast is proof of that."

A man standing at the very front folded his arms across his chest with his legs apart, like he wanted to take a stand. He hadn't said anything yet, but it was clear he was the leader of this gang.

"By the laws of piracy, we want a vote."

Her face felt cold as it paled.

"We've told you we won't accept a mutiny!" Naeem shouted, coming forward to stand next to her. "Rosetta is our Captain."

"To those who were her crew before," one of them said. "If she didn't want to be faced with the laws of piracy, then she shouldn't have taken pirates as her crew!"

The bald man at the very front gave a smirk, his face twisting into something evil. He opened his mouth for the first time to say, "She no longer has Alister Paine to protect her. Without him here, we can do what we want."

Rosetta was forced to stand her ground when she found three pistols pointed at her from below, raising up around the leader's head.

"If you shoot me," she said with an expression that hid every emotion she felt, lifting her nose up at the barrels poised to kill. "You'll be dead before you even get the chance to vote."

The narrowed, squinting eyes she received told her they knew what she said was the truth. Her men would retaliate with vengeance.

"We want to choose a new captain. You have to allow us to make a vote, and if you value your life, you will let us."

Those of her original crew stepped back and drew their own pistols or swords. They turned their weapons to those who were threatening her.

"We won't let you overtake her."

The men who wanted to vote her out faced them while drawing their swords as well. Then there was the part of her crew who were confused and scared, those who were just common thieves or sailors who may have committed small crimes – or been in the wrong place at the wrong time. They immediately backed away as not to be a part of what could potentially be a fight to the death.

Rosetta knew there were about thirty men of her original

crew left. Those who opposed her were smaller in comparison, but they looked more dangerous.

Alister had taken the murderers. The prisoners she'd taken were mostly people who had turned to crime out of desperation rather than malice. But these men...

She knew she was facing pirates, men who were just as ruthless as her. If they were just like her, and men like Alister and his crew, Rosetta knew what was going to happen if she let this continue.

It'll be bloodshed.

"Stop!" she yelled, making their heads turn to her. *I've just escaped a storm and now I'm facing a bloody mutiny!* "If I allow the chance to vote and you lose, will you concede?"

I feared this was going to happen. Her paranoia hadn't been unfounded. *I knew something was wrong.*

"You can't be thinking of agreeing," Naeem gasped. He gripped her arm and turned her to him with a frown of sincere concern. He looked so afraid, it made her own brows crinkle slightly. "You know what will happen if you lose the vote."

"What else can I do? They'll kill each other," she whispered, her eyes bowing at the truth and reality of the situation. She lifted her hands to shrug in frustration. "Then there won't be a crew to sail this ship, no matter who the captain is."

My men will fight for me. She didn't think her life was worth all theirs. She'd killed Theodore, she'd gotten to sail the Laughing Siren as her captain. She'd been blessed with mind-shattering, body aching pleasure for months, something she'd never thought she'd ever experience in her entire life – not with the way she'd been forced to live it so far.

Rosetta wouldn't be any greedier than she had already been just to live a little longer, not at the cost of this many good men's lives.

The leader stepped forward while finally pulling his own

gun from its holster. "Other than these idiots," the man said while nodding his head to her original crew. "No one else will vote for you." He cocked the hammer back. "Allow us to choose or you die."

"I'm asking if you will concede," she yelled, earning her a dark look.

The man curled his upper lips back into a mean cringe, his eyes narrowed on her in an obvious glare. In every line of his features, she could see that this man, for some reason, despised her.

"Because, as it stands," she continued. "I can either allow you all to kill each other and then none of us will be going anywhere, or I can allow this vote."

A different man stepped forward, much older and greyer than the rest. He didn't look any less violent.

"I've been a pirate for many a years. If ye win, I'll lay me gun down." But then he gave a cruel, near toothless grin. "But if ye lose, ye'll be going for a long swim, girlie. That's how it works."

She gave a huff of irritation. "Who is your choice?"

"I am," said the bald man at front. "Name's Timmy Barnes, and I used to be Captain of the Lazy Rocker before I was arrested for piracy."

"I will follow the code and allow the vote. Naeem, take the helm." He begrudgingly took it so she could step away.

Timmy started making his way up to be on the same level as her, but they stood at the top of the two different sets of stairs that led to this deck, one on either side.

He looked to be a man in his late twenties, Alister's age from what she could gauge. He was bald with a long brown beard that had been plaited and came to his sternum. He looked strong, with the cutthroat look of an average pirate.

"I have been sailing these seas since I was a thirteen-year-old boy," he shouted to the men below them. "I know how to lead a crew, far better than this pair of tits, and know these waters better than anyone. We've been following some stupid little girl whose been using her pussy to get Alister Paine to protect her! She's worthless without him."

He turned to her with his arms folded, tapping the barrel of his pistol against his bicep.

Rosetta scrunched her nose up at him with distaste.

"She hasn't got what it takes to be a captain on her own without him, and she wouldn't even have this ship if it wasn't for him. He just made her captain so he can take her hole but I'm sure, once he was done with her, he was planning on taking this ship from her."

"You have no idea what you're talking about. She took over the Howling Death and marooned him on Dunecaster!" one of her men yelled in defence. "She got the Bloody Storm of the Seas to bend to her will to get her this ship."

"She made a deal with the devil!" Keat, the man often in her crow's nest, added. "I'd like to see ye make such a deal with the likes of him. He would've sliced all yer necks before ye even got a chance ta speak to him!"

More of her men continued to give her praise.

"No one else would have the cunning to get his help and she managed to escape getting her head removed when he took it back."

"I've been sailing with her for two years and she's better than most men on the sea. Us men, we're stupid. She's got more wit in her little pinkie than you do in your whole fat, fucking, ugly head."

She gave a puff of breath through her nose, trying to stem a single laugh that tried to escape. *Bless these boys.*

"Can't even speak for yourself, huh?" Timmy asked with a humorous laugh.

"Don't get me wrong, I appreciate their help." She folded her arms across her chest to mirror him. She even started tapping the toe of her boot like she was bored. "I just don't think you're going to win no matter what you or I say."

Timmy gritted his teeth and turned forward. "Those of you who would rather see a *man* captain you, raise your hands."

Those that had stepped forward with him all raised their hands. A small handful of those who were in the back group, also raised them, although hesitantly.

"Those of you who want me to stay as your Captain, raise your hands."

When they did, and the number was obviously greater, she turned to him. "Isn't that a pity, TimTim," Rosetta sneered, shaking her head at him. It caused her nest of knots, which should really be glossy hair, to crawl across her skin. "It looks like you've lost."

"I won't be captained by a woman!"

She gave him her own cruel smirk. "That's fine with me. Was going to make you go for a swim anyway."

That smirk fell when he pointed his pistol at her. *Shit.*

She didn't have time to get her own.

Rosetta was tackled just as the gun sounded. ***Thud***. She and the person who tackled her flew through the air and she tucked her head in to protect it, rather than look up at who had saved her. They both hit the main deck without ever touching the stairs. The wind was knocked out of her as her back hit the ground and it tore a painful gasp from her chest. *OW!*

"Get him!" Naeem shouted, releasing the helm without care for the ship to grab Timmy.

All he managed to do was spook the man until he fell over the quarterdeck railing. He landed against the main deck only a few metres from her with a disgusting crack and let out a small scream.

"Kill him!" one of her men shouted.

They all ran for him as a single unit. She watched as Timmy raised his arms to block a downward swinging sword.

He let out a yell as his hand chopped away, right before someone cut his throat.

The rest of her men, including the prisoners who had voted for her, started circling those who had voted against her. There was a crowd at the front who remained dead frozen, those who were even more afraid than before.

The mutineers lifted their hands, either conceding to the vote and surrendering or realising they wouldn't win now that they understood how many were on her side.

"Are you okay, Rosetta?" John said above her, raising himself onto straightened arms.

She realised he'd been the one to save her. *Such a good man.* She gave him a broken smile of reassurance, too conflicted about what just happened to give him a real one.

"Yes, I am. Thank–"

He coughed over her before she could finish. Blood splattered against her cheek. She flinched; her eyes fluttering shut. It had been a light splatter, but Rosetta felt like his blood slapped her in the face so hard, a part of her soul left her.

"S-sorry," he choked for coughing on her, before finishing trying to get to his hands and knees above her so he was no longer crushing her.

"J-John?" she stuttered.

Her heart clenched when she realised he'd ended up taking the bullet in her stead. She'd been hoping he'd managed to get them both out of the way.

He rolled to the side, falling onto his back.

Rosetta immediately crawled to her knees, tucking her hair behind one ear so it didn't shield her vision. She stared down at the man who had a track of blood running through his always neat, white and black peppered beard.

"John?" Her voice broke an octave.

It can't be...

Tears began to well in her eyes when she saw blood was

beginning to pool beneath him. She turned him so she could see he'd been shot in the back on the right side. Rosetta knew by the wheezing, rattling, disgusting wet sounding breath he gave that he'd been shot in the lung.

"Why?" she cried, lightly slapping his chest as if that was the answer to dispelling the bullet from his thick torso. "You stupid old man! You shouldn't have gotten in the way!"

"Couldn't let it be you, love."

He raised his hand as he gave her a warm and loving smile that shattered her heart into a million little pieces. He stroked the back of his wrinkled hands, covered in the evidence of a hard-working man's life, against her cheek.

"I made you a promise." She grabbed him by the scruff of his tunic and lifted him, despite his wince. She shook him. "You're not allowed to die, you stubborn fool. I told you I'd kill you if you did."

He gave a laugh, before another cough bubbled more blood to his lips.

No, he can't do this to me. He was dying, whether she wanted him to go or not. *Oh god, no. Anyone but him.* Or Naeem. They were the only two people Rosetta didn't want to see die. She didn't think she could face the world without either of them.

"Y-you can't leave me, John. Who will help me take care of Naeem when he's too drunk to stand? Who will help me navigate the waters? Who will help me count the stocks?"

She didn't care she was being watched as she placed her forehead against his shuddering chest.

Her voice broke in different octaves, unstable and whisper-like, as she asked, "Who will be there for me when I don't know the way?"

She knew she shouldn't be letting her men see her like this, but her heart couldn't take the sickening ache in it. It felt like it was being squeezed so hard that it would burst.

"Y-You'll be fine, Rosetta." She turned her face to him, knowing by how hot it was that her face had turned bright red from her tears. "You're a beautiful woman, inside and out, just like my d-daughter. It's why I-I've always followed y-you, trying to help you find y-your h-happi-ness."

The more he spoke, the harder it seemed to be.

She wanted to scream for someone to help him, to stop the bleeding, to save him, anything, but she knew, deep down, there was nothing they could do.

John was drowning in his own blood.

He started gasping for breath, each convulsion making her feel like hers were being sapped along with him.

"P-please," she begged, looking down with a plea.

She stroked his face by running the tip of her thumb through his beard. She even wiped it over the lens of his bloodstained glasses, wanting him to see this world clearly before he left it. She wanted him to see how much she couldn't bear to let him go.

'I'm sorry' was all he could mouth before he started lightly convulsing, gasping, desperate to breathe when he couldn't.

Choking.

Then his gaze faded away to turn into a haunting, lifeless stare. *H-He's gone.*

Rosetta let out a loud screaming cry as she curled over him with shuddering breaths. For a few moments, she desperately held onto his body, heaving over it, crying over it, her heart dying over it.

She could hear no breaths, could feel no heartbeat with her hand over where it should be, and eventually, the warmth he had always held started to turn into a coldness. Bitter, bitter coldness seeped into her body to kill her own warmth.

"Rosetta," one of her crew men whispered, crouching down to place his hand on her shoulder in comfort.

She knew his voice, someone who had been with her for

almost as long as Naeem. *Keat.*

They knew. They all knew how much this man meant to her, how much she cared for him, even if she had never told them.

"Kill them," she commanded, turning her tearful face up at the men who had tried to mutiny against her.

"But the ship..." Without them, they'd struggle to sail.

"KILL THEM!" She no longer cared, not when retribution for this could be dealt. She wanted justice. "I want them all dead."

"W-wait!" one of them said, putting his hands up in surrender. "We said we would concede if we lost."

Rosetta turned her head to the man with his hand still on her shoulder and gave him a look – one he should know by now.

He sighed, standing to raise his sword. He began the slaughter of the thirty men who were the reason the man in her arms was now gone from her already sad and dreary world.

She thought that would satisfy her, that it would help to take the worst of the weight crushing down on her, would heal her pain, but it didn't.

All it did was stop her tears while her heart weighed down so heavily, it felt like an anchor had dragged it all the way to the floor so she could trample over it with her own feet.

Rosetta, covered in blood, shakily brought herself away from the floor. She left Mr Smith where he was and walked up the quarterdeck steps so she could take the helm of her ship.

She didn't say anything to anyone, didn't give any orders, and no one tried to speak to her. They started going about their normal duties without her directive. Naeem was the one to issue commands, but she didn't care enough to listen.

Eventually, she saw two people carefully lift Mr Smith's lifeless body.

She finally spoke. "If you toss him, you'll miss having

hands," she warned, unsure what they were planning on doing with his corpse. "Take him below deck and wrap him in a blanket."

"What do you want to do with him?" Naeem asked as he came up the stairs to stand beside her, worry obvious in every creased line of his face.

It was an odd expression from someone who usually held humour even in times when he usually shouldn't. She knew he must be as upset as she was about John's death was trying to hide it.

Rosetta started to steer their course from their current heading.

She couldn't face Alister, didn't care to face him with how hollow she felt inside. A big piece of her had been taken this day, and she wanted to do nothing more than fall into the ocean and peacefully float away.

Turning her head to Naeem but refusing to meet his eye, she said in a soft voice, "I want to bury him."

He at least deserves that.

The story continues...

Storms of Paine

A Pirate Romance Duology

Book Two

After the storm that separates them, Captains Rosetta Silver and Alister Paine find themselves sailing side-by-side together once more. Their passion refuses to fizzle out and burns brighter, hotter, and, frighteningly, deeper every time. Rosetta manages to convince the land hating Alister to port. They need supplies and the Laughing Siren still needs repairs.

But land may be dangerous for them – and not just because of the bounty on his head.

Emotions within Rosetta are stirring and she doesn't have a compass to navigate these unfamiliar waters. Alister's behaviour in port isn't what she was expecting, and well, she isn't a saint either – far from it.

He's like a storm, and like a savage thunderstorm, she fears he will sweep her away.

However, the more she discovers about his complicated past and the true nature of this man, the more it has her wondering if she should give herself over to her feelings... or run.